TENSION MOUNTS

It was an awesome sight. Wind was shrieking down the curve of the ramp, apparently funneled into it by the shape of the structure above. Pacifico thought it was the first time in his life that he had actually *seen* the wind. It was made visible by dust and debris: thick yellow-brown dust and a streaming blizzard of paper and assorted street trash. The scene was illuminated by dust-shrouded yellow light from ceiling fixtures. For a moment nobody spoke or moved. Then the wind seemed to turn itself up a notch.

By nightfall the wind was blowing at well over two hundred miles an hour. It took only another hour to reach three hundred. Most anemometers in the New York metropolitan area had stopped operating by that time. They had been destroyed or ripped away from their mountings, or the structures on which they were mounted had collapsed.

The wind passed three hundred miles an hour and kept increasing. Nobody was ever quite sure where it stopped.

WHO WILL SURVIVE?

DOOM WIND

DOOM WIND

Max Gunther

PaperJacks LTD

TORONTO   NEW YORK

PaperJacks

DOOM WIND

PaperJacks LTD

330 STEELCASE RD. E., MARKHAM, ONT. L3R 2M1
210 FIFTH AVE., NEW YORK, N.Y. 10010

Contemporary Books edition published 1986

PaperJacks edition published October 1987

ISBN 0-7701-0660-9
Copyright © 1986 by Max Gunther
All rights reserved
Printed in the USA

PART
I

THE
GATHERING
WIND

Who has seen the wind?
Neither you nor I:
But when the trees bow down their heads,
The wind is passing by.

Christina Rossetti

1

I WON'T DO IT!" Pacifico shouted.

"Stop shouting, for God's sake," the managing editor said.

"The hell with it. Tell Beaulieu I said the hell with it. I'm not going to do it, Charlie. That's final."

"Ah, quit complaining. How's it going to hurt? Why make such a big deal out of it?"

"It's a damned imposition, that's why. Also, it's a lousy idea. It won't work."

"Oh, for God's sake, Nick."

"I don't want any part of it, Charlie. You just tell him that."

The managing editor sighed and leaned his great bulk back in his creaky swivel chair. "You can tell him yourself. He was expecting you at eleven. You're late."

Pacifico raged up the single flight of stairs to the publisher's office. He did not respond to the secretary's friendly smile of greeting; nor did he wish her a good morning or extend any other courtesies. Instead he announced curtly, "I'm Pacifico. I understand the Old Man wants to see me."

The secretary was not ruffled by his rudeness. She was an uncommonly beautiful white-haired lady of about sixty. Her name was Mrs. Mead. It was said that she and the Old

3

Man had had a passionate love affair when they were younger, and they were still seen together from time to time in various expensive watering spots around the city, heads close, deep in earnest talk. Business or personal affairs? Only they knew.

"Ah, yes, Mr. Pacifico," Mrs. Mead said in her lovely low voice. "Will you have a seat? I'll tell Mr. Beaulieu you're here."

She pronounced the name with a loving little hint of French. The usual American pronunciation was a careless Bo-loo.

Pacifico sullenly ignored the suggested seat and stood with his hands in his pockets until Mrs. Mead told him to go in. There was an odd quality of mischief in the smile she gave him. He thought: she knows, of course.

Pacifico had been invited to the publisher's office only a few times in his career at *Seven Days*. Each time he came up here he was startled anew by the magnificence of the view. It was a huge corner office, forty-eight stories above Madison Avenue. The two outer walls were almost all glass. The view to the east was partially blocked by taller buildings, but from the southern windows, on a clear day, you could see most of the lower half of Manhattan Island.

It was not clear on this hot June morning, however. The sky was milky. No breeze blew. The air over the city streets looked steamy and unclean. It had been this way for several weeks. Meteorologists were blaming the comet.

Pacifico walked across the great expanse of beige carpet to shake hands with the Old Man, who walked around his desk and advanced with formal courtesy to meet him. Arthur Beaulieu was tall and cadaverously thin. He had enormous knobby hands. He had a hard, arrestingly ugly face with a long jaw, an eagle's beak of a nose, and shaggy gray eyebrows. Solitary and aloof by nature, he inspired fear in many of the staff members. Pacifico, however, was less easily intimidated than most and had always found the Old Man a pleasant enough fellow, though hardly amiable.

They said good morning to each other, and then the Old Man said, "I'd like you to meet my daughter Kimberley. Kim, this is Mr. Nicholas Pacifico."

"Nick," Pacifico corrected. He used his full name only in his byline, his tax returns, and a few other places. In ordinary communication he was either Pacifico or Nick to everybody except his mother, who called him Nicky despite years of protests.

"Good morning, Nick," Kimberley Beaulieu said from where she sat on a sofa behind a coffee table.

"Good morning," Pacifico replied. Not sure whether he wanted to use her first or last name, he used neither.

There was an awkward pause. Pacifico guessed he was expected to walk across the room and take her hand. He stayed grumpily where he was.

"Well, ah, let's sit down, shall we?" Arthur Beaulieu suggested. "Would you like some coffee, Mr. Pacifico?"

"No thanks," Pacifico said. He and the Old Man sat in chairs at opposite ends of the coffee table. Pacifico looked at the daughter and thought: oh boy, it's going to be every bit as bad as I feared. Worse, maybe.

She was coolly returning his gaze. On her face was a mischievous smile much like the one he had received from Mrs. Mead. She was considerably better-looking than her father, this Kimberley Beaulieu. She had blonde hair cut short, a small upturned nose, and an air of perfect poise. She was in her middle or late twenties, several years younger than Pacifico. She was a recent college graduate, the company gossip network reported. According to that same source, she had graduated at a later-than-normal age because her academic career had been interrupted. She had been kicked out of Radcliffe or some such place for chronic rulebreaking in her freshman or sophomore year and had been sent to Europe to "find herself," as the phrase went. To mature, it meant.

A spoiled rich brat, Pacifico judged sourly. Her handbag, on the sofa beside her, bore a famous designer's monogram. Her simple and elegant white dress and her preseason suntan also spelled money to Pacifico, who had scant money of his own and was not kindly disposed toward the rich. He thought she was probably the kind of girl who ran up four-figure charge accounts at Bergdorf's and, since she never saw the bills, never gave them a moment's worry.

And now she wants to dabble in a career, he thought morosely. Not because she needs the job but because she has some half-assed notion about "fulfilling herself." She'll work for a year, get bored with it, and quit. Oh boy. Great.

"As I told you," the Old Man was saying to his daughter, "Mr. Pacifico is one of our top feature writers. In fact, he may well be one of the best in New York."

Pacifico responded to this with a grin of dutiful embarrassment. It was entirely feigned. He was not embarrassed at all. He *knew* he was one of the best in New York.

Kimberley Beaulieu's smile now had a faintly mocking quality in it. She held his gaze for a second, then looked down, fished in her handbag, and pulled out cigarettes.

The Old Man turned to Pacifico and said, "I don't know how much you've been told about the, ah, the purpose of this meeting, Mr. Pacifico. Have you, ah—?"

"Charlie Broadbent told me the basic idea," Pacifico said with what he hoped was a detectable but not-too-obvious lack of enthusiasm. He wanted to state his refusal simply and directly but did not know how to do so without seeming boorish. It had been easy to shout at genial old Charlie, but one behaved oneself better in Arthur Beaulieu's office.

The Old Man said, "Well, let me tell you exactly what I have in mind. Kim here will be joining the magazine. She—"

"My father thinks I need a teacher," she interrupted. Her smile was gone. She looked—what? Pacifico thought the word might be petulant, but that was not quite right. Her pale blue eyes glinted fiercely.

"No, don't put it that way," the Old Man said. "It isn't that you need a *teacher*, exactly, What I—"

"If he's going to *teach* me, Daddy, he'll be a *teacher*," she pointed out in a tone of exaggerated patience.

Pacifico thought: she doesn't like this any more than I do. Probably thinks she should start right out as editor-in-chief. Or maybe she'd just as soon skip the whole thing and go back to the beach at Antibes.

The Old Man appealed to Pacifico. "*Teacher* really isn't the word," he insisted. "What I envision is a situation in which—well, in which an apprentice, you know, learns the trade by practicing it under a master craftsman. Not the kind of learning a student does in school, but actual hands-on experience."

The Old Man paused, watching Pacifico hopefully from under those shaggy eyebrows. Pacifico guessed he was supposed to make some noise of assent at this point, but he sat stubbornly silent.

He noticed now that Kimberley had been holding an unlit cigarette for some time, as though waiting for somebody to light it for her. Pacifico, who did not smoke, carried no matches. He had no intention of being so solicitously polite in any case. Finally she attended to her need herself with a gadget from the coffee table. It looked like a little silver urn; Pacifico had not realized it was a lighter. Kimberley looked annoyed.

The Old Man cleared his throat and went on: "To help you understand this better, Mr. Pacifico, I should tell you it's all part of a long-range plan. We've always assumed in our family that Kim would join the company someday. She will inherit my stock eventually. She can sell it off if she wishes, of course, but I've always felt—I believe she has a genuine interest in newsmagazine journalism. Am I right, my dear?"

"That's what I studied in college," she said curtly, examining a fingernail. Pacifico surmised she did not like her father to discuss her affairs with another man in this way.

Her father, seemingly oblivious to this, went on: "As Kim says, she is a journalism major. Not a rank beginner by any means. But all the college courses in the world won't teach what you can learn from a few months of real experience. Do you agree, Mr. Pacifico?"

"Right," Pacifico said without conviction.

"I want Kim to learn exactly how a good story is put together—I mean learn it by being there every step of the way, by participating in the process. I want her apprenticed to a master, Mr. Pacifico, do you see? I want her to spend a short time as your research associate and assistant writer."

Once again Arthur Beaulieu paused and waited for a response. There was no ducking it this time. Pacifico rubbed the back of his neck. He grimaced unhappily. Finally he said, "Oh boy. I don't know what to say. I think—I think maybe I'm not the right man for this, Mr. Beaulieu."

"Of course you are," Arthur Beaulieu insisted.

"But I—"

"There's something I forgot to mention, Mr. Pacifico." The Old Man gave Pacifico a sly look. "I wouldn't expect you to take on a responsibility like this without compensation, of course. I've been reviewing your salary. I believe you'll find I've come to some rather, ah, interesting conclusions."

Oh. Well, that did it. That shed a whole new light on the situation.

Pacifico's need for money was dire and incessant. He was

behind in his apartment rent, utility bills, and credit union payments. In yesterday's mail he had received a stunning new bill from his daughter's doctors. He would do almost anything for money.

Arthur and Kimberley Beaulieu were watching him, waiting to hear what he was going to say. Her teasing smile was back.

Pacifico looked at her and asked, "When are you planning to start?"

The Old Man leaned back in his chair with a sigh of evident relief.

Kimberley's smile vanished. Perhaps she had been hoping the reluctant teacher would refuse the assignment. She looked at Pacifico and shrugged. "I'll start Monday, I guess," she said with no enthusiasm at all.

"Will that fit in well with your schedule, Mr. Pacifico?" the Old Man asked.

"Well enough. Matter of fact, I'll be starting a new assignment Monday morning."

"Excellent. Kim can get in at the very beginning of it. What is the assignment?"

"The comet story. The windstorm."

"Ah. Yes, I talked to Charlie Broadbent about that yesterday. He seems to think it might be a difficult story to pull off, and I must say I agree."

Pacifico nodded and said, "Me too." That was putting it mildly. He thought the story would not only be difficult to do well but probably impossible. He did not say that, however. He said, "I think the main problem will be finding weather experts who have something interesting to say but . . . you know . . . "

"But don't sound like crackpots?" the Old Man supplied.

"Yes, those are my misgivings exactly. But I'm sure you'll find a solution. And the difficulty of it should make it all the better, you know, for teaching purposes."

Pacifico left shortly after that. He and Kimberley said good-bye politely. There was still that oddly ferocious look in her eyes, which were the color of a north sky in winter.

He looked back at her as he was walking out the door. She was reaching to put her cigarette out in an ashtray, and it seemed to him her hand shook. That puzzled him.

2

PACIFICO CELEBRATED HIS raise by having a few drinks with the gang that night at Lahière's, a favored watering spot of the *Seven Days* staff. Lahière's was reputed to have a fine Paris-trained chef and an excellent wine cellar, but Pacifico did not know anything about that. His tastes in food were simple. He did not like the complicated meals served in elegant New York restaurants, especially French ones, and as for wine, it all tasted like paint remover to him. But Lahière's did serve an honest martini at a fair price, and Pacifico's head was buzzing when he stepped outdoors into a dark blue twilight. The weather was oppressively hot. The subway would be still hotter. He decided to walk.

He lived in a shabby neighborhood on the lower west side, about three miles away. It was a walk he took several times a week. He liked the distance. It limbered the legs and sharpened the appetite. It usually took about three-quarters of an hour. Pacifico's walking pace was brisk, as was his pace in everything he did.

Tonight he walked a block eastward before starting downtown. Eastward was out of his way, but he liked the wide vistas of Park Avenue.

He began to sweat before he had gone a mile. This was unusual for him. At first he blamed the booze and felt a

11

pang of guilt. Then he exonerated himself. Booze, hell. It wasn't the booze; it was the weather.

The excuse stood up. The weather was indeed unusual. Not just hot, not just humid, but utterly motionless. The air was damp, stagnant, and unappetizing. It reminded Pacifico of the air in a high-school locker room after a track meet.

The Great Calm: that was what newspapers and TV weather announcers were calling it. It had lasted several weeks, affecting most of the northern hemisphere. Day after day, almost every city north of the Tropic of Cancer reported the same flat, milky blue skies and the dead locker-room air. The only relief was an occasional tepid, half-hearted drizzle. The calm had been accompanied by an unprecedented drop in atmospheric pressure—so much of a drop that athletic events such as track meets, which tested the limits of lung function, were more and more often being canceled. Hospitals were filling with smokers whose once mild emphysema had grown acute.

The calm would end eventually. What then? Some meteorologists predicted a windy period. A few—a crackpot minority—foresaw a wind of catastrophic power. The press had christened their vision the Big Wind. As for the comet that was supposedly behind it all, headline writers had given it many names, among them the Doomsday Comet and the Endworld Comet.

This was the story Pacifico was assigned to write next week. In his gloomy opinion, it was a nonstory. Most meteorologists seemed to doubt that anything especially noteworthy was going to happen. The press and the TV weather talkers had seized on terms like "Big Wind" and "Endworld Comet" because they were dramatic, but few journalists seemed to take the story seriously.

Nor did anybody else. The subject had made headlines when the first speculations about it came up a few months ago, but now it was demoted to the category of "other world news" in the back pages. People seemed to feel that, even if a wind did blow, it would be no worse than a lot of other winds they had experienced. So a few tree branches might break, a few power lines might come down. So what?

And so people were going about their ordinary business. Pacifico looked at the faces of people who passed him in the still, hot dusk. A pair of lovers, kissing as they walked hip to hip. A noisy group of businessmen on the way from bar to restaurant. A Japanese family gazing up at the tall buildings. Loitering hookers, sauntering lookers. Nobody was worrying about the wind.

How, then, would it be possible to write a story with life and bounce? Pacifico did not know.

* * *

He stopped at the front entrance of the New World Hotel to say hello to the doorman, an old friend. The hotel was at the bottom of the New World Center, a dazzling seventy-story tower that had been completed two years ago. It was a multiple-use building that also incorporated apartment condominiums and office space. The hotel was among New York's most expensive: an elegant, exclusive hideaway for the traveling rich. Pacifico had no idea how much the rooms went for, but the drinks downstairs in the D'Alembert Lounge cost something like five bucks apiece. He had visited it once and never made the same mistake again.

The doorman was a small, wizened old black man named Jimmy. Pacifico had never known him by any other name. The old man was standing outside the imposing burnished-bronze hotel entrance, under the vermillion canopy that stretched across the sidewalk. His ancient wrinkled face broke into a huge grin when he saw Pacifico approaching. "Hey Nick, how you been?" he shouted.

They stood and chatted companionably about weather,

prices, Pacifico's daughter, Jimmy's grandsons, and years long gone by. Pacifico's father had been a hotel doorman until his death of a heart attack nine years ago. That had been at the Hotel Martingale, an aged establishment that was now closed. Jimmy had been a bellhop there. As a boy Pacifico had often stood by the old Martingale's front entrance and listened reverently while his father and Jimmy discussed the horses and other grand matters. The boy had been fascinated by the two men's talk and also impressed by their splendid red uniforms, but his views of the world changed as he grew into his teens. He began to observe that his father and Jimmy, despite those dazzling uniforms, were not held in high esteem by the hotel's wealthy guests. The guests, in fact, treated them like trained dogs. By the time he was in his late teens, Pacifico shunned the old Martingale because he could no longer bear to witness his father's daily humiliation.

His father dropped dead on the sidewalk one hot summer day. A woman guest's Pekingese had slipped its leash, and he was trying to catch it for her. Pacifico had hated the rich unreasonably and intractably ever since.

He stood now and watched Jimmy go into action as a yellow cab pulled up to the curb. Then, after a while, he turned and went into the New World Hotel.

The lobby was large, richly furnished, and imposing. The floor was of black slate. Armchairs were upholstered in royal blue. All around the periphery were expensive small stores that were patronized not only by the hotel's guests but also by the wealthy owners of condominiums on the upper floors.

Pacifico went into the little news-and-notions shop. Cora was bending over, straightening a pile of magazines. The temptation was irresistible. Pacifico tiptoed up and slapped her bottom.

She shouted, "Get your goddamn hand off my — " Then she saw who the molester was and grinned. "Nick!" she said, and put her arms around his neck. "Nick, Nick, Nick!" She gave him a wet kiss. She was wearing strawberry-flavored lipstick. "How come I never see you any more?"

"You're seeing me now," he pointed out. He grinned down at her fondly. Cora was a short, dark woman with arresting violet eyes but acne-scarred cheeks. She was another ex-Martingale employee who, like Jimmy, had landed a job at the New World when the old hotel closed. At the Martingale she had managed the checkroom. She was five years older than Pacifico. She had introduced him to the joys and mysteries of sex when he was seventeen. The magnetism between them was still powerful.

"I close up in an hour," she said.

"Okay, I'll walk around. I'll be back."

As he went back out the front door, a shining, chauffeur-driven, gray Bentley was pulling up to the curb. Jimmy ran to it and opened the rear door. "Evenin', Mr. Pierce," he said cheerfully. "Nice to have you back with us!"

"Yes, see that my bags get sent up right away, will you? I'm in a hurry."

Pacifico thought: can't the bastard even spare an old man a smile?

He started to walk away, then stopped.

There was a cool, soft rain on his face. And there was something else . . .

Jimmy had also stopped in the act of lifting a suitcase. The two men stared at each other, astonished.

"A breeze!" Pacifico said. "I'll be damned. A *breeze!*"

* * *

It was not much of a breeze. News reports the next day

said it reached a maximum of seven miles an hour, which is designated Force Two or "light breeze" on the international Beaufort Scale. It blew for less than a day, stopping before dawn in Toronto, at midmorning in New York, and before sundown in Mexico City.

3

KIM ARRIVED FOR work at exactly nine o'clock Monday morning. She was scrupulously prompt because she did not want to give this man Pacifico an opportunity to sneer "boss's daughter."

At that hour, however, the editorial offices were eerily deserted except for a few secretaries and a boy delivering newspapers. The offices were housed in a single vast room. Since there was nobody to tell her which of the little glass-walled cubicles, if any, had been assigned to her, Kim spent twenty minutes wandering around irresolutely. The place gave an impression of haphazard growth rather than planning. It was massively untidy. Books and papers covered the desks, radiator tops, and file cabinets in wild disarray; notices, calendars, and other bits of paper were taped all over the walls and partitions. The air-conditioning seemed to be as haphazard as everything else. Some areas of the huge room were sharply cooler than others.

Kim saw the name *Pacifico* at the entrance to one of the larger, cooler cubicles and went in there to wait. She wanted a cigarette but could not find an ashtray, so she simply sat in a hard chair next to the desk and fidgeted. She was nervous. She was sure she had made a very bad first impression on Pacifico that morning in her father's office.

He must have come away thinking of her as spoiled, bored, and indifferent.

She had indeed been in an angry mood, but not because she was unwilling to go to work. Quite the opposite: Kim craved work, clung to the thought of it like a shipwreck survivor clinging to a floating plank. She had been angry that morning because she resented the need to have her father make a job for her, and also because—well, just because it was a bad morning. She had them once in a while. She had learned how to fight them and usually was able to continue functioning normally, but often, she feared, other people could see or sense that all was not well beneath the surface.

Kimberley Beaulieu was a recovered alcoholic. The terrible sickness, which usually develops slowly and strikes people down in middle age, had reached full flowering in her by the time she was twenty. Contrary to the teaching of Alcoholics Anonymous, of which she was a member, she and her family had elected to keep her condition a secret. The world believed she had been expelled from Radcliffe years back because of chronic rulebreaking and had been shipped off to Europe to find herself. The truth was that she had left college voluntarily because she could not handle the academic work while simultaneously fighting the terrifying battle against drink. Far from spending those years in Europe, as people believed, she had spent them working on an assembly line in Detroit. An AA chapter there had supported her in the fight. So had a Presbyterian church, where she contributed a clear, sweet alto voice to the choir.

Mended, she had resumed her college career. But after those years in Detroit she found it hard to take college life seriously or herself seriously as a student. AA warned that even when you have been sober for two years, for ten, you are still only one drink away from potential disaster. The precariousness of her hold on life added to her difficulties in the party-loving college environment. She graduated, but with a barely passing average.

The hunt for a job proved hard. Frightened of idleness, she abandoned the hunt quickly and acceded to her father's long-standing suggestion that she sign on at *Seven Days*.

• • •

And now here she sat, wanting a cigarette and wishing she did not. Why did the body want what was bad for it?

Pacifico arrived at nine-thirty. They said good morning politely, without warmth, avoiding the use of each other's names. Kim did not know what to call him. She certainly was not going to glorify him with "Mr.," and "Nick" also seemed wrong. She had tried that when they were first introduced, hoping they might establish a relationship of equals. She wanted to be a full partner in hard, useful work but it seemed that was not to be.

He glanced through the collection of memos and rolled newspapers that had landed on his desk, then said, "Let's go right into Charlie Broadbent's office. He wants to talk about the piece."

He was not a bad-looking man, this Pacifico, she conceded as she followed him. He was lean and medium tall. His clothes were strictly from Sears and sloppily mismatched, but that was all right; he carried them well. He radiated some kind of fierce energy. His face was quite handsome in a dark, Mediterranean sort of way.

Kim was sure she had nothing against Italians, though her family did, being of French-Swiss extraction. The Swiss imported Italians as laborers and domestic help in boom times, then stabilized the unemployment rate by sending them back home in recessions. Kim had often heard Grandmother Beaulieu speak of Italians in terms that might have been used by an old Kentucky aristocrat discussing blacks. The worst outbreak of bias had occurred when Kim, in college, elected to room with a plumbing contractor's daughter named Pizzolato. The arrangement lasted only a semester, for Kim quickly discovered, as Grandmother Beaulieu predicted she would, that she preferred to be with girls of her own social class. But she remained proud of that semester; it certified her as liberal and bias-free, she thought. She was determined now that she would not let Pacifico's background make things any worse than necessary.

If only he would try to be friendlier. He had made it plain that he did not like playing mentor any more than she liked playing student. But did he have to be so obvious about it? If he'll make an effort, she thought, I'm perfectly willing to meet the man halfway.

Charlie Broadbent, the managing editor, occupied a corner office with solid walls and a genuine wood door. He was a large fat man with gray hair and brilliant red cheeks. Kim liked him immediately, for he tried to put her at ease.

"Welcome to our chummy little group," he said, smiling at her genially as she sat. "Has anybody shown you your cubbyhole yet?"

It *was* nice to know somebody cared. "Not yet," she said, and hoped she did not sound too petulant.

He told her whom to see about that, then said, "All right, let's talk about wind." He leaned back in his creaky swivel chair and looked out the window at the dead blue-white sky. "I sure don't see any sign of wind so far, do you?"

"There was a breeze a couple of nights ago," she reminded him.

He nodded, then leaned toward Pacifico and folded his massive, meaty arms on his desk. "So okay, Nick, what do you think of the story?"

"I think it's garbage. A complete waste of time." Pacifico was sitting on the edge of a table and looking surly.

Broadbent did not seem surprised by this. He grinned at Kim and said, "Nick here isn't one of our leading optimists." He turned back to Pacifico and asked, "Why the harsh judgment?"

"Ah, you know the problems, Charlie. We talked about them last week. It's a hoked-up story. There's no foundation to it. 'Endworld' my ass. It's like finding a couple of bicycles stolen and running purple headlines about a crime wave."

"Oh, come off it Nick. I'll admit it isn't the top story of the decade, but—"

"It's dishonest, Charlie. I mean it'll have to be dishonest if I'm going to put any spark in it. It's like those pieces you see in women's magazines. You know: 'Has Your Husband Stopped Talking to You?' That kind of trash. You start by inventing some silly problem the readers didn't know they had, and then you go out and interview a bunch of shrinks. If a shrink says it's a nonproblem, you don't quote him. You go looking for shrinks who are willing to say it's the leading cause of the decline of western civilization, and that's how you—"

"Don't exaggerate, Nick," Charlie Broadbent said amiably.

"Exaggerate? *Exaggerate*?" Pacifico leaped to his feet and advanced on Broadbent's desk, gesticulating angrily. "Look, Charlie, you know what I'll have to do. I'll go to the top scientists and they'll say, 'Piss off, it's hokum, quit bothering us.' So then I'll have to go around hunting for the nuts and crackpots, just to get something I can quote. I hate stories like this, Charlie!"

"But you do them so well," Charlie Broadbent said with unperturbed good humor.

"Oh, for Christ's sake."

Broadbent glanced at Kim, as though checking to make sure she was enjoying the show as much as he was. Then he grew more serious. "Listen, Nick, I know it won't be an easy story, and my heart bleeds for you and all that—"

"But, right? The next word is but."

"Right. But. The story is scheduled, and the name on the assignment sheet is yours, buddy. It may not be a swinging piece, but we've got to have it. After all, it's a world topic, for God's sake. *Time* has already run a big piece on it, and so has almost everybody else. But us? We've just about ignored it. . . ."

As the debate went on, both men seemed to forget Kim, who sat fidgeting in her chair. She was thinking about a number of things, among them cigarettes. She had hoped Charlie Broadbent would be a smoker, but there were no ashtrays in his office either. This was a problem of the white-collar world that she had not anticipated. In the factories of Detroit you smoked in designated areas at break time, but what was the protocol governing smoking in other people's offices? She would have to find out, for like many recovered alcoholics she had shaken the big monkey off her back only to find a lesser one perched there ever more securely. With some it was food or coffee. With her it was cigarettes.

The debate was winding down. Pacifico was going through the process of capitulating while seeking concessions. "I'll tell you what, Charlie," he was saying. "Maybe we can work it this way. Why don't I put in a couple of days on that election story we've got coming up? Meanwhile Ms. Beaulieu can get started on the Big Wind. She can do some library digging, maybe some pre-interviews. Then we'll see what the story looks like and decide where we go."

Charlie Broadbent argued for a while, then gave in. Kim was delighted to learn she was to be assigned some real work. The Big Wind story was obviously not one in which her immediate boss took any real interest, but after all, work was work. It was what she wanted.

• • •

After settling the business of her office cubicle and smoking a cigarette, she reported back to Pacifico's office for instructions. He was on the phone. She sat in the chair by his desk.

"So okay, let's get you started," he said briskly as he hung up. "You can spend the rest of the day in the library. It's on the floor below this one. I'll want every major piece the *Times* has done, and also major magazine pieces, whatever we've got on microfiche. Check the *Reader's Guide* to see whether—"

"Check the what?"

"*Reader's Guide*. You mean you aren't familiar with it?"

"No, I never—"

"Jesus, what do they teach in a journalism course? Well, all right, the librarian will help you. If there are some stories that sound important but we don't have them, go over to the public library. And after that . . . You *do* know how to use the *Times* Index, I hope?"

There had been something about that in one of her courses, but she had been an inattentive student. She did not want to admit this, of course. She said, "Oh, sure."

"If a piece is really meaty, make a copy. Otherwise take notes. What I want mainly is names of sources. People we can go to for juicy stuff. But not just the cranks and the lunatics. I also want the opposing team: people who say the whole Big Wind idea is nonsense. But they have to be people who say it well. Lunatics are always colorful. The problem is to find feet-on-the-ground types who are also colorful. You follow?"

"I think so," Kim said. Actually she was confused.

He must have seen the confusion in her eyes, for he went on to explain: "Just between you and me, Charlie isn't going to get exactly the story he's expecting. I'll tell you something about Charlie: he's really quite comfortable with hokey stories. He doesn't actually *prefer* them, but it gives him no pain to print one occasionally if he thinks it'll sell magazines. Right now he'd love to have me write a dooms-day piece saying the end of the world is coming. Well, he isn't going to get it. What he'll get will be a piece that reports the plain truth: that nobody knows if any Big Wind is coming but most feet-on-the-ground types doubt it."

This had a closed-minded sound to Kim. She said, "But maybe these feet-on-the-ground types are wrong."

"Sure, maybe. We'll allow for the possibility. We'll give the crackpots their day in court."

It still seemed to Kim that a pretrial judgment was being made, but she kept silent.

"Before you hit the library," Pacifico said, "get me a cup of coffee, will you? Black, no sugar."

He began to fish money from his pocket. Kim said, "No."

"No?"

"We'd better get one thing straight, Pacifico. I'm your research assistant or whatever you want to call me, and I'll do all the honest work you want to give me. But I'm not a slave. You fetch your own damned coffee."

To her astonishment, he grinned. "Okay, Beaulieu, I was just testing you," he said cheerfully. "Glad to see you've got some fight in you."

"Fight?" She stood up, angry. "There isn't much I don't know about fighting, Pacifico. I'd guess I know a lot more about it than you do."

His grin disappeared. "I doubt that," he said.

There was a look of pain on his face. Kim did not know what it meant. She decided the best thing to do was to leave immediately.

4

KIM WAS PLEASED to discover that smoking was permitted in the company library. She was even more pleased to find the research absorbing.

The Big Wind story had begun with the sighting of a hitherto unknown comet. As was traditional, it was eventually named after its discoverer, a British amateur astronomer named Taylor. Comet Taylor seemed to be unusually large and massive. What interested everybody just as much was the fact that, as nearly as astronomers could determine, it was heading on a collision course with Earth. There would either be a direct hit or a very near miss.

As this frightening news hit the streets and airwaves, editors the world over sought out scientists for background and analysis. The scientists, trying to maintain proper detachment, pointed out that impacts and close approaches by large space-traveling objects are not merely conceivable; they are all but certain, given time. In terms of our planet's life span they are neither rare nor surprising. On the contrary, it would be surprising if they did *not* occur.

The seeming emptiness of space is filled with dark drifters, the scientists said. Some of these objects are the size of peas or tennis balls; others may be larger than Earth. Some fairly big ones are known to have hit Earth in remote times, and it is safe to predict that others will strike our planet with measurable impact in the future. In the end, perhaps, we will be struck by an object of sufficient mass to bring humankind's untidy history to a close.

Indeed, though Earth itself has withstood all impacts so far without important damage, some of these cosmic hits may have been enough to cause the mass extinction of whatever plant and animal species were then living on the land or in the seas. Many scientists—not all, but many—think this is a plausible explanation of the dinosaurs' mysterious and sudden disappearance millions of years ago. The earth may have been struck by a large comet or other celestial wanderer. The resulting explosion, perhaps mightier than the simultaneous detonation of a million nuclear bombs, could have raised a pall of dust and smoke so huge and dense that it changed entirely Earth's weather patterns. The great globe-circling cloud could have blocked sunlight, producing a ten-thousand-year winter in which cold-blooded creatures could not survive.

If this was in fact how the dinosaurs died, the perpetrator of the colossal mischief need not have been a comet. Other massive space wanderers could have produced the same result. But as Comet Taylor sped toward its rendezvous with Earth, newspapers and magazines published article after article in which such speculations were linked specifically with comets. Kim, sitting in the library, studied so many of these articles that she could predict what they were going to say.

Comets are really very interesting objects. Billions of them are thought to circle the sun out beyond the orbits of the known planets. Once in a while, for unknown reasons, one of them gets pushed into an eccentric orbit that brings it into the inner part of the solar system, where, if it is big enough, it becomes visible as a bright object with a diaphanous tail. As long as it does not hit a planet or fall into the sun, it returns to our neighborhood periodically, as Halley's Comet did in 1986.

Comets probably come in widely varying sizes. Of the few that have been studied in detail, most have seemed to be flying mountains of rock and ice a few miles across. But among their billions there are undoubtedly some much smaller and some vastly bigger. As it approached Earth, the size of Comet Taylor was calculated, and was found to be enormous. Its mass was something like one-quarter the mass of the moon.

When *that* news hit the streets, there was worldwide panic. Nobody called it Comet Taylor anymore. Now it was the Doomsday Comet or the Endworld Comet. If an object of that size should hit Earth, it was likely that all life would be wiped out.

Fortunately, the panic lasted only a day. New and more precise computations revealed that the comet was not going to strike Earth after all. Its path of approach was at roughly a 45° angle to the plane of the ecliptic. Computer simulations showed that it would pass very close to the moon and Earth, whose gravity would capture it and then release it in such a way as to bend its path and fling it toward the sun.

Like a weight whipped around on the end of a string, but on a vastly larger scale and in majestic slow motion, the huge object dominated the night sky as its path curved around Earth toward the north. It threw some people into a religious frenzy and others into a frenzy of partying. It also produced physical effects.

Its approach was close enough and its mass great enough to perturb the earth's solar orbit and also the moon's orbit about the earth—not drastically but enough to measure. It also disturbed the world's oceans. Coastal areas were devastated by enormous waves, floods, and erratic tides. The English Channel flowed like a river for a time. The

water level of the Indian Ocean dropped so far that some
port cities found themselves looking at prairies of soggy
mud where their harbors had been.

These oceanic effects were gradually diminishing as the
great comet passed to the north. They could be expected to
subside altogether as it drew away and raced toward the
sun. The effects on the weather, however, were not so easy
to predict.

For the comet had apparently pulled a substantial part of
the atmosphere toward it as it passed. There was now a
gigantic bubble or streamer of air hanging out in space
above the north pole. The bubble had grown slowly as air
flowed into it week after week from all around the globe.

One result was a worldwide drop in air pressure. The
drop posed no threat to healthy lungs, but it did make
smokers worry. Many tried to quit. Sitting in the library
now, smoking, Kim remembered joining a quitters' group
during that period. She lasted two days. The memory gave
her sour amusement.

The pressure drop had been easy to understand. But
there were also some peculiar and little-understood weather
phenomena. The southern hemisphere, which normally
enters its winter with the June solstice, was experiencing
heat more fierce than summer's. Equatorial regions were
drowning under torrential rains. Much of the northern
hemisphere had experienced a long period of rain and hail,
followed by the strange stillness that was now being called
the Great Calm. Meteorologists expected to argue for a long
time over the chains of cause and effect that had produced
these odd results. They were also finding it hard to agree on
what came next.

What was going to happen when the Doomsday Comet
went away?

Since its path had been bent so as to whip it toward the
sun, it was expected to depart much more abruptly than it
had approached. Its velocity in relation to Earth was

already increasing rapidly and would increase still more as its direction changed. Its gravitational hold on that monumental bubble of air was expected to weaken quickly.

When that happened, the air in the bubble would flow back down to its original position around the planet. There were some scientists, however, who believed "flow" was too gentle a word. They believed all that air would not merely flow down, but pour.

Some meteorologists were talking about winds of a hundred or more miles an hour. Some were talking about four hundred.

• • •

"Are you interested in lunch?" somebody was asking.

Startled, Kim looked up from the microfilm viewer and saw the company librarian standing next to her, smiling uncertainly. The librarian was a shy, painfully thin young woman with soft brown eyes behind rimless glasses. While helping Kim with the microfilm gadgetry she had introduced herself as Alice Wenska.

"It's almost one o'clock," Alice Wenska said. "I thought maybe—you know, since you're new around here—"

"Lunch sounds like a great idea," Kim said, appreciating the offered friendliness. "I didn't realize it was so late."

This was literally true. Reading about the comet, hunting for useful material and sources, trying to understand all the conflicting speculations about wind, Kim had been transported into a world in which no time passed.

She went to wash the library dust from her hands. Riding down in the elevator she asked Alice, "Where do people eat around here?"

"Well, there aren't too many choices unless you want a good long walk. There's a cafeteria in the basement. There's a coffee shop across the street, not too bad. And there's a McDonald's."

"Oh," said Kim, vaguely disappointed. She had always

supposed New York press people ate at small secret restaurants with tablecloths. Maybe that isn't true of librarians, she surmised.

Alice Wenska gave one of her shy smiles. "I know it isn't chic to say this, but I think McDonald's serves some of the best food in New York. For the money, I mean."

"Yes, it's very good," Kim agreed politely. The truth was that she had never had to care about the price of a meal except in Detroit, and there she had hardly noticed the taste.

Stepping from the air-conditioned lobby to the Madison Avenue sidewalk, they were assaulted by damp heat. Kim thought she should have been used to it after all these weeks, but she was not. It took her by surprise nearly every time she walked into it.

She and Alice walked for half a block without saying anything. Kim was puzzled by something unusual in the air, something different. What was it? She realized at last that it was the quality of the light.

She looked up. Overhead and to the south, the sky was the same milky blue it had been for weeks. But to the north it was dark gray, streaked with bands of dirty yellow light. Tall buildings were silhouetted against it in a stark way that Kim associated with bare trees in winter. Somehow, that sky looked cold. She felt inadequately clothed in her summer dress.

"What a funny sky," she remarked to Alice.

"It is, isn't it?"

Kim did not know whether it was her imagination, but the city around her seemed oddly hushed. There were plenty of people on the sidewalks, but the usual lunch-hour bustle was absent. Even the traffic on the street seemed subdued by the peculiar light.

Drivers were patient and considerate when Kim and

Alice got mousetrapped while crossing the avenue. Not a horn sounded.

"Is this really New York?" Alice asked, awed.

* * *

Inside McDonald's, however, life went on as usual. The crowd was noisy, energetic, unbeautiful, multicolored, ill-mannered, inelegant but altogether good-humored—a typical crowd drawn off a New York street at noon. Kim discovered that a Big Mac was not nearly as bad as she had been hearing all her life. Or maybe, she thought, it's just that I'm hungrier than usual.

The two young women swapped life stories. Alice Wenska came from a Chicago suburb, where she had started her career as a junior high school librarian. She had hated it—mostly, Kim judged, because she could not handle the kids. Kids can be inordinately cruel to somebody who lacks physical beauty and who, when pushed, fails to push back. Kim guessed there was not an ounce of assertiveness in this Alice Wenska.

Kim was reminded a little of her freshman roommate, "Pizz" Pizzolato. Pizz, too, had failed to push back. She was an outsider, doomed always to be excluded from the glamorous gatherings and doings of Kim's high-status group. Kim had made no effort to open the gates for Pizz; she did not see how she could. Once she had come upon poor Pizz crying alone and had felt sad and a little guilty for a day, but that had passed. A twinge of the remembered emotion pricked her now as she sat talking to Alice.

They were finishing their coffee and dessert when Kim saw Nick Pacifico, Charlie Broadbent, and some other men at a table across the restaurant. She thought: there goes my theory about where press people and librarians eat. She waved, but they did not see her.

"My boss," she said, explaining the wave to Alice.

"Do you like him?"

Kim considered this for a moment, then said, "Frankly not a whole hell of a lot. Not so far." She grinned and added, "He's an awfully prickly bastard."

"Yes, he can be that way," Alice agreed. "He'll come charging into the library and get mad if I can't find everything in two seconds. But I think he's just tense."

"Tense? About what?"

Alice shrugged. "He's had a lot of problems, I guess. The rumor around the office is that his wife left him a couple of years ago. Just ran off with some rich guy she met playing tennis. And his little girl—she's said to have some kind of expensive medical problem that causes him a lot of worry. All this is just gossip, of course. I can't document it."

"It's easy to tell you're a librarian, Alice," Kim teased.

"I know." Alice produced one of those sweet, shy smiles. "But I do like to see facts backed up. It's a mistake to believe everything people say about each other. A lot of it isn't true."

That was no news to Kim. Wishing to change the subject, she pulled cigarettes from her bag and asked Alice if she smoked. Alice said no. Kim said, "I hope you don't mind if I do. At the table, I mean. A lot of people don't like it."

"It doesn't bother me in the slightest."

"Well, it bothers me," Kim said sourly. "It's a stupid habit. Especially for somebody who likes singing."

Alice leaned forward, her brown eyes wide with interest. "You're a singer? What kind of singing do you do?"

"Glee clubs and choirs, mostly. I haven't joined any group here in New York yet, but I'm looking."

"Kim, this is amazing!" Alice said happily. "I'm a choir singer, too. It's an old church near the Village, the loveliest acoustics you ever heard. What do you sing?"

"Alto. I can fill in as a soprano if I really have to, but my range isn't all it used to be." She gestured with her cigarette to indicate the reason.

The fact was that smoking had not yet done serious damage to Kim's lungs or vocal cords. She had an exceptionally lovely, clear, strong voice. She also possessed the rare and mysterious gift of perfect pitch. More than one choir leader had told her she could develop her voice for solo singing if she wished, but she had no interest in solo singing. What she loved most of all was the sound of mixed voices singing in harmony.

Alice Wenska said, "We're always short of people. Would you like to join us in a practice some Thursday night?"

"I'd love to," Kim said eagerly.

How she would love to! It was not so many weeks since she had come to seek her fortune in New York, but the lack of music was already growing painful. A large part of her life was missing. She yearned to hear it and help make it once again: the rich, sweet harmony of male and female voices, with the alto part weaving through the center like a golden thread.

When Kim had finished her cigarette, they left the restaurant. They stopped dead on the sidewalk, staring at each other in the strange wintry light.

It was raining. The yellow-banded darkness now covered the whole sky. And a wind was blowing.

"Wind!" Kim said. "It's actually *windy*!"

For a moment, standing there with Alice, watching people hurry by in the rain, she was clutched by a feeling of dread. It was diffuse and sourceless, like the night terror that had visited her often in the days when she was drinking. But it vanished as abruptly as it had come. She and Alice walked back to work, comfortable in a new-made friendship.

• • •

It was a north wind. It reached about fifteen miles an hour—Force Four or "moderate breeze" on the Beaufort Scale. It was accompanied by occasional light rain and a modest temperature drop in most cities. In New York it blew steadily for the rest of that afternoon but subsided to almost nothing by midnight.

When the sun came up the following morning, the sky was once more hot, flat, and milky blue.

5

PACIFICO WAS SURPRISED. He had left her alone for a day and a half, expecting that she would merely play at working. She would spend a lot of time phoning friends, he supposed. She would go off for long lunches at Lutèce. Instead he had seen her at McDonald's yesterday. And now here she was in his office with what seemed like a hefty bundle of photocopied material and diligent notes.

He was just as surprised by her apparent enthusiasm. She had learned a lot about the postulated Big Wind and seemed eager to tell him about it. He interrupted her by saying, "The piece grabs you, does it?"

"Yes, but it isn't just the piece. It's the wind itself. I mean, if we do have this Big Wind, it won't just be something for us to write about. We'll be *in* it."

"Sure. *If.*" Pacifico wondered whether to deliver a lecture on journalistic detachment, then decided against it. "Listen, if you like the story you might as well go on with it. Some preliminary interviews, maybe. Are you game?"

She nodded immediately. Her pale blue eyes had the oddly ferocious look that had intrigued him several times before.

"Okay," he said. "Now on a piece like this, a good approach is to interview all the nuts first. That's stage one. Then in stage two you go to all the mainstream people, and you challenge them with what the nuts said and have them quarrel with it. So who's your leading nut?"

She continued to gaze at him without answering for a moment. He thought she wanted to argue about his use of the word "nut." But then she looked down at her notes, which were on large sheets of lined yellow paper. "Well," she said, "there's a man in California. Ferguson. Some kind of construction engineer. He's been going around saying most buildings won't take—"

"Yes, I saw him on a TV news show. But you'd better do him by phone later. Try an in-person interview first; the pace won't be so fast. Who's close by?"

"There's a man in Connecticut. Pollock, I think his name is."

"He's been on TV, too, hasn't he? Okay, hit him."

She looked perplexed. "What do I do, just walk in on him?"

"Phone first, set up an appointment. Have you ever done that?"

"Well, ah—"

"Here, you can practice on me. Pretend I'm Pollock."

For the next quarter-hour he gave her a practical training course in interviewing technique. Something told him she could be good at it—if she stuck with it.

At the end of the lesson she asked, "Can I drive there in my car? And get reimbursed, I mean?"

"Sure. There's a mileage allowance. I don't know what it is because I don't have a car." Pacifico hoped he did not sound bitter about this. He could not afford a car.

"And where can I get a tape recorder?"

"Do you think you'll need one?"

"Well, in college we—"

"Forget what they told you in college. Tape recorders are a bad habit. A lot of places won't let you in the door with one. And even when people try to be good sports, the gadgetry makes them nervous. They think every word they say is going to be used against them. A lot of times they freeze."

"But I don't know shorthand."

"Nor do I. Don't worry about it. You'll invent your own. You don't have to take down every word the man says anyhow. Nine-tenths of what people say is just noise. You ignore it."

She nodded, then stood up to leave. She gave him a sudden, cheerful smile. "Thanks for the lesson, professor," she said, and walked out.

Pacifico sat for a while and wondered about her. Then he picked up the phone and called Cora.

6

DR. SIMON POLLOCK was a small, round man with thick glasses. His eyes were watery and nearsighted. He was almost completely bald and like the rest of his face, his pate was very pink. His classmates in high school and college had called him "Squeak" because of his high voice, and he was painfully aware that his students still referred to him by that unkind name when they thought he was not listening.

Simon Pollock was a professor of meteorology. He also maintained one of the more important weather stations in the vast tri-state urban-suburban region surrounding New York City. Like all state government enterprises in the 1980s, the station was chronically short of money. It needed equipment. It also needed space, housed as it was in a crumbling old red-brick college building that should have been condemned long ago. It needed staff, too. In fact, virtually all its work was done by unpaid students and by the professor himself. But little Simon Pollock kept it up to a high standard of excellence by sheer force of will and love.

Many of the men and women in weather work would be just as happy somewhere else. They are people who drifted into it by accident, as often as not. One common route is to join the Navy without any clearly seen plan for the future. The Navy asks, "What'll we do with this guy?" and finally finds a slot in weather school. Then there are the Simon

Pollocks. He had been fascinated by weather even as a child in Nebraska. He built his first crude anemometer in the sixth grade. Like Thoreau, but in a less dreamy way, he was a self-appointed inspector of snowstorms and rainstorms. Other kids laughed at the chubby little boy who was always out getting wet, and while it would be a romantic lie to say he did not mind this, the fact is that he was able to lift himself away from his earthly troubles for hours at a time by gazing at Nebraska's vast, lonesome skies.

He had lost none of his eccentricities as an adult. He still dreamed often that he could soar among clouds like a hawk. He still loved to be outdoors when interesting weather was happening. It was a campus joke that the more inclement the weather became, the more likely it was that little Professor Pollock could be seen wandering the streets or pacing around the flat roof of that old three-story, red-brick building. "That's our Squeak!" students and faculty members would say proudly to visitors.

The roof was where the weather station's reading instruments were deployed. All were electronically connected to dials, graphs, and other displays inside; all could be monitored perfectly well without ever poking a nose outdoors. Simon Pollock went up on the roof because he habitually took readings not only with man-made instruments, but also with his own eyes and skin.

He knew he was considered odd—not quite a crackpot, perhaps, but tending that way. He was known in weather circles throughout the region as a man who did not always agree with accepted meteorological wisdom, particularly in long-range forecasting. Sometimes his forecasts were wide of the mark. Just as often they were brilliantly right when everybody else was wrong.

He was certainly out of step with the majority in his forecast of the Big Wind. Many of his colleagues and rivals believed he had devised his forecast as a grandiose publicity stunt. He had to admit it had won him a lot of space in the press and time on TV. He was about to be interviewed by a woman from *Seven Days*, and this exposure, provided the magazine was not out to make him look like an ass, would be one more feather in his cap. He did not deny he was enjoying the attention. Meteorology is not among the glamorous sciences; its practitioners are mostly obscure. When the sunshine of publicity makes one of its rare appearances, they tend to bask in it with perhaps more enjoyment than seems proper. Simon Pollock made no excuses for himself in this regard. He liked the publicity. He was guilty. He confessed it freely.

But he denied that his forecast was cynically rigged up for publicity purposes alone. It was real. True, it was based as much on hunch as on calculation, but that made it no less genuine.

Simon Pollack believed, as did a few others, that the world was going to experience a wind like nothing it had ever felt before.

●　●　●

Someone appeared in the doorway and asked, "Is this the weather station?"

"Yes," Pollock replied. There had once been a sign above the door, but it had been stolen.

"I'm looking for Professor Pollock," the visitor said. She was an extraordinarily attractive young woman with medium-short blonde hair and light blue eyes. Pollock did not recognize her. He guessed she was a summer student come to ask about something.

"I'm Pollock," he said.

"I'm Kim Beaulieu of *Seven Days*."

He was surprised. Her voice on the phone had led him to expect somebody a little older. He said, "Ah. Yes, Ms. Beaulieu. Come in. Welcome to my den."

Simon Pollock had known since boyhood that women found him uninteresting, but he kept his morale up by bantering with them and occasionally earning a smile. His visitor now rewarded him, but her smile had a nervous quality to it. She looked around the weather station uncertainly.

Probably expected a grander place, he thought as he led her to the cramped corner where he kept his desk.

The station consisted of a single large, dusty, densely crowded room on the top floor of the old brick building. The walls of the room were lined solidly with scarred old desks and rough, plywood-topped cabinets and work tables, and there was an island of tables in the central floor space. Most of the tabletop space was covered with maps, charts, ragged sheafs of teletype printout and miscellaneous books and papers. Located here and there amid the clutter were great gray machines that continuously and tirelessly printed out maps, satellite pictures, and other data from the National Weather Service, the Navy, the Canadian Weather Service, and other sources.

The professor's "office," as it was grandly called, was a small metal desk wedged into a corner behind some file cabinets. On a wall near the desk was an array of dials showing the windspeed, temperature, and other conditions being read by instruments up on the roof. Also near the desk was something else that Pollock considered important in his work: a window.

He looked out before sitting down. The afternoon was still, hot, and sunny. He could not see much sky because of a huge maple tree, which the college authorities refused to cut down despite his endless output of peevish memos on the subject, but the small piece of sky he could see was milky blue. Only the faintest breeze stirred the maple's leaves. A few students were sitting on the parched brown lawn beneath the tree, and they all looked enervated by the damp, still heat. But there was a tickle of excitement in Simon Pollock's belly. He knew the afternoon would change.

"Did you happen to look at the sky on your way here, Ms. Beaulieu?" he asked, turning from the window.

"Yes." She was sitting in the chair next to his desk, pulling a notebook and pen from her handbag. "There's a line of dark cloud in the north, coming this way, I think."

"Right on schedule," he said contentedly. He was pleased not just because it was on schedule, but because she had seen it. An observant young woman, he thought. It had puzzled and irritated him all his life to know that many people, perhaps most, can spend hours outdoors without once examining the sky.

She asked, "Is it another of those—what do you call them? Another wave of wind?"

"I've been calling them pulses, but your word is just as good. Wave." He tested the word and liked it. "Yes. Another wave is on the way. The Canadians were reporting winds over thirty miles an hour this morning."

He still had not sat down. It was going to be an interesting afternoon, and he hated to commit himself to spending a long time indoors. And so he remained standing, hands in pockets, trying not to fidget.

She asked, "Thirty miles an hour—is that what you'd call a high wind?"

"It's in the neighborhood of a 'moderate gale,' to use Admiral Beaufort's classification."

"Admiral Beaufort?"

"Sir Francis Beaufort, a British Admiral, early nineteenth century." He realized how professorial he sounded and gave her a grin to show he did not take himself that seriously.

She was making a note. "How do you spell Beaufort—the French way?"

"Yes. You'll find the Beaufort Scale in almost any encyclopedia, but I must warn you there are several different versions. Listen, Ms. Beaulieu, I have an idea. Why don't we go up on the roof?"

She looked startled, but she nodded. He led her along a dim corridor and up a flight of creaky wooden stairs.

The weather roof was a flat expanse of lumpy red asphalt. Most of the instruments were clustered in a corner, around a large brick chimney that provided the roof's only shade. Pollock pointed out the revolving cup anemometer. It was mounted at the top of the chimney, moving in lazy starts and stops, indicating an almost total lack of wind. Nearby, in a roofed wooden enclosure that needed repairs and paint, were instruments for measuring temperature and humidity. Next to the enclosure was a tipping-bucket rain gauge, and next to that was a small telescope used for visual tracking of the weather balloons Pollock launched when he could afford them.

The view from the roof, except where blocked by that hated maple tree, was magnificent. This small campus of the state university system was in an area that was partly suburban, partly rural. The campus was on a hill. From the roof could be seen a panorama of rolling Connecticut countryside, now dressed in summer green. More important to Simon Pollock, a vast expanse of sky could be seen as well.

Leaning against the waist-high parapet that surrounded the roof, he looked at that sky now and said, "Wave. Yes. I like that word. It does look like a wave, doesn't it? A gigantic wave."

"It's dramatic," she said. "A little scary, too, I think."

Looming heavily in the northern sky was a dense wall of blue-gray cloud. Its upper edge was a ragged but sharply defined line that stretched without a break from horizon to horizon. It reminded Pollock of line storms he had seen over the western prairies. He could not see its ponderous, inexorable approach with his eyes, but he could feel it in his stomach. It was coming, and nothing could stop it.

"Let's sit down," he said, and pointed to two folding canvas chairs. The hot sun was still shining in the southwestern sky, so they moved the chairs into the chimney's shadow.

"All right," he said as they sat. "What would you like to ask me, Ms. Beaulieu?"

"Whether I can smoke," she said, and gave him a mischievous grin.

"Of course." He grinned back. Using his foot, he pushed toward her an old coffee can that he used as an ashtray. "It isn't really time for my afternoon cigar yet, but I'll join you anyway."

As he lit his cigar, she said, "From what I've read about your views, professor, I gather you expect—well, what everybody calls a Big Wind."

"That's right."

"These waves—" she gestured at the darkening northern sky—"these waves will get worse and worse, then? I mean the winds will get stronger each time?"

"That's the way it looks to me. Mind you, I didn't foresee that it would happen in waves or pulses. All I said was that, sooner or later, in one way or another, the grandaddy of all winds was coming."

"Something like a hurricane, you mean?"

"Oh no. No, Ms. Beaulieu. Much worse than that. Unimaginably worse."

She drew on her cigarette and frowned at him. She looked worried, perhaps even a little frightened. This pleased him, for he had spent many weeks trying to get people to take him seriously and had not had much success. The press and TV people had given him plenty of publicity, but he suspected this was only because they thought him to be an interesting nut. Little Simon Pollock was not a man whom the world took seriously, on the whole. More often it laughed at him. Like his students, who entertained each other by imitating his squeaky voice when he was not around, the media people appeared more amused by how funny he was than impressed by things he was trying so earnestly to say. And now here was this Ms. Beaulieu of *Seven Days* frowning at him with what looked like genuine concern. How nice!

A most attractive young woman, too, he thought. Young enough to be my daughter, but by golly, I wouldn't mind having . . . well, never mind that. Attractive, yes, and also intelligent. Clearly a young woman of keen perceptions.

It had always been Simon Pollock's habit to admire the intelligence of those who took him seriously. This did not make him much different from other men and women. The distinction was that the experience happened to him less frequently and, therefore, more intensely, than to most others.

He pulled at his cigar and blew out smoke, noticing that it was carried away rapidly. A breeze had sprung up. He said, "Most hurricanes that hit land in the United States pack winds of less than a hundred miles an hour. That causes devastation enough. Even an eighty-mile wind can blow a frame house apart. But hurricane winds aren't even in the same league with the wind I'm talking about. I'm talking about four hundred miles an hour or more."

She was taking notes in fits and starts, repeatedly looking up at him with that worried expression on her face.

He thought: I've got her. That made him cautious. He did not want to lose her now by saying something she might deem overdramatic. On the other hand, he did want her to know the full extent of his concerns. He decided to risk it.

He said, "I'm not just talking about widespread damage, the kind we get with a hurricane. I'm talking about total obliteration, Ms. Beaulieu. I mean a complete wipeout." He drew on his cigar and leaned forward. "I'm talking about a wind that will blow cities down."

She stared at him silently for a second. "Cities?" she asked finally.

"Cities."

There was another silence, longer this time. The breeze was freshening. Pollock looked up and saw that the anemometer on the chimney-top was spinning steadily. The leading edge of the advancing cloud wall was now almost directly overhead.

She said, "Oh my." Her voice was low and breathy. She raised her cigarette to her mouth, then seemed to forget all about it and lowered it without taking a puff. Her pale blue eyes never left Pollock's face.

He said, "I'd better explain. You know about the comet, I suppose? And the air bubble? Or mound? Or whatever it is?" He pointed to the north.

"People talk about it drifting back to the normal configuration when the comet goes away. I've actually heard that word used: 'drift.' I'm sure sooner or later, before this is over, somebody is going to say 'waft.' What people don't realize is that air is really a pretty heavy gas. We live in it, so it seems weightless to us—just as water does to a fish. But do you know how much the earth's atmosphere weighs? I mean the whole of it?"

"I have no idea."

"In round numbers, five thousand trillion tons."

The startling figure seemed to impress her. He had hoped it would. It always impressed the more interested of his students. It still impressed him and always would.

She bent to make a note of the figure. He said helpfully, "That's a five followed by fifteen zeroes. Another way to say it would be five million billion."

"Tons, right? Not pounds. Tons?"

"Tons, Ms. Beaulieu."

"That's a lot of air."

"Indeed it is. Nobody knows how much of it is now mounded above the north pole. Several hundred trillion tons at least. And when it comes down, Ms. Beaulieu, when that huge heavy mass comes down, it isn't going to drift and it isn't going to waft. It's going to come down like several hundred trillion tons of bricks."

She looked at him for a moment, then leaned down to put out her cigarette in the coffee can. "If you're trying to scare me, Professor Pollock," she said without looking up, "you're doing a hell of a good job."

It gave him a vague discomfort to hear women use profane words—even mild ones like "hell," let alone the shocking expletives served up so casually by many of his students. He did not know exactly what the source of his discomfort was. Some old-fashioned notion about purity, perhaps. He knew this quirk of his was silly and did his best to keep it hidden.

He smiled and said, "Scaring you is my main purpose, Ms. Beaulieu. I want you to go away and write an article that will scare millions of others."

She looked at him and asked, "What you said about cities blowing down—did you mean that literally? I mean, like New York?"

"I meant it literally."

"But—but *New York*?"

"It's true air is just a gas, Ms. Beaulieu. But when it moves, when it really *moves*, it's one of the most destructive forces on earth."

He drew on his cigar, found it had gone out, leaned down and placed it carefully in the coffee can for future use. Then he sat back in his canvas chair and delivered a version of a lecture he had prepared years ago for his first-year students.

Most people, he said, find it difficult to imagine what a really powerful wind can do—especially people who have never experienced one. It often seems inconceivable that air, this gentle medium that gives us our life, can turn into a killer of man and beast, a mower of forests, and a crusher of buildings. Newly settled residents of Florida and other southeastern coastal states often blithely ignore hurricane warnings. They even hold hurricane parties as though to welcome these mighty winds, which can rip a house apart like paper.

Pollock recalled seeing a TV movie in which the characters sauntered about conversing in what was billed as a hundred-mile wind. Their teeth were appropriately clenched in the standard rictus of stress, but that was the only sign that the wind was giving them any trouble. The truth is that it is entirely impossible either to walk or to talk in a wind of such gigantic violence. Indeed, for all but the most athletic people, walking becomes impossible against winds of seventy-five miles an hour.

As Pollock spoke, the great cloud mass continued to advance overhead. It was not yet covering the sun, but the ambient light was growing subtly dimmer and bluer as more and more of the reflecting sky was eclipsed. The clouded sky in the north was growing perceptibly darker. The breeze was getting stronger.

"What we've got coming right now is a wind of thirty or thirty-five," Pollock said, "but you're going to see even that is a wind to be respected. It'll be enough to make big trees sway. Small branches will break. In a wind like that, you begin to worry about your belongings. Umbrellas get blown inside-out, awnings rip, hats blow away, loose shutters and other things get pulled off buildings."

Not only was the breeze getting stronger, but it was suddenly cooler. Pollock was warm enough in his suit, but he was concerned about his visitor in her light blue summer dress. Would she be content to stay outdoors? He hoped so.

"At around forty-five miles an hour," he continued, "you start to get structural damage to buildings, and at fifty-five you're in big trouble. Fifty-five: that's called a 'whole gale' in the Beaufort version I use. That's when big trees get uprooted and the flimsier buildings start to come apart. It's when my phone starts to ring. At fifty-five we cross the borderline into the danger zone."

He relit his cigar with some difficulty in the rising breeze. She stared at him for a second, then bent to make a note. She did not speak.

He said after a while, "What I'm saying is that winds of well under a hundred are plenty scary. Over a hundred they're absolutely terrifying. Most people have never experienced it or anything like it. They've no idea what it would be like."

"How high do hurricane winds go?"

"The National Hurricane Center divides them into five categories. The highest category is a storm with winds of a hundred-fifty-five, but that only happens once in a century. Most cities have never even experienced a hundred-mile wind. Your own city, for instance. The strongest wind New York ever felt in all its history was ninety-four."

"That's the strongest *ever*?" She was making a note.

"The strongest I've ever seen authenticated. You see news reports of higher winds, but those are notoriously inaccurate. They're usually somebody's guess. People always exaggerate when they make guesses about windspeeds."

"What's the strongest wind that ever blew anywhere?"

"Well, now we're talking about tornadoes. Twisters. They've never been clocked reliably. Some estimates say two hundred miles an hour, some say four hundred, some go higher."

"They're worse than hurricanes?"

"They're the most violent storms we've seen on earth so far. A wind like that—absolutely nothing can stand up to it for more than a minute or two. Concrete buildings crumple up like matchboxes. Topsoil gets peeled off hills. You just can't imagine . . . But the thing about tornadoes is that they're very small, usually less than half a mile across. A twister will move into an area, rip and tear at a given building for a minute, then move on. Some buildings take it, some don't. But the wind I'm predicting—the Big Wind—won't be something that goes away in a couple of minutes. It'll be a sustained wind. And a wind like that, Ms. Beaulieu, *a wind like that . . .*"

"You think it will blow cities down," she said softly.

He nodded and said, "That's what I think. Nothing man has built could stay standing for long in a four-hundred-mile wind. *Nothing.* As a matter of fact, I think very few buildings could stand two hundred. We don't know for sure, of course, because we—"

He stopped and put his hand on his bald head. He had felt a sudden spattering of raindrops.

He looked at his guest, expecting that she would want to go indoors immediately. To his delight, she did not seem to have noticed the rain. She was writing in her notebook, completely absorbed.

She looked up at him. "How much warning will we have when this Big Wind is on the way?"

Pollock shrugged. "A little, perhaps. Nobody knows."

"Is anybody trying to make predictions about it? I mean,

the waves seem to get stronger each time. Is anybody saying how long until—?"

"Until the final one?"

"Yes. Until the big one."

"Oh, my goodness, yes, there are all kinds of theories. That mound of air up above the north pole must be the most-studied atmospheric phenomenon in history. We've all got millions of dollars' worth of instruments up there, floating around under balloons. Us, the Russians, the Europeans—we're all puzzling at it, trying to figure out just how the mound is put together and how it's going to behave."

"And how *is* it going to behave?"

"Well, as I said, there are theories. The one I lean to was developed by a Canadian and a Russian, Phelps and Blagonravov. They put together a computer model, based on my published calculations. They did their studies independently but came out with the same results, and other studies since have backed them up. The model seems to show there will be two more waves or pulses after this one." He pointed to the darkening sky overhead.

"Two more?"

"Yes. They predicted *this* one right on the button. A moderate gale, they said, and that's exactly what we're about to get. Then, if their mathematical model is correct, a few days or a week from now we'll get the next-to-last wave. It will be a wind of hurricane force, seventy to a hundred miles an hour, something on that order. And then, a week or so after that, maybe two weeks, maybe three—the final one."

"The big one?"

"Four hundred miles an hour. The city-killer."

There was another sudden spattering of rain, accompanied by a gust of sharply colder wind. Simon Pollock's guest noticed it this time. She closed her notebook and said, "I think we'd better go in."

"Yes," he agreed reluctantly. He dropped his cigar butt in the coffee can, stood and looked up and around at the majestic panorama of the sky.

The edge of the cloud mass was just reaching the sun. As he watched, it began to move across the sun and eclipse it.

He was aware that his visitor was also watching, standing quietly beside him. The quick spattering of rain had stopped, but the wind was rising. It rushed noisily among the leaves of the big maple that towered above the roof. It blew against Pollock's cheek, tugged at his clothes, poked inquisitive fingers down his neck and up his sleeves. He loved the feel of it, and he would enjoy it long after he went indoors. He would carry with him the smell of clothing that has been blown fresh by a good, rude wind.

The cloud wall finally covered the sun, and the world went dark. The sky in the north was now monstrously blue-black. The wind blew the maple's leaves upward so that their light green undersides showed.

"Isn't it magnificent, Ms. Beaulieu?" he shouted, more loudly than was necessary to be heard above the wind's busy rush. "Isn't it *magnificent*?"

She nodded and gave him a look that conveyed some emotion he could not define. He wondered if she noticed there were tears in his eyes.

• • •

That third wave of wind lasted about eight hours. In the New York region it reached a sustained strength of thirty-two miles an hour, with occasional gusts to thirty-six. That is designated Force Seven or "moderate gale" in the most commonly used version of the Beaufort Scale.

In most cities the onset of wind was accompanied by a modest temperature drop and sporadic light rainfall. Meteorologists offered differing explanations of the rain. They also found it hard to explain clearly why the wave of wind made itself visible as a wall of dark clouds.

The stars came out over New York at midnight. When the people of the giant metropolitan area got up the next morning, they found that the Great Calm had ended. A very pleasant light breeze was blowing. The temperature hovered near seventy all day. The hot, damp, unappealing locker-room air had been blown away. The sky was a lovely clear blue, decorated with small, flat-bottomed white clouds.

7

TWO DAYS AFTER the third wave had scrubbed the air clean, Kim was at her gray-topped desk in her little cubicle, going over some material about tornadoes that she and Alice Wenska had dug up in the library. She was thinking of going down to the cafeteria for a cup of coffee when Pacifico appeared in her doorway. He had a file folder in one hand and a brown paper bag in the other.

"Coffee?" he asked.

"Sure," she said, startled. She did not know what to make of this.

He unloaded the bag's contents on her desk; two lidded plastic cups of coffee and a handful of sugar cubes and miniature creamers.

"I didn't know how you like it," he explained, "so I brought cream and sugar on the side."

"Black," she said. She was bewildered. "Thanks."

He sat in the visitor's chair that was wedged between the end of her desk and the cubicle's outer partition. The cubicle was so small that his legs stuck out into the doorway.

"I've been going over your Pollock interview," he said. He put the file folder on the desk. It contained her typed report on the interview plus some of her library gleanings.

"The first thing I have to say about it is that you're a lousy typist."

She was so disconcerted that she could not immediately tell whether the criticism was intended seriously. Then, to her relief, he grinned. He had an absolutely charming grin, she thought, even though it was on an Italian sort of face.

"Your typing is as bad as mine," he said. "You a two-finger person?"

"Two fingers and a thumb."

"Well don't worry about it. A great typist you'll never be, but I'll say this, Kim, you've got the makings of a reporter." He tapped the folder. "This is good. I mean *good*."

She was overwhelmed with pleasure and relief. Only later did she realize he had addressed her for the first time by her given name.

"Lots of nice sharp observations," he continued approvingly. "You've got a good feel for the details that count. One thing, though: always include a physical description. We've got to help the readers see the guy talking. What does he look like?"

"Well, he's a kind of funny little man with glasses. He's almost bald. He has this high squeaky voice."

Pacifico penciled some notes in the margin of her typed report, muttering to himself: "Little . . . bald . . . squeaky."

"He smokes cigars," Kim added.

"Smokes *cigars*?" Pacifico looked delighted. "That's great!"

Kim did not understand what was so great about it. Pacifico must have seen the puzzlement in her eyes. He sipped at his coffee and explained: "Cigars—that's an idiosyncracy, you see? It gives me a way of saying how odd the guy is. I can't come right out in print and say he's a kook. That's libelous. But—you know, a little squeaky guy who smokes cigars. There are ways of saying that so it's simply a statement of fact, not a judgment. But if I do it right, the reader will get the point."

"The point being that Pollock is—a little peculiar?"

"Right."

Kim thought about this and did not like it. She had grown fond of that funny little Professor Pollock, so earnest, so anxious to be taken seriously. It wasn't *his* fault that he had a squeaky voice and didn't look like Cary Grant in one of those old cap-and-gown movies.

She said, "The thing is, he isn't really nutty."

Pacifico looked at her over the rim of his plastic cup. "You were quite taken with the man, weren't you?"

She shrugged, then nodded. "Yes. I guess I was."

He nodded to himself, as though this were something he had expected. "You'll get over it. It happens to all of us at first. We fall in love with people we interview. But you've got to train yourself not to do that. You've got to look at them objectively."

"But he's such a nice little man," Kim said unhappily. "I'd hate to think of him being hurt, you know?"

"Sometimes," Pacifico said, "you've got to be willing to be a bastard. As a matter of fact, almost any story worth doing is going to make somebody mad."

"But—"

"Don't worry, I'm not planning to make a complete ass of the guy. But we do have to tell both sides of the story, right? I made a few phone calls this morning, and there *are* a lot of experts who take this Big Wind business with a pinch of salt. The U.S. Weather Bureau, for instance. Their official position is that they aren't making any predictions at all. Whatever happens will happen when it happens."

"A typical government bureau," Kim said scornfully. "Play safe. Say nothing."

"They do have a point, though. They say there aren't enough data to make predictions with."

"But couldn't they just say *maybe*? I mean, if we're going to have the kind of wind Professor Pollock talks about, it will kill people. Shouldn't the Weather Bureau be telling people to take precautions, just in case? Shouldn't *we* be telling them that?"

"Think how silly we'll look when nothing happens."

"Well, sure, but wouldn't it be worse the other way around? Suppose we said pooh-pooh, it's all bullshit, and then everything gets blown down?"

He frowned at her. "Jesus, this Pollock really got to you, didn't he?"

"He made a lot of sense, I thought. I mean—oh hell, I don't know what I mean."

She sipped her coffee. Her pleasure at learning she had done good work had turned to disappointment at learning Pacifico planned to make light of it. Or at least to treat it as less portentous than she had thought. She wanted to go on protesting. She opened her mouth to speak, then abruptly changed her mind and took another sip of coffee instead.

No, she thought. I'm not going to spoil it.

Pacifico gave her a quick glance, as though making sure her protests were really concluded. Then he flipped through her report until he came to a passage he had marked. "There are a couple of things to look into," he said. "One is this business about New York's record wind— ninety-four miles an hour, the professor says. First check to see if that's really true and documented. Then see if you can find figures for some other cities. Chicago, maybe. Moscow."

"Would that be in the library?"

"I don't know. If it isn't, get on the phone." He located another passage. "And we need more details on this Canadian and Russian who say we've got two more waves of wind coming, a hurricane-force one and then the big one. Phelps and Blagonravov. They rigged up some kind of computerized mathematical model based on some theorizing by your man Pollock, is that right?"

"As I understand it."

"Okay, but it's all a bit vague. We don't have to give the readers more than a couple of sentences on it, but we ought to understand it as well as we can ourselves before we start writing about it. See what you can dig up. And then maybe tomorrow afternoon, I thought we'd go out and do an interview together." He gave her another of his appealing grins. "Maybe I can give you some pointers on how to interview people without falling in love with them."

"I did *not* fall in love. I only—"

"Just kidding. There's a man in New York who sounds like he's worth an interview. A structural engineer. George Hoch-something. I'm not sure how it's pronounced."

"Hochenauer," Kim said. She assumed it was pronounced in an Anglicized/Germanic way, the first syllable rhyming with *poke* and the last with *hour*.

"Right, Hochenauer. He's been turning up in a lot of news stories lately. Sounds nice and controversial. See if he'll talk to us this afternoon some time."

They discussed scheduling for a few minutes, and then he departed, leaving her to clean up the coffee litter on her desk.

8

GEORGE HOCHENAUER HAD told the *Seven Days* people to come to his office, which was on the south or low-rent side of the grimy old Flatiron Building. He would rather have met them at Booker's, his favorite saloon, but it always got too noisy in there toward five o'clock. And so he waited for them in his dim, dingy, and dusty little office, occasionally refilling a paper cup from the bottle of Mother Fletcher's whiskey that he kept in his desk drawer.

It was much quieter in his office than in Booker's. In fact it was depressingly quiet. The phone had not rung all afternoon, except for that one call from the *Seven Days* woman. George Hochenauer's business was not very active.

"George Hochenauer & Son, Consulting Engineers," it said on the pebbled-glass upper section of the door. The son had left years ago for the more promising environment of Silicon Valley, California, but George Hochenauer had allowed the "& Son" to stay there on the door. He had no strong feelings about it. He had simply never gotten around to deleting it.

The firm consisted in its entirety of Hochenauer himself, with occasional clerical and bookkeeping help from his wife, Wilma, when she was sober. She had planned to come here this afternoon and act the role of receptionist to impress the magazine people. However, she had not turned up, and

Hochenauer guessed she had stopped at Booker's for a quick drink. For Wilma, of course, there was no such thing as one quick drink at Booker's. Hochenauer figured he would go down there and join her when the interview was over. He would grumble about her forgetfulness but not seriously.

Big fat Wilma: she was even more of a drinker than he. But he loved her even at her worst. They were a pair of disgusting slobs, he often thought, but each unaccountably loved the other, and thus they were redeemed.

Hochenauer weighed a good deal less than his wife. He was a little skinny guy with a spectacularly ugly face. It was a rat's face, long and sharp-featured, with eyes like little black marbles. The somewhat sinister look was intensified by a thin black mustache. Nobody would ever have bought a used car from Hochenauer. He looked greedy, dishonest, and unscrupulous. In fact, he was none of these; but if one's face is one's fortune, his had never been of the slightest value to him.

He was just pouring himself a refill of Mother Fletcher's when he heard the grind and clank of the elevator arriving in the echoing hallway outside his door. That was one thing about these old buildings: you could hear your visitors coming. Hochenauer smoothed back his thin black hair and ran a hand over his bony jaw, which he knew would sport a greenish beard shadow at this time of day. It would give him an unwashed look, though he was in fact a man of scrupulous cleanliness. It was another of his cosmetic problems. He knew that they could not be solved and had long ago stopped trying, though he had not altogether stopped worrying.

The *Seven Days* people introduced themselves as Nick Pacifico and Kim Beaulieu. Nice-looking pair, Hochenauer thought. The guy, Pacifico, had one of those handsome Italian faces. His nose was too big, but he had a good strong chin with a cleft in it, the kind of chin Hochenauer had always wished to have. As for the girl, she was a real dish. Hochenauer offered them some Mother Fletcher's, which they declined, and then the three of them settled down for the interview. Hochenauer had no comfort to offer them but two straight-backed metal chairs, but at least Wilma had dusted them a few days ago.

The Beaulieu girl began by repeating what she had told him on the phone, that they had seen him quoted in *Newsweek* and thought they would like to know more about his uncharitable views of construction methods. Hochenauer grinned at her and said it was very flattering to have all these big magazines paying attention to him. He did not allow the grin to remain on his face for long, however, for some of his teeth were misshapen in such a way as to give them a fang-like appearance. The girl grinned back.

What a babe! It certainly was nice to be famous, if only for a short while, and have babes like this come to your office. It had all begun when Hochenauer, in a fit of pique one day, dashed off a bitterly scornful letter to the *Structural Engineering Reporter* on the subject of buildings and weather. It was a knowledgeable letter, for the subject was more or less Hochenauer's specialty. The editors printed it as a full-dress article. Some newspaper reporter, looking for something sensational to say about the Big Wind, saw the article, phoned Hochenauer, and got him to say some still more sensational things, which he later tried to modify without success. Other feature writers saw the newspaper story, and before he realized what was happening to him, George Hochenauer was a minor celebrity.

Most of the interviews had been by phone. He was presented to readers in terms suggesting the firm of George Hochenauer & Son was a large thriving business. A couple of TV shows had sent scouts around to look him over. The scouts had gone away mumbling politely, never to be heard from again. Hochenauer thought his two visitors this afternoon might also be experiencing some disappointment.

Pacifico was saying, "Before we get into your views, Mr. Hochenauer, can we get some of your background? You're a structural engineer with a special interest in weather, is that right?"

"Yes, that's right." Hochenauer understood that he was being asked to present his credentials and defend the shabbiness of his office. "Most of my work these days, I'm an expert witness in court cases."

The girl was taking notes. Pacifico asked, "How does that work? I mean, who pays you to do that?"

"Okay, let me give you a frinstance. Case I'm working on right now. There's this big shopping center, see, and one day they have this real bitch of a rainstorm, if you'll pardon my language, Ma'am, and the whole place floods up, and a lot of the merchandise in the stores gets ruined. So the merchants, they go to their insurance companies, and the insurance people, *they* turn around and go to the developer who built the place. You get the picture, right? The insurance people are saying, 'You screwed up by putting in lousy drainage, so you gotta pay,' and the developer is saying, 'No way. My drainage system conforms to all local codes and shows proper prudence and all that. You wanna sue somebody,' he says, 'sue God. I ain't paying a nickel.' That's what we call an act-of-God defense, see. So okay, the insurance people hire me to go into court and say the flood wasn't God's fault, it was the lousy drainage. It was, too. We'll win the case easy."

"How did you get into this weather specialty?" the girl asked.

Hochenauer knew his visitors had read the story in *Newsweek* and wanted it retold for their own use. It was a good dramatic story. Hochenauer did not mind repeating it. He sipped from his paper cup, stacked his feet on his desk, moved them so that they did not block his view of the babe, and launched into the well-remembered narrative.

As a young engineer he had been involved in the design of an indoor sports arena. He became convinced that the wide-span roof supports were not strong enough to hold up a heavy accumulation of snow. Since the design changes he recommended would add greatly to the cost, his boss and everybody else told him to go away and shut up. As it turned out, the supports were adequate for average weather, but the structure's third winter was unusual. There was a lot of snow combined with unrelieved, intense cold. Week after week, snow piled up on that roof without melting. Finally, one night, the roof collapsed during a basketball game. More than thirty people died. George Hochenauer became a popular hero during the ensuing investigation. One news photo showed tears running down his bony cheeks.

That was the story he told for publication. What he did not add was that the episode was professionally disastrous for him. He became known in the business as an idealistic young wiseass who wanted to design buildings for freakish weather regardless of the cost. That was only a slight exaggeration. He did, in fact, want to make buildings more weather-resistant. He became a crusader on the subject. This did not endear him, of course, to contractors, real estate speculators, and financiers who wanted to hold down costs. He became all but unemployable except at the lowest levels, and finally he had to go into business for himself because there was no other way to make a living.

When he had finished telling his story, Hochenauer poured himself some more Mother Fletcher's. There had been a time in his life when he had done much of his drinking in secret, but he made no attempt to hide it anymore. He was a functioning alcoholic, knew it, and did not give a damn.

Pacifico asked, "Now what about the Big Wind, Mr. Hochenauer? I understand you're—well, pessimistic, is that right?"

"Not about the wind itself. I mean, I got no crystal ball that says whether any wind is coming. But if it does come, then we got trouble."

"You think a lot of buildings won't take it?"

"*Most* won't take it. Not if it's four hundred miles an hour, they won't. Maybe not even if it's two hundred."

"Do you have proof of that?" Pacifico asked this question in a tone and with a look that was not especially friendly, and the girl seemed to hunch down over her notebook as though wishing to disassociate herself from the implied distrust. Hochenauer sensed that he was getting through to her more than he was to the guy. At least, he thought, she had come up here with an open mind. Or maybe better yet: maybe she had come with a predisposition to believe him.

"Proof?" he said, replying to the question. "No, proof I can't give you. No building has ever been tested against a sustained four-hundred-mile wind. Nor against two hundred. Nobody really knows what would happen. I don't know—nor does the architect who says he's sure his building is going to stand. But I'll tell you. With wind loads like that, you're not gonna find *me* on the top floor of any building. Where you'll find *me* is in a hole in the ground."

Hochenauer paused to collect his thoughts. His visitors sat silently looking at him, the girl with an encouraging small smile, the guy deadpan.

He went on to outline his view of the construction business as a gigantic gambling game. If you had unlimited money, he pointed out, you could build a house to withstand virtually any kind of cataclysmic weather. Unlimited money is never available, however. And so every structure is made just well enough to withstand the normal run of weather in its particular region. When abnormal weather comes along, structures leak and buckle and fall. It is a long-running game of chance. Starting with the original builder, each owner of a building hopes the local weather will stay within average limits until he sells to the next owner.

"People don't like to be told their own house is a gamble," Hochenauer said, "but it's the plain truth. Like, you take down in Florida, for instance. If they ever had a freakish cold spell down there, half their pipes would bust because the pipes aren't protected right. But when it comes to wind, they spend more money because high winds are part of their average weather, you follow? Even the regular little ticky-tacky frame houses down there, a lot of them, they can take a hurricane wind. They bolt them together good down in Florida. Use a lot more sill bolts and corner bracing than we do around here. But up in New England, it's the other way around. In New England they spend money protecting their pipes from freezing, but they don't spend so much on wind because they only get a full-force hurricane once in a great while. So in New England, when you got any wind more than seventy or thereabouts, you got houses coming apart."

His two visitors were still looking at him silently. The girl looked worried; the guy looked skeptical.

Hochenauer thought: I know this guy's type. I've met him all over. He's proud of how hard it is to con him. He's so proud of it that he doesn't want to listen at all.

Hochenauer plowed on: "So okay, now we got this Big Wind on the way, supposedly. I seen all sorts of guesses on how strong it'll be, but let's take the number four hundred. That's the number you hear most often. This weather professor up in Connecticut, Simon something—what's his name?"

"Pollock," the girl supplied.

"Yeah, Pollock, you keep reading about this Pollock

talking about the wind, and four hundred is the number he keeps mentioning. So let's say he's right and that's what we get, a four-hundred-mile-an-hour wind, okay? Now there are a couple of things you ought to know about wind load. Wind load: that's the lateral push against the side of a building. Engineers have been worrying about it ever since they built the first tall cathedrals in the Middle Ages. And one thing about wind load is, it increases as the square of the wind speed, you follow? So if you get a four-hundred-mile wind, you don't just have four times the push of one hundred. You have just about sixteen times."

He took a sip of Mother Fletcher's. It was a cheap brand but mighty satisfying. "At four hundred miles an hour," he said, "with most buildings, you're looking at wind loads like you wouldn't believe. With most, the wind load figures out to more than the entire weight of the building." He paused, then added, "including the foundation."

Nobody spoke for a few seconds. The girl recrossed her long legs. Hochenauer shifted in his chair so he could see them better. Then he went on: "The taller your building is, the worse your problems get. Because of the leverage against the top, you follow? It's hard to calculate what would happen. One thing sure: something has to give. Either the building busts up, or it gets uprooted like a tree. Four hundred—I'll tell you, that is one bitch of a wind."

Hochenauer flattered himself that even the guy, Pacifico, now looked impressed. The girl looked scared. After staring at him for a moment she said, "My God, Mr. Hochenauer."

"Yeah," he said, and nodded.

"If all this is really true—I mean if it actually happens—where would people be safe?"

"Underground. Or maybe—just maybe—in an old heap like this one." He waved an arm to encompass the Flatiron Building.

He thought his admiration for the building was more sentimental than anything else. He had had his office here for twenty years. But the sooty old building did have a wind-resistant look. Built in 1902 when Twenty-Third Street was "midtown," it was one of the first steel-skeletoned buildings in New York. Its twenty stories made it the city's tallest building for several years. Its nickname came from its odd triangular cross-section, which was dictated by the shape of its plot. The narrow point of the triangle pointed northward. Hochenauer thought that might be helpful in facing a north wind. The building would be crudely streamlined like the prow of a ship. Until all the north windows blew in. And until . . .

Oh well, there was no sense in having nightmares about it. Hochenauer swallowed some more whiskey.

Pacifico was saying, "If all this is true, Mr. Hochenauer, then there's something that puzzles me. Why do only you and a few others seem to be worried? Why is everybody else so calm?"

The girl looked quickly at Pacifico, then down at her notes. Hochenauer chuckled sourly. "It's the way the world works Mr. Pacifico," he said. "You admit you got a problem, you got it. Like, you take city governments, for instance. They admit they're worried about the wind, then they gotta spend money on shelters and other stuff. Can you imagine some bureaucrat taking that risk? Or some politician? He asks himself, suppose the wind don't come? Next election I'm gonna have my opponent pointing out how I got six million cases of food rotting down in some subway tunnel someplace. No, it's a hell of a lot easier to pretend the problem don't exist."

Hochenauer finished his drink, thought of pouring another, decided against it, and dropped the paper cup into the dented metal wastebasket next to his desk. He knew from long experience that he was at the borderline beyond which the liquor would affect him in unpredictable ways. Normally articulate, he sometimes became boringly garrulous when drunk—or, conversely, slurred and stumbled his way into a morose silence. His hard, bright mind either started to explode with visions like a Fourth of July night sky or turned into a cold gray lump. He felt like tying on a good one tonight, but this was not the place. He would do it later with Wilma, and they would get home by leaning on each other.

He continued: "Now you take the building establishment. You think *they're* gonna say they're worried about wind? Ha. I got a life-size picture of some architect standing up and saying, 'Oh my, I'm scared my building will fall down.' Or some developer with a bunch of office space to rent. Or some hotel guy."

Pacifico nodded, shrugged, seemed satisfied. After a few more questions, the interview was over.

Hochenauer thought he had put his points across well to the girl but not so well to the guy. He wondered if they teamed up that way deliberately. Like the way cops teamed up in pairs to interrogate a suspect. If the hard guy couldn't make the suspect crack, maybe the soft guy could.

A few minutes after his visitors had left, Hochenauer locked the office and went down to drink the night away at Booker's.

9

AN EXTRAVAGANT, GAUDY and impossible sunset was in production in the western sky when they stepped out of the Flatiron Building. The meteorological show was so spectacular that it interrupted their argument and left them dumb and gaping. They had not been able to see the sky from Hochenauer's office, whose single small window afforded a view of another building's wall, and to step out unexpectedly beneath a sky like this was like being hit in the face with a bucket of ketchup.

It was a madness of red and purple. Orange-reds alternated in streaks and stripes with dark rose-reds and outrageous mauves. The pretty little flat-bottomed clouds that had sailed in the sky all week now came in assorted shades of purple and indigo, rimmed with flame. There was too much color. It spilled down over the city, drenched building walls, ran along the gutters, and turned the sidewalks pink.

The Flatiron Building's neighborhood normally has a no-nonsense quality to it, an air of harsh economic reality. It is a neighborhood of small businesses struggling to survive. The stores are only stores, not salons or boutiques or anything so grand. The office buildings are not monuments but simply buildings containing offices. The restaurants are places where you eat if you are in the neighborhood. Nobody comes here except on business. But on this lunatic

red-and-purple evening the pragmatic old neighborhood
had a dreamlike quality. People moving along the sidewalks
gave an odd impression of floating rather than walking.

"It looks like the last sunset of the world," she said.

He nodded. They stood for a moment longer, trapped in
a melancholy enchantment. Then he shook his head
abruptly and said, "No. End of the world? What kind of
baloney is that? You've been taking the Pollocks and
Hochenauers too seriously again."

Their interrupted argument was resumed. She said, "You
mean everything Hochenauer said—it didn't make *any*
impression on you?"

"A little. Not much. Let's listen to the other side before
we make any judgments. We're seeing that architecture
professor in New Jersey tomorrow, right? Let's listen to
him and *then* see what we think of Hochenauer."

"You just won't give an inch, will you, Nick?"

"Now look, you know the rules by now. We're reporters.
We're supposed to be impartial. We can't take sides on
issues. We aren't crusaders."

"Why not? What's wrong with a worthwhile crusade?"

"Nothing, in the right place. But we can't just give free
space to every lushed-up crackpot with a theory to sell."

She stared at him angrily. "That isn't fair," she said.

"What isn't?"

"Calling the man lushed-up. His drinking problem is a
private affair of his own. It has nothing to do with us."

He shrugged. "Okay, we'll forget that. But the fact
remains: this guy Hochenauer has a far-out theory. And if
we quote somebody like him, then we've got to quote other
people arguing with him."

"Your precious feet-on-the-ground types."

"Well . . . yes."

"How do you know Hochenauer isn't a feet-on-the-
ground type?"

"Him? I doubt it. What he is, is a guy trying to save a

dying business. What he's in this for is publicity."

"Those weren't the vibes I got. It seemed to me he was really interested in this, this crusade of his."

"Interested in your legs, too."

"*What*?" Her anger exploded so loudly that people drifting past on the sidewalk turned and stared. "What makes that your damned business? I'd just like to know! You're my guardian now, are you?"

"I just thought I'd mention it. Don't be so prickly."

"Prickly? *Prickly*? That's what you call it? My God. You people are all alike. You think a woman is just—"

She stopped abruptly.

"Which people are those?" he asked after a while.

"Nobody. Forget it. I just meant men in general. New York men."

"It didn't sound that way to me."

"Now who's being prickly?" She gave him a quick, angry glance, then turned and started to walk away. "I'm going home," she said over her shoulder. "Good night."

She stepped to the curb and held her hand up for a cab. Pacifico watched her for a moment, then turned and began to walk downtown.

"Nick!"

He stopped and looked back. She was walking toward him across the pink sidewalk.

"Listen," she said, "please forget I said that. It was my family background talking, not me. It was stupid. I apologize."

"It's okay. But what, your family has something about Italians, is that it?"

"They were French-Swiss."

"Ah."

"You know the Swiss."

"Not personally, but I used to hear my father talk about them."

"Apology accepted?"

"Of course. Come on, I'll buy you a drink."

She hesitated, then said, "No. I'll buy *you* a drink. Let's go to the—no, wait. I've got an even better idea. Let's let my father buy both of us a drink." She smiled with delight at the mischievous idea. "He got us into this, so let's make him pay some of the costs, right? We'll go to a place where I can sign onto his charge account. How about the D'Alembert? It's in the New World Center."

• • •

The D'Alembert Lounge was a dark, intimate place, trimmed in red and gold. A woman in a long white satin evening dress sat at the piano, singing what was no doubt intended to be a restfully mournful song about lost love. But her singing had an oddly jittery quality in Kim's ear. The voice kept breaking out of control and sharping high notes. Despite its low volume it did not sound sad; it sounded shrill and worried.

The cocktail crowd had the same nervous quality. At some tables people sat stiff and silent; at others the gestures and facial expressions seemed agitated. Waitresses moved about with grim, darting purposefulness, looking as though they had not been smiled at all evening.

At a table near the door a woman sat angrily, arms folded, pointedly looking away from the man who was arguing with her. Kim overheard him as she walked by. "But if it's gonna be a goddam hurricane wind," he was saying, "I gotta go up there and move the goddam boat, don't I?"

Kim wondered if people were growing more concerned about the Big Wind. According to the Phelps-Blagonravov computer model, the next-to-last wave could be expected some time in the next few days, and it would be a wind of hurricane force. Did this explain the jittery quality of the D'Alembert Lounge? Or, Kim wondered, am I merely picking up vibrations from inside myself?

She and Nick Pacifico sat at a table. A waitress appeared quickly. He ordered a Bombay martini. She asked for plain ginger ale. "Please bring it in the bottle," she requested of the waitress, "and pour it at the table."

This was a routine that she had picked up from an old AA member in Detroit. Convinced that one sip of alcohol could start her once again on the spiral to disaster, she was terrified of being served an alcoholic drink by mistake in a busy restaurant. And so she insisted on verification.

The procedure is common with recovered alcoholics, but the waitress was young and had obviously had a hard day. She looked tired and irritable. She said, "Madam, I'm afraid we don't have individual bottles of ginger ale."

"All right. Coke, then."

"All our soft drinks come in big bottles," the waitress said stubbornly.

Kim saw Nick Pacifico looking at her with a disgusted expression. He and the waitress both think I'm doing this just to be difficult, she thought, annoyed.

She looked up at the waitress and said, "Bring me some ginger ale in a big bottle, then. Just so it's poured at the table."

"Well, I don't know—"

"If you don't want to do it, let me talk to the headwaiter."

The waitress walked away stiffly.

There was a tense silence at the table. Then Pacifico said, "Just because you're rich, Kim, you don't have to bully people."

Her first impulse was to stand up and walk out. Controlling that with an effort, she lighted a cigarette with hands that shook. Finally she said, "What did you think all that was about? Did you think I was just being bitchy for fun?"

"Well? What the hell *was* it about?"

She drew a deep breath and said, "I'm an alcoholic,

Nick. I have to be sure I get the right drink."

He looked at her for a second. Then he reached across the table and covered her hand with his. "Forgive me," he said.

It was an evening for apologies. She wanted to say something about that but could not think of anything graceful. It turned out that nothing needed to be said anyhow. It was a situation best allowed to develop itself without words.

The waitress returned with their drinks. She plunked Pacifico's martini before him and then, still more sullenly, thumped a filled glass in front of Kim.

"It's ginger ale," the waitress announced. "We had some individual bottles after all. Here's your bottle." She put an empty Canada Dry bottle on the table next to Kim's glass.

Kim sighed. The waitress obviously wanted to win this fight. Perhaps intentionally, she had failed to comply fully with the difficult customer's wishes. Kim started to protest, then changed her mind. She had had enough strife for one evening. She decided she would simply make do without a drink.

The waitress turned to go. Pacifico said, "Miss."

The waitress whirled back to glare at him. "Yes?"

"I'm afraid you didn't understand. We wanted the ginger ale poured at the table. Will you try again, please?"

The waitress took Kim's drink and walked off, furious.

Pacifico held up his martini and asked, "Does it bother you? Watching me drink?"

"Oh no. Most of us aren't troubled by that at all. It's hard to explain. Your drink is *your* drink, so it doesn't tempt me. I can even enjoy watching you enjoy it. But if something is served to me, then it's *my* drink, and that's different. Or a bottle of liquor that's nobody's drink yet— that can be a temptation, too, in some situations. I don't know if any of that makes sense, but what I'm saying is you can enjoy your martini with me just as you would with anybody."

Pacifico opened his mouth to speak but was interrupted by a loud voice a few tables away. It was the man who was worrying about the hurricane wind. "All right,' he shouted at his wife or woman friend, "I'll just let the goddam boat sink, then!"

The waitress came back with Kim's drink. She poured it in bad-tempered silence and departed without a word.

Kim talked about her life. She was an only child. Her parents were separated before she reached her teens. She loved her father, who, she said, was not as frosty or forbidding as the *Seven Days* staff believed. She also loved her mother, Angela, but in a different way. Her love for her father had a large component of admiration in it, but she felt no admiration for her mother.

"My mother is one of those useless rich women who jet around attending parties," Kim said fondly. "She has more money than she can ever spend, but she's doing her best to get rid of it. She bought a two-million-dollar condominium right over our heads, as a matter of fact." Kim pointed at the ceiling.

"Here at the Center?"

"On the sixty-eighth floor. It's magnificent. Glass all around. Like my father's office but grander."

Pacifico's story was more commonplace. He had simply been one of a horde of kids in the city school system. Finding in himself a love of language, he had had the good luck to meet some excellent teachers, who boosted him toward a journalist's career.

She said, "Somebody told me you, ah, had a wife."

"Yeah, once I did. Gloria and I had a lot of problems, mostly about money. We're divorced."

"Children?"

"A daughter. Danny, we call her. Daniela. She's nine."

"Does she live with you?"

"No, with Gloria. I see her often enough, though. Gloria is decent about that. Matter of fact, I'll be picking Danny up tomorrow after we finish with that Rutgers professor. I'll leave you to find your way back to New York by yourself. Hope you don't mind."

"No, that's fine. Your daughter is in New Jersey?"

"Yes, not far from Rutgers, that's where Gloria lives."

"I was told Danny has some—some medical problem."

"That's putting it mildly." He smiled down at his drink bitterly.

"I'm not being too nosy? You're not mad at me for asking?"

"Why should I be mad at you? As Hochenauer's friend put it, if I want to sue somebody I won't sue you, I'll sue God."

She frowned at him. "What is it?"

"Bone cancer. Ewing's sarcoma, it's called. In her leg."

There was a silence. Then she said, "I think maybe another drink wouldn't do you any harm, Nick."

He signaled to the waitress. The loud drinker was still shouting about the hurricane winds and his boat. People were getting annoyed. At a table behind Kim somebody growled, "Why doesn't he shut up? I hope the wind blows his freakin' boat to China."

Kim said, "Listen, Nick, I have an idea. Why don't we drive to Jersey in my car tomorrow?"

"Sure. If you want to."

"And after we've seen the professor, we'll pick up Danny and I'll drive the two of you back to New York. Unless that next wave of wind stops us, that is."

"You really worried about that?"

She shrugged. "I don't know. Maybe. Yes, I guess I am."

10

THEY WERE DRIVING north on the New Jersey Turnpike. Ahead of them and over them loomed a massive wall of blue-black cloud.

"Can you drive when the wind blows, Kim?" Danny asked from the back seat. She did not sound at all worried.

"Count on me, kiddo," said Kim easily at the wheel. She and Danny had taken an instant liking to one another.

Pacifico sat relaxed in the front passenger seat. He did not anticipate any problems.

The radio news report said winds near seventy-five had been reported by the Canadian Weather Service. Police in the tri-state New York region were urging motorists to get off the roads as soon as possible and cancel all unnecessary trips. Pacifico did not clearly see what all the fuss was about. Seventy-five did not sound like much of a wind to him. He had toyed briefly with the idea of pulling in at a motel but had dismissed it. Why not simply drive home to New York? It should not take more than an hour, given a little luck with the traffic.

It was mid-afternoon. The leading edge of the cloud mass was just covering the sun, plunging the world into an eerie daytime darkness. Ahead, near the horizon, the sky was gigantically black. Cars on the turnpike had their headlights on.

"It's scary, isn't it?" Danny said. The tone of her voice suggested that she meant enjoyably scary, in the manner of a monster movie or roller-coaster ride. Pacifico looked back and saw that she was grinning. He reached back and gave her small, thin hand a hard squeeze.

How he loved this Daniela! She was nine. She was full of love and good humor. She had dark straight hair, a small heart-shaped face, and enormous dark-brown eyes. She was small-boned and too thin—an effect of the sarcoma itself and also of the radiation and chemotherapy treatments, which affected her appetite. But Pacifico thought she would become a stunningly gorgeous woman—if she became a woman at all.

A brief, violent squall of rain drenched the highway and then stopped. A hard wind came suddenly from nowhere. Tree leaves and stray bits of paper and a green-and-white thing that looked like a tennis visor went bowling across the road. The little red Volvo swayed and fishtailed in the gusts. The wind was cold. They closed the car windows. Kim put out the cigarette she had been smoking.

"You okay, Kim?" Pacifico asked. She was wrestling with the wheel to hold the car on course.

"I think so. For now, anyway."

Nobody spoke for a long time. The cold wind rushed around them. The sky was darkening malevolently.

It was happening just as the Phelps-Blagonravov model had predicted. Here came the hurricane-force winds—somewhat earlier than expected, but still roughly on schedule. Pacifico was perplexed. He had held steadfastly to a belief that the whole Big Wind story was little more than a journalistic fraud. But if this prediction was correct, might the other also be? Could it be true, after all, that city-killing winds of four hundred miles an hour would follow in a week or two?

The wind was rising rapidly. Ahead of them, a green Volkswagen with a lone driver suddenly swerved onto the grassy verge and ran out of control for a moment before struggling back onto the roadway. The air was full of flying flotsam. An empty paper cup hit the Volvo's hood, rolled up the windshield, and vanished over the roof.

There was another hard, quick shower of rain. The wind rose alarmingly. Something large and flat, perhaps a sheet of plywood, cartwheeled across the turnpike and hit the side of a truck.

The green VW, a light car with no passengers to give it weight, was in serious trouble now. The driver seemed to be a woman or teenaged girl. She could not hold the little car in its lane. She wandered to the left, nudged a larger car that was creeping past, then veered sharply to the right as a violent new wind gust caught her in its grip. The little green car went bouncing over the roadside grass and came to rest in the midst of a stand of trees.

"You know what I think, Nick?" Kim said.

"Yes, We'd better get off the highway. Find a motel or something." He had to shout to be heard above the thunder of the wind.

"That's exactly what I think." There was no panic in her voice, but Pacifico noticed that her knuckles were white on the wheel. It kept jerking spasmodically, as though it were a live animal trying to escape.

"Want me to take over?" he asked.

"Maybe in a while. I'm okay for now."

They were close to an exit. Unfortunately a lot of other drivers had had the same idea. A long line of cars crept down the exit ramp as the wind howled and shrieked around them. The Volvo jiggled and swayed.

Danny was silent. Pacifico looked back and saw her gazing out the window with large, round eyes.

No toll collectors were on duty. They had either been sent home or had deserted. The cars rolled through the gates and crept away in several directions.

"Which way?" Kim shouted above the wind.

Pacifico had been looking for a "food and lodging" sign but had seen none. He had a vague impression that they had passed a cluster of shops and gas stations not far back on the turnpike, so he suggested turning back southward.

The wind was now mostly behind them. "My God, I can feel the rear of the car lifting up!" Kim said. Pacifico climbed between the bucket seats and sat on the rear seat to distribute the weight better. He put his arm around Danny and hugged her. "How are you doing, Miss Mousy?" he asked.

"I'm scared, Daddy."

"No you aren't. People turn green when they're scared."

"Oh Daddy, that's silly."

Pacifico knew it was silly, but he had to keep their morale up somehow. He had never imagined a seventy-five-mile wind could be this formidable. Maybe it's more than seventy-five, he thought.

They came into a broad street lined with large old homes and tall, stately old trees that swayed and thrashed wildly. The wind blasted through their upper branches with a colossal roaring sound. The air was full of flying green leaves and twigs. Branches and other debris littered the street.

Ahead was what looked like the center of a small town. Cozy little stores were lined up on both sides of the street for two or three blocks. There was nobody on the sidewalks, and most of the stores also looked dark and deserted. But a few had their lights on.

"Maybe one of them is a restaurant," Kim shouted, wrestling with the wheel. "You hungry, Danny?"

"No, thirsty."

"Okay. We'll see if—"

Kim's words were drowned out by a tremendous crash that could be heard above the thunder of the wind. Half a block ahead of them, one of the huge trees had fallen directly across the street.

Kim inched the car up to it and stopped. There was no way to go around it. It had been uprooted in a lawn on one side of the street, and its top branches lay in somebody else's lawn on the other side. The root end of the massive trunk, where it lay almost touching the street, made a barrier as high as the Volvo's hood.

They were trapped in the residential part of the street. The first of the stores was half a block ahead.

Kim looked back at Pacifico. "Do you want to drive us out of here? My arms are tired."

"Sure," he said. She climbed into the front passenger seat, he into the driver's seat. He shifted the Volvo into reverse, preparatory to backing away from the fallen tree. But a glance in the rearview mirror told him he was not going anywhere for a while. He turned off the headlights and the ignition.

"Look behind us," he said.

Several other cars, probably also refugees from the turnpike, were stopped at odd angles behind them. The blacktop around their wheels was rapidly being buried in debris, including some large branches. The street looked impassable.

It was just after three o'clock. The sky was the color of a wet street. They sat helplessly in the car as the wind screamed around them. Kim pulled out cigarettes, then put them away again.

Ahead of them, the modest little downtown area was tantalizingly close but unreachable. Pacifico saw a jewelry store with its lights on, a liquor store, a real estate and insurance agency. Farther away was a red-bordered Texaco sign on a tall pole. The sign looked as though it was shuddering in the wind.

An empty garbage can rolled crazily down the street, bounced onto the sidewalk, and smashed into the glass front of one of the stores. Something that looked like a shed door danced along the sidewalk end-over-end and disappeared around a corner. A hanging traffic light near the Texaco sign was swinging wildly over an empty crossroads, unlit.

All the store lights on one side of the street suddenly went out. A power line must have come down.

Pacifico looked around and saw that the homes on the same side of the street had also lost their lights. But on the other side, his right, lighted windows still shone cheerfully, gold and orange. They looked like islands of peace in a world gone mad.

Directly to his right was a big, rambling old gray house with a white-pillared porch that surrounded it on three sides. It was the house to which the uprooted tree belonged. Some of its lower windows were lighted. It beckoned.

"Do you think we could reach that house?" he shouted.

"Let's not even try," Kim shouted back. She had to lean close to him to be heard. "Remember what Professor Pollock said about walking in a seventy-five-mile wind."

Pacifico had read it in her report but had not believed it. He still was not convinced, though his respect for wind was growing. He did acknowledge, however, that it would probably be impossible for Danny to walk in that mighty blast. Her leg was weak. She walked with difficulty even under the best of circumstances. He did not know how he would get her to the old gray house.

But he thought he would have to do something soon, for it was growing cold in the car. All three of them were in light summer clothes. It was not a wintry cold—sixty degrees, perhaps—but it was enough to chill anyone who had to sit still in it. It would be particularly hard on Danny.

The circulation in her leg was poor. When that leg got chilled, the diseased bone area hurt intolerably.

Pacifico thought of running the car's heater for a time, but when he turned on the ignition he saw that the gas tank was nearly empty. Kim gave him a questioning look. He explained about Danny's leg. She looked back at Danny, then leaned forward and switched on the radio.

"Maybe somebody can tell us how long this is going to last," Kim said.

But few stations seemed to be on the air at all. When a voice did come through it was distant and indistinct.

Horizontal rain lashed the windows and then stopped. The car pitched and shuddered on its springs as the mighty wind yelled around it. Pacifico realized suddenly that the car was being pushed toward the tree trunk inch by inch. The front end was almost touching the trunk, and the rear end was moving to the left.

The Texaco sign began to flap crazily, then went down. The hanging traffic light was gone.

The lights on the right-hand side of the street all went out.

The glass front of the real estate office burst inward, then outward again. Pieces of glass flew down the street. The wind then went into the office like a huge violent hand and scooped out everything that would move. A blizzard of debris exploded out through the opening: papers, books, a chair, a hat, a thing that looked like a raincoat.

Kim finally found an audible voice on the radio. It was a man's voice and sounded close to hysteria. It said winds gusting over eighty had been clocked at Kennedy Airport. All air and ground transportation around the city was halted. Virtually all services were suspended. The voice started to say something about a report from Chicago when the transmission failed. The voice vanished. Kim turned the radio off.

Pacifico looked back at Danny. Her small heart-shaped face was pale. He asked, "Leg hurting, Miss Mousy?"

"No. A little, maybe."

He knew that was a lie. He took off his sport jacket and handed it back to her. "Use it as a lap robe," he said.

"But you'll get cold, Daddy."

"He's your father, don't argue with him," Kim said, turning to grin at her. The grin was unconvincing. Kim looked drawn.

For the second time she pulled cigarettes from her bag and put them back again. Pacifico thought she did not want to smoke in the closed car. He wondered if the closeness of the liquor store was troubling her. Its glass door had been blown open.

Something bounced off the car's roof and fell against the downed tree. In the fraction of a second before it flew away, Pacifico saw it was a wooden sign. It said, "John Grunwald, DDS."

He noticed now that the old gray house to the right was starting to come apart. Its lights had gone out some time ago. Gutters and downspouts had ripped off. A piece of porch furniture had blown through a side railing and was lying in some shrubbery. And now one corner of the porch roof was beginning to lift off its supporting white pillars. It was flapping up and down.

Kim looked back at Danny again and said, "You're shivering, kiddo. Maybe we can keep each other warm." She climbed into the back seat, put her arm around Danny and hugged her close.

Pacifico did not like the pinched look on Danny's face. He knew the pain was growing sharper. He thought about getting her suitcase from the car's trunk; perhaps it would yield a sweater or something else to keep her warm. Then he remembered that she had brought only a little overnight case, as she often did. He kept some of her clothes in his apartment. On short visits there was no need for her to carry a lot of luggage back and forth.

He shouted back to Kim, "I don't suppose you have a blanket in the trunk?"

She shook her head.

In that case, he decided, there was only one thing to do He would make his way to the nearest house and borrow some blankets.

The old gray house was the nearest. The wind had half-turned the car so that its right front quarter was toward the house. Pacifico climbed into the passenger seat. When he tried to open the door he found that the wind was pushing directly against it. He struggled with it. The door opened an inch, then slammed shut again.

"What are you doing?" Kim shouted from the back seat.

"Going to borrow a blanket," he shouted back.

She said something he could not hear. He pushed against the door with all his strength. There was a brief letup in the wind's force—he found himself thinking of George Hochenauer's engineering term, "wind load"—and the door opened and he was out. The door slammed shut violently behind him. At the same time, the wind slammed him against the car.

He had not been prepared for it. The strength of the blast was appalling. It rolled him forward and pushed him down on the car's hood. He pushed back, struggling to get himself upright. The wind's direction shifted slightly, and he found himself on his hands and knees in front of the car. The huge tree trunk was above him. He got his hands on it and pulled himself up. He stood there for a few seconds, belly against the trunk, hands and feet braced, lurching wildly.

The air was full of flying things. Something small and sharp stung his cheek. A medium-sized tree branch, fully leafed, came flying along the street and fetched up against the great trunk a few feet away from him. He had a ridiculous thought: "Wind load is hazardous to your health." The noise was gigantic: a shriek, a howl like nothing he had ever heard before. He could actually feel his ears flapping. When he turned his head to look at the old gray house, he found his vision impaired because the wind was pushing and poking at his eyeballs. The result was that the scene kept shifting and jumping like a movie taken by an amateur with a hand-held camera.

Something hit him hard in the back.

He started to work his way along the trunk toward the house. He came to a pile of branches, brush, and other debris that had become jammed against the trunk, found he could not get over it or through it and started to go around it. This meant letting go of the trunk. He managed to stagger a few steps, but then the wind overpowered him. It blew him into the brush pile on his back. There was nothing to hold onto. He found he could not stand up.

He lay there struggling helplessly. He shouted curses at the top of his lungs, but he might as well have whispered them. He could not even hear his own voice.

Then he saw that this short, desperate journey was all for nothing. The old gray house was coming apart.

The loose corner of the porch roof was flapping harder and harder. Shingles tore off. One of the white pillars came loose and fell away. Then the entire porch roof lifted, buckled, writhed like a gigantic snake and disintegrated. Shingles, boards, and rafters sprayed upward against the house like a flight of startled birds. Naked without its porch skirting, the old house shivered.

A corner of the main roof had also lifted and was beginning to shiver itself to pieces. An entire dormer had ripped away—roof section, window, and all. The two walls that joined under the lifted roof corner had started to separate. The crack widened as the wind pried at it like a colossal crowbar. A large section of the front wall suddenly folded away from the house and ripped loose, exposing a bedroom with striped wallpaper. It should have made a lot of noise, but Pacifico could hear nothing above the roar and shriek of the wind. The old house seemed to be coming apart in eerie silence.

He stared, hypnotized, momentarily forgetting his own problem. He thought: if this is only an eighty-mile wind, what would two hundred be like? Or four hundred? *My God, how could anything stand up to it?*

That afternoon, before picking up Danny, he and Kim had interviewed a professor of architecture at Rutgers. The professor had assured them that people like George Hochenauer were crackpots. No wind could seriously threaten a well-made building, the professor said. Wind was just air in motion. How could air pose any threat to steel and stone?

Pacifico had come away believing him, planning to quote him approvingly.

But it seemed to Pacifico now that he would have to rethink the story. Wind was more to be feared than he had ever dreamed. He was filled with a sense of helplessness and dread.

Something struck him hard on the forehead. The blow made him struggle with extra urgency to get out of the brush pile. The wind abated a little. He finally managed to roll out of the pile and struggle to his feet, clutching at the great tree trunk. Once again he looked up at the old gray house that had been his destination.

The process of violent destruction was continuing. The entire roof, one side wall, and most of the front wall were now gone. The wind was scooping furniture out of the exposed rooms and ripping away interior walls. A large section of the striped-papered bedroom wall came loose, flapped toward Pacifico in a freakish wind eddy and then swerved away. It was followed by something big and heavy that fell end-over-end and crashed into the lawn not far

from the tree's torn-up roots. Pacifico realized that it was a
bed. It had landed upside-down with its mattress partly
beneath it, but as he stared at it, the wind ripped sheets and
blankets away from it and hurled them down the street.

One blanket got snagged in the tree's tangled roots and
stayed there. It took Pacifico several seconds to realize that
the wind, which had prevented him from going into the
house for a blanket, had perversely delivered one to him
outdoors.

Inch by inch, fighting the mighty wind all the way, he
reached the blanket, untangled it from the roots, and
struggled back to the car. He was not sure exactly how he
had managed it. When he climbed into the car and collapsed on a seat he found that the wind's terrible yell had
completely deafened him. Kim and Danny were passing the
hours by singing together, and he could tell they were
singing at the top of their lungs, but he could not hear their
voices. He heard nothing but a gigantic roaring that seemed
to be both outside the car and inside his skull.

They spent the rest of the afternoon and much of the
night in the back seat—all three of them under the blanket,
with Danny sandwiched in the middle. Pacifico's hearing
returned slowly, and as the wind began to abate he was able
to join in the singing. He had an untrained voice but a good
ear for relative pitch. Danny also had a natural musical ear
and a sweet, high little voice that responded malleably to
Kim's tutoring. They had to hold their heads close to hear
each other above the wind, but under Kim's direction they
achieved some fine, clutching harmonies that made Danny
squeal with delight.

There were times when they sat silent, resting their
voices, listening to the wind. Pacifico was warm enough
under the blanket and he thought Danny was tolerably
comfortable, too, but he was aware that Kim shivered
occasionally. She kept staring toward the liquor store until

total darkness fell. Though Pacifico could not see her after that, he had the impression that she continued to stare into the dark, cruelly attracted yet repelled by the doom that she saw out there. He thought cigarettes might help her get through times like this, but apparently out of consideration for her fellow prisoners in the car she had not smoked since they left the Turnpike. He started to say he did not mind if she smoked, then held his tongue. She seemed to be balanced on a razor's edge. It would not be a good idea, he thought, to meddle in a problem he did not fully understand.

She seemed to grow more tranquil as the wind abated. It finally died away altogether at about ten o'clock. An hour later a gibbous moon came out from behind clouds and illuminated a scene of awful desolation. Many of the old houses lay in ruins, and so did several of the stores farther down the street. The Volvo was pushed hard up against the big tree trunk and was buried hood-deep in a winddrift of brush and debris.

The car's three occupants got a door open and thrashed their way out of the pile. Together with some other stranded motorists they went to one of the less-damaged houses in search of food and water.

● ● ●

News reports the next day said the National Weather Service's anemometer on top of the Empire State Building had recorded a gust of eighty-four miles an hour. In most versions of the Beaufort Scale, anything above seventy-five is designated Force Twelve or "hurricane." There is no higher designation.

Throughout the northern half of the world, official survey teams and individual citizens spent the next few days looking over the damage. Most steel-skeletoned and concrete city buildings turned out to be substantially unscathed. Some older brick buildings were dangerously weakened, and some tall brick structures, such as factory chimneys, were blown down. The worst devastation was found in suburban towns. All across America and western Europe, wood-framed houses had been severely mauled. The Russians and Chinese were secretive, as usual, but there was no reason to suppose the wind had treated their towns more gently than those of the west.

As a general rule, the wind had been at its most powerful in northern cities, gradually abating as it moved south. Oslo reported sustained winds of nearly ninety, as did other cities near the sixtieth parallel. Tokyo, some twenty-five degrees to the south, measured sustained winds of slightly more than seventy. Cities south of the Tropic of Cancer felt nothing more than a gale.

This was the general rule. As is always true of weather patterns, however, there were exceptions and anomalies. For unknown reasons, Rome was blasted by stronger winds than was London. Some Chicago suburbs were flattened, while most Detroit suburbs seemed serenely unaffected. The wind spawned tornadoes in some regions but not in others. It brought bitter cold and snow to San Francisco, while in Paris it actually caused the ambient temperature to rise.

Some scientists now began to talk with new respect of the Phelps-Blagonravov computer model and the Simon Pollock theories on which the model was based. The model appeared to have predicted the hurricane-force wind accurately. But many scientists, perhaps most, still remained skeptical of the model's final prediction—that there would eventually be a wind of city-killing violence. They found the prediction too bizarre and sensational for their taste. With the scientific caution that had been pounded into them ever since they fidgeted through their first high-school physics lessons, they insisted on more study and verification before making up their minds.

This skepticism was volubly endorsed and actively encouraged by most of the world's government agencies, which wanted an excuse for inaction; and by the world real estate and construction community, which was already losing money and feared worse to come. Those who did speak up in Phelps-Blagonravov's favor tended to get shouted down. When New York's commissioner of buildings, Jake Barnes, suggested in mild terms that occupants of high-rise apartments in the city might consider making preparations for shelter lower down, he was subjected to a public chorus of jeers and catcalls. He also received a private phone call from Mayor Millington, who told him politely but unequivocally to keep his mouth shut. Decisions and comments on scary topics such as the evacuation of tall buildings, the mayor told Barnes, were to come only from the mayor's office.

The heat of the public debate rose abruptly when a new issue of *Seven Days* hit the streets.

11

THE ARTICLE WAS flagged on the cover. "BIG WIND COMING?" the banner line bellowed, stark black on school-bus yellow. "WILL IT BLOW CITIES DOWN?"

In terms of newsstand sales, that week's issue became one of the most successful in the history of *Seven Days*. The first reports coming back to the circulation director sent him hurrying upstairs to tell Arthur Beaulieu the good news. On the basis of preliminary figures, the circulation director said, it looked as though they were going to have a near-record week on the nation's newsstands. He thought it might even turn out to be the second-best ever. The all-time record was held by a mid-1970s issue whose cover, lasciviously pink and purple, had squealed in happy shock over a Washington call-girl ring.

After being banished to the back pages for many months, the Big Wind was hot news again. The recent blow, which had topped eighty miles an hour in some cities and caused heavy damage in suburban areas, had made people start asking questions once more about a subject they had been ready to forget. It was *Seven Days*'s luck to hit the stands at just the right time.

Many people read the wind story with avid interest. Some who read it were frightened. Some were enraged.

• • •

Peter James Schenker read it over a late breakfast on the patio of his home at Monterey, California, high above the cold blue Pacific. The low, concrete-walled house, designed to stand Pacific storms, had sustained only light damage in the recent high wind.

Schenker was an architect of international repute, a tall, thin-wristed, somewhat effeminate man with flowing white hair. He and his partners had designed many of the world's best-known buildings. He reacted to the article at first with lofty amusement. It was amazing how little the press and public knew about architecture! His amusement turned to irritation, then to rage. He threw the offending magazine across the patio. "What nonsense!" he shouted, his voice rising shrilly. "What absolute fucking *nonsense!*"

"You call, Señor?" his Mexican houseboy asked.

"No, Ramon, no, I was just—listen, bring me a phone, will you?"

• • •

John R. ("Jelly Jack") Barrow read it in his Houston office. He was not much of a reader, usually preferring to get his news from TV, but after Schenker's call he sent his secretary out to pick up a copy of *Seven Days*.

"Jesus," he mumbled as he read the article. "Schenker was right. A thing like this—Jesus, it could knock the shit out of the market."

Jelly Jack Barrow, a mountainously fat man, headed a company with extensive real estate interests in Houston, Minneapolis, New York, and other cities. Its name was New World Development, Inc. It had started out many decades ago as a device for channeling cash capital from organized crime into legitimate investments, and it still served as a laundry for large amounts of drug, gambling, and prostitution money. But a good deal of blameless public capital had come to flow in New World's veins as it grew, and its stock was traded on the Big Board. Its main business was office and apartment buildings. In recent years it had also begun to move into the hotel business. Its crowning achievement was the New World Center in midtown New York, a dazzling new seventy-story tower designed by Peter James Schenker. The Center was a multiple-use building: hotel, restaurants, and shops on its shimmering lower floors; offices in the middle; and apartment condominiums at the top. Its rentals and condo prices were so high, however, that the company had had trouble filling it.

And articles like this one in *Seven Days* sure as hell weren't going to help, Barrow thought angrily. What were they trying to do, for Chrissakes, bankrupt the whole real estate and construction industry? Jesus. Times were tough enough without shit like this.

He picked up his phone and barked at his secretary: "Get me Joe Lemkin."

Joe Lemkin was the company's stockholder relations director. When he came on the phone, Barrow asked him, "How's the stock doing? I haven't seen a paper in a couple days."

"Well, it's down, Jack," Joe Lemkin said mournfully. "Closed at twenty-two yesterday, off a point and a quarter. As of noon today we're down another three-quarters."

"Jesus," Barrow groaned. "Off two in two days, huh?" Since he had somewhat more than 100,000 shares in his personal portfolio, this meant he was some $200,000 poorer on paper than he had been yesterday morning. That hurt.

"A lot of other real estate and hotel stocks are down, too," Lemkin added.

That did not make Barrow feel any better. "What's doing it, Joe?" he asked. "The *Seven Days* thing?"

"That's got to be part of it, sure. But it takes more than one lousy magazine article to move the market. I think people were worrying about the wind anyhow—you know, after that eighty-mile blow we had. *Seven Days* just gave them a push."

After hanging up, Barrow sat and thought for a long time about various ways of applying push in the opposite direction. His thought processes were slow but orderly. When he had decided what to do, he picked up his phone again.

• • •

Spencer Millington had already read the story when Barrow called. Millington agreed that it was a terrible piece—one-sided, unnecessarily scary to the ill-informed, and damaging to a lot of people's interests, including his own. He agreed that somebody ought to do something about it.

"Right," Jelly Jack Barrow said. "Somebody should. Namely you, among others."

"Me?"

"Yeah. You."

Millington sighed unhappily. He was not a doer.

Spencer Millington was the mayor of New York. He was a member of an old New York family, a family that had once been wealthy but had been on the skids for several decades. The mayor was a handsome, urbane man of forty-five whose political success was founded on the idea that one must, above all, avoid giving offense. This meant shunning action and avoiding stands on issues, but that was no great hardship to Mayor Millington, for he had no strong beliefs of his own—nothing but a trendy and fuzzily thought-out liberalism plus a fondness for personal comfort. His pliability had brought him to the attention of some powerful interest groups, who had made use of him as their point man. Nobody harbored any great fondness for Millington, but then again, hardly anybody seriously disliked him either—and in politics, sometimes, that can count for a lot. Millington was beginning to believe he might have a shot at the governorship next year.

On the phone, Jelly Jack Barrow reminded the mayor that New World Development belonged to a business consortium that had contributed generously, and not entirely legally, to his last campaign. If there was to be a run for the state capitol next year—well, that would be a still more expensive campaign, and a man would need all the friends he could get, right? Millington did not need this reminder. He never forgot who owed what to whom, nor who wanted what.

He did not need to be reminded, either, that he had taken care of a potentially costly building-inspection problem for the New World Center when it was under construction—a problem having to do with grades of window glass. Nor was it necessary to remind him that, in return, New World had placed some large orders with the Millington family lumber company.

Jack Barrow may have guessed that these reminders were all unnecessary, but he offered them anyhow. Barrow was a careful man. He liked to have things spelled out, not assumed. Having satisfied himself that Mayor Millington's position was clearly understood, Barrow returned to the subject of the *Seven Days* article. "I seem to remember you know the publisher of this goddamn magazine, right?" he said. "What's the guy's name, Boolow?"

"Beaulieu," Millington said. He made it his business to know many of the city's top media people. "I don't know Arthur very intimately. But my wife and his wife—his ex-wife, I should say—they're old friends, college classmates, in fact."

"Yeah, I remember you saying something about that one time," said Barrow, who, like a mythical elephant, forgot nothing. "I also seem to remember this woman, Mrs.

Beaulieu, she bought a condo at the Center, didn't she?"

"That's right, yes."

Barrow was silent for a moment, as though trying to put ideas together. Finally he said, "Well, I don't know how you're gonna use that, but maybe you'll come up with something."

Millington did not understand. "What is it you want me to do?"

"Find a way to lean on this bastard so he doesn't print any more shit about wind."

"You think he's planning a sequel?"

"I dunno. It's what people tell me. But it stands to reason. Everybody's expecting this Big Wind some day soon, right? So he hits the streets with this sequel before the wind gets here, he sells a hell of a lot of copies."

Millington thought that was a plausible analysis. In all likelihood, a sequel was even now in preparation for next week's issue. The sequel would almost certainly be hurtful to the interests of people in the construction and real estate industries. Most newsmagazines and major papers had adopted a cool, distant, and uncommitted attitude toward the talk of looming danger, but *Seven Days* seemed bent on stirring up a national panic. That first article had been full of scary talk about wind load and unkind comments on the failure of government agencies to make emergency plans. Millington could well understand why Jelly Jack was upset.

"I don't know if there's much I can do," Millington said.

"You'll think of something," Barrow said in a tone that did not encourage arguments. "Don't worry, we'll be backing you up. We're leaning on some TV people for starters. We're gonna get our side of the story told one way or another. So you won't be working alone. Anyway, you owe us, Spence, you know that."

"I know that, Jack."

● ● ●

Angela Beaulieu did not usually read *Seven Days*. It was too strongly associated with her former husband. She wanted as little as possible to do with Arthur. Indeed, on several occasions she had gone out of her way to give gossip columnists the deliciously spiteful intelligence that she preferred *Time*. But she did read the wind story, for it represented the first career effort of her beloved only daughter, Kimberley.

Dear Kimberley! She was trying so hard to become an adult, but she was still a child in many ways. She had phoned Angela repeatedly during the time she was working on the article, bubbling over with tales about the wonderful world of journalism and the behavior of some dreadful Italian-surnamed man who seemed to be her boss. Just like a little child: "Watch me, Mother, I can swim!"

It was important to Kimberley to be "taken seriously," as she put it, and for her, at this point in her life, this meant showing the world that she could work successfully at a career. Angela did not know how long this journalism fad would last; not long, she suspected. It was Kim's way to get wildly enthusiastic about things, then get bored with them rapidly and drop them. When she was ready to drop journalism, Angela would not object, though she was sure Arthur would. He had a lot of old-fashioned Calvinist ideas about the ennobling qualities of work, but the fact was that Kimberley did not really need to work. Angela had never earned a paycheck in her life and did not feel she had missed anything important. Still, she intended to support her daughter staunchly while this earn-my-own-living phase lasted.

Thus it was that the wind story had been required reading for Angela. She had sent her maid, Edna Jane, out to buy a copy as soon as the issue was on the stands. Edna

Jane, who had been with the family since Kim was a little girl, also bought a copy for herself.

And thus it was that Angela had read the article when she received a phone call from her old friend Sarah Millington, the mayor's wife.

After chatting about this and that for a few minutes, Sarah got to her point. She said, "Angela, love, you once told me you dreamed of giving a party so absolutely noteworthy that it would make the front page of the *Times*. Is that still true?"

Of course it was. A born and bred socialite, Angela Beaulieu lived for parties. What else was more important, after all? Angela worked hard to get her name and occasionally her picture on the society pages. She particularly enjoyed being photographed next to contemporaries who were going to seed, for she was still slim, attractive, and golden-haired at age fifty. She dazzled people at parties. That was good fun. But to make the *front* page . . . what a triumph of partygiving that would be! She believed Truman Capote had done it once, just once. Had anybody else?

She answered Sarah Millington's question by laughing and saying, "Of course, Sarah dear. Who wouldn't want that? If only it were possible!"

"Maybe it is, love," Sarah said quietly.

"Are you serious?"

"Quite serious. Did you see the latest issue of *Seven Days*? With that article about the Big Wind?"

"Yes. As a matter of fact, my Kimberley helped write it."

"Oh?" Sarah sounded as though she did not welcome this piece of information. She was silent for a moment, and then she said, "Oh. Well, maybe you aren't going to like this idea after all."

"What *are* you gibbering about, dear heart?"

"I was going to suggest a Big Wind party. You know, like the hurricane parties they're always having in Florida. I

know how you love to needle poor Arthur. Well, here would
be a way to needle him on a grand scale and grab headlines
at the same time." Sarah's voice was rising with enthusiasm. "Don't you see the beauty of it, Angela? Here Arthur
publishes this solemn article saying how scared we all ought
to be, and you turn around and throw the season's biggest
party in the middle of a windstorm in that lovely apartment
of yours at the top of the New World Center. Think of it!"

Angela thought of it.

"It's a sneaky, dirty idea," she said after a while. "You
ought to be ashamed of yourself for suggesting it, Sarah."
She waited a beat. "I love it."

"What fun, right? I'll help you organize it, if you like."
Sarah loved organizing parties. "I think what you'll have to
do is pre-invite people without knowing the date. Then,
when we get word that the Big Wind is finally on the way,
we get on the phone. Maybe we can work out a telephone
chain. We could—"

"Suppose the wind is in the morning?" Angela asked.
She was beginning to have doubts.

"Well, in that case—I don't know," Sarah said, sounding
deflated. Then her voice brightened. "In that case we'd
make it a brunch. Not knowing—that would make it twice
the fun!"

"Do you really think people would come, Sarah? I
mean—you know—"

"The Newsworthies?" This was a term that the two
friends had used since college days. "I'd bet my boopsie on
it, love. People are always looking for some new kind of
party, especially when they think somebody with a camera
will be around. We'll be sure to tell the press about it, of
course. People will jump at the chance to come to this,
Angela! You can count on Mayor and Mrs. Millington, for
starters."

"Won't he be at City Hall? I mean, with the emergency

and everything?"

"He gets busy after, not during. While the wind blows, everything shuts down. *Everybody* will come, Angela. There won't be anything else for them to do!"

"Well—" Angela was still hesitant.

"You aren't scared of wind, are you? I mean, you didn't take that article seriously?"

"No, of course not." This was perfectly true. Having been rich all her life, Angela had not often needed to be concerned about weather. There was somebody to take care of it. Heat wave? Somebody made sure the air conditioning kept functioning properly. Cold spell? Somebody was down there somewhere, tending furnaces and pipes and things. Angela did not know who did these things or exactly how they were done; she knew only that if weather presented problems, they were not allowed to become *her* problems. She assumed that if something needed to be done about the wind, somebody would do it.

No: it was not worry about wind that made her hesitate; it was worry about Kimberley. What would Kimberley say if her mother threw a highly publicized Big Wind party, demonstrating that she did not take the article seriously?

That could be a problem. On the other hand . . . what fun the party would be! And how newsworthy! And what a slap in the face for Arthur!

Their divorce had not been amicable. They had fought bitterly over money and other matters. What made Angela wildly angry was that he had thrown her over for a woman ten years older than she: his long-time secretary, Julia Mead. A woman of his own age. That witch. Julia's hair had been graying even back then. Now it was snow-white, but Julia and Arthur were still seen together around town after dark. What kind of witchcraft did the woman practice?

Angela remembered something Arthur had said during a hurtful argument just before they agreed to divorce. "I'm tired of playing in this kindergarten," he had told her. "I've found a *woman*." Angela would never forget that.

She sat now in the enormous living room of her apartment on the sixty-eighth floor of the New World Center and imagined it filled with a festive crowd. The place had cost her more than two million dollars, but it was worth every dime, she thought. It was a corner apartment. One great window of the living room faced north; the other looked westward to New Jersey. The decorator had used color sparingly, in bright splashes here and there. But the walls and carpeting were eggshell white. The effect was one of great space, floating high above the streets of New York. It was a setting designed for history-making parties, Angela thought.

The party would be a black-tie affair, of course.

"Let me think about it for a day," she told Sarah Millington. "I'll call you."

● ● ●

Professor Simon Pollock was delighted with the article. It quoted him accurately, abundantly, and, on the whole, approvingly. It also quoted many others, of course—some saying things he could agree with, others not—but he thought he emerged as one of the story's more sympathetic characters. That young woman reporter—by golly, she was obviously a person of high intelligence. She would go far in her profession!

A network TV news show phoned him the day after the magazine hit the stands. Would the professor like to come to New York and participate in a live hour-long special on wind? All at network expense. Night in a hundred-dollar hotel. Steak dinner—anything you want. We'll even send a car up to Connecticut to get you and take you back home, professor.

Not often in his life had Simon Pollock been treated so

royally. He accepted with pleasure.

The show was to be at night, but he was asked to turn up at the studio right after lunch to be briefed and pre-interviewed. The pre-interviewers were two young women, one of whom seemed quite unconcerned about the Big Wind, while the other was plainly frightened. It did not surprise Pollock to find such wide divergence of feeling. Some are exhilarated by violent weather and some are scared of it, while still others, absorbed in indoor lives, have virtually no interest in weather at all.

The pre-interviewers asked him if he was still expecting a Big Wind. He replied in his squeaky voice that he was.

"But how can you be so sure, Professor Pollock?"

"Well, our instruments still find hundreds of trillions of tons of air stacked up above the north pole. When that huge heavy mass is released . . ."

"Will these four-hundred-mile winds really be as power-ful as people are saying?"

"Oh my, yes. Look what tornadoes can do, for instance. In Oklahoma once, a tornado carried a grand piano half a mile. Another tornado picked a railroad locomotive off its tracks and rolled it *up* a hill. Is that powerful enough for you?"

"Yes, thank you, professor. We're expecting this wind in the next couple of weeks, is that right?"

"Something like that, yes."

"Could it be longer?"

"Oh, certainly. These are educated guesses, nothing more."

"What kind of warning will we have?"

"Well, it's possible that mound of air will undergo a change in shape just before it—just before. If it does change, the instruments will tell us . . ."

It was about three o'clock when the pre-interviewers released him with an admonishment to report back at seven. All that talk about the Big Wind had made him tense. There was a twitchy sensation in the back of his legs. Undoubtedly, he thought, his body was preparing itself to run away—only there was nowhere to run to. He decided that what he needed was a walk brisk enough and long enough to tire him.

Stepping out onto the sidewalk, he was startled to find that the afternoon, which had started out clear, had turned cool and cloudy. He realized that he had just emerged from the most indoor of all indoor environments. The studio was not only climate-controlled but also windowless. There must be people, he reflected, who did not see the sky all day long. There must even be some who commuted by subway and got to their office buildings by walking in New York's maze of pedestrian tunnels, and those people would not see a daytime sky except on weekends. Simon Pollock could not have tolerated such a life. Yet he knew there were many who found it congenial and thrived in it.

The network had provided him with sumptuous accommodations at the New World Center. He stopped there to leave his tie and suit jacket in his room. His students in Connecticut expected him to be weather-rumpled, but it would not do to appear that way on nationwide television. He put on an old blue zipper jacket and went out toward Central Park for a walk.

He saw and sensed the same divergence of feeling throughout the city as he had noticed in the two pre-interviewers. Some were taking the Big Wind lightly or making a commercial venture out of it. He passed a clothing store that was advertising a "Gone with the Wind" bankruptcy sale. Women's shops were promoting perfumes with names like Nightwind. The music industry was also cashing in. Pollock stopped outside a record store to hear an old ballad that was enjoying a revival: "Down in the valley . . . hear the wind blow." The mournful harmonies moaned like wind in lonesome places. Next came a song about love's tornado. Pollock walked on.

The crowds jostling him on the sidewalks seemed expectant and excited. He recalled reading in the morning paper that growing numbers of employees were staying away from their jobs. They claimed worry or psychosomatic distress brought on by the expected wind, but many simply wanted to make it the basis of a holiday. Dozens of Big Wind parties were being planned in private homes and nightclubs, an article on the society page noted.

The fools, Pollock thought. They're just like Florida newcomers and their hurricane parties. They think weather is something concocted for their *entertainment*.

But he saw many others who were obviously taking the Big Wind more seriously. Walking across Central Park, he saw a congregation listening in respectful silence while a man and woman in clerical garb took turns preaching about the cleansing wind that was soon to destroy wicked Sodom. Strolling down Park West, he saw a man stop a car and climb out for what appeared to be the sole purpose of examining the sky. "Nothing to worry about," the man reported to a passenger as he climbed back in. "Just a regular cloudy sky, looks like." Pollock, who was alert to such manifestations, observed that people on the sidewalks seemed to be glancing upward much more often than was normal.

He was in the Times Square area when it started to rain gently. Normally he enjoyed rain as much as any other weather, but he suddenly felt a strong need to get indoors. He was filled with a sense of terrible foreboding. He knew the Big Wind was not on the way yet, but he needed to comfort himself by calling the weather station and getting a status report from his graduate assistant. He quickened his pace and hurried through the rain to his room.

●　●　●

It was still raining when he returned to the TV studio later in the evening. He was puzzled by a felt change in the studio's emotional atmosphere. At first, he thought he was picking up nothing more than the jittery vibrations that must be common before any live show went on the air. Then he began to feel that the change had something to do with him. People seemed embarrassed, reluctant to talk to him. The two pre-interviewers avoided him with the greatest care. The hostess and chief on-camera interviewer of the show, a woman named Darlene Dorsey, greeted him brusquely and then also avoided him until air time.

He was startled to learn, just before air time, that he was to be the first guest interviewed. He had understood that he was not to appear until the second half of the show. An assistant director hustled him into the interviewee's chair and clipped on his lapel mike while he tried to collect his thoughts.

Darlene Dorsey began the show by reading a rambling, disorganized preface about disasters, rumors, hysteria, and other topics whose relevance was not altogether clear. It seemed to have been written in a great hurry. Pollock was perplexed by her tone, which was one of tolerant amusement over the idiocy of crowds. This was not what he had been led to expect.

Nor were her questions the ones he had been told to expect. "Professor Pollock," she asked, after establishing his credentials, "you've been saying you expect winds of four hundred miles an hour. But how is it possible to predict wind velocity with such certainty?"

"Oh, I didn't say that. I said *two* to four hundred. I—"

"Ah, so you really *don't* know what kind of wind we might see?"

"Well, I—"

"All this talk of four hundred miles an hour is really just—well, it's just a guess, isn't it?"

"Yes, in a way. It's—"

"An educated guess. I believe that's your own phrase, professor?"

"Yes, but—let me explain—I—"

And so it went. The only thing merciful about it was that it was brief. Pollock saw that he had been set up so the other guests could have the fun of knocking him down. He was followed by a meteorologist who doubted there would be any Big Wind at all. Then came a psychiatrist with jargon-clogged comment on the fear of storms in children and adults. Then came Spencer Millington, the handsome and urbane mayor of New York. Millington perfectly reflected Darlene Dorsey's air of tolerant amusement. He said it would be impossible to run a city like New York if the government panicked over every predicted disaster. A few months ago, he recalled, everybody was worrying about a flu epidemic, and just before that it was an invasion of man-eating ants, or something.

Darlene Dorsey and the mayor enjoyed a companionable chuckle.

Simon Pollock's face felt hot. He squirmed in his chair in alternating embarrassment and rage. He was also baffled. Until tonight, all the staff people connected with this show had treated him with friendly respect. He had understood that viewpoints other than his own were to be presented, but all were to get fair coverage with a minimum of editorial bias. But *this*, he thought—this wasn't a news show, it was a public execution! What had happened to change the nature of the show so suddenly? Had somebody gotten to the producers? Some big-money interests, perhaps, who had something to lose from the idea of a dangerous wind?

The second half-hour of the show was a copy of the first. The straw man, set up to be knocked down, was a structural engineer named Ferguson. Pollock remembered seeing him quoted in the *Seven Days* article, along with another engineer named Hochenauer. Ferguson believed few buildings could survive a sustained two-hundred-mile wind without serious damage, and as for four hundred, it would flatten everything. He was not permitted to say this in front of the camera, however, for Darlene Dorsey cut him down as skillfully as she had Simon Pollock. The next guest was the renowned architect Peter James Schenker, designer of the New World Center. Schenker commented on Ferguson in tones of amused contempt. Pollock was unable to stand it any longer. He fled the studio while the show still had twenty minutes to run.

It was still raining. For a while he walked the wet streets, letting his anger cool. Then he realized he was ravenously hungry. He had done a lot of walking that day and had not yet eaten dinner. A wicked idea came to him. Since his hotel bill was being picked up by the network, he would avenge himself by buying the most expensive dinner on the menu at the New World Red Room—which was, he had been told, one of the priciest restaurants in the city.

He gorged himself on lobster, a luxury that he had never been able to afford for himself. Afterward he decided to let the network buy him still another unaccustomed luxury. He went into the D'Alembert Lounge for a glass of brandy and a cigar.

To his astonishment, an elegantly dressed and rather attractive woman sat on the bar stool next to his, ordered a tall drink and started to talk to him. She seemed to be in her early thirties. She introduced herself as Heidi.

"Didn't I see you on TV earlier tonight?" she asked, examining his face.

"Yes, I was on that special about wind."

"Yeah, I thought I recognized you. What did you think of the show?"

He shrugged gloomily. "Well, I didn't get much of a chance to say what I—"

"Yeah, I noticed that. Like they had it all loaded against you, the bastards. But you're really worried about this Big Wind, aren't you?"

"Yes, I suppose I am."

"Me, too, you wanna know the truth. I've had this kind of phobia about wind ever since I was a little kid. Had to crawl in bed with my mother when there was a thunderstorm."

She seemed genuinely disturbed. They talked about wind for a while longer. Then, during a lull in the conversation, she abruptly leaned over and whispered in his ear, "You wanna spend some money?"

Simon Pollock's experience with women was limited. He had never married, had had sexual intercourse only once, awkwardly, as a teenager, and had never in his life been solicited by a prostitute. Even whores found him uninteresting. Thus he did not immediately understand what Heidi meant.

Then understanding dawned. "Oh," he said. "You mean—uh—?" He waved his hands helplessly.

"That's what I mean, honey." She put her hand on his thigh and caressed him a little.

It was one of the most wildly exciting moments in Simon Pollock's lonely life. The preachers in Central Park had called this city a Sodom, and how right they were! And if it was about to be destroyed, why not enjoy one of its last nights? The trouble was that Simon Pollock had no idea what one should expect to pay for such a service. He stammered, "When you say—uh, money—what is the, I mean how much?"

"Hundred dollars for the regular, more for specials. You want me to stay all night, three hundred."

Pollock's face fell. For a state university professor, those were substantial sums. He had only some fifty dollars on him in any case. Sadly, he told Heidi so.

"Oh well," she said. She sighed and stood up. "Have a nice night, honey." She patted his arm and walked off.

Five minutes later she slid back onto the stool next to him. "Give me the damned fifty," she said, sounding irritated.

"What?"

"I don't know, I guess I like you. You're a gentleman or something. Can we talk about the wind some more—later?"

"Of course, but—"

"Come on, let's go up to your room before I change my mind. Jeez, I ought to have my damned head examined."

She stayed all night. Simon Pollock had never had such an experience in his life. In the morning he ordered them an extravagant breakfast in bed, billing it to the network. They talked about the Big Wind a lot.

● ● ●

George Hochenauer had enjoyed the *Seven Days* article. Indeed, he found it a pleasant surprise. That guy who interviewed him, Pacifico, had not seemed to buy much of what he was trying to say. Hochenauer had expected to find the article slanted against his viewpoint. Instead, it quoted him more or less accurately and without any editorial prejudice that he could call objectionable.

It also quoted another engineer, a fellow from San Francisco named Ferguson. Hochenauer thought he had met Ferguson once, long ago, at some engineering convention. Ferguson held substantially the same views on buildings and weather as Hochenauer did. The major difference between them was that Ferguson was a man of somber and impressive appearance. He was a tall, craggy fellow with a face something like Abraham Lincoln's. Hence it was Ferguson's picture, not Hochenauer's, that accompanied the *Seven Days* article. Ferguson had also appeared as a guest on several TV talk shows.

Oh well. Hochenauer was used to that kind of rebuff. He

was consoled by the thought that not every TV interview was pleasant.

"That Darlene Dorsey is poison," he commented to his wife, Wilma. They were watching the hour-long wind special while sitting at the long bar at Booker's. "Shit, poor old Ferguson. He can't get a word in edgewise."

"Yeah, him and that Pollock, that weather professor," Wilma agreed. "But you notice when she's got some asshole like the mayor up there, he gets to talk all he wants. I'll have another a these if you don't mind, Jimmy." She held her glass out to the bartender.

They watched in silence while Darlene Dorsey finished dismantling Ferguson. Then Wilma said, "You know what the trouble is? That Ferguson, he's too polite. They shoulda had you on there, Hoke."

"Shit."

"Yeah, I mean it," she said loyally. "Hey Kramer," she called down the bar. "They shoulda had Hoke on there, right?"

Kramer shrugged morosely, indicating that it made no difference to him. Kramer was a habitué of Booker's, as were Hochenauer and his wife. Nobody knew anything about Kramer except his last name. He seldom said anything except the few words that evidently summed up his philosophy of life. "Who cares?" he would grumble. "Who gives a shit?"

"See," Wilma said to Hochenauer, "Kramer thinks you shoulda been on there, Hoke." It was a Booker's tradition to make fun of the silent Kramer.

Hochenauer grinned and drained his sixth shot of Mother Fletcher's. Wilma was drinking her habitual vodka and orange juice. Hochenauer suspected her large daily intake of this drink was partly responsible for her condition of gross overweight, and he sometimes tried to get her to moderate the habit. "At least wait till after breakfast, Wilma," he would plead. It was not that he found the fat objectionable; on the contrary, skinny little Hochenauer was sexually aroused by his wife's huge breasts and her great jelly of a bottom. What troubled him was the fear that the overweight condition might shorten her life. However, she had no intention of changing her drinking habits, and most of the time he kept quiet and hoped for the best. He would have prayed if he knew how. He could not imagine life without Wilma.

She said, "Well, I don't give a shit whether Kramer gives a shit. I think you oughta been on that show."

"Nah. Not me. I'm too ugly."

She patted his bony, ratlike face. "Not ugly," she said fondly. "You ain't ugly, Hoke. You just look *unusual*, that's all."

He grinned with gloomy humor. "Yeah. Well, at least people wanna hear me talk. Never heard that phone ring so much."

The *Seven Days* article had brought him a flood of publicity, though no invitations to show his face on TV. He had received calls from other magazines, newspapers, radio stations. And also from people who wanted him to shut up. One call had come from a former boss, a Florida contractor who said he was working on a deal to build a high-rise condominium complex. "With talk like you're talking," the man shouted angrily, "I'm losing my backers. The god-damn market is drying up. I'm telling you, Hochenauer, you better keep your yap shut, you hear me? Or maybe, someday, somebody is gonna shut it for you!"

Hochenauer took this for an idle threat. He had heard others like it during his life. Such talk was common in the construction industry. It did not worry him.

There was one phone call that did worry him, though he

could not say why. It had been this afternoon. The caller, a
man, did not give his name. He asked, "Can I talk to
George Hochenauer?"

"You got him."

"You the guy they quoted in that magazine this week?
The engineer?"

"Yeah, that's me."

The man hesitated, then said, "Listen, you gotta help
me. I—"

There was another pause. Then the caller hung up.

•   •   •

Ed McRoyden had been unable to go through with it. His
plan—well, no, not a plan, just a vague intention—had been
to tell the story without identifying himself. Use George
Hochenauer as a confessor. Pour it all out, all the pain and
worry. Hochenauer was a fellow engineer, and judging from
that magazine article he was a guy who could sympathize
with this kind of problem. McRoyden needed desperately
to talk to somebody, hear some soothing words of absolu-
tion. But as soon as he got Hochenauer on the phone,
McRoyden's voice froze.

Ed McRoyden's conscience had troubled him for more
than two years, but he had clung to the comforting belief
that his sin was only a sin against money and hence, in
God's eyes, trivial and forgivable. The article in *Seven Days*
had removed that emollient, however. He had read the
article with mounting dread. It made him fear his sin might
turn out to be a sin against people. It might even turn out
to be murder.

He emerged from the coffee shop phone booth after
trying to talk to Hochenauer and walked outdoors. The
afternoon was cool and sunny. A block away was the New
World Center, seventy stories of shining metal and glass.
He gazed up at it. It reared gigantic against a blue sky in

which small white clouds moved lazily. Their motion created the illusion that the top of the colossal building was moving—leaning, *falling*. McRoyden wrenched his eyes away, dizzy and frightened. He staggered against a woman passing on the sidewalk. She muttered an unforgiving comment at him and hurried away.

He leaned against a wall and looked up at the New World Center again. He wanted to forget it but could not. He was drawn to it as though by some dark magic that overcame his own will.

Ed McRoyden was a big man with blue eyes and reddish, sandy hair and beard. He was an inspector in the city's Office of Building Construction. It was his job, in essence, to haunt construction sites and make sure each structure conformed to its officially approved plans and specifications as filed with the Department of Buildings. The city could not afford to hire enough field inspectors, and so they had to spread themselves thin. Like income tax agents, they relied heavily on random spot-checking, hoping that their mere presence would keep people honest. The system worked poorly, as all such systems do. A lot of substandard materials, badly thought-out design concepts, and sloppy workmanship got by. A further result of the tight budget was that there was no effective system under which one inspector spot-checked the work of others. Such a system existed on paper, but in practice it was unreliable.

It was a situation in which cheating was not only possible but easy. Ed McRoyden had resisted temptation for many years but then had begun to ask himself why. A slow accumulation of irritants led to this change. Perhaps the most telling of them was the arrival of his fortieth birthday. He was forced to acknowledge that, unless some fairy-tale miracle took place, he was probably not going to reach the heights of success he had dreamed of as a young man. In fact it was beginning to look as though he was dead-ended.

He had been passed over for promotion twice. "It isn't anything you did *wrong*, Ed," his boss tried to explain kindly. "It's just, you know, some guys have this leadership ability and some don't." McRoyden knew there was a lack of assertiveness in him and knew other men detected it quickly. Dead-ended at forty! And with two teenaged sons to put through college and a wife who was turning sour after years of penny-pinching. Her sister, married to a successful commodities broker, had received a Russian sable coat for *her* fortieth birthday, a coat as black and deep as the sky between the stars and worth more than Ed McRoyden's entire net worth. His wife was not so cruel or so stupid as to point out this fact to him, but they were both keenly aware of it.

McRoyden concluded in time that his habitual, rigid honesty was not going to pay off as handsomely as the priests and nuns at school had always said it would. Assigned to the New World Center project, he let it be known that if anyone wished to say anything to him in private, he was willing to listen. This resulted in his earning some $26,000 in cash payments during the course of construction. The contractor and others—he was never sure who supplied those fat envelopes of cash—saved millions. Nothing dangerous was done; McRoyden would never have gone along with that. Just little things: fewer bolts and rivets than the design engineers had specified in some of the joints; a slightly cheaper grade of steel in some of the spandrel beams; three-eighths instead of half-inch sheet-rock in some interior walls.

There was one close call. A discrepancy having to do with grades of window glass somehow came to the attention of somebody who was not supposed to know. McRoyden braced himself for trouble, but it never arrived. Unaccountably, miraculously, a soft thick blanket of silence came down over everything. Who arranged for this cover-up, or how, McRoyden never knew. His impression was that the orders came from high in the city government. He asked no questions. He recognized that he had been saved by powerful crosscurrents of motivation that were far above and beyond his ken, the way an ant on a sidewalk may be saved when a man swerves to look at a pretty girl.

McRoyden had expected no trouble from his other moneymaking ventures around the project. Even if somebody discovered something amiss in some future year, he told himself, it would be virtually impossible to affix blame. Indeed, it was unlikely that anyone would even *try* to affix blame. Buildings never functioned right, yet it was rare that anybody was called to account. People just shrugged and said, "Oh well." Even when something went drastically wrong, as in the 1981 collapse of walkways in that Kansas City Hyatt Hotel, nobody could say where the fault lay. Deliberate corner-cutting? Shoddy materials? A mistake by some sleepy engineer who specified the wrong kinds of bolts? Negligence by a work-crew foreman with a hangover? The truth would never be known for sure, though lawsuits arising from that horrifying disaster might drag through the courts for years.

Nothing so drastic would happen to the New World Center anyway, McRoyden had thought. In his mind, the worst-case scenario was something like that of the famous Boston building whose windows kept falling out when it was new. Nobody ever took complete or final responsibility for that. In the end, people shrugged and said, "Oh well." People don't *expect* buildings to work right, McRoyden thought. No suburban homebuyer is ever surprised to find his basement leaking in wet weather—even though every town building code on earth says basements must be dry. McRoyden worked in an industry in which malfunction is routine.

These comforting thoughts had been chased from

McRoyden's mind by the article in *Seven Days*. He had no idea what might happen to a carelessly built structure in a two- or four-hundred-mile wind, but the possibilities seemed nightmarish. He wanted to talk to a fellow engineer who would understand what he was going through.

He went back into the coffee shop. He was going to try calling George Hochenauer again.

But there was a woman in the only phone booth. She saw him waiting, smiled, and held up a finger to signal that she would not be long. She was about his age, brown-haired, with a round placid face and big round glasses.

While waiting, McRoyden looked out the window and up at the massive new building down the street. He was overcome by another wave of vertigo. He staggered against the corner of the phone booth and stayed leaning there, eyes closed.

"Are you all right?" It was the woman who had been in the booth. She had finished her call and was standing there looking up at him. She was short and slightly plump. She wore a dowdy brown suit. Her gray eyes behind her glasses were worried.

He looked at her and opened his mouth to speak, but no sound came out.

She reached out and put her hand gently on his arm. "You really don't look too good. Why don't you sit down a while?"

He let her lead him to one of the plastic-topped tables near the window. He sat. Part of his mind registered surprise when she sat too, but the other part was in a dreamlike state in which illogical events went unquestioned.

A waiter came. The woman looked at McRoyden and said, "I'm going to have a cup of tea. Why don't you have one too? It might do you good."

He nodded dumbly. The waiter left.

She said, "You aren't ill, are you?"

"No," he said, speaking for the first time.

"I didn't think so. Something's troubling you, isn't it?"

Her gentle, soothing voice was more comforting than he would have thought a stranger's voice could be. He grinned and said, "Does it show?"

She smiled back. "Yes, it does."

They sat silent for a while. The waiter brought the tea.

She asked, "Would it help to tell a stranger about it?"

"I don't think so."

She nodded, sipped her tea placidly, and made no effort to press him farther.

As she had predicted, the tea made him feel better. Or perhaps it was simply her presence that calmed him. She was tranquil and accepting. He felt she would understand his problem if he chose to pour it out to her. Since he did not, she accepted his silence. They sat at the table for a long time without saying a word. McRoyden felt his tense facial muscles relaxing. His big, red-fuzzed lands lay quietly on either side of his teacup.

She finished her tea, wiped her mouth with a paper napkin, and picked up her old, scuffed handbag. "May I make a suggestion?" she asked.

McRoyden shrugged.

She said, "Whatever it is that's troubling you, perhaps God can help. He usually does, you know."

McRoyden doubted that. He had been raised as a Catholic in a very pious household, but by the time he left high school he had lost interest in religion. He had no strong feelings about it; it was simply a nuisance that he preferred to avoid. The woman's suggestion brought a cynical reply to his tongue, but he censored it. He did not want to make her angry. He said mildly, "You could be right. I don't know."

"Why not try prayer? Do you belong to a church?"

"Not really. Catholic, I guess."

"Well, any port in a storm, you know. When you need to pray, you can do it anywhere. There's an Episcopal church not far from here. Would you like me to go with you?"

"No, I—listen, who are you?"

She smiled. "A busybody, I suppose. That's what you're thinking, isn't it?"

"No, I didn't say that. I just—"

"Actually I'm a minister. United Church of Christ—used to be called Congregational."

"A minister?" McRoyden was puzzled.

"Yes." She saw his puzzlement and smiled. "We've had women ministers for years."

"Is your church around here?"

"No, I have no parish at the moment. I'm unemployed. I'm living in New York with my sister till something turns up."

McRoyden grinned and said, "A shepherd without a flock. So you go around looking for little lost lambs."

She did not respond to this immediately, and he thought she might have found it unfunny. But in a moment she smiled and said, "Well, how else can I keep myself from going stale?"

McRoyden wanted her to know he did not intend to make a joke out of her concern, so he said, "Anyway, I appreciate it. I really do."

She stood. "I'll be going now. But if you want somebody to talk to—I stop in here for tea just about every afternoon at this time."

McRoyden nodded.

She leaned forward, touched his hand, and walked away. He sat and watched the coffee shop door close behind her. He continued to watch until the little brown-clad figure disappeared into the afternoon crowds, and it came to him that he did not even know her name.

12

NICK PACIFICO AND Kim took a cab downtown for their interview with Mayor Millington. They did not speak much. Pacifico commented on that fact as the cab pulled up at City Hall. "You're kind of quiet this morning," he said.

Kim shrugged bad-temperedly. She felt his eyes studying her but had no wish to return his gaze. She stared out the window in silence.

Out on the sidewalk she said, "Listen, Nick, I'm sorry. Don't pay any attention to me. I'm just in a prickly mood, that's all."

He nodded, and she thought he probably understood.

She was having one of her bad mornings. Her body felt achy and lacking in spring. There was a tenseness behind her eyes, not actually a headache but a sense of pain lying in wait. It was an effort to find joy in anything—in the pleasant morning sunshine, in people's smiles. Older members of AA had told her such mornings would come less frequently as time went on. That was nice to know, but meanwhile she had this day to get through. What made it worse was that she wanted a cigarette. She had not smoked since that day in the windstorm in New Jersey. She was determined to quit for good this time. Why, oh *why* did the body harbor these perverse urges to poison itself?

When they arrived at the reception room outside the

mayor's office, Kim was annoyed by its opulence. She remembered reading or hearing that the previous mayor had been a man of simple tastes—or at least had found it politically expedient to appear so—and had used the reception area mainly as dead-storage space for old files. Mayor Millington, however, had spent a good deal of the city's money surrounding himself with luxury like some Oriental potentate.

Kim and Nick walked across a meadow of thick beige carpet to the receptionist's desk. The receptionist, however, was talking on the phone and gave no sign that she knew they were there—or, for that matter, that she cared. The conversation was personal, not business. She was telling a friend about a recent shopping experience at Bloomie's.

Kim knew this kind of discourtesy was common in modern urban life, and a voice somewhere inside her was saying soothingly that no good purpose could be served by getting upset. Still she felt her irritation rising as the receptionist continued to ignore the two visitors who stood like supplicants before her desk. Evidently the young woman had been mounting clippings in a scrapbook before the phone claimed her attention, for there were scissors and an open pot of rubber cement on the desk. Kim contemplated the delightful idea of picking up the scissors and cutting the phone cord, then thought better of it. Finally she turned to Nick Pacifico and said in a loud voice, "I'm tired of waiting. Let's go in and announce ourselves."

He grinned, obviously delighted. They walked toward a closed door that seemed to lead to inner offices.

"Hey!" the startled receptionist shouted. Into the phone she said, "Hold on, I'll be right back." Then she jumped from her chair looking flustered and angry. "You can't go in there! You got to wait till I—I mean I got to take your names and announce you."

Kim said, "We waited. Nothing happened."

"Well, I was onna phone. Couldn't you see I was onna *phone*?"

"Right," Kim said, "and I got tired of waiting. Now I figure I've got maybe ten seconds of patience left. So if you want to announce us, get your fanny back in that chair and start announcing."

Flabbergasted, the receptionist flopped back into her chair. "Boy, some people!" she said. "You think you can just waltz in here and—"

"We're Beaulieu and Pacifico of *Seven Days*, and we have a ten o'clock appointment with the mayor."

The receptionist gave Kim a surly look and picked up the phone. Kim looked at Pacifico, who had stood watching the exchange without saying a word. There was a grin of perfect enjoyment on his face.

Mayor Millington was suave and smilingly polite when he greeted them in his big, elegant office. Kim knew, however, that it would please him if they were both to drop through a hole in the floor and vanish forever from his life. The mayor very definitely did not want to grant this interview. He had agreed to it only when Pacifico, on the phone, had suggested that a refusal could be made to look very, very bad.

"You mean if I refuse," the mayor had said, "you'll say so in your article?"

"I don't see how I could avoid it, Mayor," Pacifico had replied, grinning at Kim, who had sat listening in his office. "We're going to a lot of other big-city officials. Chicago. Moscow. People are going to say, well, okay, but what about New York? I've got to put in *something* about New York."

And now Mayor Millington sat behind his enormous, polished desk, wearing his standard news-media smile. "So," he said, "you're writing a sequel. It'll be a bit less— ah—shrill than your first one, I hope." The mayor held up a copy of the current *Seven Days* with the gaudy cover that shouted, "BIG WIND COMING? WILL IT BLOW CITIES DOWN?"

Pacifico said, "We didn't think it was shrill, Mayor. We just reported what some scientists and engineers told us."

"A lot of people thought it was needlessly frightening," the mayor said. He was still smiling. Kim thought: he really is a handsome man, this Spencer Millington, and he has lots of nice white teeth. But if he doesn't wipe that silly smile off his face, I'm going to lean over his desk and bust him one.

Pacifico was saying, "Well, Mayor, I'll grant it was scary, maybe. But that wasn't because of a shrill tone of voice. It was the subject matter. I mean, if we've really got a four-hundred-mile wind coming, that's scary."

The mayor shrugged, still smiling. Then he looked at his watch. "Well, let's get on with it. I've got a full calendar this morning. What was it you wanted to ask me?"

"Just one main question," Pacifico said. "The whole thrust of this second piece will be the precautions people are taking. So okay: New York. What's New York doing? What preparations?"

"Preparations?" The mayor was still smiling. Reneging on her promise to bust him one, Kim contented herself with writing in her notebook: "Preps? Loopy smile."

Pacifico was elaborating. "Yes. Like—well, in Moscow, for instance, they have a plan to shut down the subway system so people can shelter in the tunnels. They're working on plans for food, water, first aid—or at least they claim they are. In other places, nobody seems to be doing much of anything. So we wonder where New York fits on this spectrum."

Kim knew from correspondents' reports and her own telephone research that very few American or West European cities were making more than token efforts to prepare for the wind. She doubted that the Russians were preparing half as efficiently as they said they were, but at least, she thought, totalitarian governments always do have an edge when it comes to mobilizing for an emergency. One of democracy's problems. has always been its inherent untidiness.

Mayor Millington was enumerating the actions he had taken in New York. Kim listed them derisively in her notebook, using the journalistic shorthand she had developed in the past busy week: "Alerts hosps. Sets up study grp. Stays close touch police cmish."

In short, the mayor of New York had done virtually nothing to prepare his city for the expected wind.

Pacifico and Kim exchanged a quick glance. Pacifico said, "You mentioned hospitals, Mayor. I'm sure it's a good idea to alert them. But according to the experts we've talked to, most people won't be able to get to hospitals—certainly not during the wind, maybe not after it either."

"In fact," Kim said, "hospitals themselves might be destroyed."

Mayor Millington was still wearing his smile. "But that's just guesswork isn't it?" He answered his own question. "Of course it is. We've never had any four-hundred-mile wind around here. We may never have one, but even if we do, nobody has the faintest idea what damage it will do, if any. And I'm not going to get this city all stirred up over somebody's guess. I'm not going to rush around spending the taxpayers' money. I'm not going to have people panicking."

"I understand the problems," Pacifico said. "But isn't it a worse risk to do nothing?"

The mayor's smile abruptly vanished. "*Nothing*? What do you mean nothing? I've told you the steps I've taken!"

Neither of his visitors said anything. The mayor looked worried. "You're *not* going to accuse me of doing nothing, are you?"

"We'll report just what you told us," Pacifico replied.

Kim consulted her notes. "You said you've alerted hospitals and set up a study group, and you're staying in close touch with the police commissioner."

The mayor evidently realized how thin that sounded, for he now hastened to add to the list. He said something about the fire department. He mentioned water supplies. He talked about an alleged plan for shutting down the subways. Kim caught another glance from Pacifico and knew exactly what he was thinking: that, in all likelihood, none of these ideas had occupied the mayor's mind until this very moment.

The interview ended, and Kim felt dissatisfied with it. Practiced politician that he was, Mayor Millington had generated a lot of words while saying hardly anything. He could not be accused of refusing to answer questions, nor even of answering evasively. He had seemed laudably forthcoming. Yet what she had in her notebook, Kim knew, was trash.

As she and Pacifico walked back out through the reception room, Kim felt a stab of remorse over her ill-tempered treatment of the receptionist before. This was not a new experience for Kim; she often regretted the results of her irritability on bad mornings. Perhaps, she thought now, a gracious and pleasant farewell would be acceptable as a token of apology.

"Good-bye," she said to the receptionist, with a friendly smile. "Have a nice day."

The receptionist was working on the scrapbook. She gave Kim a surly glance and returned to her work without saying anything.

"Well, all right, don't have a nice day," Kim said. "Have an awful day. Have a *miserable* day."

Pacifico was waiting for her at the door, grinning appreciatively. He looked as though he were about to make a wisecrack.

"Don't say anything," Kim warned. "Not one *word*."

He held up his hands to show he meant no offense.

"And don't give me that superior look, either," Kim snapped.

"Sorry. Bad day, huh?"

"Oh, shut up. No, don't shut up. Let's find some coffee and a doughnut, Nick."

• • •

Jelly Jack Barrow unlocked a lower drawer of his desk and removed a telephone from it. The phone was an old rotary-dial model, black and unremarkable except that the usual plastic number disc was missing from the dial's center. The number of this phone was not on record anywhere except at the telephone company's office and in a few private files and notebooks.

Barrow dialed a number in a distant city. A man's voice answered. Barrow recited a code phrase, then hung up and sat back to wait.

For a few peaceful moments he let his gaze wander over the attractive Houston skyline outside his office window. But then his eye fell on the *Wall Street Journal* that lay on his desk. He regarded it with loathing, as though it were a poisonous reptile. Unable to stand the sight of it any longer, he picked it up and flung it into his wastebasket.

Things were not going well for Jelly Jack or for New World Development. The trading price of the company's common stock was now down seven points and still dropping like a duck with its tail shot off. In terms of that one investment alone, Jack Barrow was some $700,000 poorer on paper than he had been before that infuriating *Seven Days* article hit the streets. If he were also to count the probable losses in the market value of his home and other personal real-estate holdings, he had lost something like one and a half million dollars in a few hellish days.

The entire construction industry was on its knees. So was

the real-estate industry. Nobody in his right mind wanted
to buy any kind of building until the expected big blow was
over, except at distress-merchandise prices. In the suburbs,
people with houses to sell were finding that the only buyers
in sight were speculators. If you were desperate to sell, a
speculator might give you half what you thought your home
was worth a week back. It was the same in the cities. Places
like the New World Center in New York, with expensive
apartments and office space to unload, were finding the
stream of potential buyers reduced to a trickle. It was even
getting hard to attract lessees.

According to reports Jack Barrow had received from
several different sources, most people reacted with amusement or indifference to the wild idea that something like the
New World Center might be blown down. Only a minority
took that nightmare seriously. But many people did seem to
think minor damage was possible—broken windows, perhaps. And so the question everybody asked was: "Why buy
trouble?" They were all going to hold onto their money
until the big blow was over. Meanwhile, a sad crowd of
suburban homeowners, building contractors and develop-
ers like New World were left holding the bag.

Barrow was not worried about the immediate loss of
money. He could presume, or at least hope, that real estate
values and stock prices would recover after the blow. What
concerned him was the possibility that they wouldn't
recover completely for a long time, maybe not for decades.
This whole comet-and-wind episode was making people
think more than ever before about buildings and weather.
They were listening to crackpots like that jackass Hochenauer. Barrow could not predict exactly what the long-term
results might be, but he harbored a gloomy suspicion that,
in one way or another, it was all going to end in his retiring
a good deal poorer than he had planned.

The black phone rang. "It's me, Jack," said a man's
voice.

"Yeah, good to hear your voice, Al. How's Brenda? The kids?"

They small-talked for a short while. Finally Al asked, "What's up?"

"Well, we need a job done in New Jersey," Barrow said. "You've read that *Seven Days* article, right? Yeah, shit like that we can live without. So now it turns out what we guessed all along, they're doing a sequel. Could be even worse than the first one. Unless we do something about it."

"Ah," said Al.

"Yeah."

"You need some pressure."

"We need some pressure. Now there are different ways it could be done. There are two reporters working on the article, a guy called Pacifico and a chick. The chick, she's the publisher's daughter."

"The publisher of the magazine, you mean."

"Yeah, Arthur Beaulieu. That's an obvious place where we could put on pressure, but I dunno yet, I'm still thinking. Meantime, I want you to go to work on this Pacifico. We found out he's got a daughter. She's a grade-school kid, name's Daniela. Lives with her mother in New Brunswick, that's where Rutgers is."

"This Pacifico is divorced, then."

"Yeah, or separated. His wife is in the phone book under her married name, Gloria Pacifico, we checked that. So here's what you do. Pick two of your ugliest goons. Like that big guy with the cauliflower ear I seen you with, the mean-looking guy. Him and his skinny sidekick. You know the guys I mean? Okay, have them make like they're gonna kidnap the kid."

"Make like it but not do it?"

"Right. I don't wanna get involved in no kidnapping. Also, I don't want the kid hurt. You got it?"

"I got it."

"All I want is, the kid gets the scare of her life. The goons try to grab her and force her into a car, something like that. They scare her so bad she wets her pants, but she gets away and runs home to mama."

"And mama calls papa."

"Right, you got it. Meantime this Pacifico, he gets a phone call telling him he's got to quit writing these stories, getting people all worked up. Now timing is important, Al. I want it all to happen tomorrow."

"Tomorrow? Jeez, that won't be easy, Jack."

"You want easy, get yourself an honest job."

Al chuckled. "Okay. Okay. But it'll cost you."

"It always does."

"Twenty-five large plus expenses."

"Twenty-*five*? You're dreaming, Al!"

"I don't think so, Jack. This kind of work, it takes experienced men. It takes finesse, you know? Maybe I can get the two guys you're thinking about and maybe I can't, but whatever, I can't just send a couple of kids down there to New Brunswick. 'Specially not the kind of kids we got these days. The men we're gonna need, they won't work for no minimum wage, Jack."

"We'll pay fifteen."

"*Fifteen*?" Al gave a snort of derisive laughter.

They finally settled on twenty. The money would be withdrawn from a special cash fund and delivered in cash by courier. No record of the transaction would ever reach the Internal Revenue Service.

Jelly Jack Barrow locked the black phone in its drawer and sat for a while organizing his thoughts.

For the moment, he thought, everything that could reasonably be done was being done. Everything short of violence, at any rate. Jelly Jack disliked violence. He was capable of resorting to it when backed into a corner, but in his experience it was seldom necessary. With a little care and thought, most problems could be solved more elegantly without it.

A case in point was that TV show the other night, the special on wind. Barrow grinned contentedly when he thought of it. Darlene Dorsey certainly made mincemeat out of that Professor Pollock! The little jerk had originally been cast as one of the show's heroes, but there was some heavy rewriting at the last minute. And it had all been accomplished without violence. A little money here, a touch of discreet blackmail there, some career threats, some promises. Elegant! A textbook case!

Barrow could not take personal credit for that manipulation, though he had been consulted about it. It had been carried out by other powerful real-estate interests, ordinarily New World's competitors but now allies in adversity. It comforted Barrow to know he had such allies. He couldn't be everywhere, but they were.

• • •

Ed McRoyden returned to the coffee shop down the street from the New World Center. It was afternoon, near three o'clock. The Congregational minister said she usually stopped in for tea at about this time, and—yes, there she was, sitting quietly at a table. It was a relief to see her round placid face. She was wearing a rumpled, tweedy gray suit that would have looked at home, McRoyden thought, in some small town in far northern New England. It did not look at home in summertime New York, on a street of trendy boutiques one block from Park Avenue. But somehow, the street seemed more out of step than she did.

"Mind if I join you?" McRoyden asked.

"I've been kind of waiting for you," she said.

He ordered tea from a passing waitress, then sat. "We don't know each other's names," he said. "I'm Ed McRoyden."

And I'm Amanda Grewen." She spelled her last name for him.

"What do I call you, Reverend Grewen?"

"Amanda is good enough."

The waitress brought the tea. They sipped in silence for a few moments. It was remarkable, McRoyden thought, that with this dowdy little minister there was no pressure to fill every pause with words. He could not explain it. The silence was not tense but soothing and companionable. And here was another peculiar thing: he had never liked tea before. He still might not like it in other situations. But here in this coffee shop, at this little plastic-topped table with Amanda Grewen, the flavor was cheering and relaxing.

"Listen Amanda," he said finally, "can I—do you have time to listen to a long story?"

Her gray eyes flashed with merriment behind the big round glasses. "I'm unemployed, remember? If there's one thing in the world I've got, it's time."

And so McRoyden told her all about his work with the Office of Building Construction, his fall from grace at the New World Center, and his nightmare on reading the *Seven Days* article.

"The thing is," he concluded, "I'm afraid maybe I've helped build a death trap. That building—" he gestured in the direction of the Center—"it would have been all right in ordinary weather. What I did was dishonest, but it wasn't *dangerous*. I mean I didn't allow anything that would have put people's lives in danger. Just some substandard materials here and there, some run-of-the-mill shoddy workmanship. I could live with myself when I thought that's all it was. But now—" He gestured helplessly.

She finished the thought for him. "You're afraid what you did wrong is going to get wronger in un-ordinary weather."

"That's it exactly. When I did it, it was just a sin against money. Now it's against *people*, Amanda."

He was afraid at that point that she might try to console him with psychiatric banalities about misplaced guilt or browbeat him with thoughts from the Bible. To his relief, she did neither. She simply finished her tea and allowed the soothing silence to wash over him.

After a while he said, "It's a relief to have told somebody at last."

She smiled and nodded. "I thought it would be."

"Funny how I couldn't get it out till now. I couldn't tell my wife. I couldn't tell anybody." The truth was that his marriage had been souring for years, and his wife was no longer a person in whom he could confide. But he thought he would have hesitated to tell her even if they were still wrapped in their honeymoon closeness.

"It often is easier with a stranger," Amanda said. "There's no long relationship to worry about. Nothing to protect."

"Maybe that's it."

"You know—" she leaned across the table and touched his big, red-fuzzed hand—"there's somebody else you could talk to, if you felt like it. Maybe it would make you feel even better than talking to me. You know who I mean, don't you?"

"I guess you mean God."

She nodded. "There's an Episcopal church a couple of blocks away. I think I mentioned it last time we were here. You weren't ready then. But the offer is still open." She smiled.

He looked at her for a second, then asked, "You'll go with me?"

"Of course."

"Okay." He finished his tea, then put the cup down and grinned at her. "I've got to say your prescriptions have been pretty good so far, Doc. You've even got me liking tea. So if you say going to church will help, I'm willing to give it a try."

"Good. Satisfaction is all but guaranteed." She picked

up her old, scuffed handbag and began fishing in it for money.

"The tea is on me," McRoyden said.

"Oh no. There's no reason—"

"It's your fee. Don't argue. An out-of-work preacher shouldn't be turning down free tea. And besides—" McRoyden hesitated.

"What?"

"There's another favor I'd like to ask of you. I don't know, maybe it's too much."

"Try me."

They were standing now. He looked down at her, trying to figure her out. He thought perhaps she was incapable of saying no to anybody's need, in which case it would be exploitive to ask for a favor one did not really have to have. He genuinely liked this tranquil, little round-faced woman and did not want to take advantage of her. On the other hand, he thought, maybe she knew no greater pleasure than to be of service to others.

He decided to go ahead and ask. "There's a man I've been wanting to talk to," he said, "but I've been putting it off. I want to tell him the same story I've just told you. I think maybe it'll be easier if—if you go with me. Will you?" He added hastily, "He's in New York."

"Of course I will. Who is this man?"

"He's a construction engineer. Name's Hochenauer."

● ● ●

George Hochenauer took an immediate liking to the big, red-bearded man and the funny little woman minister who turned up with him. Wilma seemed to take to them, too—which surprised Hochenauer, for Wilma tended to be uncomfortable and cranky with nondrinkers.

The four of them sat in a booth at Booker's. Hochenauer was drinking Mother Fletcher's, though in moderate amounts so far. He thought he might get drunk later, but it was still early evening. Wilma was knocking back her usual vodka and orange juice. The big man, McRoyden, was nursing a bottle of beer. The little gray-suited preacher woman wasn't drinking anything. She just sat in a corner of the booth with her hands folded quietly on the table. But Hochenauer detected no hint of prim disapproval in her manner. On the contrary, she looked around Booker's with lively interest, even with delight—like a kid seeing a lot of strange new animals at a zoo, Hochenauer thought.

Hochenauer had listened with interest and sympathy to McRoyden's story. It seemed to Hochenauer that the big man was heaping more blame on himself than he deserved, and Hochenauer said so. "It don't sound to me," Hochenauer said, "like you did anything that would have much effect on the structural strength. And anyhow, what difference is it gonna make? If this Pollock is right and we got a four-hundred-miler coming, then what the hell. Maybe a bomb-proof concrete blockhouse will stand up to it, but nothing else will, no matter how well it's built. *No* building is made to take that kind of weather."

McRoyden did not seem convinced. He said, "But listen—"

"Don't argue with Hoke, Ed," said Wilma, who was already well on the way to being drunk. "Believe me, Hoke has been studying up on weather for years. It's all he ever thinks about. Shit, he even talks about it in bed." She elbowed her husband in his bony ribs. "When he oughta have his mind on other things. Ain't that right Hoke?"

"Can't you ever get your mind off sex?" Hochenauer grumbled. Then he looked at Amanda Grewen and said, "Excuse the loose talk, Ma'am."

"Aw, the Reverend don't mind us talking," Wilma said confidently. "Do you, Rev?"

"Of course not, why should I?" Amanda replied with a

smile. "If the good Lord invented sex, I'm sure he expects
us to talk about it."

"Yeah, right!" Wilma said enthusiastically. She was
obviously taken with the idea. "Hey, Kramer!" she called
to the morose and solitary drinker at the end of the long bar.
"Church lady here says the good Lord wants us to talk
about sex. So say something sexy for us, Kramer."

Kramer gave her a look of gloomy indifference and
turned his attention back to his drink.

"Doesn't that man ever smile?" Amanda asked.

"No, that's Kramer," Wilma explained. "He lives here.
He was on that barstool when they built the place." Wilma
finished her drink and handed the empty glass to Hochenauer. "Get me another a these, will you, Hoke?"

Table service at Booker's was provided by the customers
themselves. Hochenauer walked across the grimy vinyl-
tiled floor to the bar. "Refill for Wilma, Jimmy," he said to
the bartender, who needed no further instructions. Hochenauer returned to the booth and gave his wife her new
drink.

"So, Ed," Hochenauer said as he slid back into his seat,
"what are you planning to do?"

McRoyden shrugged. "I don't know. That's why I
wanted to talk to you. What would you do?"

Hochenauer gave him a wry grin. "Maybe I'm not the
best guy to give advice on that. You know my story, I guess?
Yeah, well, I didn't handle it too good. Shot off my mouth
too much."

"Hoke is too honest for his own good," Wilma told
McRoyden. Then she turned to Amanda and said, "Too
honest, that's his big problem. Too damn honest." Wilma's
voice was shaking.

Hochenauer shrugged his skinny shoulders. "I don't
know about honest. Stupid is more like it, maybe." Hoch-

enauer did not usually talk about his life in this way, but he felt drawn to a fellow engineer in trouble. "You want my advice, I'll give it to you. Don't make a martyr of yourself."

They all looked at him in silence. He went on: "I mean, if you got it in mind to make some kind of public confession—well, ask yourself what the hell good it's gonna do. You'll only get everybody beating on you."

"What makes you think I want to confess?" McRoyden asked.

"I dunno," Hochenauer said, studying him. "Just something about you. An impression I get."

"I've had the same feeling, Ed," said Amanda.

McRoyden looked at her, then nodded slowly. "Maybe I've been playing with some idea like that," he acknowledged. "But the idea isn't to make me a martyr. It's to save people."

"Get them out of the building, you mean?" Hochenauer said. "Get them underground?"

"Right."

"Well, okay, that's a fine idea. But why just the people in the New World Center? Why not other buildings too? In a four-hundred-mile wind they're *all* unsafe."

McRoyden looked doubtful. Hochenauer pressed the point: "Look, you got this idea you wanna make amends or something, right? I can buy that. But there's no sense destroying yourself doing it."

"Hoke is right, Ed," said Wilma. "There's no sense destroying yourself." She shook her head. "No damn sense in it. No sense at all." She started to cry.

Hochenauer put his arm around her shoulders and gave her a fond squeeze. "Ah, come on, old lady, cheer up," he said.

Wilma cheered up instantly. "Don't pay no attention to me," she told the others with a grin. She wiped a tear from the corner of her eye, using a cocktail napkin. "Now, Ed, you listen to what Hoke says. Old Uncle Hoke, he'll always steer you straight."

"I'm listening," McRoyden assured her. "But look, Hoke—it's all right if I call you Hoke?—I don't quite understand what you're suggesting. Let's say you're right and I want to make amends without destroying myself. Okay. How? What would I do?"

Hochenauer waved his hands helplessly. His thinking had not progressed that far yet. To his relief, Amanda picked up the ball. "I think Hoke is suggesting some kind of crusade," she offered. "A publicity campaign, maybe."

"Right!" Hochenauer agreed. "Tell people they got to get underground when the wind starts blowing! You wanna do a penance, Ed, here's your penance!" Hochenauer's quick mind was overflowing with ideas now. "A crusade! Yeah! You tell people they got to find their underground place now, before they need it. And they got to put together a pack of food and water to take down there. Warm clothes, a blanket. They're on their own, see, that's what you got to tell them. Nobody else is gonna do anything for them. Millington, he's just sitting on his ass. So are all the rest of the bureaucrats."

"Yeah, that Millington, what a jerk," Wilma grumbled. She was beginning to slur her words. "They wanna have a mayor, they oughta have you up there, Hoke. How come an asshole like Millington gets to be mayor?" She appealed to Amanda. "Life sure is unfair, innit, Rev?"

"It often seems that way," said Amanda.

Wilma began to cry again. Tears ran down her plump pink cheeks. "How come God don't straighten it out? Come to think of it, what's he sending us this wind for? Punish us, or what?"

"Ah, come on now, cut the crap," Hochenauer said. He gave his fat wife another affectionate squeeze, which stopped the flow of tears as abruptly as though he had turned a faucet. Wilma smiled happily and dabbed at her cheeks with a damp napkin.

" 'Vengeance is mine, saith the Lord,' " Wilma quoted. Hochenauer did not clearly understand the relevance of that, but Wilma seemed to find it pleasing in some obscure way. "Hey Kramer!" she called to the lone drinker. "The Lord's vengeance is gonna strike us all down, Kramer!"

Kramer shrugged. "So who gives a shit?" he said.

"Ah, that Kramer, he don't care about nothin'," Wilma complained. Hochenauer was afraid she was about to start crying again, but instead she finished her drink. "Get me another, huh, Hoke?"

"In a minute," he said, judging that she needed to slow down.

There was a short silence, and then Ed McRoyden said, "Getting back to this crusade idea, Hoke . . ."

His voice trailed off. Hochenauer guessed he was asking whether it was all right to interrupt Wilma now. Hochenauer gave him a green light by saying, "Yeah, you like the idea?"

"Well, I guess so. I mean I do like it basically. But the thing is, see, I'm no publicity man. I wouldn't know how to put together a campaign like this. What do I do? Where do I start?"

The big man obviously lacked leadership qualities. He was a follower, Hochenauer thought, but the thought had no taint of scorn in it. A man like Ed McRoyden might achieve success in a different kind of world.

While Hochenauer was trying to frame an intelligent reply to McRoyden's question, Amanda Grewen once again came to his rescue. "It doesn't sound too tough to me," she said to McRoyden. "I'll help you."

"Yeah, so will I," Hochenauer said. An idea came to him. "Tell you what. We could start by calling those people at

Seven Days. They seemed to like what they heard from me last week. I'll introduce you as this big city inspector, and then you tell them what you think."

"About people getting ready to go underground, you mean?"

"Yeah, with packs of food and water. They got to get these packs ready now, see, that's the important thing."

"Call them survival packs," Amanda suggested.

"Right," said McRoyden. "Survival packs. That has a good urgent sound." Hochenauer was pleased to detect a note of rising enthusiasm in the big man's voice. He was even more pleased when, immediately afterward, McRoyden came up with an original idea. "And these survival packs," McRoyden said, "they ought to have one more thing in them. A flashlight. Candles. Some source of light."

"You think that's important?" Hochenauer asked.

"I know it is. If we're going to have the kind of destruction you talk about, buildings will lose electric power, right?"

"Right."

"And if people are underground in the dark, they'll panic. Also, people will be trapped in building cores, trying to run down the stairs. No daylight ever reaches the core. They'll need light or they'll kill themselves."

"How about emergency generators?" Hochenauer asked.

McRoyden thought for a moment. "There's a city law about generators. I forget just what it says. Buildings over a certain size are supposed to have a generator in good working condition. Or buildings with automatic elevators, or something. I'll have to look that up." He grinned sourly. "But there's one thing I can tell you right now. Whatever the law is, it's pretty much ignored. Some generators I've seen are so old they'd explode if you tried to fire them up. Other places, they've got a new generator but nobody ever bothered to lay in a fuel supply."

"That'll be another part of the crusade," Amanda said.

"Landlords are going to hate me," said McRoyden. Then he shrugged. "Ah, what do I care?"

"You'll be okay," Hochenauer tried to assure him, though Hochenauer was not himself sure about this. "Just don't act like a wiseass, that's all." Hochenauer thought of adding that this was the mistake that had ruined his career, then censored the thought. He really did not like dwelling on what might have been or examining the turning points of his life. Somehow, he was not sure exactly how, he had achieved a state of tolerable contentment with Wilma in spite of everything. He was not a subscriber to the Socratic bromide that the unexamined life is not worth living. On the contrary, in Hochenauer's philosophy, which he based not only on his own life but on the stories of other people he knew, some lives are worth living only because they *are* unexamined.

Amanda was saying, "Let's get started. Can we call your friends at *Seven Days* now?"

"It's nearly seven," Hochenauer said. "I don't know how late they work."

"Let's try anyway."

Hochenauer understood her impatience. She did not want McRoyden to lose momentum. Hochenauer nodded.

* * *

Two days later, Arthur Beaulieu tossed a dog-eared yellow manuscript on his desk and said, "I like it. It's solid. Lots of zing."

"I thought you would," said the managing editor, sprawled untidily and bulkily in a corner of the long sofa.

"Now we come to the big question," Arthur Beaulieu said. "Do we publish it?"

Tall and gaunt, he sat fencepost-straight behind his desk and looked around at the others. Next to Charlie Broadbent on the sofa sat Beaulieu's daughter, Kimberley. On her other side, in the sofa's other corner, sat Nick Pacifico. The fifth person in the big office was Adelaide Kent, the executive editor, who sat rather primly on a straight chair with carved mahogany arms.

"I say go ahead and print it," Pacifico said, answering the publisher's question. "That's what Kim and I wrote it for."

"But this kidnapping threat against your daughter," Arthur Beaulieu said. "It doesn't worry you?"

"Sure, it worries me. But I'll be damned if I'll let some bunch of anonymous hoods tell me what I can write."

Kim gave Pacifico a worried look as he was speaking. Arthur Beaulieu noticed it. He had also noticed that the two of them were sitting closer together than was necessary. He wondered if they were falling in love. Remembering their coolness toward each other when they had first met in this office, he thought that would be a pleasingly romantic outcome. He believed he was free of the family's anti-Italian bias. Looking at Pacifico, however, he was disgusted to find the ultimate test of the bigot being rudely shouted in his mind: "Would you want your daughter to marry one?"

He asked Kim, "What are your feelings, my dear?"

"I think Nick is the one with the most to lose," she said. "It's his daughter. The decision ought to be his, without pressure from the rest of us."

"No, you rate a vote," Pacifico said to her. "After all, you were threatened too, weren't you?"

"Threatened?" Arthur Beaulieu was startled. "Threatened how? You never told me anything about a threat, Kim."

"Oh, it was nothing much," she said with a shrug. "I didn't want to worry you. *I'm* not worried. It was just an anonymous phone call. A man. He said I'd better stop writing articles about buildings falling down, or else."

"Or else what?" Beaulieu was seriously concerned. He loved this Kimberley. She had caused him a lot of grief during her young life, but he loved her desperately.

She replied, "Or else I'd regret it, or words to that effect. It was just one of those vague threats. Just words. It didn't mean anything."

Beaulieu looked at her for a long moment, then looked down at his big bony hands, which were clasped on his desk. "Anonymous threats," he said. "I hate them! They're so cowardly. And since you never know who they come from, you don't know how seriously to take them." He looked up at the others. "Threats against the publisher are routine, of course. They come with the job. But when these people start harassing individual reporters—"

"You've had threats?" Kim asked.

"Oh, of course," Arthur Beaulieu replied with a dismissive wave of his hand. "I'm used to it. The publisher is the natural target. Every time we do a story on abortion, I get threats. Every major piece about Jews and Arabs—"

"What kinds of threats?"

"Oh, letters and phone calls." Beaulieu waved dismissively again. "Threats to bomb the building, threats to shoot me. But I disregard them because I've learned they're never meant to be taken literally. They're just people blowing off steam. In all my years as publisher, nobody has ever actually assaulted me."

"Well," Kim said, "if you're not worried, why should I be?"

"Because it's different when they seek out an individual reporter. I'm just a figurehead. One of my functions is to be somebody people can get angry at. But a reporter—that kind of threat is more serious."

"That makes sense to me," said Adelaide Kent. She was a small-boned, chic woman in her middle forties. She looked concerned. "That Big Wind story did stir up a lot of passion. The letters department is swamped. I wouldn't dismiss these threats too lightly. I like this second story—"

she gestured at the yellow manuscript on Beaulieu's desk—
"like it a lot—but I wonder if we really want to take the risk
of printing it."

Arthur Beaulieu asked, "Have you taken any precautions, Mr. Pacifico? In regard to your little girl, I mean."

"Yes, I've brought her to New York with me. My wife
was so upset she had Danny hysterical, afraid to leave her
room. That's my daughter's name, Daniela. But I've talked
to Danny since she calmed down, and my impression is that
there isn't really much to be scared of."

"Why do you say that?" Beaulieu asked.

"Well, Danny has this feeling—or a bit more than a
feeling, a theory—that there wasn't any real intent to
kidnap her. What happened, see—she's walking home from
a friend's house when two men pull up in a car and stop her.
Two real goons, sounds like. One guy has a cauliflower ear.
So they kind of surround Danny, make a lot of menacing
noises, start pushing her toward their car. And then they
just plain stand there and let her go."

"As though all they wanted to do was scare her," Kim
explained. "And scare Nick." Arthur Beaulieu nodded.

"My theory," Pacifico went on, "is that there's something they didn't know about Danny until they saw her.
She's crippled. She can't run. The best she can do is a fast
hobble. I think they rigged up the whole scene with the idea
that they'd pretend to grab her, but then she'd wriggle out
of their grasp and run. That was how it was supposed to
happen. When she didn't run, all they could do was stand
there with their mouths hanging open. It was so obvious
that even a scared nine-year-old picked it up."

"So what you're saying," Adelaide Kent interpreted
slowly, "is that they didn't succeed. Is that right, Nick?
They didn't scare you. You still want to run the sequel."

"That's what I'm saying," Pacifico agreed.

She looked unconvinced. "The sequel seems to me to be

just as strong as the first piece. If the first piece made some people mad, the second will make them madder." She looked at Pacifico. "What if this attempted or faked kidnapping was some kind of warning? What if they *really* come after your daughter when they see the sequel?"

Pacifico said, "I've thought about that. There are things I can do to protect Danny. I'll be ready."

"You really want to run the piece?" Adelaide Kent asked.

"I really want to run the piece."

She shrugged. "All right then. I sense I'm the only one who was even thinking about voting no. Is that right?"

All except Arthur Beaulieu nodded immediately. He hesitated for a moment, looking at his daughter, worried. He did not want to expose her to danger, yet he knew she would be angry—and justifiably—if he denied her the opportunity to make her own decision. It was a good decision and a brave one. Arthur Beaulieu was in a trap; whatever he did would be wrong. Finally, reluctantly, he nodded.

Adelaide Kent shrugged again and said, "Then let's run it."

"Bravo!" said Charlie Broadbent, obviously pleased with the outcome. "It's a fine piece. We'll have another fifteen percent jump in newsstand sales if we handle it right. I want another of those poke-you-in-the-eye Pelham covers."

Lloyd Pelham was a hot young artist who made a substantial part of his income painting *Seven Days* covers. Arthur Beaulieu thought he could predict what Adelaide Kent was going to say, and he was correct. She said, "No, let's not use Pelham again so soon. His work is clever but shallow. It makes us look cheap."

"But it sure as hell sells magazines," Broadbent said. "Look at that last cover. It was our second-best seller ever."

"It wasn't Pelham's art that did the selling," Adelaide

Kent responded. "It was the subject matter. *'Big wind coming? Will it blow cities down?'* How could people *not* buy that issue? They would have bought it no matter who the artist was. It could have been my two-year-old nephew using Crayolas. We'd still have had a best-seller."

"I doubt it," Charlie Broadbent insisted. "Pelham's art made the subject matter stand up and shout. It's what stopped people."

"It had a cheap gaudy look to me," Adelaide Kent said. Her fine nostrils dilated momentarily as though detecting the effluvium of some nearby dungheap. "School-bus yellow. Magenta. Passionate purple—now *really*. I think we should use Pelham a lot less than we do."

Charlie Broadbent stuck stubbornly to his view. "Only one thing counts," he said. "Does the cover grab people? I mean *people*, not just the curator of some art museum."

Arthur Beaulieu listened to the debate with growing contentment as it crashed and banged along. His two top editors held a similar debate almost every week, and Beaulieu was always delighted. In these two, he believed, he had just about the perfect combination of editorial talents. Charlie Broadbent had a sure sense of popular tastes and an instinct for aggressive journalism, the kind of journalism in which the object was to build circulation at almost any cost. As for Adelaide Kent, she knew elegance when she saw it and knew how to create it. She fought hard and sometimes bitterly to defend *Seven Days* from the lapses of taste into which Charlie Broadbent would surely have led the magazine if unopposed. The result, Arthur Beaulieu believed, was a delicate and appealing balance. The magazine managed, in most of its issues, to reflect the best qualities of both personalities.

In the end, the two editors came to a compromise agreement: they would assign the cover to an artist who was known for flamboyant commercial work but was also capable of subtlety. Her name was Thoma; she never used any other name but that.

"I hope she works fast," Arthur Beaulieu said. "We'll need it by tomorrow."

"At the prices we pay," Charlie Broadbent said drily, "she'll work at any speed we ask for."

"It won't be a complicated cover anyway," Adelaide Kent said. "I think the main feature of it could be just one word in big block capitals: SURVIVING. Just that. And behind it some kind of design suggesting a high wind."

"I like that," Pacifico said. "Surviving. Yeah, that's what the story is about."

"Well, I don't know," Charlie Broadbent said dubiously. "I think I'd like it better if the cover suggested a bit more of the story's focus. There are two main elements in it right? One: building owners and government bureaus deny there's a problem or don't want to hear about it. So two: citizens have got to take steps on their own, survival packs and so on. If we could find a way to get both these elements on the cover, it would be stronger."

"Maybe, but it might also get too cluttered," Adelaide Kent said. "I'd rather see it simple and stark."

"Why don't we see if Thoma has some ideas?" Arthur Beaulieu suggested.

"I'll phone her right away," Adelaide said. "If you'll all excuse me." She stood and walked out.

Kim and Nick Pacifico also stood. "We've got some final fact-checking to do," Kim said, "so we'll be going too." They walked out together. Arthur Beaulieu watched them, then turned and found Charlie Broadbent watching him.

Charlie grinned. "Good-looking couple," he said.

"Are they a couple, Charlie?"

The managing editor shrugged his meaty shoulders. "I don't know, Arthur. I really don't have a clue. What do you think, Mrs. Mead?"

Arthur Beaulieu's secretary of many years, Julia Mead, had entered the room a few seconds earlier. "I'm afraid I haven't a clue either," she said. Beaulieu guessed she might be more frank with him that night over dinner. She was always more discreet in the office.

She laid some papers on his desk. "Something for you to sign, Mr. Beaulieu," she said. They always used each other's last names in the office. "It's for the air-conditioning contractor."

"All right, Mrs. Mead, I'll get to it right away," he said. "Let's hope the job gets done right this time."

"We can hope, I suppose," she said with wry pessimism. The air conditioning had completely failed on several of the building's lower floors. It was a problem that cropped up almost every summer.

Julia Mead left. Charlie Broadbent heaved his great bulk from the sofa, started to go, then paused. "I'll tell you one thing I've noticed about Nick," he said. "Some kind of change has come over him in the past week or so."

"What change is that?"

"He started out hating this story. Now look at him."

13

THE ISSUE OF *Seven Days* with the stunning Thoma cover was a runaway best-seller. It was swept up from newsstands by tens of thousands of people who had seldom or never read any newsmagazine before. In total sales it was by far the biggest issue ever published by *Seven Days*.

Thoma had painted a stark silhouette of a great tree bent by a wind whose scream could almost be heard. Behind the tree was a dark, turbulent, stormy sky that moved if you stared at it long enough. Superimposed on this magnificent painting—Thoma's very best work to date, some said—was the word "SURVIVING," and below that, in smaller type, "*Why You Are On Your Own.*"

Within hours after this issue hit the streets, supermarkets from coast to coast were mobbed by people preparing survival packs. Hardware stores, discount stores, and others quickly sold out of flashlights, batteries, gasoline and oil lanterns, even candles. Union Carbide and other battery manufacturers were hit by the biggest tidal wave of store reorders they had ever seen. Manufacturing plants went into three-shift operation, sending out recruiting teams to hire teenagers off street corners, drunks off bar stools, and derelicts off park benches.

The buying panic was less pronounced in the New York area because the local daily news media had already been talking about personal survival efforts for two days. Ed McRoyden had managed to get himself interviewed by several newspaper, TV, and radio reporters. Many people considered him a standard end-of-the-world nut, and in support of that assessment there was plenty of loud jeering from the real estate industry, building contractors, architects, and others. Some more muted scorn emanated from government offices, including that of New York's mayor. Still, there were others who took McRoyden more seriously.

The *Seven Days* article was his first national exposure. On the day it was published, McRoyden was approached by a production assistant from a popular prime-time TV talk show. Would he care to appear on the show and state his views? Of course he would, he responded. The production assistant said fine, she would call back with the details. He never heard from her again. He was almost sure he knew what had happened. Somebody rich, powerful, and persuasive had convinced the show's producers that to have a guest such as Ed McRoyden would not be a good idea.

The next day, he lost his job.

He was shocked by the suddenness of the firing. He had been using accrued vacation time during the past week or so while wrestling with his personal crisis, but he had stayed in touch with his office by phone. If his public activities of the past several days had displeased his superiors, they had had plenty of opportunity to say so. Nobody had said a word. McRoyden had assumed his case was covered by a pious pronouncement made by Mayor Millington many years ago on taking office: "The attitude of this administration is that in most circumstances a city employee's off-the-job activities, political and otherwise, are his or her own affair."

The pronouncement was typical of the mayor's trendy liberalism. Most of the city's employees took it to mean that one was free to do anything that would shock conservatives.

You could espouse homosexuality, attend an America-bashing rally at the U.N., or try to prevent a nuclear-powered Navy warship from sailing into New York's harbor. As several employees found out, however, this benign tolerance did not extend to activities such as writing articles that criticized the mayor or speaking at a fund-raiser in support of a political opponent. McRoyden had assumed that his own activities—the public talk of danger in a high wind and of the need for personal survival preparations—were politically neutral in this context. He was careful never to criticize the mayor or anybody else. But it was obvious that he miscalculated.

"I'm sorry, Ed," his boss said, "you're just stirring up too much heat." The firing was conducted by phone.

"But I don't understand," McRoyden protested. "How is it affecting my work? Or our office? I'm telling people we're concerned about their safety. Isn't that what we want?"

"Don't make it tough on me, Ed. My hands are tied. It's orders. You're out." McRoyden could imagine his boss squirming.

"Orders from where, Wes?" McRoyden asked.

"Higher up."

"How much higher? Who?"

"I don't ask questions. It ain't good for my health."

McRoyden's boss was an aging bureaucrat marking time until retirement, his whole attention fixed on his pension and his condominium in a golden-years community in Florida. Arguing with him or questioning him would be futile. McRoyden sighed.

"There's one other thing, Ed," his boss said. "I been told to tell you this. You wanna go around stirring up people, that's up to you. It's a free country. But you gotta do it as a private citizen, y'unnerstand? You ain't a New York City building inspector no more. Whatever you wanna do, you gotta do it without using the name of this office."

"Well," McRoyden said, "I'm an *ex*-inspector. I'm free to say that, I should think."

"No you ain't!" his boss shouted, growing angry and flustered. "You ain't ex-anything! You ain't nothing! You're Ed McRoyden, that's all. I don't want you using the name of this office nohow, no *way!* I don't want you screwing me up, Ed!"

The man was terrified of being blamed for something and losing his pension. McRoyden felt no sympathy. He said, "I'm free to tell the plain truth, Wes. Up 'til today, I was a New York building inspector. Today I was fired. Those are the facts. If I want to give out the facts, I'll give them out."

"You keep this office out of it!" his boss yelled. "You hear, Ed? You listen to me, now. You listen good! I won't have this office mixed up in it. I don't want no part of it!"

McRoyden thought of George Hochenauer's advice: *don't destroy yourself.* He had tried to heed that advice, but not hard enough, it seemed. Somehow, despite his caution, he appeared to have ended by destroying himself anyway. In his shock and confusion over the sudden firing, he did not clearly understand what he had done to deserve the fate. He also remembered Hochenauer's other warning: *don't be a wiseass.* He had been meticulously careful about that. He had not thrown blame at anyone—indeed, had pussyfooted in cowardly retreat whenever questioning reporters gave him openings to complain about corner-cutting construction practices or governmental inaction. Yet here he was, in the soup anyhow. He felt a great wave of rage rising within him.

"You hear me, Ed?" his boss was shouting. "This office stays out of it, y'understand? You ain't gonna go around flashing our name like some kind of badge! You're a private guy on his own, you got me, Ed? That's it. I ain't gonna—"

"Wes."

"Yeah?"

"Go screw yourself."

McRoyden hung up. Seldom in his life had he relieved himself of anger in so simple and direct a way. It felt good.

● ● ●

The first signs of a change in the air mound over the North Pole were detected at about 5 P.M., U.S. Eastern Daylight Time. It was a Tuesday. At that hour people in the New York area were closing their offices, gathering for end-of-day drinks and commuting home to supper. People in California still had several hours to work before granting themselves the evening's rewards. In West Europe they were watching the late movies on TV and getting ready for bed. In Moscow they were sound asleep, while in Tokyo they were sitting down to breakfast.

The beginnings of change in the air mound were picked up simultaneously by several monitoring posts inside the Arctic Circle. One of the biggest and best-equipped posts was maintained by the Russians on the remote, frozen island of Novaya. The Russians may well have been the first to see the developing outline of the change and understand its potential meaning, but they were tripped up by their chronic passion for secrecy and their nation's ponderous bureaucracy, in which a dozen officials had to be consulted before any announcement could be made. And so the earliest announcement came from the world's second-biggest country, Canada.

The Canadians had a monitoring station on the bleak island of Ellesmere, on the Arctic Ocean just west of Greenland. They had operated this station for years. It was used by the Canadian Weather Service and also by several different military task groups and other, more mysterious government agencies. Because of its role in national defense, it was more liberally supplied with money than is commonly the case with weather installations outside Russia. The living quarters were underground, warm, and comfortable, and the instruments were the finest available anywhere.

It was here that Dr. Gerard Phelps had done most of his work on what later came to be called the Phelps-Blagonravov Model—the computer model that attempted to predict the air mound's behavior. And it was here that Dr. Phelps and his colleagues, monitoring the continual input of new data into the model on that Tuesday evening, began to see an alarming change.

Air pressure inside the colossal mound had suddenly started to increase rapidly, an early warning that the mound might be in the first stages of collapsing in on itself. A similar pressure jump had occurred just before the hurricane-force blow two weeks back, but this new jump was much more pronounced.

That alone made Dr. Phelps abandon all thoughts of a peaceful evening drink and dinner, but there was more. Something strange appeared to be happening at the top of that gigantic mountain of air. A huge, slowly rotating cavity seemed to be developing up there. It was something like the cavity that forms in water running out of a bathtub.

"Oh boy," Dr. Phelps said to an assistant.

"It this it, sir?"

"I wouldn't be surprised."

"Shall I get on the phone?"

"Not just yet. Let's watch it a while longer."

● ● ●

In Houston at that moment, Jelly Jack Barrow was picking up the numberless black phone in response to its ring.

"It's me, Jack," said Al. "I got your message. I had a

hunch you'd call."

"Yeah, why is that?"

"Well, I saw the new issue of *Seven Days*. Looks like scaring that kid wasn't enough, right? They went ahead and shit on you anyway."

"They sure as hell did," Barrow said morosely. "Our goddam stock is off another four points. It's lost half its value, Al!"

"Well, it could be worse, Jack. You seen the prices of insurance stocks lately? Shit. We got one fire-and-casualty outfit, its stock went from over thirty to eight and a fraction."

"My heart bleeds for you," Barrow grumbled.

"Yeah, I knew it would. So let's talk business. What is it you want this time?"

Barrow hesitated, grimaced, then said, "Acid."

"What?" Al sounded startled. "On a little kid?"

"No, no. I'm talking about the broad. Beaulieu's daughter. I figure we give her a face treatment, we'll convince all of those bastards we mean business."

"Jeez, Jack, they really got your back up, don't they?"

"You're goddam right they have. I'm through tippy-toeing around. They want it the hard way, well, okay, that's what they're gonna get."

"Okay, Jack."

Barrow's voice took on the tone of one pleading for understanding. "You know me, Al," he said. "I don't go for violence much. I always give people a chance to do things the easy way, right? I bend over backwards to be reasonable, ain't that so, Al?"

"Yeah, Jack, you do, that's the truth."

"So I've tried and tried with these magazine people, but they just won't listen. I gotta *make* them listen, Al. Somehow I gotta make them listen."

"I understand that, Jack."

"So okay. You got a man who knows anything about acid?"

"Yeah, I got a guy. Matter of fact, it's the same guy I sent down there to scare that kid in Jersey for you. The big guy with the ear. Him and his partner. They always work together, but just the big guy does the acid. He's one mean son of a bitch, lemme tell you. Shoot his own grandmother for a buck and a half."

"He's done acid before?"

"Yeah, a couple times. It isn't something we get a lot of calls for."

"How much will it cost me?"

"Hundred large."

"A *hundred?*"

"Yeah, that's what the market is, Jack. Throwing acid in somebody's face, that's a big-ticket item. Guy gets caught, he's looking at twenty years in the zoo. Life, maybe. Also, this kind of work, it calls for a special kind of guy. Me, I couldn't do it, I'm too squeamish. Most guys couldn't do it. But there are some—you know. And you don't hire them for no five bucks an hour, Jack."

"We'll pay seventy-five grand."

"No, a hundred, Jack. This time I really gotta stick. If it's any less than a hundred, I don't want the business."

Barrow thought for a while, then asked, "You'll arrange it for tomorrow?"

"*Tomorrow?* Jeez, you don't believe in giving a guy a lot of notice, do you, Jack?"

"Set it up for tomorrow and we'll pay your price."

"This broad, she'll be in New York?"

"Far as I know. Check with Spence Millington; he'll know how to find her."

"Okay, you got yourself a deal, Jack."

"Good. Now listen, Al—let me think a minute." Barrow

paused to mull over some problems of logistics. "A hundred grand, that's a lot of cash. I don't think I wanna trust it to the usual pipeline. So what I'll do, I'll deliver it myself. I'll be flying to New York tonight. I'll stay in the company suite at the New World Center. Tomorrow after the job's done, you give me a call there, okay?"

"Okay. I always enjoy a trip to New York. So I'll see you tomorrow. Maybe we can have a drink together."

"Sure, we'll do that," Jack Barrow said.

● ● ●

The cavity at the top of the air mound was growing more pronounced, wider, deeper. Its speed of rotation was increasing. Moreover, a twenty-mile-wide cylinder of air in the very center of the prodigious mound was also beginning to spin. Air pressure within and next to this cylinder fluctuated wildly.

The analogy to water flowing out of a bathtub was still accurate. Dr. Phelps watched the incoming data closely. At any minute, he expected, the data would show that the spinning cylinder was actually an enormous funnel of air spiraling downward.

"This is really it, sir, isn't it?" his assistant asked.

For several seconds Phelps was silent, stunned by the unimaginable size and power of the weather event he was witnessing. Then he shivered, though the big computer room was maintained at a constant, dry seventy-two degrees.

"Yes, this is it," he replied finally. "I think we'd better tell the world the time has come."

"Time to see how right our model is, sir." The assistant's tone said he intended this as a question without a question mark.

Phelps said, "Partly, I suppose. But don't forget that no

computer result is any better than the human thinking it's based on. There's always got to be a human brain in there at the root of it."

"Are you talking about Simon Pollock, sir?"

"Yes, I am. We're about to see how right Simon Pollock was."

• • •

Dr. Simon Pollock happened to be spending that night in a New York hotel, an old but tolerably clean place called the Prince Albert. He had been drawn there by his passion for the only woman who had ever shown him any sexual kindness.

The passion was ungovernable. It was an obsession. He recognized it as a species of insanity, driving him to do things he knew were stupid. He *knew* it was stupid to leave his Connecticut weather station at this time, of all times. He *knew* he should be staying close to the station, watching his instruments, reading the printout, waiting for the great wind that might come any day. He knew all that. And yet here he was.

Heidi had hit him hard. She had knocked the intellectual legs right out from under him. Nothing like her had ever happened to Simon Pollock in his entire life. She was really too big a dose for him to take all at once. He was like a long-starved man who eats a six-course meal and almost kills himself. His system needed more time to get used to her. It would have been better for him if, somehow, she could have happened to him in easier stages.

He had fought for days against the urge to return to New York, but the pull of Heidi was irresistible. He had given in, rationalizing in ways that a more sane Simon Pollock would have found laughable. Well, it's only for one night, he had told himself. I'll catch the earliest train back to Connecticut on Wednesday morning. What can happen in one night?

Chances are, nothing. And just in case something does, I'll leave word where I can be reached.

And so he had given the Prince Albert's name and phone number to a graduate assistant, drawn Heidi's fee and some extra cash out of his meager savings account, and boarded a train for wicked Sodom.

A saner Pollock would have been more careful. He would have left the Prince Albert's name with more than one person, or would have written it down somewhere or phoned back from New York to verify that all was well. In the tempest of his emotions, he did none of these things. He gave Murphy's Law a chance to operate, and as he should have expected, it did.

His instructions to the graduate assistant were that the instruments and printout should be monitored at least till midnight, at which time the station could be closed for six hours as long as nothing interesting was happening. The assistant broke up the monotony of his long vigil by phoning friends. In the course of doing that, he got wind of a beer party that sounded like fun. He found another graduate student, a young woman, who was willing to cover the station in his place. He left her in charge. Unfortunately, he neglected to give her the information about where Professor Pollock could be reached. Nor did he give her more than a vague idea of his own projected itinerary for the night.

Thus it was that she could not offer any help when Dr. Gerard Phelps phoned from Canada at about seven o'clock. Dr. Phelps was apparently in a state of high agitation. She knew who he was and recognized the importance of the call. She said she would do her best to track Professor Pollock down. At that instant all the printers and fax machines in the big, dusty room seemed to burst into frenzied activity at once. It did not take the graduate student more than a minute to understand what was happening. Within an hour she found herself fielding a steady cannonade of phone calls from newspapers, magazines, and TV and radio reporters. They all wanted the professor's comment on the changes taking place up there in the Arctic. They not only wanted comment; they wanted it *now*.

The harried young woman embarked on a frenzied telephone hunt for the graduate assistant who had left her with this mess. After going through a long chain of people she found out about the beer party, which was being held illegally in a nature conservancy. There were no phones in the woods, of course. After trying unsuccessfully to dispatch a message via a friend in a car, she finally, reluctantly, called the police. It was now nearly eleven o'clock.

The police sergeant who answered the phone was no dunce. He had heard about the Arctic developments by radio, was fully aware of their implications, and was familiar with Professor Pollock's name and reputation. He accordingly dispatched a patrol car to the nature conservancy immediately.

"Find out where Pollock can be reached," he instructed, "then get back to your car pronto and call in."

"What'll I do about the beer party?" the patrolman wanted to know.

The sergeant thought for a second. Then he said, "Take all their names, make them clean up, send them home, give them a good scare, and then forget it."

It was past midnight when the phone finally rang in Simon Pollock's hotel room. He was alone in the room at the time. Heidi had gone down to the lobby for Cokes.

As soon as Pollock heard the graduate student's voice, he knew what had happened. "Oh boy, Professor Pollock," she said, "am I glad I've finally found you! You wouldn't *believe*—"

He hardly needed to listen to the rest of what she said. He

knew. Of all the nights he could have chosen for his adventure with Heidi, he had chosen the worst.

After thanking the student for her hard work and resourcefulness, he scrambled out of bed and barefooted over worn carpet to the chair where he had hung his clothes. He began to pull on his underwear. He had no idea if any kind of transportation plied his homeward route at this time of night, but he could not stay in this room any longer—not at a time like this. He thought: I'll take a *cab* if I have to.

The phone rang as he was buttoning his shirt. It was a New York *Times* reporter who had obtained the name of the Prince Albert by calling Pollock's weather station for the sixth or seventh time. Evidently the graduate student was still loyally standing by at the station.

Pollock answered the reporter's questions as succinctly as he could. Yes, it did seem that something unusual was happening up there above the North Pole. Yes, this could well be it, a wind such as we've never seen before. Yes, you can quote me . . . Yes, it should arrive in the next twenty-four hours . . . Yes . . .

Pollock was thirsty. Where *was* Heidi? He had barely hung up after talking with the *Times* man when the phone rang again. This time it was a radio reporter, a woman. Could she ask the professor some questions and tape his replies? As long as it's brief, Pollock agreed. He wanted to say no, but his innate politeness forbade such a rejection.

The radio reporter asked substantially the same questions as the *Times* man. Pollock's throat was dry and scratchy when he finished that interview. Where on *earth* was Heidi? He went back to the business of getting dressed. He pulled on his socks, then his pants. It was while he was buckling his belt that he came aware of something wrong. It took him a few seconds to determine what that something was, and then understanding dawned.

Throughout his adult life, Simon Pollock had habitually carried his wallet in his left rear pants pocket. Whenever he pulled on his pants, he unconsciously expected to feel the wallet's bulk against his left buttock. It was the absence of that bulk that was disturbing him now.

He felt with his hand. Yes, it was true. His wallet was gone.

His unhappy gaze wandered to the top of the scarred old bureau. He had placed his watch there when Heidi complained that it was scratching her. The watch was gone too.

He sat on the bed and stared sadly at nothing for a moment. Then, slowly and methodically, he pulled on his shoes and bent over to tie the laces.

So it was over. He would never see Heidi again. He had learned something, perhaps. He did not know if he would ever want to risk his equilibrium with another woman in the same way. In all likelihood, he thought, the opportunity would never arise, for it was not the nature of his life to offer such opportunities routinely. But if he did happen to meet somebody else . . . he did not know.

At least he would always have the memory. The adventure had been brief and had ended painfully, but he believed a time would come when he would be glad it had happened. Better to have plucked a rose and been scratched than never to have held the rose at all.

Or so he had heard. He hoped it would turn out to be true.

The phone rang again. He debated not answering, but after the fourth ring his deep-rooted courtesy forced his hand to the receiver. The caller this time was a Deborah Mints. She represented one of TV's biggest morning talk shows.

"I'm *delighted* to find you in New York, Professor Pollock!" she said. "We'd like to invite you to be our guest on the show this morning." She spoke very fast.

"This very morning?" Lacking a watch, Pollock was confused.

"Yes. You know about the weather news from Canada, I suppose? Yes, well, we're going to devote a lot of the show to that. We'll be asking all these big scary questions. You know—what will today be like? Is it the last day of the world?" She did not sound scared, nor even mildly worried. Probably an indoor person, Pollock reflected. She hurried on: "So we were wondering, since you *are* in New York—"

"Oh, but I'm afraid that won't be possible," Pollock said, finally collecting himself. "I'm hoping to be on my way home to Connecticut very soon."

"You couldn't wait till after the show? We'd put you on as early as possible."

"No, I'm afraid it wouldn't work out. I really must get back to my weather station. I'm sure you understand."

"Oh dear. Well, if it has to be, it has to be. Some other time, perhaps, professor. Nice talking to you."

Deborah Mints hung up before he had a chance to mumble a farewell. Remembering his last TV appearance, in which he had been unexpectedly bludgeoned by Darlene Dorsey, he was glad to have a legitimate excuse for shunning this one.

The phone rang again as he was leaving the room. This time he resisted the impulse to answer, shut the door, and walked away.

Down in the lobby, he turned in his room key and said he was checking out. The night clerk was a young black man dressed like a bank teller in a white shirt and dark blue suit. He did not seem surprised to find a guest checking out in the middle of the night. No doubt he had seen Heidi leave and could make his own guesses.

Pollock's credit-card imprint had been taken when he checked in the previous day. As the clerk was preparing to fill out the voucher, Pollock said, "Wait! I wonder—uh—"

The young man looked up. Pollock stumbled on: "I—uh, this is really most embarrassing, but you see—I've lost my wallet. All my cash, all my credit cards. So I was wondering—ah—"

The clerk had heard it all before. He offered a sympathetic smile but shook his head firmly. "I'm sorry, sir. Hotel policy. No cash advances."

"But couldn't you just—"

"I'm sorry, sir. I'd help you out if I could. But if I break the rules I lose my job."

"But what am I going to *do?*" Pollock asked, aware that his squeaky voice was rising to a wail. "How will I get home if I can't even buy a bus ticket?"

"Well, sir," the clerk said soothingly, "why don't you wait till morning and call a friend?"

"But I don't *know* anybody in New York!" Pollock realized with chagrin that he had almost stamped his foot in frustration. Soon he might begin to weep if he did not control himself. He finished in a quieter voice: "I really am a complete stranger here."

"A bank? A brokerage, perhaps? There must be somebody you do business with." The clerk had the modulated, faintly British-accented voice of an actor. He was probably looking for work in the theater. He added a new thought: "Or perhaps you can get a cash advance from your credit-card company."

Pollock nodded, but not optimistically. His dealings with the company to date had not been such as to inspire confidence in its generosity.

Then an idea came to him. Deborah Mints!

He searched all his pockets for telephone change but could find only seven cents. "May I use a phone?" he asked the clerk.

The clerk gave him an unhappy look. "Oh boy. I'm really not supposed—"

"It'll just be a local call!" Simon Pollock was not normally so insistent or assertive, but now he was desperate. "Please! I've got to make a call!"

The clerk sighed. "All right. This is probably a firing offense too, but—in the back office there. Use the phone on the desk."

Five minutes later he was talking to a surprised Deborah Mints. He told her he had changed his mind about appearing on the show, and then he came haltingly to the heart of the matter: "You see, the reason for all this is that I've had my—ah—I've lost my wallet. I have no money or credit cards. So I was wondering—uh, it occurred to me that you might sometimes offer a fee. An honorarium, perhaps."

"I see."

"Is that ever done?" Pollock was writhing with embarrassment. He would never have requested such a fee under any normal circumstances.

"Hold the phone a moment, professor," Deborah Mints said. He heard a few brief bursts of high-speed conversation. Then she came back on the phone and asked, "Would a hundred dollars solve your problem, professor?"

"Oh, my goodness, yes!" Simon Pollock slumped in his chair as a wave of relief washed over him.

"Good." The brisk and businesslike Ms. Mints then gave him some instructions about when and where to present himself. She added, "I presume you have no way to buy breakfast. If you'd care to come early, we always have coffee and buns on hand."

Pollock expressed his gratitude and hung up.

He went out to walk the night streets of New York. It was a clear summer night, comfortably cool. The stars shone peacefully. There was very little wind so far. He wondered when it would begin to build up.

The streets and sidewalks were more crowded than

Pollock would have thought normal for this time of night. It was nearly two o'clock. The great city's morning awakening should not start for four or five more hours, yet Simon Pollock had an impression of daytime bustle around him. He wondered if people were simply apprehensive, restless, and unable to sleep, as he was. In support of that theory he was able to pick out men and women on the sidewalk who seemed to be ambling aimlessly, pacing to nowhere, lost in thought. But there were many others who had the appearance of heading for destinations. The street traffic, too, had a busy and hurried quality. There was a lot of impatient horn-thumping.

Many people on the sidewalk carried small containers: everything from elaborate knapsacks to rumpled paper bags. Pollock guessed these were the survival packs that people had been advised to keep handy. Pollock thought with annoyance of his own pack, prepared with great care but left absentmindedly on his desk at the weather station. He had not been thinking rationally yesterday.

He noticed other characteristics of these puzzling nocturnal walkers. Many carried suitcases. Others had children with them. He found that particularly odd. The only places where you commonly see a lot of children walking about at night, he reflected, are airports and other transportation terminals. Then it came to him: he was witnessing the start of a mass exodus from New York. Some people, at least, seemed to be taking seriously his public warnings about the power of the coming wind.

But where were they going? Where did they think they would be safer than underground? Were they going to huddle in frame houses in the suburbs, where they would be in as much danger as anywhere? He did not know. He thought many were fleeing the city through sheer panic. They had not thought much about where they would run *to*, just as long as they could find the emotional release of running.

"But we don't have the *time!*" a woman said to a friend as they hurried past him. There was definitely panic in her voice.

Others, however, were treating the situation as a lark. Pollock walked past a tavern with a propped-open door. It was crowded with happy patrons, arms over each other's shoulders and around waists, singing in boozy harmony. "Hear the wind blow, boys!" they sang. "Hear the wind blow!"

Simon Pollock walked on. A heartbreakingly pretty girl danced by him on the arm of her lover. She had dark eyes that flashed with merriment in the light from a store window. "Oh, Johnny, isn't it *fun!*" she exulted.

Pollock kept walking through the turbulent night. He did not know what experiences awaited that pretty girl over the next twenty-four hours or so. He did know she would not find them fun.

The last day had begun.

PART
II

THE
LAST
DAY

Nature with equal mind,
Sees all her sons at play,
Sees man control the wind,
The wind sweep man away.

Matthew Arnold

14

WEDNESDAY MORNING DAWNED bright and pretty over New York City and its vast three-state suburban region. Those who were up early enough saw a fetching blue-and-pink sunrise. By nine o'clock, when the sun was fully risen, anxious sky-watchers saw nothing to alarm them. The sky was mostly clear and blue. There were some high, wispy clouds that seemed to be moving southward rather fast, but they were in no sense ominous.

The temperature that morning was pleasantly cool for midsummer, ranging from the middle seventies in southern New Jersey to the high sixties in parts of Connecticut. As the climbing sun warmed the land, temperatures were rising. But the rise was slower than normal and by mid-morning would come virtually to a standstill.

There was a breeze, and it was freshening. At about seven o'clock most anemometers in the tri-state region recorded windspeeds of four to seven miles an hour. That is designated Force Two or "slight breeze" on the Beaufort Scale. It is the lowest windspeed that can be felt as air in motion against the face. It makes leaves rustle faintly but is not enough to blow paper or dry leaves around.

By nine o'clock the anemometers were detecting speeds in the neighborhood of ten miles an hour—Force Three or "gentle breeze." This is the speed at which a light flag will drift away from its pole, and the very smallest tree branches quiver.

The usual morning invasion of commuters into the city was much diminished on this Wednesday morning. People had heard about the Arctic developments on TV or had seen the morning's banner headlines on the front pages of newspapers. "BIG WIND COMING?" one newspaper yelled, plagiarizing *Seven Days*. Many companies told employees to stay home. Many commuters stayed home because they and their families were genuinely afraid of the wind, while others seized on the news as an excuse for an unauthorized vacation day of picnics and parties. Still others—almost certainly a plurality—simply went on with their lives as usual. They did whatever they would have done on any other Wednesday morning. They commuted, they got the kids ready for summer day camp, they went shopping.

Little knots of people gathered here and there to speculate on what the day might bring. They gathered on city street corners, at suburban back fences, in shopping-plaza parking lots. They looked at the sky. They told anecdotes of windstorms they had experienced in other years. The gentle breeze caressed their faces and played with their hair.

● ● ●

Arthur Beaulieu had been awakened at about five o'clock that morning by a phone call. The call reached him at his townhouse on Central Park West. The caller was a *Seven Days* junior editor who was taking his turn at the rotating night duty.

The night staff had standing instructions to get Arthur Beaulieu out of bed when news of great importance was breaking. Since it was left to their judgment to decide what "great importance" might mean in any particular situation, there was always some hesitation about making a middle-of-the-night phone call. As a result, he was usually allowed to sleep longer than he might have wished. Such was the case this morning. However, he did not complain. He appreciated the staff's wish to protect the Old Man from unnecessary curtailment of his sleep.

"Is this the day?" Julia Mead asked him as he hung up the bedside phone. She was sitting up in bed next to him. She had heard his side of the brief conversation.

"It looks as though this is the day," he replied.

"Oh damn. I was felling sexy this morning, Arthur. I mean I really had the hots."

"I know the feeling." He slipped the top of her nightgown down, exposed a breast, and kissed it.

"Stop that, you idiot. You'll make it worse."

"Yes. Forgive me. I couldn't resist."

Mornings were their favorite time. At night, after a long day's work, a woman of sixty-one and a man of sixty-seven often found libido burning low. But mornings could be glorious.

He grabbed a handful of her luxuriant, sleep-rumpled, snow-white hair and kissed her on the forehead. Then he began to untangle his long, bony frame from the covers. "You stay in bed a while," he suggested. "There's no good reason why you have to be out wandering the streets at dawn."

"Stay in *bed*?" she asked, astonished. "On a day like this? Arthur, that's crazy!"

He paused, considering her statement. Then he nodded. "Yes," he agreed, "I suppose it is."

Five minutes later he was on the phone to Adelaide Kent, the executive editor. He said, "I'm concerned about the staff, Adelaide. I think we should tell them not to report to work."

An elaborate network of telephone chain calls existed for this purpose. The network had proved effective in blizzards and other emergencies over the years. But Adelaide's reaction was much like Julia Mead's. "I don't know, Arthur," Adelaide said. "This isn't just another storm. This is a world news event. We're news people, aren't we?"

"Yes, but—"

"I can tell you *I'm* not going to stay home today. Are you?"

"Well . . . no."

"Of course you aren't. And if you want my guess, Charlie Broadbent and most of the others are going to feel the same way. The only way to keep Charlie home today would be to handcuff him to his bed."

"I imagine you're right, Adelaide."

"Of course I'm right, Arthur." Adelaide Kent was a woman whose opinions were always clear in her own mind and firmly expressed.

"What would you suggest, then?" Arthur asked.

"Well . . . " Adelaide paused, then said, "Why don't you, ah, give Mrs. Mead a call and see what she thinks? I'd trust her instincts completely in a situation like this."

"Yes, I'll do that. Thanks, Adelaide."

He hung up, amused. Adelaide could probably guess, he thought, that Julia Mead spent many or most of her nights at his townhouse. He and Julia did not advertise their relationship but, on the other hand, did not make any extraordinary efforts to hide it either. Still, they addressed each other in the office as "Mr. Beaulieu" and "Mrs. Mead." They felt comfortable doing that because they were different people in the office than after hours. Their relationship was different. When Julia put on a business suit, she *became* Mrs. Mead to him, not a lover or companion anymore but only a highly regarded business colleague.

He was sure his diurnal plumage brought about the same change in her response to him. The senior editorial staff, affectionately tolerant, went along with this funny little charade.

He padded barefoot into the living room, where Julia was beginning her usual half-hour of morning calisthenics. He explained the problem to her. She paused, thinking it over while lying stretched out on her back on the carpet. Finally she raised herself on her elbows and said, "I think maybe this is a case where the best decision you can make is no decision."

"Play the weasel, you mean."

"Well, if you must be so blunt about it—yes. Whatever you tell people to do, they'll resent it. So tell them nothing. They're got to make their own decisions."

He thought about that. Finally he said, "You're right. I think what I'll do is let people come to work—those who want to, that is. If some of them stay home, I'll say nothing."

"That's what I'd do, Arthur. And some time around noon, or whenever the wind starts rising, we can spread the word that we want people to go home."

"Even then, not everybody will."

"Of course they won't. But it's a personal decision. It isn't one you can try to make for people, Arthur. These are adults, and pretty bright adults at that. They'll figure it out for themselves. All you can do is let them know they're free to choose."

He nodded. It seemed right.

She returned to her exercises. He stood and watched her for a few moments. She was remarkably lithe for a woman of sixty-one, he thought admiringly. In fact, not to mince words: this Julia Mead was a beauty, in face as well as figure. She worked hard to keep herself fit. She had also had good luck in the roulette of heredity: she possessed a body, face, and skin that aged well. Arthur Beaulieu was always proud to be seen with her. He enjoyed the astonished looks of other men when he introduced her.

He turned and went into the bathroom to shave. His face gave him no pleasure. Unlike Julia's, it was an old face: full of lines and sags and exaggerated bony bumps, very obviously the face of a man nearing seventy. But his body was not so bad, he thought. He got plenty of exercise; walked a lot, usually rode a bike to and from work. He ate sparingly, avoiding heavy dinners and big breakfasts. There was not an ounce of excess fat on his knobby frame, not even around the belly. His blood pressure was that of a much younger man. Heart and lungs were in robust condition. So was his sexual equipment, a fact that particularly pleased him.

Still, he had no illusions. He and Julia were not a couple of twenty-year-old youngsters. They were in their sixties. No matter what you do with it, the human body *does* age. There is no escape from this pitiless law of nature. A sixty-year-old skin lacks the elasticity of youth. The aging process can be slowed by exercise and moisturizing creams and other defensive efforts, but it cannot be stopped. In time, the final collapse sets in. And at last, no matter how you might have struggled to ward off the inevitable outcome, you're dead.

But the lucky thing, he often thought, the merciful thing is that I don't know when the end will come. I know I'm going downhill but I don't know how fast. That's one of nature's kindnesses.

He had been intrigued years back to hear a Frenchman refer to the moment of sexual climax as *la petite mort*—the little death. Apt, Arthur had thought then. But today he no longer thought so. His feelings were precisely the opposite. To him, the climactic moment was the moment of eternal life. The orgasms he experienced today were in all ways equal to those he had known in his youth.

Indeed, perhaps they were better, for he and Julia had the experience to know how to please each other in ways that no twenty-year-old ever dreamed of. So in this respect—this one respect, if no other—he could believe that his aging body was not aging after all. In this one delightful circumstance, he could deny the otherwise all-too-obvious effects of being sixty-seven. This, he knew, was as near as mortal man can ever come to immortality. He loved Julia Mead for many reasons, but high on the list was the fact that she was stopping him from dying.

They had met about twenty-five years ago. He was just then beginning to make *Seven Days* into a respected rival of *Time* and *Newsweek*. She walked in off the street and asked for a job—a beautiful but bewildered woman, fresh from what he judged had been an inordinately painful, drawn-out marital breakup and divorce. His own marriage, to Angela, had been slowly souring for a long time. He and Julia became lovers within weeks.

That hastened the end of his marriage. He and Angela were happy to see the last of each other. His chief regret was the need to leave behind his only daughter, Kim. At the time he and Angela parted, Kim was a very young child. She had been born late in the marriage, when he was thirty-nine. He loved her very much. He and his lawyer fought hard for a flexible visitation schedule, and he cheated on it whenever an opportunity arose. He could never see enough of Kim.

"It's taking you a long time to shave today," Julia was saying behind him. She had come into the bathroom for her shower.

"Yes, I know," he said. "I'm slowing down. It's a sure sign of age."

"You're not getting older, dear, you're getting better,"

she said. She gave him a fond pat on the fanny as she
stepped behind him to get into the shower.

He rinsed and dried his craggy face. He shouted to Julia
over the noise of the shower water: "What do you hear
about Kim at the magazine? Do people talk about her?"

"Oh yes. She's well liked, I think."

"Respected?"

"A good deal, as far as I can tell. She seems to have
convinced people she's going to stand on her own feet."

"That's good to hear."

"Yes. I don't think you need to worry about her any
more, Arthur. She's grown into a fine young woman."

"She'll make it?"

"No question, Arthur."

"You're not just saying that to make me happy?"

"No. It's my true belief."

He nodded at himself in the mirror, hoping he could
believe her. Unlike Adelaide Kent, Julia did not always say
what was on her mind. Julia used words as a diplomat does,
to calm, to soothe, to please, to sugar-coat painful facts and
scary possibilities. This was one reason why she was such a
good executive secretary, Arthur supposed. For twenty-five
years she had listened to him talk about his daughter. In the
days when Kim was reeling from one alcohol-fueled disaster to another, Julia had comforted him. In particular, she
had tried to help him banish the nagging suspicion that
Kim's alcoholism was connected in some way with his
absence as a father.

Julia would do or say anything to make him feel good
about Kim, he thought. Still, he felt he had objective
reasons to be optimistic about his troubled daughter at last.
She seemed to be making her AA program stick. And she
seemed serious about her newly begun career at *Seven Days*.
Those two Big Wind articles she had turned out with

Pacifico were excellent. At the age of twenty-eight, he thought, she has finally gotten her life properly launched.

He dressed rapidly, breakfasted on grapefruit juice and a single slice of buttered toast, and headed for the front door. "See you at the office, Mrs. Mead," he called.

"I'll follow you in twenty minutes, Mr. Beaulieu," she called back from the bedroom.

They always made it a point not to arrive at the office together.

• • •

Angela Beaulieu was on the phone soon after breakfast. It was going to be an exciting day. She had to talk it over with her best friend, Sarah Millington, the mayor's wife.

"This is the big day, Sarah!" she said happily. "Time to get Operation Telephone rolling. You *will* help me, won't you?"

"Of course, dear. It was my idea to begin with, you may remember. Do you think I'd let you down at the crucial moment?"

The two friends had spent a good deal of time planning and organizing the Big Wind party. Angela's secretary had sent out an initial batch of a hundred-fifty expensively engraved invitations. When regrets and acceptances seemed to be running in roughly a fifty-fifty ratio, she had sent out more, ending with about one hundred putative guests. All were told to expect a phone call notifying them of the party's date and time. Angela expected some attrition in her guest list during the waiting period, but not a great deal. After all, this was to be one of the most important parties of the year. If you were invited to such a party, you did not casually fail to appear.

While the invitations and responses were fluttering politely through the mail, Angela was busy making arrangements with a caterer and attending to other preparations. She was particularly concerned with publicity. This was to be a party that the world *must* know about! While she had no luck with TV and radio people, she did manage to plant advance mentions of the party in several newspaper gossip columns, magazine trivia pages, and elsewhere. A few publicity plums fell into her lap. One came from *Town & Country* magazine, which sent a reporter and photographer around to record step-by-step the process of organizing a party for the rich, the famous, and the beautiful. Another plum came from the New York *Times*. Moira Shepherd, the paper's restaurant critic and occasional reporter on Hollywood and high society doings, said she would like to attend the party with a view to telling her readers about it. Angela said that would be wonderful.

And now, at last, the climactic day was here. "The timing is just perfect, Sarah!" Angela exulted. "The experts all think the height of the wind will be tonight sometime. It just *couldn't* be better!"

"So we invite them for—when?"

"Seven, I should think."

"Well, okay, but—look, we don't really know how hard the wind will be blowing then, do we? Maybe it'll be blowing so hard at seven that people will be afraid to drive, or something."

"Then they can take a cab," Angela said, dismissing the problem. Weather had never been permitted to interfere with her plans.

"I think this is something we should think about," insisted the more practical Sarah. "Just in case, you know?"

"Well, all right, what *do* we tell them?"

"I think—I think we should give them a whole lot of leeway. Let's tell them seven is the tentative time we're thinking of. No, make it eight. But tell them if the wind starts really blowing earlier than that, they can show up any time they like."

"Any time from five on," Angela amended.

"All right. But make sure they know how flexible you are. We'll just have to count on people to use their heads. I think I'll wear my new red taffeta, Angela. Do you think it's too—well, *young* for me?"

"You're as old as you feel, dear heart."

"That's a lot of poopsie-pie, and you know it, Angela. You're as old as you are."

"All right, put it this way. You're as old as you can make people believe. Is that better?"

"Maybe. But you still haven't answered my question . . ."

The two friends discussed the troublesome experience of aging for a while longer, then got back to the business of the invitations. They divided the guest list more or less alphabetically and agreed to set up sub-chains of deputized callers where practical. Angela was not in the least concerned with the fact that some prospective guests were as far away as California and Europe. She herself thought nothing of taking the Concorde to Europe for an important party. She had even flown to Paris one day for lunch.

The phone rang as soon as she had finished talking to Sarah. It was her daughter Kimberley. Angela had been expecting the call and had been wishing there were a graceful way to duck it.

"This is the day of your big decision, Mother," Kim said without preamble. "So tell me what it's going to be. Are you still going ahead with this Big Wind party?"

They had been arguing over the subject ever since Kim read a gossip-column item on it three days ago. Kim persisted in talking as though the party could still be called off—as though such a horrendous upheaval and unforgivable social gaffe were merely a matter of making one simple decision. To Angela, however, the fact of the party was already carved in granite. She could not cancel it even if she wanted to. She did not want to in any case. She thought it was going to be wonderful fun, perhaps the high point of the New York summer season.

She said all this to her daughter. "But Mother," Kim protested, "it's going to be *dangerous*. Don't you understand?"

"Don't talk to me as though I were a child, dear," Angela rebuked mildly.

"But Mother—oh *damn!*" Kim sighed with exasperation. "Listen, I'll be coming up to see you some time today. How about lunch? Will you feed me a sandwich?"

"Of course, dear. I'll tell Edna Jane to make some of those special cucumber sandwiches you like. You know I always love seeing you. But Kim, I'm not going to sit here and listen to a lecture."

"Mother—" Kim sighed again. "Oh, Mother, you're such a dope, and I love you!"

* * *

Pacifico and Daniela were riding up Madison Avenue in a cab. This was not his normal way of getting to work. Most mornings he either walked uptown or took the subway. But he wanted to protect little Danny against kidnapping and other potential threats, and he felt safe in a cab.

He was keeping her close by his side twenty-four hours a day. It had been his plan to take her to Vermont for a month-long stay with his cousin Rose Ann and her husband. They were a loving couple with a lot of kids. Danny always enjoyed visits with them. Unfortunately Rose Ann had herself been away on a visit and was not expected home until today.

And so he was bringing Danny to the office with him every day. She seemed to find it a grand adventure, though he was sure there were periods of boredom for her among all the adults. The office staff had welcomed her hospitably, as he had been sure would happen. It would take a cold heart indeed, he thought, not to be melted by a child so full of grace and good spirits. She spent a lot of time with Kim, of course. She also seemed to enjoy time spent in the library with Alice Wenska.

As the cab pulled away from a traffic light and started to veer toward the *Seven Days* building's main entrance, Pacifico reached down to give his daughter's small thin hand a squeeze. In that instant he felt her hand tense suddenly, and she clutched his fingers with her other hand.

"Daddy!" she whispered. She sounded frightened. "It's them! I see them!"

"Who, baby?"

"The man with the funny ear. And the thin man. That's them, Daddy! By the doors. It's *them!*"

Danny had been having recurrent nightmares about the pair who had menaced her in New Jersey. Pacifico felt he knew them personally, though he had never seen them. He looked now and saw two men leaning against the wall of the *Seven Days* building, near the entrance. One was a big, beefy man in a chocolate-brown suit, carrying a black briefcase. Pacifico thought there was something odd about the man's ear but was too far away to see it clearly. The other man was very tall and thin. He was wearing a light gray suit and carrying a rolled-up newspaper. They might have been two businessmen enjoying the morning sunshine while discussing the day's plans.

"Duck down!" Pacifico told Danny quickly. He was afraid they might see her. As far as he could tell, however, they were not watching the passing traffic with any great interest. They seemed more intent on the faces of those walking by on the crowded sidewalk. Still, Pacifico did not want to take any chances.

To the driver he said, "I changed my mind. Don't stop here. Take a left at the corner and I'll tell you where to drop us off."

Pacifico studied the two men as the cab crept past them in heavy traffic. The big, brown-suited man definitely did have a misshapen ear. His hair was sandy and cropped in a short crewcut. The thin man wore a gray felt hat that looked at least a size too big for his narrow head. Both men wore dark glasses.

"Are you sure those are the men?" Pacifico asked Danny. She was curled on the seat next to him, still clutching his hand.

"Yes, Daddy. I'm sure." She held his hand tight to her cheek and looked up at him with frightened eyes.

"Really sure?" he prodded.

"Really, *really* sure!"

He looked back as the cab passed them and turned the corner. They showed no interest in anything but the passersby on the sidewalk. They were still standing in the same spot as before. They were obscured from view by the corner of the building.

"You can sit up now, Miss Mousy," Pacifico said.

Danny only curled herself more tightly against him. "They scare me, Daddy!" she said.

"I know, baby. I know they do." He stroked her hair with his free hand. "But I don't think they're standing there waiting for you. Why should they be? What would make them think they'd find you here?"

She said nothing. He did not know the answer to his own question, and it puzzled him.

He directed the cabdriver to stop near the entrance to a parking garage down the street. There was a pedestrian tunnel from the garage to the *Seven Days* building. He and Danny gathered their survival packs and other belongings, scrambled out of the cab and hurried underground.

• • •

Simon Pollock got to Grand Central Station at about nine-thirty with the TV network's hundred dollars in his pocket. It had taken longer than he had hoped to find somebody in the accounting department to issue his check, and then to find somebody else to cash it.

In contrast to his previous experience at the hands of Darlene Dorsey, this morning's interview had been pleasantly bland. He was asked to give his opinions; he gave them, and that was that. He did have a moment's misgiving when he passed Peter James Schenker in a corridor just before the show. He remembered that the flowing-haired, mellifluous-voiced architect had been part of the opposition in the Darlene Dorsey show. In a brief flurry of panic he wondered: am I being set up for another public execution? But such was not the case. It turned out that Schenker's presence in the studio that morning had nothing to do with Simon Pollock. The publicity-loving architect was in New York to star in a special on urban renewal.

And now Pollock was at Grand Central, hoping to find an early train home to Connecticut. His hope dimmed when he found the huge building densely crowded with other travelers—most of them, apparently, trying to find a way out of the city. Clumps of people stood about with suitcases and survival packs, talking, arguing, looking harried. There was a lot of jostling as rivers of people weaved among the standees. Ribs were being elbowed, suitcases kicked over, packages dropped. The crowds were not bad-tempered but were not patient either. There was a sense of urgency and hurry in the air.

Pollock made his way to the great, high-ceilinged main hall. There were long lines in front of the ticket windows. The ticket sellers all seemed to be holding heated, arm-waving arguments with frustrated passengers. Pollock picked a line at random and appended himself to the end of it. After waiting twenty minutes and shuffling forward no more than three lengths of his overnight case, he decided to try something else. He would find a homebound train, board it without a ticket and pay the fare to the conductor. A train-times display told him there was a train to his part of Connecticut in half an hour. He pushed through the milling crowds to the designated departure gate, and there he stopped, baffled.

Several hundred other people had evidently had the same idea. A heavy iron-barred gate had been pulled across the opening. In front of the gate was a large, angry crowd. Behind it was a red-faced, harassed conductor with a wispy ginger-colored mustache.

"I told you," he was shouting, "we can't let nobody else on board! The train's full!"

"But I've got a *ticket!*" somebody shouted. Several others yelled that they had too. They all waved their tickets at the conductor.

"You'll have to get a refund," the conductor said.

"Yeah? Where? Where do I get this refund?"

"At the ticket window. Or you get it by mail."

"Yeah, great. Meantime, how the hell am I supposed to get where I'm going?"

The conductor shrugged. He didn't know and he didn't care.

A woman asked, "Are you going to run more trains?"

"I don't know, Ma'am. That isn't up to me."

"Who *is* it up to?"

"You'll have to ask at Information over there."

"Have you seen the *lines* at Information?" the woman demanded, exasperated. "Why doesn't somebody take some responsibility?"

There was a chorus of agreement from the crowd. The conductor's ginger mustache was slowly vanishing as his face grew redder. "I'm sorry, lady, I'm doing the best I can," he said.

"Yeah, you only work here, right?" shouted a man near the front of the crowd. He turned to address his fellow travelers. "It's the same old story. He only works here. He doesn't give a damn!"

"Yeah!" the enraged crowd shouted. "Right! Right on!"

The woman fired a parting shot as the browbeaten conductor turned to go. "And that's the *dumbest* mustache I ever saw!" she shrieked. The crowd applauded lustily.

After that, the crowd gradually dispersed, muttering. Pollock and some others stood still for a time, trying to decide what to do next.

The woman who had commented on the conductor's mustache was picking up her suitcase and handbag. "Boy," she said, "this whole thing can sure make you lose your temper!" Pollock happened to be standing near her. She gave him a smile of such radiant good humor that it startled him. He could not help smiling back.

"I think you had every right to lose your temper," Pollock said.

"Oh, I don't know." She shrugged. "It really wasn't that poor man's fault. None of this is anybody's fault. On a day like this, what we need most of is patience."

Pollock stared at her, entranced. There was something about her that clutched him. In all of his cloistered life, he had never experienced the magnetism that can spring up suddenly and shockingly between strangers in a public place. He did not know what was happening. He knew only that he was in the grip of a profound and mysterious spell.

She was in her forties, he judged. She had an arrestingly pretty face and heavy brown hair that fell over one eye. She was exactly his own height and slightly built.

"How will we ever get out of here?" Pollock asked.

"I don't know." She gestured at some other nearby departure gates, all of which were locked shut and surrounded by baffled crowds. "I don't think there's any hope of getting a train out of New York in any direction. Do you?"

"It doesn't look promising."

She gave him a quick, searching gaze. Then she said, "Maybe we'll have better luck at the bus station. Want to try it?"

Pollock was astonished to realize she was inviting him to be her traveling companion. He thought sadly: I've missed too much in my life. Too much. He said, "Do you know the way?"

"Yes, it isn't far. Ten minutes' walk, maybe fifteen with these crowds."

Pollock picked up his overnight case. "You think it'll be easier to find a seat on a bus?"

"Who knows? It could be bus companies are more flexible. Maybe it's easier to add extra buses than extra trains. We ought to *try*, at least."

"I agree. Lead the way."

They had to weave their way out of the station single-file, so they talked little until they were outdoors. The Forty-Second Street sidewalk was crowded, but not as densely as Grand Central. Pollock and the woman were able to walk abreast most of the time. She said, "You're a stranger in town, I gather?"

"Yes, pretty much so. My name's Simon Pollock. I—"

"Oh, you're the weather man! I had a feeling I'd seen you somewhere before. On TV, wasn't it?"

They exchanged stories and explanations. Her name was Cecilia Medina, but she had been answering to the name Cissy so long that she had given up trying to do anything about it. She was a suburban teacher, housewife, and mother of three. She had come to New York to see a play and spend time with an old friend. She was supposed to be back in her third-grade classroom tomorrow.

"I sure hope I make it," she said.

"Oh, you'll make it," Simon Pollock said with more confidence than he felt. "If we can't get to Connecticut one way, we'll find another. With me, it isn't just a matter of hoping. I've *got* to get there. Today. This afternoon at the latest."

They turned south on Fifth Avenue and walked the pleasant block dominated by the imposing public library building. The broad steps leading up to the front entrance were filled with people. In stark contrast to the nervous and hurried crowds at Grand Central, the crowd here was leisurely, settled, and satisfied. These were obviously people who had decided to stay in New York and see what happened. Most of them seemed to be enjoying themselves. Pollock saw one group of young men and women passing a wine bottle around. An older group had a bottle of Jack Daniels. It was only ten-thirty in the morning, but a mass outdoor party seemed to be in the making. Pollock also thought he caught a whiff of marijuana on the strengthening breeze—a smell with which he had become familiar during his many years on a college campus.

The breeze was just beginning to stir bits of paper and raise small puffs of dust from the gutter. It was not strong enough, however, to make women hold down their skirts or men their hats. Pollock judged from these clues, and from its feel against his skin, that it was in the neighborhood of fifteen miles an hour. Admiral Beaufort called that Force Four, a "moderate breeze."

●　●　●

Amanda Grewen was having a morning cup of tea at the coffee shop down the street from the New World Center. Around her neck she wore a four-inch wooden cross on a chain—a handmade gift from a parishioner of long ago. She also had with her an ancient Bible, bound in pebbled black leather, that had been given to her by her grandfather.

She did not know what this day might bring. Before it ended, she thought, there might be some who wanted God's comfort or guidance. And so she had decided to advertise her ministry by wearing the large cross and carrying the Bible. If people wished to seek her out, she would be there for them, ready to help.

It was unconventional, but that was entirely in keeping with the traditions of the United Church of Christ. Formed out of several different Protestant strains, the church emphasized the independence of congregations and was all in favor of experimentation. Women were serving as Congregational ministers long before most other religious sects even dared think about the idea. Congregational churches were holding jazz services as far back as the 1930s, when such an innovation was sacrilege to any conventional religious mind. Amanda knew her unconventional ministry would win the approval of church elders if she should ask their opinion—which she was not required to do in any case.

She sipped her tea quietly. She wondered if Ed McRoyden would turn up. He had said he would join her if he could. He had not been very hopeful, however, and neither was she. The balky diesel generator at the New World Center was giving him a lot of trouble.

He had started working on the engine yesterday. After talking publicly for days about the need to check out emergency generating equipment, he had taken it on himself to see what response there had been at the Center. He got answers by showing his city inspector's card. The card was no longer valid, but nobody at the Center seemed to know that. The news of his firing had not yet been widely publicized. Thus he discovered that as far as anybody could recall, one of the three big stationary diesel engines had not been serviced or tested once since it was installed. There was not even any fuel in its tank.

McRoyden bought fuel with his own money, but the engine would not start. Amanda had last seen him early this morning, when she went down to the basement generator room to take him a container of coffee. He was puzzling his way through an oil-smudged service manual. He looked tired but oddly content.

Amanda understood. He was engaged in an act of atonement. During the past several days he had begun this atonement by warning people of the coming need for shelter, food, and sources of light. But those ideas were largely other people's; he was only a spokesman. This work on the generator, by contrast, was entirely his own. Amanda thought it was the best possible answer for him.

Now she sat in the coffee shop, finishing her tea. It was past ten-thirty. She decided he was not going to take a midmorning break after all. She paid her bill and dropped the change in a pocket of her old brown suit. She was carrying no handbag because she did not want to be encumbered by anything but her Bible. She went out to walk.

In front of the New World Center was an attractive plaza paved with some kind of stone that sparkled in the sun. There was a reflecting pool surrounded by stone benches, and between the benches, young sycamore trees stood in squares of earth blocked out of the pavement. The breeze was rippling the water and making the trees' top branches sway gently.

A young black woman was sitting on one of the benches, hunched over, holding a tiny baby. As Amanda walked past, she saw that the woman was crying.

Amanda paused, undecided. It was never possible to know for certain whether one's help was wanted. Either decision could be wrong: to intrude where one was not welcome, or to walk away from a situation in which one kind word might make a difference. Finally she decided to take what seemed like the lesser risk. She stopped by the bench and asked, "Is there something I can do?"

The woman looked up. As soon as Amanda saw the tear-streaked face, she knew this was not a woman but a girl, probably not more than sixteen years old.

The girl looked at Amanda's Bible and at the wood cross on its chain. "You some kind of preacher woman?" she asked.

"That's right. I'm a Congregational minister."

The girl glanced down at her baby, then at the water in the pool, then back at Amanda's face. "I be scare," the girl said, and then immediately amended that to schoolbook English. "I'm scared." She started to sob.

Amanda sat next to her on the bench. "Scared of what, dear?"

"We all alone, my baby and me. Ain't got no place, ain't got nobody. And here come this Big Wind, and us out on the street! What they speck us to *do?*"

"Nobody expects you to stay on the street. What you have to do is get underground. Go down in the subway."

"Can't afford no subway. I ain't even got a dime!" The girl hugged her baby and cried miserably.

"That's easily fixed," Amanda said. She found a few dollar bills in the pocket of her suit jacket. She held them tentatively toward the girl, but the girl looked away. Amanda went on: "You won't need money anyway. All these buildings have basements. People aren't going to lock you out. Not a mother with a tiny baby."

"No? Who says? People been locking me out of places all my life."

"There's really a lot of love in people's hearts, dear. Sometimes you have to help them bring it out."

"Yeah? What you know about it, white lady?" The girl turned on Amanda in sudden anger. "What *you* know, huh? You and your Bible. What *you* know what it's like to raise up a baby all by you se'f? You ever try it, huh?"

Amanda hesitated, then said, "Well, as a matter of fact, yes. I've tried it."

The girl stared at her with tear-filled dark eyes.

"My baby died when he was a year old," Amanda said. "He was born with a heart defect. But while he lived—oh yes, I know all about it."

"You din have no husband?"

"No."

It was Amanda's pregnancy out of wedlock that had caused her to be dismissed by her last congregation. The vote had been close, but the conventional minds had won. It was a story she rarely told to anyone. Telling it now to this misfortune-dogged waif on a city street, Amanda felt oddly comforted.

They sat without speaking for a few moments. The girl kept looking at Amanda, then looking away, as though trying to arrive at some conclusion. The breeze sighed through the sycamore trees. Finally the girl said with a shy smile, "I reckon I take that money off you, you don't mind. I ain't et for a time. And the baby, he need some milk."

Amanda handed the money over. "After you get some food, come back here," she said. "I'll be somewhere around this building all day. And I guarantee I'll find you a free basement."

"Sure, I be back," the girl said, standing. Amanda was not sure she meant it.

The girl gave Amanda a parting nod and walked off. Amanda sat alone on the bench for a while, watching the ripples chase across the surface of the pool. She was surprised to find a tear running down her cheek.

15

THE WIND'S STRENGTH increased abruptly during the last hour of the morning. By noon it was in the neighborhood of thirty miles an hour. Admiral Beaufort called that a "moderate gale" and designated it Force Seven.

A wind of that strength will cause all but the very thickest-trunked trees to sway. It makes power lines and TV antennas sing. It whistles and moans going around corners of buildings. It is the kind of wind that traditionally accompanies movies about haunted castles. It snatches hats off people's heads and loose awnings from the fronts of stores. It measurably impedes walking. While the extra exertion of walking into a Force Seven gale is not inordinately taxing to people in good health, it can pose serious problems for those with arthritis, lung ailments, and heart conditions.

With the increase in wind force came a peculiar change in the sky. Great masses of dark cloud seemed to appear from nowhere. The clouds were in constant motion. They whirled and tumbled, as though the sky were starting to boil.

* * *

Jelly Jack Barrow had arrived at the New World Center the previous evening. He had had a long night's sleep and a late breakfast. He had held a midmorning meeting in his hotel suite and had taken care of a few other items of business. Now he had nothing left to do all day but wait for a phone call from Al and hand over the agreed-upon cash fee.

He wished the transaction were over. He hated to think what the $100,000 fee was buying. He knew Al would want to stay for a couple of drinks after collecting the money, but Barrow wanted neither a drink nor a prolonged dose of Al's company today, much as he liked Al under normal circumstances. Barrow's breakfast was not sitting easily in his stomach. He felt a bad attack of indigestion coming on. It was hell what you had to do to get ahead in this lousy world, he thought.

He wandered around the hotel lobby. There were three taverns in the hotel, and all were doing a lusty business. They were so crowded that patrons were beginning to spill out into corridors and stairways. Barrow was sure that at least half a dozen police and fire department regulations were being jovially breached. He walked to an outside door and looked out at the darkening day. Street traffic was moving so turgidly that pedestrians felt free to weave among vehicles at will. Some pedestrians were hurrying, while others were just ambling or standing about, feeling the wind, looking at the sky. A lot of drinking was going on out there, too. Barrow saw one group holding a tailgate party at the curb. The atmosphere was much like that of a college football stadium before a big game. People were getting started on what was obviously intended to be an all-day party.

A young woman pushed the door open and walked into the hotel. Her clothing and makeup were exotic. As Barrow moved ponderously aside to let her pass, he was enveloped in a wind-borne gust of strong perfume. He guessed she might be a call girl. He stood and watched the swing of her splendid bottom as she strode down a corridor. He wondered if that was what he needed now: something to take his mind off things while he waited for Al's call and the dreaded words, "The job is done." A good healthy roll in the hay might even cure his indigestion, he thought.

He had a phone number for use in such need. He started to follow the young woman down the corridor toward a bank of phone booths, but even as he walked, he knew his heart was not in it. His libido was rising so sluggishly that any distracting thought could cool it. The distracting thought occurred when the young woman's eye was caught by one of the chic little shops that lined the corridor. It was a shoe shop. As she stopped and turned to look at the window display, Barrow stared at the sweet curve of her young cheek and jaw. Illuminated by yellow light from the window, the smooth skin shone with golden radiance.

Barrow stopped in his tracks, gaping like a fish. A horrifying vision was superimposing itself on the reality of what he saw. For one ghastly second, he saw that lovely golden cheek pitted, ridged, and scarred by acid.

The young woman saw him staring and gave him a hostile look. "Something bothering you, mister?" she asked.

"No, I'm sorry," Barrow said hastily, and lumbered away.

He went into the central lobby area and spent a few minutes trying to compose himself, leaning against one of the great pillars that dominated the spacious room. The pillars were sheathed in the same lustrous black marble that covered the floor. The marble was cool. Barrow put his hands behind his back and pressed his damp palms against the cooling surface. It made him feel better.

Across the lobby he saw a news-and-notions shop. Perhaps a good cigar would make the world look brighter, he thought.

He made his way toward the shop, weaving clumsily among armchairs and clumps of standing people. There was a painful tightness in the area of his diaphragm. He was out of breath when he got to the shop.

The dark-haired, small woman behind the counter wore a plastic name tag introducing her as Cora. Barrow did not pay a great deal of attention to her until he had selected the cigar he wanted to smoke. Then he looked at her face. She had arresting violet eyes and delicate features that might have been called beautiful if her luck had been better. But her cheeks were scarred with acne.

Barrow stumbled out of the shop without buying his cigar. He boarded an elevator and rode up to his room. Only one thought was in his mind. He had to call off the acid attack.

He had a good idea where to find Al. When in New York, Al and his friends almost always stayed at an obscure small hotel downtown. By a long-standing agreement, Barrow and Al communicated as infrequently as possible, generally restricting themselves to conversations over the secure phone in Barrow's Houston office. But this was an emergency. Barrow argued his way through a long chain of people and finally got Al on the phone.

"Yeah, who is it?" Al asked. Barrow recognized the voice.

"It's me," Barrow said. Both were careful not to use names. You never knew who might be listening in a hotel.

"Some problem?" Al asked.

"Yeah. I want today's assignment called off."

"Called *off?* For Chrissakes, why?"

"Never mind. I'll tell you some other time."

"Called *off!* Jeez."

"Will you take care of it?"

"Sorry, no way. The guys are on the street. How am I gonna get in touch with them?"

"Oh shit." Barrow felt the tightness growing around his

diaphragm again. "You mean the—uh, operation is—uh . . . ?"

"That's right."

"How far along would it be?"

"Search me. All I know is, the guys couldn't get here till this morning. So last night, they phone a friend of theirs and get the friend to—uh, acquire the—uh, subject for them. So this morning, the friend fingers the subject, and they take it from there. That's all I know."

Barrow understood from this that Al's two men had hired a friend to find out what the Beaulieu woman looked like. One common way to do this is to pose as a poll-taker and visit the target person's home. Then this morning, presumably, the friend found some way to point out the target to Al's men as she left her apartment or arrived at her office building for work.

"We gotta find them and call it off!" Barrow insisted.

"Find them how? Where you wanna look?"

"Round the building, maybe. I mean where this B—where the subject works." Barrow had almost said "this Beaulieu broad" but caught himself just in time. "I mean, if they were starting up the operation this morning—"

"Yeah, maybe. But it don't make no difference anyhow. Even if I did know where to find them, how am I gonna get up there? Have you seen the traffic this morning?"

"Take the subway."

"Shit. Every time I ride the subway in this town, I either get lost or get my pocket picked. Whaddya think I am, crazy?"

"But it's an emergency!" Barrow shouted.

"Well, okay, go out and find them yourself. You're a hell of a lot closer than I am. You're only a few blocks away."

"Is that right?" Barrow asked dubiously. He did not know where the *Seven Days* offices were.

"Right. Five minutes' walk, tops. But listen, one thing.

The money. However it turns out, you still owe us. Right?"

"We'll talk later," Barrow growled, and hung up.

The room was not hot, but he was sweating. He loosened his tie and collar. He found a Manhattan phone book and looked up *Seven Days*. The listing gave him both street address and phone number. He dialed the number with a fat finger that trembled.

The operator connected him to Kimberley Beaulieu's office phone. The phone rang for a long time, and then a woman answered. "*Seven Days* editorial," she said.

"Kimberley Beaulieu, please?"

"Hold on, maybe I can catch her."

Barrow waited with desperate impatience. She's *got* to be there, he thought.

"I'm sorry, but you just missed her," the woman told him.

"You mean she just left?"

"Yes, for lunch. Not more than a minute ago. If you'd like to leave your name—"

"No, I'll call later, thanks."

So the operation had not yet been completed. That was a relief, but there might not be much time left. Perhaps, Barrow thought, Al's men were planning to waylay her somewhere around the office building. He envisioned them lurking, following her, waiting for the right place, the right moment.

She would be a young woman with lovely fresh skin. Barrow had never seen her, but he had heard Spence Millington describe her. Barrow saw her in his mind as a golden girl. She had luminous golden cheeks like that girl looking into the shop window.

Barrow hurried down to the ground floor and out into the blast of the Force Seven gale. He was not perfectly sure he could pick Al's men out of a crowd, for he had seen them only a few times and only briefly. Still, he had to try.

He turned westward toward Madison Avenue. The wind was not strong as he made his way along the side street. It came in gusts that blew first one way, then another. People were collecting against the sheltering buildings along the north side of the street. Barrow pushed past them more roughly than was usual for him. He had been fat since his teens and normally took pains not to accentuate his great bulk by blundering about like an elephant. But today he did not care. All he wanted was to get to the *Seven Days* building, find Al's men or find the young Beaulieu woman, stop the horror he had started.

"Hey man, watch where you steppin', huh?" shouted an angry black woman. He had bumped her arm, causing her to spill part of a drink she was holding in a paper cup.

"Sorry," Barrow mumbled.

"Yeah? What good sorry gonna do? Look at my pants! Sorry gonna pay the cleanin' bill, is it?"

Barrow hurried on as she hurled a final inelegant term of opprobrium at his back. His diaphragm area was hurting badly now. The pain was spreading all through the center of his body. It felt as though a huge balloon, or perhaps a basketball bladder, was lodged down there and was gradually being inflated. The bigger it grew, the harder he found it to breathe.

He was already gasping when he reached Madison Avenue, turned north, and found himself heading directly into the teeth of a boisterous thirty-mile gale.

There was a lot of Jack Barrow to catch the wind. His enormously wide suit jacket billowed out like a blue pinstriped sail. Unprepared, he staggered back for two paces before adjusting to the frontal force and regaining his equilibrium. But forward motion taxed his strength to the utmost. At nearly three-hundred badly distributed pounds, Barrow found walking hard under the best of circumstances. Even a slight incline winded him. This part of

Madison Avenue sloped upward gently. The slope and the buffeting wind together were more than he should have attempted, even if he had been feeling good.

He had gone about half a block when he realized something was seriously wrong. The giant basketball bladder expanded to fill his entire body cavity. It seemed to be popping out of his throat, choking him. It expanded downward into his belly. He thought he might explode. He knew he was soiling his pants but could not do anything about it. The street whirled about him. He stumbled and fell against a parking sign. He grabbed at it weakly for support, but there was no sensation in his hands. He heard people's alarmed voices and was dimly aware that they were reaching out to help him, but his vision was darkening.

This must be death, he thought. I wish it could be a little more dignified.

He was unconscious before he hit the sidewalk and dead only a short time later. Jelly Jack Barrow had become one of the wind's earliest casualties.

● ● ●

Ed McRoyden had spent the morning trying to get a recalcitrant diesel engine started.

It was one of three main diesel-powered generators at the New World Center. Designed to kick in automatically if the building's normal supply of electric power were to fail, the engines would not produce enough current to satisfy the Center's huge everyday appetite to the full, but they would be adequate for emergency needs. They would at least provide light for corridors and stairwells and would bring all elevators down to the ground safely.

Two of them seemed to be in ready condition. They responded instantly when McRoyden and a building-staff engineer started them manually, and though the generators were cold, they did not sound too bad. This third one

apparently had been neglected. McRoyden did not know
why. Such things happen in a large building, most often as
a result of staff turnover. A new employee stepping into a
job may get poorly briefed or hardly briefed at all. Nobody
tells him he is supposed to be the nursemaid of the Number
Three diesel. As time goes on, everybody assumes somebody else is taking care of it.

It was a 500-horsepower Cummins engine. When it had
its generator spinning, it would be able to produce 450
kilowatts of electric current. But it refused to start. Big,
square, ugly, buff-colored, about the size of a station
wagon, it sat stubborn and silent on its bolted-down base.
Nothing McRoyden could do would bring it to life.

The big twelve-volt batteries were lively enough. They
cranked the starter motor in the usual diesel way: so slowly,
laboriously, and groaningly at first that you thought the
whole inside of the great engine must be jammed and glued
together. But then the starter would pick up speed, and
finally it would whir and clank briskly. But there was no
other response. The diesel cylinders never fired. As soon as
McRoyden cut off battery current to the starter, it clanked
to a cold stop.

He and the staff engineer checked the engine over as well
as they could. Though neither was a diesel specialist, they
were able to arrive at a fair understanding of the way this
brown behemoth was supposed to work. Unlike a standard
gasoline engine, which explodes fuel in its cylinders by
means of electric sparks, a diesel gets the same effect by
squeezing its fuel until the heat of compression causes the
desired explosion. Once a diesel engine gets running and
the cylinders are all nice and hot, it is about as trouble-free
as any engine can be. The problem is getting it started:
creating enough heat in those cold cylinders to produce the
first explosions. There are many approaches, none of them
foolproof. There are many things that can go wrong.

The staff engineer finally said he was going to phone around for a Cummins service representative. He left, then came back half an hour later to say that every diesel specialist in New York seemed to be out on house calls. McRoyden could not reasonably complain about that, since it was mainly he who had publicized the need to check out emergency generating equipment. The staff engineer left again to try some more phone calls. McRoyden sat at a rickety table in one corner of the basement room, finished some lukewarm coffee, and idly flipped through an oil-smudged diesel service manual.

Somebody appeared in a doorway across the room. It was a small man with snow-white hair parted exactly in the middle and combed neatly to the sides. He had a small, trim, snow-white mustache. He was neatly dressed in a button-down white shirt, maroon tie, and tan poplin jacket. The jacket was tidily zipped partway up, and the tie was clipped to the shirt to keep it out of trouble. McRoyden thought the man was almost certainly an engineer. In all likelihood he wore both belt and suspenders.

"Are you Ed McRoyden?" the white-haired man asked.

"That's me."

As the man approached, McRoyden saw that he had sky-blue eyes behind steel-rimmed spectacles. There was something familiar about the face.

"I'm Jake Barnes," the man said, holding out his hand. "The commissioner."

No wonder the face was familiar. This was Jacob J. Barnes, New York City's commissioner of buildings. It was from his department that McRoyden had recently been fired. The two of them had never met, but McRoyden had heard the commissioner speaking a few times at engineers' and architects' gatherings.

"I had a devil of a time finding you," Commissioner Barnes said as they shook hands. He looked McRoyden straight in the eye and came directly to the point of his visit with no preliminary shuffling around. "I wanted to find you because there's something I want you to know," he said. "Firing you wasn't my idea. I didn't order it. I made about twenty phone calls trying to get it stopped."

"Who did order it?"

"Don't ask me that."

McRoyden nodded. He was all but sure the impetus behind his firing came from Mayor Millington's office.

"I also want you to know I'm not going to let you get thrown to the wolves," the commissioner said. "When all this is over, you want a new job, you come and see me. There are places I can send you, doors I can open."

"Thanks," McRoyden said with genuine appreciation. A recommendation from Commissioner Jake Barnes could be valuable. Barnes was widely known and highly respected in structural engineering circles. He was universally thought to be a man of impressive competence and integrity. It was felt that he ran his big, untidy, harried agency as well as was humanly possible in the face of formidable difficulties, among them a shrinking budget, an inadequate staff, and a need to rely too heavily on spot-checking in the eternal effort to secure obedience to the city's massive and elaborate building code.

Having briskly achieved the purpose of his visit, the commissioner seemed to relax a little. He looked around at the big Cummins engine and said, "They told me you were having trouble with this brute."

"Yes, it doesn't want to start."

"Hasn't been serviced in a while, I suppose?"

"That's how it looks."

Barnes nodded sadly. "It's frustrating, isn't it?" he said. "I mean the way you can't depend on people to do things right. I've been out touring construction sites this morning, and I've already found half a dozen serious violations. I'm not talking about trivial rulebreaking, I'm talking about real live danger. How can people be so stupid?"

The commissioner's habit of inspecting construction sites in person before major storms was well known in the building-trades community, though not to the public-at-large. Whenever a significant wind was forecast, Barnes would leave the departmental offices on Wall Street, find a car and driver, and visit major building projects. The reason for doing this was that in New York, as in all tall-built cities, poorly buttoned-down construction sites had always been the leading source of danger on windy days.

Barnes would cruise up and down the avenues, making sure all his department's rules were being observed. Mobile cranes were supposed to be lowered all the way to the ground. Often they were not. In a crowded and cluttered building site, it took a certain amount of ingenuity and work to find a space in which a long crane's boom could nestle horizontally. Fixed cranes at the tops of buildings were left in place, but the department's rule was that they should be allowed to "weathervane" or swing about freely. This rule, too, was frequently ignored.

So were the rules about loose objects that could fall into the streets. "I almost got killed half an hour ago," Barnes was saying. "I was climbing out of my car when *wham!*—a hell of a big piece of timber hits the ground ten feet away from me. I look up. About thirty stories high there's a catch floor that nobody has bothered to think about. I can see the planks moving in the wind. It's obvious they'll all be blown down sooner or later."

A catch floor was supposed to be a safety measure. When a building was in its skeletal stage, the city required that temporary floors be installed below high work areas to prevent dropped parts and tools from hitting people on the ground. Such a floor might be nothing more than a few dozen planks laid across steel beams. It could save lives. But if nobody thought to remove it or secure it during a windstorm, it could change suddenly from safety measure to lethal hazard.

"Why don't people use their *heads*?" Commissioner Barnes complained. Then he sighed. "Oh, well. Why get excited? Listen, McRoyden—Ed—I can use a short break and a cup of coffee. Care to join me?" Barnes held up a dented metal lunchbox that he had been carrying. It was the only untidy thing about him—probably a sentimental relic of the days when he had earned his living as an engineer on site.

McRoyden understood that the commissioner wished to make a friendly gesture. The time was eleven-thirty, close to lunch. McRoyden did not really want more coffee but felt it would be unkind and ungrateful to say no. After all, the man had not been required to pay this visit. Most people in the same circumstances would never have thought of it. McRoyden held out his paper cup and said, "Half a cup would be nice."

The commissioner sat at the rickety table, pulled a Thermos flask from the lunchbox, and poured the coffee. He sipped from his plastic cup. "This may not be elegant," he said, gesturing at the bare concrete floor and walls around them, "but at least it's quiet. That wind can make your ears ring."

"How hard is it blowing?"

"Gale force, the radio said. And rising. And so is my blood pressure, I'm afraid." The commissioner gave McRoyden a quick, direct look with his blue eyes. "I'll tell you frankly, Ed, I'm worried."

McRoyden shrugged. "So would any sane man be."

"I know. But I'm supposed to project this image of cool confidence. It's part of the job." Barnes suddenly grinned. "You wouldn't want to take over my job for a few days, would you?"

McRoyden grinned back. "Thanks, but no thanks."

Barnes's grin disappeared as suddenly as it had come. "Four hundred miles an hour," he said. "If that's what we've really got coming, then I don't know what to expect. Even three hundred—even *two*—winds like that are way over our tolerances."

"I know," McRoyden said in what he hoped was a soothing tone.

New York City's building code specified the wind loads that must be withstood by buildings of various heights. The very tallest were required to take loads of forty pounds to the square foot. Such a load would be exerted by winds in the neighborhood of 125 to 130 miles an hour. No such wind had ever blown in New York. Nor had any such wind ever been *expected* to blow there. The code was felt to provide for an ample safety margin. Indeed, some architects and developer-speculators had long grumbled that it was too ample. In their view, the high wind-load provisions added unnecessarily to the cost of tall buildings.

"Suppose we get real damage," Commissioner Barnes said. "I mean *real* damage. Buildings toppling." He stared at McRoyden, and McRoyden saw the nightmare in the man's eyes. "What's going to happen? Will I be lynched? Will people say we should have written a tougher code?"

McRoyden had thought about that. "I'm sure some will," he said.

The commissioner nodded morosely. It was the answer he had expected. "And yet if we'd tried to write higher wind loads into the code," he said, "everybody would have screamed. We wouldn't have been *allowed* to toughen the code even if we'd wanted to. It all comes down to economics, doesn't it?"

"Economics," McRoyden agreed, nodding. "Another thing people are going to say is that we should have done more to enforce the code we did have. But I remember the last time you went around asking the city for more money, they sent you away without a nickel."

Barnes gave him a searching look. "We really could use a bigger inspection force, couldn't we? And more pay for those we have."

"I think so." McRoyden was tempted to bring up the subject of bribery. He remembered being taught in parochial school that confession makes you feel good. He had found that to be true sometimes. But now he decided to keep his mouth shut. Barnes was undoubtedly aware that in any group of law enforcers, including building inspectors, some are more honest than others. What can I gain now, McRoyden asked himself, by telling the commissioner that I was one of the rotten apples in his barrel?

That thought was followed by a more startling one: maybe he suspects it anyway. The man isn't dumb. He must have asked himself why I conducted a crusade about survival and why I'm monkeying with this diesel. Why am I going to all this trouble? He might suspect it's all some kind of penance.

As though catching a stray wisp of McRoyden's thoughts, the commissioner stood and walked over to the big Cummins engine. He walked around it and examined it while wiping his neat white mustache with a handkerchief. "Funny," he said, "this big baby *looks* as though she wants to run, doesn't she?"

McRoyden belonged to a younger generation of engineers who did not commonly refer to machines as "she." But he unconsciously adopted Barnes's jargon. "She does," he agreed.

Barnes pointed to thick cables that led out of the generator end of the machine. "Where do they go?" he asked.

"This machine serves mainly the condominium tower," McRoyden said. "Elevators, hallways, stairwells."

"It'd be pretty scary, stuck up there in the dark, wouldn't it?" The commissioner walked around the engine one more time. Then he said, "These batteries are okay?"

"Sure are. The starter revs up just fine."

"Let's hear how she sounds."

McRoyden stood, walked to the side of the engine and flipped the starter switch. The motor groaned, heaved, clanked, gradually gained speed. Soon it was whirring steadily.

The commissioner leaned close to the engine and sniffed. "No fuel smell," he commented. "There *is* fuel in the tank, I suppose?"

"Oh yes. I filled it myself."

"You mean it was empty?"

"Just about."

"Ah!" Commissioner Barnes straightened up, unzipped his jacket and began to take it off. "Could be she's airbound. Either that or there's water in the fuel, from condensation inside the tank. That often happens if you let these big tanks stand empty. Let's find a bucket."

McRoyden found a bucket in a supply room. When he returned to the engine room, the commissioner was rolling up his white shirtsleeves. McRoyden was amused to see that Barnes, as he had guessed, wore both belt and suspenders.

"You sound as if you know diesels," McRoyden said as he handed over the bucket.

"Well, I've worked at a hell of a lot of different jobs in my time." Barnes closed a valve in the fuel supply line from the tank, then spread his handkerchief on the concrete floor near the engine's fuel filters. He kneeled on the handkerchief and slid the bucket under the lower of the two filters. He felt under the white cannister, said "Ah!" when he found a petcock, struggled with it and finally got it open. Fuel poured into the bucket.

When it stopped draining he closed the petcock and

reopened the valve in the supply line. He wiped his hands with his handkerchief.

"Sometimes you have to do that over and over again before anything happens," he said. "Other times, just once will do the trick. Keep your fingers crossed."

"Shall I try it now?"

"Try it."

McRoyden flipped the switch. The starter went through its usual repertory of complaints, then slowly got itself turning. And suddenly, with a bellow so loud that McRoyden and the commissioner both jumped back, the huge engine came boisterously to life.

There was a silencer in the exhaust system, but an engine of that size does not submit easily to attempts to quiet it. For a time, the two men did not try to talk above the thundering. The commissioner carefully unrolled and buttoned his sleeves, adjusted his tie, put on his jacket, zipped it, and picked up his lunchbox. He held out his hand to McRoyden.

"They always make a lot of noise when they're cold," he shouted, leaning close as they shook hands. "She'll quiet down. Let her run a while or she'll give you more trouble. She may anyway."

With a parting wave, Commissioner Barnes left.

● ● ●

Kim left the *Seven Days* building shortly after twelve o'clock. The distance to the New World Center, where she was going to have lunch and, she hoped, a sensible talk with her mother, was only a few short blocks south and one long block east. On an ordinary day it was a walk that might have taken ten minutes. Today, she quickly realized, it was going to take a lot longer.

The Madison Avenue sidewalks were so crowded that it was impossible to walk more than a few steps in a straight

line. Two street vendors had parked their wagons near the
building and were selling fruit juices and hot dogs at grossly
inflated prices to a horde of eager buyers. People stood
around munching, sipping, looking up at the darkening,
turbulent sky. Their clothes and hair flapped and whipped
and streamered in the rude thirty-mile gale. People had to
lean close to each other and shout if they wanted to
converse. Many were enhancing their lunch-hour enjoyment with alcohol. Kim saw one man buy a paper cup of
fruit juice from the vendor, swallow some and spike the
remainder with whiskey from a pocket flask. He sampled
the resulting drink, looked doubtful for a moment, then
smiled contentedly. The vendor was watching mournfully.
The man offered some whiskey to the vendor, who accepted
with evident gratitude.

Meanwhile, drivers and riders in the stop-and-go street
traffic were less content. Pedestrians seemed to be the main
problem. With the sidewalks growing ever less navigable,
people with places to get to were taking to the blacktop.
Kim joined a stream of hurrying, windblown people who
dodged among cars and buses, provoking much angry horn-
honking and many arguments in English, Spanish, and
variants.

Directly in front of Kim, a yellow cab tried to slip into an
opening and narrowly missed a small dark man who ran in
front of it. "Ey, mon, watch where you drive, uh?" the
pedestrian shouted. "You almo' bost my kneecap, mon!"

"So get back on the goddam sidewalk where you belong!" the enraged cabdriver shouted back.

"You almo' kill me, sunnabitch bastard!"

"Up yours, Pedro." The cabbie thrust a brawny arm out
and executed the international middle-finger sign as he
slowly pulled away.

"Yeah?" howled the equally enraged pedestrian. "Op you
twice!" He thrust both middle fingers at the departing cab.

The cab had barely passed Kim when she heard its tires screech behind her. She looked back and saw that the same driver had narrowly missed another pedestrian, this time an elderly woman.

At the edge of her field of vision, then, Kim saw something else, or thought she saw it. Very briefly, perhaps thirty or forty feet behind her among the cars and pedestrians, she thought she glimpsed a big man with a crewcut and a chocolate-brown suit. At the instant she looked at him, he vanished behind a delivery van.

Danny had talked often and fearfully about the two men who had frightened her in New Jersey. Apparently Danny had seen them again this morning as she and her father arrived at the *Seven Days* building in a cab. Nick had called the police as soon as he got to his desk. Nothing had come of that, for the police were busy preparing for the wind and in any case were finding it increasingly hard to move around town in their patrol cars. Meanwhile, Kim had tried to comfort Danny and had heard the two men's descriptions again from the little girl and also from Nick. Kim had developed a peculiarly stark mental picture of the big man. With his bulk, cropped hair, cauliflower ear, and chocolate-brown suit, he seemed full of menace. Kim did not know exactly why. Perhaps she had simply absorbed some of Daniela's fear.

She stood looking at the delivery van for a second, then decided she was suffering from an overactive imagination. It was that kind of day. She turned and continued walking south down Madison Avenue. The wind blew her skirt against the backs of her legs and made her hair flow past her face, tickling her cheeks and forehead. She knew she would arrive at her mother's apartment looking rumpled and would have to find a mirror and tidy up. It had puzzled her throughout her girlhood and still puzzled her today that her mother never looked rumpled no matter what the weather was like. Angela Beaulieu always looked as cool, smooth, and elegant as a porcelain doll. How did she do it? By simply *refusing* to let a wind or anything else interfere with the way she wanted to look, Kim thought.

A flurry of white, pink, and yellow paper rushed past Kim, and simultaneously she heard a young woman squeal behind her: "My God, the sales reports! My boss will *kill* me!" Several young women ran past in pursuit of the escaping papers, but their luck was not good. The colorful flurry got caught in an updraft and swooped up toward the sky. "My *God!*" screamed the distraught custodian, watching helplessly, hands against her cheeks. "What am I going to *do*? My God, Paula! I might as well shoot myself!"

Leaving Paula to comfort her friend, Kim walked on. The wayward papers had drawn her attention to the sky. It was filled with moving masses of cloud, and its colors were increasingly strange. Mixed with the heavy blue-blacks and dark grays were swirls of pale yellow and yellow-green. Blue-sky openings appeared from time to time, shone for a few minutes, and then rapidly closed up. Occasionally, shafts of golden sunlight pierced the tumbling clouds, creating an eerie illumination that somehow made the day seem darker.

Turning east off Madison Avenue, Kim looked back. It was a casual glance; she did not really expect to see anything alarming. But to her surprise, she once again glimpsed the man in the chocolate-brown suit.

The frightening thought came for the first time: he is following me.

It could all be a silly mistake, she knew. But the fact was that she *had* received a threatening phone call warning her off the subject of buildings and high winds.

She stood still for half a second, irresolute. Her attention was distracted by a loud cracking noise next to her. A carelessly secured tarpaulin was pulling loose from a pickup truck. Ropes still held one end, but the free end was flapping and slapping in the wind. When Kim looked again for the big man, he was gone. But she did see a gaunt man in a gray suit, holding down an oversized hat that the wind wanted to tug from his head.

It could all be my imagination, Kim thought. And yet . . .

Suppose, she thought, just suppose Danny was right. Suppose the two men Danny saw outside the building this morning really were the same two who scared her in New Jersey. Could it be they are here now to intimidate a different target?

Kim started to walk east. In the lee of buildings along this side street, the al fresco lunch-hour party was especially dense. Making headway through it without rudeness was all but impossible. Kim managed tolerably well by setting her face in an apologetic smile and making a lot of polite noises. The crowds were essentially good-humored, but she sensed a powerful, pent-up excitability just beneath the surface. Any belligerent shoving or careless elbowing could provoke a flare-up of hot tempers.

In any case she did not want to seem to be hurrying. Nor did she permit herself to look back. For she was aware that she had a tactical advantage over her pursuers, if they were indeed pursuers. If this episode was not merely a concoction of her imagination, or Danny's, or both, then Kim's advantage was that she knew she was being followed and knew by whom. Their disadvantage was that they did not know she knew.

And so she deliberately avoided the appearance of fleeing. The yearning to look behind her was nearly intolerable. It was an itch between the shoulder blades, a physical twisting of the neck. She fought against it and barely won. She entered the New World Center by one of its side doorways and found herself in a wide corridor lined on both sides with expensive little shops. She walked down the corridor and came out into an open area dominated by the D'Alembert Lounge, which was doing a thundering business. Beyond that was the glittering lobby of the hotel, and on the other side of the lobby were the elevators.

As a multiple-use building, the New World Center had three distinct sets of elevators. One set served the hotel on the lower floors; a higher-rising set served offices in the middle of the building; and finally the highest-rising set—the so-called tower elevators—were the exclusive province of apartment condominiums at the top. It was possible to interchange among the sets on a few floors, but on the whole the elevators were planned and placed so that traffic from one set would not trip over traffic from another. Kim found the tower elevators. While waiting for an available car, she finally permitted herself to look around.

The two men were standing right behind her, studiously examining the floor and ceiling.

There was now no further doubt in Kim's mind that these were the men of Danny's nightmares. The big man had a swollen, misshapen ear. There was something frightening about him. Kim did not know exactly what it was. A lack of warmth, perhaps, or an indefinable meanness about the eyes or mouth. He looked like a man who was capable of using violence coldly, perhaps even with relish, to achieve his ends. With his crewcut hair and pale gray eyes he had a Nazi look, Kim thought.

He carried a black briefcase, but not by its handle. Instead he held it hugged against his side with one arm and elbow. The other hand rested on its top, as though he wanted to be ready to reach into it at any moment. What could be in it? A gun? A knife?

Kim was badly frightened. She knew it would be a mistake to get into a tower elevator with these men. Traffic to the upper floors was not heavy. Indeed, at this very moment there seemed to be no other prospective riders waiting to go to the condominiums. If she were to get into an elevator, Kim realized, in all likelihood she would find herself shut up alone in it with her pursuers. She did not know just what the big man had in his briefcase or what he had in mind, but she was perfectly sure she did not want to find out the hard way.

The two men were carefully looking everywhere but at her. She responded by keeping her eyes off them. They still seemed not to know she was aware of them as pursuers. That meant they would not be prepared for a surprise move on her part. But what could that move be?

Kim felt panic rising as she searched for a useful idea. Her mind screamed with questions to which there were no answers. Should I run? Scream for a security guard? But suppose that provokes them into a desperation response? They'll know they aren't hidden anymore. Will they decide they might as well assault me in public?

She felt herself starting to tremble, but then her AA training came to her aid immediately and automatically. There are many ways to conquer the shakes; you experiment until you find what works for you. With Kim, it was adding sixes. She drew a deep breath and added multicolored sixes in her head. A red six and a blue six produced a purple twelve, which faded to white. A green-and-yellow six now produced a chartreuse eighteen. . . .

It was a form of self-hypnosis. The relief of muscular tension was instantaneous and complete. Kim felt tight tendons loosening in her neck and shoulders. She knew, with a confidence born of years of experience, that her nervousness now would be virtually undetectable to anybody who did not know her well.

But the trick of adding sixes did not solve the objective problem at hand. Just as a bright golden emerald-encrusted thirty-six was coming to radiant life in Kim's mind, an elevator arrived and the doors slid open.

Time, she thought. I need more time.

She looked at her watch and frowned, trying to give the impression that she had just remembered a forgotten errand. Then, without hurrying, she walked away from the tower elevators.

She paused, looking around, undecided. She could phone for help, perhaps. Or find a security guard and try to explain her problem to him. But would her story be believable? "I'm being followed by two sinister-looking men, officer." Wouldn't that just get her laughed at?

While she was trying to resolve this dilemna, people bustled by her. A business-suited man walking backward, taking leave of a friend, bumped into her and apologized with an embarrassed smile. She realized that she was standing in the outflow from the office-level elevators. Not far away was a display board bearing the names of office tenants.

She walked to the board. A half-formed idea was in her mind now. It took shape more clearly when she scanned the names on the board. There were many well-known corporate names here. One that caught her eye randomly was GTE. A huge, international company such as that, involved in defense work, undoubtedly concerned about terrorists, political fanatics, crackpots, and other unwanted visitors, would certainly have some kind of security provisions in its reception area. Kim noted the floor number of GTE's office suite, then marched resolutely to the elevators.

In contrast to the tower elevators, these were larger and comfortingly crowded. Kim boarded an elevator with a dozen other people. When she turned to face front, she saw that the two pursuers had also come on board.

She started to tremble again. She added sixes with visual aid from the lighted floor-number display above the elevator doors. That calmed her. She was also reassured by the warm and solid bulk of other people separating her from the

crewcut man and his briefcase. But she was troubled by a
sudden *what if* speculation that intruded among the sixes.
What if all these good people got off the elevator at some of
the lower floors?

Luckily that did not happen. And when she stepped off
the elevator at GTE's floor, she saw immediately that her
thinking had been correct. She found herself in an elevator
lobby from which they were only two exits. One was a
solid-looking door, undoubtedly locked. The other way out
led past a glass-enclosed security desk, behind which sat a
uniformed guard.

Without needing to look behind her, Kim was certain the
two pursuers had stepped off the elevator with her. She
walked up to the security desk. The guard was a black man
with a polite but brisk manner. He asked Kim how he could
help her. She had pulled her wallet from her handbag, and
now she found her press identification card and pushed it
through the guard's window slot.

"I'm Kim Beaulieu of *Seven Days*," she explained. "I'm
supposed to meet my partner here. Is it all right if I wait?"

"Do you have an appointment?"

"I think so, but my partner was going to handle that. He
should be here soon. If I could wait . . . "

The guard gave her a skeptical look, then examined her
ID card. It bore her photograph and certified that she was
a member of the *Seven Days* editorial staff. Nick had told
her she would not need it often, but there would be times
when it could get her in and out of tight situations. This was
its first test.

The guard finally slid the card back to her. "Have a seat
over there, Ms. Beaulieu," he said, pointing to a waiting
room area furnished with armchairs and a sofa.

Kim settled herself in an armchair and watched the two
men in the elevator lobby. She would have been amused by
their dilemma if she had not been so scared. They could

neither leave the lobby nor stay in it. The guard was eyeing them sharply, as they were surely aware. They fidgeted, paced, held a whispered consultation. Finally the guard stood and called to them over the top of his glass shield: "Can I help you gentlemen?"

Kim saw that he was armed. Without doubt, too, the electronic equipment on his desk included some means of summoning help quickly if he should need it.

The gaunt man replied, "No, we—uh—"

"Seems like we got the wrong floor," the big man said.

"Yeah, right," the gaunt man agreed. He hurriedly pressed the elevator "down" button.

The guard remained standing, watching them silently. At last an elevator came and they were gone.

A wave of relief washed over Kim, but its soothing effect did not last long. She had escaped, but probably only temporarily. The two pursuers did not look like men who would give up easily. Whatever they wanted from Kim, they had already gone to a lot of trouble to get it and undoubtedly would be willing to go to a lot more. If she went back down to the lobby, she could find one or both waiting for her.

She gave herself a wry internal grin and thought: all right, Miss Smarty-Pants. *Now* what?

She sat. The guard glanced at her curiously once a minute. He plainly was not going to let her sit there unchallenged for any great length of time.

A door near the guard's desk opened and an excited group of people poured out toward the elevators. They greeted the guard cheerily. Kim gathered that they were employees who had been sent home early because of the rising wind. More waves of people followed. The elevator lobby filled with a happy throng. Kim wondered if she could elude the pursuers by burying herself among all these people. Could she ride down to the lobby and slip away unobserved? She quickly decided that her chances of pulling that off were pitifully small.

What *am* I going to do, then?

Well, if I can't ride down, I might as well ride up. Maybe one of Edna Jane's cuke sandwiches will help me think.

She stood and walked past the watching guard to the elevator lobby, where she pressed the "up" button. She asked a man if he knew where she could change to a tower elevator. He said he thought it could be done on fifty-five.

When her elevator arrived, she looked inside before boarding. The only other passengers were three women. At the fifty-fifth floor she once again looked about warily before committing herself and leaving the elevator's sanctuary. There was no sign of the two men. She walked along empty, echoing corridors until she found the tower elevators.

Her mother's floor was sixty-eight. She rode to sixty-seven instead. She did not know how much the two men knew about her, but she thought it was possible they were aware of her mother's residence at the New World Center. They might be waiting for her up there right now, or one of them might be. If that were so, and if she were to arrive in an elevator, she would be trapped. And so she planned to walk the last part of the journey.

On the condominium floors of the Center, stairway doors were in the elevator lobbies. The stairs were of concrete and steel, so it was possible to climb them absolutely silently in stocking feet. Kim took off her shoes and padded up to the sixty-eighth floor. For a while she listened with her ear to the heavy steel-clad firestop door. She heard nothing but a low-pitched hum—the sound of a thousand distant and diverse mechanisms at work in various parts of the gigantic building. Then, very carefully, she opened the door a crack and peered into the lobby.

It was empty.

A minute later she was hugging Edna Jane Cullum, the nurse and maid who had become a well-loved friend.

• • •

Kim walked into the huge living room and found her mother on the phone. While Angela continued to converse into the phone, the two of them exchanged a cheek-to-cheek embrace of genuine affection. Kim then walked to the great north window and looked up at the dark, sun-shot sky. The wind blustered against the window and moaned around the building's corner. Overhead was an almost perfectly round blue-sky opening in the clouds. Within the opening Kim could see white streaks of higher cloud, immeasurably far away. The effect of enormous, lonely distances brought a feeling of fullness into Kim's throat, the feeling that precedes tears. But as she watched, the opening elongated into an eye shape, and the eye quickly squeezed shut.

She remained at the window while her mother finished talking on the phone. Kim gathered that the other party to the conversation was Sarah Millington. She gathered further that her mother and Sarah were pleased because the guests coming to the proposed Big Wind party were displaying resourcefulness. Many had checked into the hotel downstairs, with plans to stay at least until tomorrow. Thus they would not need to be concerned if the wind disrupted transportation. Other guests had checked into an equally expensive hotel down the street. As is true in many parts of New York, this neighborhood was honeycombed with underground shopping arcades and pedestrian tunnels. It was possible to get from one hotel to the other without ever exposing oneself to the weather outdoors. Most guests were planning to arrive at the party without even getting their hair mussed.

Kim's mother was winding up the conversation. "Listen,

dear heart, I really must go," she was saying, "I've got a million things still to do, and Kim is here for lunch. I'll talk to you later."

Hearing the sound of the phone receiver being replaced in its cradle, Kim whirled around. "Mother," she said, "I really must talk to you about this party. You've got to—"

"Enough!" Angela Beàulieu said sharply, jumping to her feet with one small hand held out in a "stop" gesture. She was smaller than Kim and had a fragile look, but she was still capable of exercising maternal authority on the rare occasions when she chose to do so. "I'll say this just once, Kim," she went on in a more controlled voice. "I won't listen to lectures about my party. One more word about it from you and out you go. Clear?"

It was clear. Kim stood looking down into her mother's sky-blue eyes and knew it would be pointless to argue. There was some kind of steel in this mother of hers. It seldom showed because Angela Beaulieu, rich at birth and still richer by marriage, had not lived the kind of life in which steel is needed often. But when circumstances did call for it, there it was.

Kim said, "You mean you'd turn me out without even feeding me?"

"Of course not, dear heart. What I mean is that I'll tell Edna Jane to put your cucumber sandwich in a paper bag, and you can go and eat it at your office."

"Well, I guess I'd rather stay."

"You'll be good?"

Kim sighed and nodded. "I'll be good."

They hugged each other fondly. Kim's mother said, "I thought we'd eat in the library. Anywhere else, we'll be in the way."

Kim heard the clink and rattle of party preparations in the kitchen and dining room. "That'll be nice," she said. "May I make a phone call first?"

"Of course, dear."

Kim thought of using the phone in her mother's study for privacy, then decided that would exaggerate the call's importance in her mother's mind. Her mother, she knew, had no compunctions about eavesdropping on phone calls when her curiosity was aroused. And so Kim made the call from the phone that stood on an antique desk in a corner of the vast living room.

She was calling Nick Pacifico. She knew he would understand about the two pursuers without her needing to do a lot of explaining. He would not laugh at her story or her fear and perhaps would be able to help her elude the two men.

Unfortunately he was not in his office, and nobody knew where to find him. She next thought of calling her father but was dissuaded by the sight of her mother across the room, carefully rearranging some flowers in a vase but quite obviously listening with full attention. Kim knew her story of pursuit would require more explanation to her father than to Nick, and the explanation would undoubtedly upset her mother.

She decided to wait half an hour and try Nick again. She and her mother went into the library, where Edna Jane had already set up little folding tables bearing cream of asparagus soup, cucumber sandwiches on thin pumpernickel bread, and iced tea, all tastefully dressed and garnished. It was the kind of light but fussy lunch Kim had not enjoyed for a long time. She had grown used to the hearty, nononsense fare and surroundings of McDonald's.

"My, such elegance!" she commented, partly to tease and partly because she found the change pleasing. "So this is how the rich live, is it?"

"Haven't you been eating well?" asked her mother, looking worried.

"Oh, stop being so motherly, Mother. Of course I eat well—just in a different style, that's all."

"Different how?"

"Oh, we eat at luncheonettes, McDonald's, places like that."

"Who is 'we'?"

"The staff. The people I work with."

"Including that Nick Pacifico? The man you were just trying to call?"

There was a not-quite-finished smile on her mother's face. Kim did not know whether the question was meant teasingly or should be taken as a more serious probing. She decided to respond casually. "Sure," she said, "he eats with us when he's around. Or if he and I happen to be out on assignment together—"

"Are you sure there isn't more to it than that?"

"What *are* you gibbering about, Mother? He's my mentor, that's all."

"Really all?" That mischievous half-smile was still on her mother's face. "I've been hearing you talk about him for weeks now, and it sounds to me—"

"Your imagination needs cooling off, Mother. Have you been at the hashish again? What gives you such a nutty idea?"

"Kimberley Kim. I'm your mother, remember me? I've known you longer than you've known yourself."

Kim suddenly decided to stop arguing. She looked at her mother, shrugged, grinned, and bit into a delicious cucumber sandwich.

Maybe her mother was right, she thought. There was something she felt when she was with Nick Pacifico. There was *something* between them. But whatever it was, it was formless and unnamed. Neither one of them had ever done anything about it or sought to explore its nature. All Kim knew about it was that it was pleasant and exciting, and it seemed to ask some questions to which the answers, though hidden, hovered somewhere nearby.

"You really are a smarty-pants, Mother," she said finally.

Her mother smiled at her but said nothing.

They finished their lunch companionably, talking of family trivia. Kim made another attempt to phone Nick, but he was still away from his desk. The wind howled around the building more loudly than before, Kim thought. Its strength must be increasing. She was anxious to get back to the office. She decided to find a phone booth in the lobby downstairs and call her father.

"Where will you spend tonight?" her mother asked as they were parting.

Kim stared at her mother, momentarily speechless. Where *would* she spend this scary night? Alone in her apartment? She had not faced the question squarely before, but now she knew the answer without needing to think about it. She wanted to be with Nick and Daniela.

It was exactly the right question for her mother to have asked. Kim replied by kissing her mother and saying, "I don't know yet. I love you. Tonight, Mother . . . please be careful."

●   ●   ●

The elevator took her down to the ground-floor lobby without incident. To her relief, several other riders boarded on the way down, so that she stepped out in the lobby cozily enclosed in a little clump of people. The clump dispersed immediately, but she saw no sign of the two pursuers. She looked around until she saw a sign indicating where she could find public phones. She started in that direction, thinking that a phone call might be unnecessary after all. Perhaps the pursuers had given up. Perhaps they had intended only to scare her in the same way as they had scared Danny. Perhaps the whole episode was a product of her imagination, as she had thought when it began.

But then she saw the gaunt man. He was in between her and the phones. He was walking toward her through the crowds, watching her unblinkingly.

She turned. The big man was behind her, his briefcase hugged to his side.

She panicked. She made a right-angle turn and fled toward a revolving door that led out to a side street.

The wind had risen markedly. Though this street was protected by buildings, strong gusts blew from one direction to another, making it hard to walk. The air was full of flying things: bits of paper, somebody's hat, a sheet of torn plastic. Kim plunged through the sidewalk party, which was still in progress despite the strengthening gusts. She no longer tried to hide the fact that she was fleeing. When she looked behind her, she saw that the two pursuers were only a few paces back.

She thought it likely now that they intended to grab her or somehow attack her physically in public. They knew she had spotted them as pursuers, so they could no longer hope to achieve their ends by trickery. They must calculate, she thought, that their chances of getting away with a public assault were good on a day such as this. The streets were a nightmare of confusion. Police patrol cars would not be able to get through the jammed traffic, and Kim saw no foot patrolmen.

Heartbeat thumping in her ears, she struggled on through the wind-buffeted crowds. She saw suddenly that she had turned the wrong way in her panic and was headed toward Park Avenue instead of Madison. But there was no hope of turning back.

The wind grew stronger as she approached the Park Avenue corner. She felt a spray of cold water on her face. It was not rain; it was water being blown from the surface of a reflecting pool in front of the New World Center. The pool was surrounded by young sycamore trees that were thrashing wildly in the gale. Their leaves and twigs mixed with other debris in the rushing air.

Kim looked behind her as she turned north and headed into the wind. The two men were now almost close enough to grab her. She saw that the big man was withdrawing something from the black briefcase. It was neither a gun nor a knife. Kim could not identify it for a moment. Then she recognized what it was, but the recognition only increased her fear because she did not understand its purpose. It was an ordinary, short-spouted plastic squeeze bottle, the kind used in diners to dispense mustard and ketchup. The plastic was translucent. Kim's impression was that the bottle contained a clear, yellowish liquid.

The big man handed the briefcase to his partner. Kim was running now, terrified, looking back, bumping into people. The big man removed a cap from the bottle's spout.

"Please help me!" she shouted to some people who were hurrying past. "Find a policeman!" But they could not hear her above the roar of the wind. They only stared.

Then something big and shapeless flew past her. She had a brief impression of green and white stripes. There was a shout from the big man behind her. When she looked back she saw that he was struggling with a large piece of striped canvas that had wrapped itself around his head and upper body. There were metal eyelets along one edge of the canvas. Another edge was ragged and torn. It was apparently a piece of a store's awning that had come loose and been ripped away by the gale.

The big man staggered back, blinded by the canvas, pushed by the wind. He fell on the sidewalk. And then, to Kim's astonishment, he screamed.

"My hand! Jesus Christ, my hand!" he howled hoarsely from under the stiped awning. Kim saw the plastic bottle roll away down the sidewalk, spilling liquid. The gaunt man dropped the briefcase and squatted down to help his partner get free of the canvas. "Get some water!" the big man was shouting. He struggled free and jumped to his feet. He saw the reflecting pool not far away and ran to it. When he got to the edge he fell to his knees and plunged his entire arm into the water, up to the shoulder. Before his hand disappeared under the surface, Kim saw that the skin was bright red.

She understood now. She had had a very narrow escape. She had been saved by the wind.

She felt dizzy and weak. Her knees felt as though they might give way at any moment. She managed to stumble forward into the thundering gale until she reached the next uptown corner, where she turned west toward Madison Avenue. The walking was easier here in the lee of buildings, but the jelly-kneed feeling persisted. Kim pushed weakly through the crowds for a short distance, then decided she had better rest for a while and compose herself.

Ahead of her, a street vendor had parked his cart in the entrance to a parking garage. The location was well sheltered from the wind. A big, friendly crowd had collected there. Kim stumbled through a thicket of hands holding the vendor's doughnuts, coffee, and fruit drinks. She came to a low wall where she would have liked to sit, but people were perched along it solidly like birds on a telephone wire. Overcome by a wave of dizziness, Kim swayed against a woman who was standing next to her.

"Hey!" the woman said. She was a large black woman with a single streak of pure white in her hair. When she saw Kim's face she looked concerned. "Hey, are you all right, honey? You don't look too good. Are you sick?"

Kim made no attempt to deny it. She passed her hand across her forehead, feeling dazed. She started to sway again, but the big woman caught her firmly by the arm.

"Here, you need to sit," the woman said. She led Kim to the low wall. A teenage boy was sitting nearest to Kim. The big woman said, "Hey you! Kid! Off the wall! This lady's sick."

The boy hesitated for a fraction of a second, obviously wondering whether anything could be gained by challenging this large person's authority. Quickly deciding not to try it, he slid off the wall. Kim sat gratefully.

"Oh boy," she said to the big woman. "Thanks."

"Right," the woman said, "now you just sit there, honey. I'm going to get you something to drink."

Kim sat slumped, hugging her handbag. The wind blew and the crowd shouted and laughed, but she hardly heard anything. She was conscious only of her own rapid breathing.

Time must have passed, but she was not aware of it. The big woman abruptly appeared in front of her, holding out a drink in a paper cup. "It's a special fruit punch this man makes," the woman said. "You'll like it."

Kim sipped. The drink had a pleasant grapefruity taste. She felt her composure returning. She drew a deep breath and smiled up at the big woman, who was watching her with a worried frown. "This was just what I needed," Kim said. "How much do I owe you?"

"You don't owe me anything, honey."

"But these street prices aren't cheap. I—"

"No, I was a Girl Scout once," the big woman said with a grin. "I'm supposed to do a good deed once in a while. Listen, do you think you're going to be all right now?"

"Yes, I just had a dizzy spell. I'm feeling fine now."

"Well, all right. But if you need me, I'll be right over here." The woman went to rejoin some friends.

Kim sat and finished the drink. She could feel her tense body relaxing. Her breathing slowed. There was a pleasant warmth in her belly. It was spreading up her chest. She felt as though she were an empty vessel being filled with hot soup. But it was not soup; it was love. She felt a great and glowing love for all these people who were crowded around her, companions for a brief moment along the lonesome road of life. The world was no longer a lonely and frightening place, not with good people like these all around. Would any of them remember her a year from now? Kim hoped so. She was sure she would remember them. She *loved* them!

Suddenly she knew what was happening to her. She recognized these banal and sentimental thoughts. With a strange double shock of pleasure and terror, she realized she was getting drunk.

The cause became apparent immediately. Wandering jovially through the crowd was a barrel-bellied man in what Kim thought was a Navy or Coast Guard uniform. This sailor had obviously been drinking for a long time. His lee scuppers were under. He was waving a half-full bottle of vodka in the air, inviting everybody in sight to have a drink on him. Whenever anybody thrust a paper cup toward him, he sloshed liquor into it.

"More?" he asked Kim. He stood swaying in front of her.

Her first thought was: no. Then she asked herself why it was necessary to turn the man away so hastily. She thought: why not give myself time to decide? She held out her paper cup. The man poured in several ounces of vodka.

Alcoholics differ widely in their reactions to drink. Some, after a period of abstinence, find they have lost all interest in alcoholic beverages. Some find they still like the flavor and effects but are no longer tempted to overindulge. These lucky men and women return to controlled, harmless social drinking and maintain this sobriety for the remainder of their lives. Some find they can drink socially for a time, but that time is limited. After a few months or a year they gradually return to the behavior that can destroy them. And some, taking a first drink after long abstinence, experience a rush of drunkenness and a loss of control so swift and pervasive that nothing seems possible but to succumb to it.

Since the hereditary, physical, and emotional factors responsible for these varied results are not understood, AA members are counseled to assume they belong to the latter group. Kim had always assumed she did. Now she was discovering that the surmise was correct.

She stared at the vodka in her paper cup. How nice it would be to give in to the pull of it. How nice to sink into its warm embrace!

Then she thought: no, no, *no*! Before she could change her mind, she emptied the vodka onto the ground.

She was immediately sorry she had done so. What a foolish and hasty act! How could one more drink do any harm? She should have taken a sip of it, at least.

She stood and pushed through the crowd toward the sailor with the vodka. She wanted to ask him for a refill. But when she got to his side, she saw that his bottle was almost empty. He was trying to pour the last of it into somebody's cup, but a good deal of it was spilling on the ground. "Hey, save some for me!" Kim said, but nobody heard her. Immediately ashamed, she crumpled her paper cup in her fist and walked out of the sheltered area to the street.

A side entrance to the New World Center beckoned. She went in and wandered around the great lobby until she found the D'Alembert Lounge. Drinkers were three deep around the bar. She pushed her way close but was unable to get a bartender's attention. "Hey, what do you have to do to get a drink around here?" she shouted. Some patrons looked at her oddly. Ashamed again, she left quickly and walked up and down. She came to the Center's front entrance and stood for a while looking out at the thrashing sycamore trees and the wind-whipped water of the pool.

Jesus and Mary Macadamia, she thought, inventing a saint because she needed one all her own. What now? What am I going to do?

16

Early in the afternoon, most anemometers in the tri-state region were recording sustained winds in the neighborhood of fifty miles an hour. Admiral Beaufort had called that a "whole gale" and would have entered it on his numerical tabulation as Force Ten.

A whole gale is a powerful and dangerous wind. It can uproot large trees. It can turn ordinary objects into lethal projectiles. It will rip loose shingles, shutters, and TV antennas off houses. It scoops sheets of plywood and other wide-surfaced materials from construction sites. It makes driving a car or truck difficult, except at the slowest speeds.

A whole gale is the highest windspeed in which it is possible to walk and make reasonable headway. People with sound legs and lungs can walk in higher winds, but only with great difficulty. A whole gale allows you to walk if you must.

This is not to say it is a good idea to go out into a whole gale, particularly in an urban or suburban environment with projectiles flying through the air. Throughout the tri-state region that afternoon, people were being urged to keep their cars off the streets and themselves indoors. But of course there were millions who failed to pay attention.

Officialdom was doing its best. Many summer schools, day camps, and other children's activities had been closed for the entire day; and of those that did open, virtually all were closed by noon. Adult activities were also closing down. Many office and factory workers had stayed home, some on orders, some on their own initiative. Most of those who reported for work were on their way back home by mid-afternoon. The twin towers of the Port Authority's World Trade Center in downtown Manhattan, 110 stories high, were evacuated at two o'clock at the strong urging of the Department of Buildings. Some other tall structures were also cleared of people, but this evacuation effort was, on the whole, not very successful. There was a lot of resistance, particularly from residents of high-rise apartments. The effort might have worked better if it had been preceded by a more carefully designed public-education campaign.

The Port Authority began closing the three major metropolitan airports at about one-thirty. Incoming flights were permitted to land until everybody was out of the sky, and that was the end of all flying for the day. The Tappan Zee Bridge was closed not much later when light cars proved unable to handle the rising winds that came howling down the Hudson River. Some officials wanted to close the George Washington Bridge, too, but decided that would cause a riot on the Manhattan side of the river. Instead, all lanes but one on both levels of the bridge were designated west-bound, for use by traffic leaving the city. People who wanted to drive into the city were discouraged by the single lane, as intended. Most turned back while they still had the chance in New Jersey.

Emergency command centers were being activated throughout the region. In Manhattan, the main center was set up at the Police Department's headquarters. Representatives of various city agencies gathered there: Buildings, Traffic, Transportation, Hospitals, Sanitation, Water, the mayor's office. Included in the group also were officials of the local telephone and power companies. The command center was a potentially useful idea that had worked well in many emergencies in the past. On this occasion, however, many of the officials found themselves frustrated by disorganization and confusion. It would all have worked better if somebody such as the Mayor had exercised leadership and begun organizing it several days back.

Overhead, the boiling sky grew ever darker and more strange. Clouds tumbled and whirled around each other. Shafts of golden sunlight still appeared from time to time, piercing the heavy blue-black mass. But these sun shafts were becoming more rare, and the rarer they got, the more startling they were to the eye.

● ● ●

Simon Pollock wished he could see more of that magnificent sky. He and Cissy Medina had managed to clamber aboard a Connecticut-bound bus after three frustrating hours of waiting at the Eighth Avenue Terminal. The fare of $30, payable in cash to the driver, who then kicked back part of it to a dispatcher, was more than three times what one would normally expect to pay for this trip. Despite that, the bus was jammed. Cissy had a seat near the front, while Pollock, a standee, got squeezed toward the rear.

An hour after leaving the terminal, the bus had traveled fewer than ten blocks. It was now stopped dead in traffic. The traffic was so hopelessly dead that drivers were no longer sounding their horns. The wind whistled and roared around them.

Pollock had been unable to see a street sign for a long time. "Does anybody know where we are?" he asked.

"Forty-ninth, I think," said a plump woman seated near him. "Jeez, this is really something, innit?"

"Yeah, and to think it's costing us thirty bucks," said a man sitting next to her. He was a big, muscular man, totally bald, with a waxed-tipped Hercule Poirot mustache. "Hey driver!" he shouted. "How long are we gonna have to sit here?"

"How'm I supposed to know?" the driver grumbled. "I look like I got a crystal ball up here, do I?" The driver was obviously just as exasperated as his passengers.

"Maybe we'll sit here forever," said a man standing next to Pollock. He was a wiry young black man with a transistor radio hanging from his shoulder on a long strap. "This is it, man! Terminal gridlock!" He grinned cheerfully, evidently finding the concept amusing.

"We'll sit here till we starve, looks like," the plump woman predicted gloomily. "Year from now, they'll find our skellintons."

"Hey Mama, I got to pee!" a teenage girl called out, affecting a child's squeaky voice. Her friends shrieked with glee.

"Hey, driver!" the big bald man shouted. "How about I get my thirty bucks back? I want off!"

"Yeah? What for?" the driver snarled.

"This bus ain't *going* anyplace."

"Relax, will ya? We'll get there."

"Yeah? When? Next Christmas?"

"Right!" chorused a dozen other passengers. There was a scramble of movement as people started making their way along the crowded aisle to the front of the bus. They were shouting that they wanted to get off the bus and wanted refunds. The driver turned in his seat, looking belligerent. But when he saw the determined passengers advancing on him, including the formidable-looking bald man, he grew instantly polite. He set his parking brake, rose from his seat and turned to face the passengers. He held up his hands in a placatory gesture.

"Okay, okay," he said. "You want refunds, you'll get refunds. I ain't gonna argue. You want off the bus, it's up to you. But listen. You get off, where you figure to *go*?"

"There's a luncheonette right across the street there," the bald man said, gesturing with his thumb.

"And a bar next to it," somebody else pointed out.

"Yeah," said the bald man. "One way or the other, I figure I'll be better off out there than sitting in this thing. So how about my money?"

"Okay." The driver shrugged and pulled a fat wad of money from a pocket of his jacket. "Anybody who wants off, I'll refund twenty."

"Whaddya mean, twenty?" thundered the bald man. "I paid you thirty, friend!"

"Well, you gotta get the other ten from the dispatcher," the driver explained optimistically.

"Never mind that shit!" the bald man roared. There was a solid chorus of agreement from his fellow passengers. "I paid thirty getting on, and by God I'll collect thirty getting off!" The crowd howled and hooted in hearty endorsement.

The driver saw immediately that he was in a debate that he could not win. The only question was how painful he wanted his defeat to be. He elected to take it the easy way.

As passengers climbed off the bus with refunds in hand, others settled into vacated seats or stood irresolutely, trying to sort out the tradeoffs. The young black man standing next to Pollock seemed to be having a lot of trouble making up his mind. "You staying?" he asked Pollock.

Pollock shrugged. "For a while. There's no hurry, seems to me."

"Figure you'll get off later, you mean?"

"If the bus doesn't move."

The young man nibbled at a thumbnail. Finally he said, "Ah, the hell with it. Reckon I'll go get me something to eat."

He started to walk off. Pollock said, "Wait!"

"Yeah?" The young man looked surprised.

"That radio of yours. Does it work?"

"Sure."

"Would you—uh, care to sell it to me?"

After some good-humored haggling, they settled on a price of thirty dollars, not including the carrying strap, which was a gift from the young man's sister. The little radio worked well. Several news broadcasts were coming in loud and clear.

Passengers continued to trickle off the bus one by one. Pollock finally found a seat next to Cissy Medina. As he did so, unexpectedly, the bus lurched forward. They traveled for nearly an entire block before once again coming to a halt in gridlocked traffic.

They were in a grimy old neighborhood of small, sooty buildings. A block to the north a tall, shiny office tower loomed against the rushing dark sky. Nothing else in the neighborhood was new. Near the bus was a large, busy cafeteria, and not far from that, inevitably, a bar. The bar sought dignity by calling itself a cocktail lounge, but the pink neon sign flickered uncertainly, lacking confidence in its own statement. The cafeteria and bar both had a dingy and shadowed look, darkened by the residue of yesterday's soured dreams. The wind blew dust and paper along the unswept sidewalks. Gridlocked motorists and bus passengers looked out at the neighborhood and longed for destinations far away.

"Do you think we're right to stay on the bus, Simon?" Cissy asked.

"I think so. For the time being." As a meteorologist, Pollock was good at calculating odds and felt comfortable dealing with uncertainties. "If this traffic ever gets moving, we could be in Connecticut in an hour and a half."

"Is that enough time? I mean before the wind gets too high?" In the past few hours he had told her much about his expectations of the coming wind.

He replied, "It could be. At the moment I think it's a chance worth taking. I think—let's stay here a while and see what happens."

To his astonishment, Cissy suddenly reached out and took his hand. "I'm glad I'm not in this all by myself," she said.

"Me, too," Pollock said. He wished he could have thought of something wittier or more urbane to say, but he had never been known for the sparkle of his conversation.

"I'm kind of scared," she said.

"Yes." Once again Pollock tried to think of a clever rejoinder, and once again he failed. He finished by saying lamely, "If you want the truth—me, too."

Yes, Pollock was scared. But he was also exhilarated. The reasons he had given for a decision to stay aboard the bus were perfectly sound, entirely logical. But there was another reason, an overridingly powerful one that he could not have explained clearly to anybody else and did not fully understand himself. It was simply this: he wanted to be out in the weather.

He recognized the illogic of this huge, vague motive. He knew he could have monitored the wind just as well by sitting comfortably in the cafeteria window with a mug of coffee. But here on the bus, he was not looking out *at* the weather; he was *in* it. Or so he felt.

He watched wind-bullied pedestrians struggling along the sidewalks. He thought he would like to be out there with them, arguing with the gale, feeling its mighty push and joyfully pushing back. But he was also enjoying Cissy Medina's closeness and the warmth of her hand. He stayed where he was, surrounded by the wind's loud fury yet protected from it.

If the traffic did not loosen and open up soon, he knew, it would be sensible to leave the bus and seek shelter in a building. Sooner or later, the wind would rise to such force that walking would be impossible. Any passengers who were still left in the bus at that point would be trapped in it. So it would be prudent to keep monitoring the radio news broadcasts and keep watching pedestrians on the sidewalks. Pollock knew he would be able to tell when the time came to leave the bus.

At the moment, most people on the sidewalks were getting where they wanted to go. A frail old woman was having some difficulty but was being helped along by two young women. In stark contrast, two kids with skateboards were having the time of their lives.

The bus crept forward once more. But after traveling less than its own length, it stopped again. The passengers all groaned.

I won't give up on the traffic yet, Pollock thought. If we can once get rolling, Connecticut isn't very far away.

•   •   •

Kim did not know how long she had been standing at the front entrance of the New World Center, gazing out at the windy world without seeing it. She was standing near a ceiling-high pane of glass between two revolving doors. The glass was tinted smoky gray. It looked and felt soothing. She rested her forehead against it and closed her eyes.

"You look troubled," said a soft voice. "Can I help?"

Kim opened her eyes and was surprised to see a woman standing next to her. The woman was short and round-faced. Her eyes were gray. She looked at Kim from behind a pair of small, unstylish glasses. She wore a dowdy brown suit. A large wooden cross hung from a chain looped around her neck.

"My name's Amanda," the woman said. "I'm a Congregational minister. If I'm intruding, just tell me to go away."

"No, don't go!" Kim said, startled by her own instinctive response. She realized she must look and sound frightened.

She tried to soften that impression by smiling, but knew the smile was not convincing. Then she asked herself what was the sense of trying to fake a cheerfulness she did not feel. She said, "You're right, I'm in trouble. I don't know what to do. I mean I know what I *should* do, but I don't know what I *want* to do. I mean—"

She realized she was babbling and stopped. A tear ran down her cheek. She wiped it away with a knuckle.

"We can sit down over here," the minister said. In the Center's outer lobby there were a few backless stone benches, matching the ones outdoors around the pool. Kim followed the little brown-suited woman and sat on a bench next to her.

They sat in silence for a short time, the minister with her hands folded quietly on her lap, Kim with fists clenched against her mouth. Kim relaxed gradually and lowered her hands to her lap. The minister reached over, gave Kim's nearest hand an easy pat and then a squeeze, and withdrew. She still said nothing, but the gesture seemed to say, "I'm here if you want to talk to me," It also said, "And if you *don't* want to talk to me, that will be all right, too." Kim felt no coercion or sense of hurry.

Kim finally said, "Would you like to hear a long, dopey story?"

"Dopey?" The minister smiled. "Well, why don't you tell it and we'll see what we can make of it."

Kim paused to collect her thoughts. Then she said, "I'm an alcoholic. Do you know anything about alcoholics?"

"I attended a week-long seminar on alcoholism some years back. I can't say that makes me an expert, but—yes, I've counseled alcoholics. I think—I hope I've been helpful a few times."

Kim nodded, encouraged. At least she did not have to go through the basics with this dowdy little minister. She did not have to waste her time and energy battling the centuries-old belief that alcoholism is a moral problem rather than a physical one. She said, 'It began early with me, in high school. I was a sort of awkward kid. Alcohol was a wonderful discovery. It helped me become the person I'd always wanted to be, glamorous, witty—you know. I liked myself better after a drink or two. . . ."

The minister listened attentively as Kim told her story. It is a rare skill to be a good listener, Kim had often thought. In her troubled lifetime she had tried to explain her problems to many: teachers, psychiatrists, specialists in alcoholic counseling. Most of these people had been rather poor listeners because each had his or her own special agenda to impose or province to defend. Instead of hearing what she was saying, they heard their own conceptions superimposed on her words. "Ah, yes, Kim, I believe what you are *really* saying is . . ." More than once she had wanted to stand up and shout, "I'm saying what I'm *saying*! Why can't you listen?"

And here was this perfect stranger, this little wandering minister, doing exactly that. When Kim had finished, the minister looked at her placidly for a moment, then looked out at the windy street, digesting what she had heard. Finally she looked back at Kim and said, "You started out by saying you were confused about what you should do and what you want to do. But I've got to say I don't hear very much confusion in your voice."

"You don't?"

"Not really. Should and want: it seems to me they're the same in your case. Aren't they?"

"I don't know. I—"

"Unless there's something wrong with my ears, what I hear is that you want to go back to your office. You want to be with this man Nick and his daughter Danny. Isn't that so?"

"Of course! But—"

"You want that an awful lot more than you want another drink, it seems to me. At least, I think that's what you've been telling me. Isn't it?"

"Yes."

"Well, all right, then. Why all this shilly-shallying around?" The minister jumped to her feet and held out her hand. "Come on. Let's go."

Kim was startled. "You mean you'll walk it with me?"

"Yes, of course."

"But the wind—"

"Oh, it isn't blowing that hard, yet. Besides, there isn't a great deal of me to catch it. But we'd better get started. Come on."

Kim took the offered hand and allowed herself to be pulled to her feet. She and the minister locked arms and went out into the howling gale together.

* * *

Pacifico and Danny were waiting in the ground-floor lobby of the *Seven Days* building. The magazine's staff had been dismissed, as had the staffs of other corporate tenants in the building. Some had swept unfinished work into desk drawers and left in happy haste. Those who were more conscientious, or who enjoyed their jobs more, had stayed to finish what they were doing. The lobby was crowded with people carrying survival packs.

Pacifico and Danny were watching the main doors that led out to Madison Avenue. They were hoping to see Kim. She had said she was going to the New World Center to have lunch with her mother. She should have returned half an hour ago.

"I don't know, Miss Mousy," Pacifico said dubiously. "I think maybe we'll have to give up on her. If we don't get to the subway soon, it may be too late."

His plan was to spend the night in the basement of his

apartment building downtown. It was a three-story brick building in an area of other small buildings. He felt it would be about as safe as anywhere in the city. He would have preferred to take a taxi for Danny's safety, but one look at the clogged street traffic had told him it would have to be the subway, like it or not.

"Let's wait five more minutes, Daddy," Daniela urged, squeezing his hand. "Just five. Please!"

"All right. Five minutes. Then we really must make tracks."

"Come *on*, Kim!" Danny said, hopping with urgency on her good leg.

Pacifico was not perfectly sure whether it had been his own idea or Danny's to ask Kim to spend the night with them. He was not even sure whether it would be necessary to ask her. In some odd way, with no words directly spoken, the arrangement seemed to be understood.

He did not know how it had all come about. What he did know was that his wish to see Kim coming through those doors was every bit as strong as Danny's. Probably stronger.

"Come on, Kim!" Danny pleaded. Her voice was full of frustration. She sounded close to tears.

Pacifico felt as though he might be able to weep, too. He had in the pit of his belly a feeling that the people of New York City faced a night such as they had never known before. It would be a night of catastrophic upheaval. Loved ones would be separated. People would die. Friends and family members would lose track of each other, perhaps never again to pick up the threads. Kim had to come through those doors now because later would be too late. If she did not appear *now*, Pacifico thought, he would never see her again.

"Come on, Kim, come *on*!" Danny said miserably.

She looked at the clock on the wall, then looked quickly at her father to see if he had seen her looking. He gave her thin shoulder a squeeze. "Yes, I know," he said. "The five minutes are up."

"Just a few more minutes, Daddy! Please, *please!*"

"Yes, okay, we'll wait a while longer."

The truth was that he did not need Danny's urging to make him extend the wait. Kimberley Beaulieu, he thought. You troubled and lovely woman. You must come through those doors. You *must.* For I cannot face the rest of my life without you.

A familiar figure appeared at the doors, struggling to make headway in the wind. But it was not Kim. It was Alice Wenska, the librarian. She pushed her way into the lobby, saw Pacifico and Daniela, and walked up to them. She was wind-rumpled and out of breath.

"Oh, boy," she panted. "What a wind!"

"Where are you coming from?" Pacifico asked, puzzled.

"Lexington Avenue. I wanted to take the subway to my apartment, but it turns out the subways are all closed."

"*Closed?*"

"Yes. There are crowds of people down there looking for shelter. They're starting to spill along the tracks, so I gather the mayor or somebody ordered all the electric power shut off."

"Leaving a lot of us stranded."

Alice Wenska shrugged. "It looks that way," she said mildly.

Pacifico was not so even-tempered. "A typical Millington muck-up," he said sourly. "If he'd announced last night that he was going to close the subways at a certain hour, people could have planned around it. What a jackass! He doesn't anticipate events. He just stands there till they hit him on the head."

"Oh, well." Alice shrugged philosophically again. "At least we all have survival packs. We won't starve."

Pacifico carried emergency supplies in an old airline bag, Danny in a canvas book bag, Alice in a plastic shopping bag from Macy's. "Sure," Pacifico growled. "We won't starve. No thanks to the mayor."

"Oh, maybe he's just overworked," Alice suggested generously. "Nobody can think of everything."

"Don't make excuses for the man, Alice. He's an incompetent jerk. He—"

"Daddy, Alice!" shouted Daniela joyfully. "Here's Kim!"

They saw Kim make her way to the doors, arm-in-arm with a small woman in a brown suit. The small woman shouted something in Kim's ear, then turned and went back in the direction she had come from. Kim pushed into the lobby. Her cheeks were wind-reddened. Her short blonde hair was in wild disarray. She saw Pacifico hurrying toward her. She threw herself into his arms.

"I thought maybe I'd lost you," he said into her ear. "Sweet Kim. Don't scare me like that any more."

"I won't, Nick, I promise," she said, hugging him.

He saw Alice and Daniela watching. Alice looked startled. Danny was wearing a big, open-mouthed grin.

Kim broke away from him and said, "I left my survival pack on my desk. Wait for me." She gave Danny a kiss and Alice a hug. "Oh, it's so good to be back with all of you!"

"You talk as if you've been a million miles away," Pacifico said, perplexed by an overtone of meaning he could not define.

She looked at him for a moment, then said, "I have."

Pacifico watched her board an elevator. He did not understand what she meant. But he did understand that, in some unknown way, she had come perilously close to vanishing from his life that afternoon.

17

ABRUPTLY, WITH NO warning, the wind increased to hurricane force late in the afternoon.

In Admiral Beaufort's classification, any wind higher than 56 knots, or about 67 miles an hour, was a hurricane. The admiral called that a Force Twelve wind, and there he left it. He made no attempt to divide hurricanes into categories. It is not known whether he ever experienced a hurricane in person. But as an officer of the British Navy, which ruled most of the world's seas in his time, he undoubtedly knew what a hurricane was. He knew that this was a wind of such terrible violence that no ship had any reasonable hope of surviving in it. Since all hurricanes meant death to a sailor, all hurricanes were essentially alike.

But in later years, the U.S. National Weather Service did classify these prodigious storms that came shrieking out of the Caribbean Sea. Admiral Beaufort's deadly Force Twelve winds are now thought of as coming in five gradations. The least destructive is a wind of up to 95 miles an hour, and is designated Category One. The most destructive is Category Five: a wind of more than 155 miles an hour.

Hurricanes of Category One are common. It is not unusual for half a dozen or more to develop in a single autumn season. Though they can cause deaths, injuries, and property damage, they are not greatly feared. People of the Caribbean speak of them, on the whole, as just another of life's damned nuisances.

Hurricanes of Category Five are too frightening to think about. They are considered hundred-year storms—meaning that, statistically, such a storm should be expected to develop roughly once every century. A hurricane that hit New England in September, 1938, may have been the only Category Five storm of the twentieth century so far. An observatory at Harvard University measured gusts over 180 miles an hour, but anemometers back then were notoriously unreliable in dealing with high wind speeds. Many meteorologists believe that storm may have been only a Category Four. That was bad enough. In terms of deaths and property damage, it was a worse disaster than the Chicago fire and the San Francisco earthquake put together.

● ● ●

Simon Pollock had been half-dozing. It had been a long, hard day. He had not slept since he was awakened by his graduate student's phone call in the middle of the night. Now he was sitting in the bus, listening to the wind. Some other passengers were snoring. Cissy Medina's head was resting on his shoulder, but he did not think she was asleep. He liked the faint, soapy fragrance of her thick dark hair.

Suddenly he realized that the bus was rocking and shuddering on its springs. At the same instant he saw that the two boys who had been skateboarding on the sidewalk were in serious trouble.

In the past hour or so the bus had moved one block north. To the right was a collection of the small, sooty buildings that were indigenous to this neighborhood: some dingy stores, some tenements, a grimy hotel. To the left was the interloper he'd seen earlier: a tall new office tower, no doubt built by speculators who had taken advantage of cheap land and hoped it would soon become less cheap. The broad, empty sidewalk in front of the tower was ideal for skateboarding. The two boys had been having too much fun to stop, though both had fallen once or twice. They would whip around the northern corner of the building, race southward down the sidewalk with the gale at their backs, and finally swoop around the southern corner at dizzy speed and come to rest fifty yards down the side street.

They had rested for a time, and now here they came again. As soon as they came around the northern corner and started to pick up speed on the straightaway, Pollock could see they were going much too fast. The wind was screaming. One boy recognized his miscalculation immediately and tried to cut his losses like a good speculator, by stepping off his skateboard. He was not prepared for his own wind-driven forward motion. His body was ahead of his feet. He pitched forward, slammed into the sidewalk and slid on his face. Pollock winced in sympathetic pain. But the boy rolled over with all four limbs apparently still working well, struggled to a kneeling position and crawled to shelter in the building's doorway.

The other boy elected to stay on his board. He must have known it would be impossible to make the southern corner at the ferocious speed he had reached, for at the last moment he covered his head with his hands. He tried to make the turn, but the wind would not let him. He kept going straight. He went off the curb and crashed into a parked car with bone-breaking force. He slid down the side of the car as limply as though he were made of rags, glued to the car by the force of the wind. Finally he slipped down out of sight.

Pollock now knew that he, too, had made a serious miscalculation. To confirm what he was already sure of, he switched on the little radio he had bought. Many stations seemed to have disappeared off the air. Of those that were still broadcasting, most were sporadic and indistinct. Pollock finally found a voice he could understand. The voice said sustained winds of more than 120 miles an hour were now being clocked at Kennedy Airport. Immediately after that, the voice said a new bulletin had just been received. The number was raised to 150.

"Category Five," Pollock mumbled.

"What's that, Simon?" Cissy asked drowsily.

"I'm afraid I've made a bad mistake, Cissy." Pollock was aware his voice was trembling. He tried to prevent it from rising to a squeak. "A very bad mistake. You depended on me . . . I gave you bad advice. I'm sorry."

Cissy sat up. "Simon, what on earth are you talking about?"

"The wind has picked up very suddenly. It caught me by surprise. It's almost up to the strength of a Category Five hurricane—that's the worst kind of all. Walking in that wind out there would be impossible. We're stuck, Cissy. I'm sorry." Pollock felt tears gathering at the corners of his eyes.

Cissy's response surprised him. She took his face in both her hands and kissed his eyes, then his nose, then his forehead. "Don't take blame for what isn't your fault, Simon," she said. "You used your best judgment. We all make wrong calls once in a while." She paused, then added, "I've made some beauts in my time, believe me."

She was giving him a look he could not interpret. He must have frowned a question, for after a while she said, "Like marrying the wrong man."

Pollock stuttered, "You—uh—did?"

"I did." She sighed. "Why couldn't we have met years ago, Simon? I wish—oh, well. All the words of tongue or pen, and all that."

"If only," Pollock agreed.

"Maybe—" she looked at him shyly, "—maybe we can talk about that when this is over."

"Yes, I think we—"

Pollock was interrupted by a sudden commotion in the front of the bus. At the same time he felt a strong eddy of cold wind. He saw that the driver had opened the bifold doors and was in the act of clambering out of his seat. Several passengers near the front were shouting at him.

"I'm leaving!" the driver was yelling. "You want my advice, you'll do the same."

"You mean you're just gonna walk off and leave this bus inna *street*?" asked a woman, sounding incredulous.

"Lady, this bus ain't goin' no place. Look, see that car next to us there? You see any driver at the wheel? You see *anybody* in that car? Yeah, right. And up ahead there, see that yellow Toyota?"

"I wouldn't know a Toyota from a—"

"That yellow car there, I'm talking about. The little one. And off to the side there, the Ford pickup, see it? Well, I been sitting here watching, and I seen everybody get out of that car and that truck a long time ago. I tell you we got abandoned vee-hickles all over the streets! I guarantee you this bus ain't goin' noplace for a hell of a long time. Maybe it'll sit here till it rusts, for all I know."

There was a pause while the passengers digested this. The mighty wind howled and screamed past the open doors. The bus rocked and jiggled.

"But what about us?" the woman finally shouted.

"What do you want me to do, lady?"

"You can't just abandon us! We're your *passengers*! You can't just abandon passengers inna middle of a street!" The woman turned to her fellow passengers for support. "Ain't that right? Must be some kinda law about it."

"Yeah, lady's right, man!" a man shouted.

"Well, what do you want me to *do?*" the driver asked again. "This is a bus, not a goddamn bulldozer! How am I gonna drive this bus through all them abandoned vee-hickles? You wanna tell me that? You got any good suggestions?"

The passengers had no suggestions to offer. The driver stepped down into the stairwell. "Hey!" somebody yelled. "How about our thirty bucks?"

"You see that bar down there? That's where I'll be. You meet me in there."

"Well, at least leave us the key to the bus!" somebody else requested.

"Keys are in the ignition," the driver said. "Traffic opens up, you move the bus over to the side."

"Sure, we'll be happy to do the favor," said the woman who had been arguing with him before. "Seeing you been so good to us. Bastard."

Pollock shouted to the driver, "Don't go out there! You can't walk in this kind of wind!"

The driver shrugged and turned to leave. But a big, bearded black man suddenly jumped to the front of the bus and grabbed the driver by the collar of his jacket. The wind was roaring so loudly now that Pollock could not hear everything that was said, but he thought he heard the word "money." It was evident that the black man was having none of the driver's promise to refund ticket money in the bar down the street. The passenger wanted his refund now.

"Don't go out there!" Pollock was yelling. "You can't make it! You'll kill yourself!"

There was a scuffle in the stairwell. The driver's jacket ripped open. Somehow the driver broke free and fell backward to the street. Pollock watched through a window, horrified. The screaming wind scooped the man up to his feet, then forced him to run at an impossible speed, bouncing and rolling down the right side of the bus toward the rear. He fell to his knees, then got scooped up again. He ran wildly past the rear end of the bus and slammed into the radiator grille of a little red sportster. His jacket snagged on the hood ornament. He kept going: over the hood, over the canvas top and down the back, where he was lost to view. His jacket ripped to shreds instantly. The money he had so stubbornly protected went flying down the avenue like a miniature snowstorm, dispersed and disappeared.

The voice on Pollock's radio was saying something about 190 miles an hour. The transmission was indistinct and kept fading in and out. In one brief spell of clarity, a woman's voice said reports of 240 miles an hour had been received from Chicago. She added, "As far as can be determined, all communication with Chicago is now—" Her voice faded out.

Pollock stood and walked to the front of the bus. Through the big windshield he had a clear view of the fantastic, rushing sky. It was a sky like none he had ever seen before in his life, but it brought back amplified memories of the vast stormy skies he had watched as a boy in Nebraska, and it brought back his lifelong fantasy of soaring among clouds like a hawk. What a sky this was! It flowed like a flood-swollen river. Massive cloud shapes, black and blue-black, brown and green, formed and swirled and re-formed. Pollock was stunned by the terrible beauty of it.

"That's a sky to remember," said a voice at his elbow.

It was a young Japanese man in a business suit. He was sitting in the driver's seat with his square, competent-looking hands resting on the wheel. He had managed to get the bifold doors closed while Pollock's attention was on the sky. It was still windy inside the bus, but the strength of the eddies had diminished markedly.

Pollock replied, "Yes, I never saw a sky like it. It's magnificent."

"Scary as hell, too. It's getting dark fast."

"I think it is, yes." The sky on the northern horizon was monstrously black.

A sudden shower of hard small particles struck the windshield and roof of the bus. They sounded like hail. A few of them got wedged briefly under a windshield wiper. The young Japanese leaned forward to get a closer look. "I'll be damned," he said. "They look like glass." He looked up at Pollock, puzzled. "Little chunks and slivers of glass."

"Oh boy," said Pollock unhappily, realizing immediately what they were. "Windows. Bits of broken windows. Could be from miles away."

"We're in for quite a night, aren't we?"

"I'd say so. Can you operate this bus if we get a chance to move it?"

"Oh sure. I used to drive a bus in California. But I don't really think we're going anywhere."

"Neither do I. I was just asking."

● ● ●

At first Angela Beaulieu was a little disappointed in the turnout. Some of the more dazzling jewels on her invitation list had failed to appear. The French ambassador had been called back to Washington. Lauren Bacall said she had a cold. Other guests, having failed to plan ahead, had been stranded in far places by the breakdown of the nation's transportation system. That annoyed Angela. She would have expected the transportation industry to be more reliable. Whatever happened to old-fashioned resourcefulness? You just couldn't *depend* on people these days!

But Angela's disappointment was mild, for she felt it was still going to be a memorable and newsworthy party. Nearly a hundred of the beautiful, the famous, the influential, and the rich flowed through her apartment's huge rooms as the unnaturally early darkness fell. They were in evening dress. They glittered. They were all gorgeous, even the ugly.

They exclaimed in rapture over the view from the huge north and west windows of her living room. The fantasy sky streamed overhead for their pleasure. Far below, the streets of New York sparkled in the gathering dusk. And the party music was provided by the wind. It moaned, whistled, and crooned against the windows.

Angela's initial disappointment evaporated completely as she watched the party catch fire. Thoroughly experienced as both hostess and guest, she knew the earliest symptoms of party success and failure. She could usually predict within the first hour what the outcome was going to be. Failure, in particular, tended to make itself felt promptly. The guests would seem to congeal into little silent clumps. Corners of the room would grow dark as loneliness seeped in through the cracks. Being at such a party was like being a defendant in a Kafka trial: accused of some unspecified crime under unknown laws, eager to admit guilt but forced to endure the trial anyhow, for the trial was also the punishment. Angela had squirmed through many such experiences.

But this party was going to live! Frozen clumps of people began to thaw and break up. Reluctantly at first, then more boldly, the guests were venturing outward, circulating, testing themselves against strangers. Who could say how many lives would be changed as a result of this party? Perhaps the course of history will be altered, Angela thought. In this very room, at this very moment, statesmen were meeting philosophers; musicians were meeting sculptors; politicians were meeting businessmen. Love affairs were starting. The foundations of future marriages and friendships were being laid. Seeds of grand ideas were floating about, to land on who could say what fertile soil? And it's all because of me, Angela thought. Me! She felt godlike.

She circulated contentedly. Leaning against the great black bulk of the grand piano, splendid in a midnight-blue tux, was Peter James Schenker, the architect who had been principal designer of the New World Center. He had accepted Angela's invitation tardily and, it seemed to her, reluctantly. She wondered whether somebody had pressed him into it for publicity purposes. He looked distinguished with his flowing white hair and long bony face—an artistic face, Angela thought—but he seemed worried and aloof. She introduced him to an impossibly handsome young actor, and that seemed to pep him up.

Near a table of canapes, filling her belly as usual, was fat Moira Shepherd, restaurant critic and occasional high-society reporter of the *New York Times*. Angela did not begrudge her the food; the tubby epicure could stay and stuff herself all night if she wanted to. The same went for the shaggy young photographer who had come with Moira, though Angela considered asking him to put his camera away. Angela did not like either of them personally, but what good was a history-making party if the world did not know about it?

Standing near the great west window, already somewhat tipsy and apparently enjoying herself, was Sarah Millington, Angela's good friend. Sarah was wearing a bright red dress and drinking her favorite cocktail, the so-called "perfect" Manhattan—a taste that had been seized upon and publicized by New York civic boosters. Sarah was a dark, intense, small woman who drank and smoked too much and who, perhaps as a result, was aging visibly faster than her handsome husband. Angela looked around for Spencer Millington and was not surprised to see the mayor engaged in earnest talk with a stunning, six-foot-tall black actress.

There were several other stage and screen folk at the party. They had been invited because they could be counted on to add dazzle to such an affair, but Angela disliked them, on the whole. They were always performing. They all had great mouthfuls of expensive teeth. Angela preferred people among whom she herself could glitter. There were a few corporation presidents and other business leaders here tonight; she liked their relaxed good manners. There were a couple of Congress people. A women's college president. An Air Force general. And of course a black African statesman, a bearded Arabian oil minister, and an agricultural bureaucrat from India. It was virtually compulsory in New York these days to invite some U.N. types to a party such as this.

The party was growing louder, but the music of the wind was still clearly audible. Its noise level, too, had increased. It was howling magnificently. Angela was delighted with the way it was cooperating. It made the party more fun, more—what? Cozy! Yes, that was the word! Why did people come to a party, after all? They came because they wanted it demonstrated to them and others that they were members of an in-group. The world outside might be lonely and unfriendly, but inside, in the warm embrace of the party, each member gorged on a feast of concentrated love and affection. That was what parties were for, Angela believed. The wind underlined it.

She spoke briefly to her maid, Edna Jane Cullum. Edna Jane and Branch, her husband, were a black couple who had been in Angela's employ for years. Both had pearl-gray hair. They were so attractive and competent that they were constantly turning away job offers from other wealthy individuals and families. Thus far they had remained loyal to Angela. Tonight, with their usual quiet efficiency, they were supervising a platoon of temporary helpers supplied for the party by the caterer.

"It's going beautifully, Edna Jane!" Angela said happily.

"Yes, Ms. Beaulieu, it mostly is," Edna Jane nearly agreed. She was a perfectionist for whom nothing was ever perfect. "Some of these temporary folks, though, they think they here for fun instead of work, seem like. Caught two of them sneaking a drink."

"Should I talk to them?"

"No, I reckon Branch and me can handle them."

"You're a jewel, Edna Jane."

"I know that, Ms. Beaulieu," Edna Jane replied with a mischievous grin.

A jewel indeed. She and Branch were always solving such problems for Angela. They shielded her against life's little irritations. She did not know what she would do without them.

The party rumbled on. Outside, the wind's sound rose to a shriek. Some kind of heavy fog or dust must have come with the wind, for the lights of the city streets grew dim and then vanished altogether.

• • •

They had taken refuge in the *Seven Days* building's basement: Nick Pacifico, Kim, Danny, Alice Wenska, and several hundred other people. There were several basement levels. The accommodation was roomy, reasonably warm, and comfortable. They might have been content to stay there. But after a short time they began to smell oily smoke. It grew thicker rapidly. People began to cough. Eyes stung and watered.

"Land sakes, *that*'ll clean out your sinuses!" commented a tiny old lady. She wore her white hair in an old-fashioned bun and had a brown, wrinkled face that looked as though it had spent a lot of time outdoors.

"What do you suppose it is?" somebody asked.

"Oh, it's diesel fumes," the old lady said, in a tone indicating that this should have been obvious. "Probably some nitwit checking out a generator. Forgot the first commandment: make sure it's vented right."

"Hey, what's this, Granny, you an engineer?" asked a young woman with bizarre orange hair and a black leather cap. Pacifico recognized her as one of a pair of street musicians who played clarinet duets on midtown corners. Her partner, leaning on a wall next to her, was a young black woman who habitually wore huge, gaudy earrings and a white leather cap.

The old lady replied, "Engineer? Me? Land sakes, no! But I ran a farm for twenty years after my husband died. Kept the machines running all by myself. When it's either starve or learn, you learn."

"That's as true as the morning dew, Granny," the young black woman said.

"What, you a poet or something?" Granny asked, looking at her with interest.

The young woman shrugged but did not reply. Pacifico said, "Look, we'd better get out of here before we choke to death."

"I was going to suggest that very thing," said Kim. "I went to a lot of trouble to quit smoking. I don't need this."

"There's a tunnel to the parking garage across the street," Pacifico said. "Let's try that. Leg holding up okay, Danny?"

"It's fine," Daniela replied. He judged from her face that the answer was probably true. She looked excited with the adventure she was having with all these interesting adults. She was holding Kim's hand. Pacifico took Kim's other hand and led the way. Several dozen people followed.

As soon as they entered the tunnel they found themselves leaning into a blast of wind. The wind dissipated the choking diesel fumes, and Pacifico's first thought was that it was nice to be able to breathe again. His second thought was a question: why was it windy underground?

The answer became plain as they emerged into the cavernous parking garage. This was a building devoted almost entirely to the formidable problem of what to do about cars in midtown Manhattan. Except for some restaurants and stores on the street-level floor, the aboveground parking levels were all fully open to the weather. The only completely closed-in floor was this one below street level. If you wanted to park down here, you paid a stiff extra fee for the weather protection. But there was no such protection today. An exit ramp curved up to street level, and evidently this ramp was placed and shaped just right for catching the wind.

"My God, *look* at that!" said the orange-haired young woman.

"Unreal!" her friend agreed. She sounded exultant.

It was an awesome sight. Wind was shrieking down the curve of the ramp, apparently funneled into it by the shape of the structure above. Pacifico thought it was the first time in his life that he had actually *seen* the wind. It was made visible by dust and debris: thick yellow-brown dust and a streaming blizzard of paper and assorted street trash. Included in this rushing river were cartwheeling pigeons, dazed or dead, most of their feathers torn off. The scene was illuminated by dust-shrouded yellow light from ceiling fixtures. For a moment nobody spoke or moved. Then the wind seemed to turn itself up a notch, for some larger objects came tumbling down the ramp. One was a metal folding chair. Another was a brown-and-white spotted dog. Its head flopped loosely. Obviously its neck was broken.

At the bottom of the ramp, dust and debris were piling up against parked cars and against a concrete-block wall. Set into the wall was a pair of plywood doors, fastened in the middle with a thumb latch. The doors were painted glossy dark green, a texture and color that Pacifico disliked but saw all over New York. He theorized that a paint company had manufactured an excess billion gallons of the stuff years ago and ever since had been trying to get rid of it at bargain prices. A two-foot-high drift of dust, paper and dead pigeons had accumulated along the doors' lower edge.

Pacifico and a young man with thick glasses tried to open the doors, but they were locked or bolted from the other side. The young man said something, but Pacifico could not hear a word. They were standing directly in the path of the mighty jet of air from the ramp. Dust and blurred shapes flew all around them as they staggered to stay upright.

Then there was a sound like thunder from above, clearly audible over the wind's howl. A second later, the wind funneling down the ramp increased enormously in strength. Apparently something up above had moved or been blown down or ripped away. It might have been a partition wall. Whatever it was, it had been partially screening the wind but now was no longer there. The force of the new blast hurled Pacifico and the young man against the plywood doors. Screws were ripped out of the wood. The bolt let go. The doors flew open violently. Pacifico found himself tumbling into a dark room, along with the young man and a blizzard of trash and dead pigeons.

Other people struggled through the wind to look into the room. Some had pulled flashlights from their survival packs. The beams, shining through whirling dust, revealed what seemed to be a storage room. Crates and cartons of food were stacked along the walls. It was probably a storage facility for a restaurant. Orienting himself to a remembered plan of the street above, Pacifico thought he remembered seeing a high-priced Italian restaurant at about this location. Since he had never had any interest in elegant dining, however, he had never been inside the place nor paid more than passing attention to it.

It was windy in the storage room but less so than at the entrance where the plywood doors were. Perhaps that was because the wind had nowhere to go. As far as airflow was concerned, the room was a dead end. As people continued to make their way into the room, seeking its shelter, Pacifico and some others explored it.

Somebody found a light switch. Feeble ceiling bulbs came on, enabling people to turn off their flashlights. The ceiling bulbs revealed a flight of stairs that led up to a glossy green steel-clad door. It probably opened into the restaurant. The young man with the thick glasses, obviously well endowed with the gift (or curse) of curiosity, went up the stairs to try the door. As expected, it was securely locked or bolted from the other side.

At the far end of the room, opposite the plywood doors, there was another flight of stairs. These led up to a pair of black iron doors set in the ceiling. They were undoubtedly sidewalk delivery doors. They were shivering and bouncing up and down in the thundering wind that blew across their upper sides, trying to pull them open. A thick bolt on the lower side held them shut. They rumbled, rattled, and clanked loudly in their iron frame.

The young man with the glasses mounted the steps. He was reaching up for the bolt when he was stopped by a shouted warning from the old lady who had identified the diesel fumes. "I wouldn't do that, sonny!" she yelled urgently.

He blinked at her. "You wouldn't?"

"I surely wouldn't. Those doors open out on the sidewalk. You don't want to poke your head outdoors in a wind like that."

"Yeah, that's good advice," Pacifico agree. "Remember that dog we saw on the ramp? That wind is a bonebreaker."

The young man thought about that for a second, nodded, and came back down the stairs. "You're right," he said simply. He grinned at Alice Wenska, who was standing nearby looking worried.

"That's an intelligent young man," the old lady said to Pacifico. "Takes advice from his elders." Pacifico did not know whether she was serious or joking.

People at the other end of the long room were trying to get the plywood doors reclosed so as to block out the wind. It was proving difficult. They had to push against both the wind and the dust and debris on the floor. The two street musicians were trying to slide the piles of debris away from the doors with their feet, but the wind kept delivering more of it. The work progressed inch by inch. Finally the doors were almost closed. There was about a hand's-width gap between them in the middle. That was the best that could be done with the tools at hand. A man and woman secured the doors by sliding heavy cartons of canned soup against them. The doors shuddered and wind whistled fiercely through the gap, but the arrangement held.

Thirty-odd people began to relax. They found cartons and crates to sit on. Some sat alone, some in groups.

"We'll be here a while, I think," Kim said to the group around her. "So we might as well know each other's names. I'm Kim, and this is Nick, and Alice. And the pretty one here is Danny."

"Oh, man, what I wouldn't give for eyes like that!" the orange-haired young woman remarked, studying Danny. "Oh, well, you can't have everything, right? At least I've got gorgeous hair." She grinned around at the group, revealing that she had a front tooth missing.

"Her hair's a fright, but it makes her happy," her black partner said affectionately. "So okay, names. We answer to a lot of names, but mostly I'm Trish and my friend is Suzanne. Suze, they call her."

"And if our music makes us famous and we go on TV," Suze added, "we'll call ourselves the Scotch. That's for, you know, Black & White."

"I like your earrings, Trish," Danny said shyly.

"Why thank you, baby," said Trish, pleased. She was wearing huge, spoked gold earrings that looked like wagon wheels.

"Now how about you, Granny?" Suze asked.

"Well, you won't believe this," the old lady replied, "but my name's Mary Smith."

"You're right, I don't believe it," said Suze. "So if it's all right by you, I'll go on calling you Granny."

The old lady shrugged contentedly and said, 'You won't be the first, child, and won't be the last."

Alice Wenska and the young man with the thick glasses had been sitting together, talking about vision and trying each other's glasses on. Alice announced shyly to the group that his name was Walter. "He's a computer trouble-shooter," she added.

"Hey, that's a poem!" said Trish, delighted. She repeated the words in exaggerated singsong style, swaying and snapping her fingers to the rhythm: "He's a comPU-ter . . . troubleSHOO-ter!"

"I also like woodwind music," Walter said. He gestured at the two musicians' clarinets in their black cases. "Do you suppose we can have a concert?"

"Maybe later, Walter," Trish said, still happily swaying to the music in her head.

Pacifico and Kim were sitting close on a long wooden crate that seemed to contain lettuce. She was wearing a plaid-lined British raincoat that was smudged from her work at the plywood doors. Pacifico had an arm about her waist and a hand in her pocket, so he could feel the warmth of her thigh. They had stopped listening to the conversation around them.

"Does anybody ever call you Nicky?" she asked.

"My mother does. Anybody else would get punched in the nose."

"Oh. Well, all right, then tell me this. What are your

feelings about sex?"

"I rate it A-plus."

"You've made a study of it?"

"Not as much as I'd like."

"Me, too." She snuggled against him. "It's such interesting stuff, isn't it? Let's study it a lot when we get the chance. When we get out of here, when this is all over—let's go somewhere and just do nothing else for *weeks*!"

"What do you think I am, Superman?"

"We'll find out."

For a long time, nobody noticed the changes that were taking place at the plywood doors. The fury of the funneled wind was increasing steadily. Despite the heavy cartons that were placed against them, the doors inched open. The gap between them slowly widened. However, this did not result in an increase of wind inside the storage room, for as the gap grew wider, it also grew shorter. The drift of dust and debris outside the doors rose to a height of four feet, then six. Finally it rose all the way to the ceiling, plugging the gap completely.

There was no longer any wind inside the room. But the doors continued to inch open, pushed by the mound of trash, which in turn was pushed by the tremendous force of the wind behind it.

As the gap widened, dust and trash and dead pigeons began to push into the storage room.

• • •

Julia Mead and Arthur Beaulieu had sought refuge in a part of the *Seven Days* building's basement that was not seriously affected by the wayward diesel fumes. The area they chose was far from the ill-vented engine and one floor lower. It was also served by excellent ventilation and was designed to be fireproof and even resistant to a nuclear bomb attack.

It was the area where the magazine's morgue was maintained: microfilms, microfiches, computer tapes, file folders, and other repositories of records bearing on many decades of news-gathering. This archive was one of Arthur Beaulieu's pet projects. As a young soldier in Europe during the Second World War, he had been appalled by the widespread and careless destruction of valuable old records and libraries, many of which were without duplicates and, therefore, impossible to replace or reconstruct. When he took control of *Seven Days* upon inheriting his father's voting stock, he made it his business to ensure, to the extent possible, that no detail of events as witnessed by the magazine would ever be lost to future journalists or historians.

Julia had heard him say many times, "This isn't just a magazine. It's a historical document." He said it to young editors and reporters who seemed insufficiently awed by their responsibilities and were letting their work grow sloppy. There was a certain pomposity about the statement, and Julia was quite sure the younger staff members amused themselves by mimicking it when out of earshot of the forty-eighth floor. But she knew Arthur believed it with all his heart. To him, *Seven Days* was not only a business venture but something in the nature of a public trust.

There was a large, comfortable lounge room attached to the morgue. Julia and Arthur and two dozen other people were in the process of settling down in this room, preparing for a long night. Julia had had to exert a good deal of persuasive power to make him retreat underground like this, for like all good journalists he wanted to witness events with his own eyes, even at the risk of his life. Many of the staff people had been just as unwilling to leave their posts. But when windows began bursting on the higher floors and communication lines with the rest of the world were cut off one by one, it became apparent that time spent aboveground was going to bring inexorably increasing risks, accompanied by steadily diminishing returns.

The magazine collected news from around the globe by many means, from the seemingly archaic to the futuristic. Correspondents and stringers in some parts of the world had to send dispatches by mail just as though they were still in the nineteenth century—indeed, in some cases (Afghanistan, for instance) had to depend on horseback couriers and other slow delivery systems to start a dispatch on its way. At the other end of the spectrum, news came in via the most advanced satellite technology.

But all these systems, from the oldest to the most modern, were turning out to be equally vulnerable to the wind. Communications satellites were serene in their orbits high overhead, unaffected by anything that might happen in the atmosphere below them. But a satellite was only a conduit. It would not report news or generate messages by itself. Every news report depended on people and equipment on the ground at both the sending and receiving ends.

Reports from northern cities had stopped coming in during the early part of the afternoon. While New York was still experiencing nothing stronger than a gale, wire-service reports from Stockholm, Anchorage, and other cities near sixty degrees north latitude were talking of winds above two hundred miles an hour. All communication from the sixtieth parallel ceased soon after that.

Slightly to the south, Moscow began talking of even higher winds a few minutes later. A lone Associated Press reporter there, a woman, kept transmitting for several minutes after everybody else had vanished. The Russians appeared to be making no attempt to censor her report, probably because the devastation and confusion in the city were too great. She said she had picked up a Soviet military weather report giving the windspeed at four hundred seventy-five kilometers an hour. Several large buildings in Moscow had toppled. She also had it from a reliable source that the Kremlin itself was seriously damaged, in many

places beyond repair. The Kremlin was very old, and many
of its walls were of brick. The aging mortar, weakened by
more than a century of weather, airborne chemical pollu-
tants, and vibrations from the streets and subway, could not
take wind loads such as these. The AP reporter began to
speak about Muscovites' efforts to find shelter, but then her
report stopped abruptly.

London was the next big city to be cut off, quickly
followed by almost all of western Europe's major cities.
Oddly, reports of severe trouble came next from Tokyo.
That city is on the thirty-sixth parallel, which runs between
Los Angeles and San Francisco on the other side of the
globe. But while neither California city was reporting
unusual winds in the middle of the afternoon, Tokyo—
where it was then morning—was experiencing not only a
wind such as it had never seen before, but also terror from
the sea. Gigantic storm surges—sea waves estimated at
sixty to ninety feet high and spaced ten or fifteen minutes
apart—were smashing into the Japanese coasts, rolling over
towns and villages and sending great walls of frothing salt
water far inland.

Very soon after Tokyo stopped communicating, the wind
in New York rose abruptly to hurricane force. Jake Barnes,
the commissioner of buildings, appeared on local TV and
radio broadcasts to urge people to seek shelter underground. Those local broadcasts then began to wink off the
air one by one. Finally Julia was able to convince Arthur
that the time had come to save themselves.

They sat now on a sofa in the underground lounge,
surrounded by *Seven Days* staff members and other refugees from some of the building's tenant companies. Arthur
looked glum.

Julia leaned against him and looosened his tie. "I'm
doing this so I can call you Arthur," she explained,
unbuttoning his shirt collar. In the office he habitually wore

white shirts and dark ties, usually dark blue with discreet stripes. The difference between that stiffly business-suited man and the man she knew after hours was amazing, she often thought. Amazing—but funny and pleasing, too.

He started to raise his big knobby hands as though to stop her from carrying out this transformation, then slumped in acquiescence. He gave her a weak grin, which quickly evaporated.

"Oh, come on, Arthur," she said. "Cheer up."

"It's my magazine," he said unhappily. "I hate to walk away from it like this."

The way a captain hates to abandon his ship, she thought. "But even if you'd stayed upstairs," she pointed out, "there wouldn't be anything you could *do*."

"I know. I understand that. But—"

"But understanding it doesn't make you feel any easier about it."

"That's just the problem, Julia."

"I know." She took one of his hands in both of hers and squeezed it. "I wish I could do something to help."

Seven Days was the main hinge of his life, she knew. It had been acquired along with sundry other business properties by his father, a Swiss financier, who had died just after the Second World War. Under the terms of his will, family members were granted a good deal of leeway in deciding how the estate should be divided among them. Arthur got one of the least valuable properties: *Seven Days*, then a struggling publication with an uncertain future.

It was his by his own request. Nobody else in the family had wanted it, but he had coveted it for many years. Journalism was in his blood, particularly journalism as practiced in America. In anticipation of taking over the magazine, he had served as a U.S. infantryman during the war. The reason for doing so was that it enabled him to obtain U.S. citizenship rapidly. He was Swiss by birth, but

his dreams of the future all took place in America. Under
U.S. law in those years, a foreign man or woman who
served with the country's armed forces was usually deemed
worthy of citizenship by virtue of that fact alone, and the
usual long-drawn-out procedures were waived.

By the time Julia came to *Seven Days* in the early 1960s,
Arthur had already lifted it to prominence among newsmagazines. Julia bore no special feelings about journalism at
that point in her life. She was simply looking for a job, any
job. She needed deliverance from the emotional and financial wreckage of a marriage gone wrong. She quickly found
that *Seven Days* was the kind of safe harbor she had been
seeking. It was an organization to which she could devote
herself for life. That would have been true, she thought,
even if she had not fallen in love with its chief.

She squeezed his hand again.

"I love you, Arthur," she said into his ear. Oh my, how
I do love this aging man. Without him and the magazine he
built, my life would have been—what? I cannot imagine
what would have become of me. She said, "No matter what
happens upstairs tonight, you've still got me down here."
She meant that from the heart but realized it sounded
banal, so she quickly added: "You've got all this, too. The
archives. This is where *Seven Days* really lives, Arthur. This
is the immortal part of it."

"Yes, that's right, isn't it?" The thought seemed to cheer
him. "The soul." He grinned at her and returned the
pressure of her hands.

At that moment the building shook. There was a loud
rumbling that seemed to come from all around. The vinyl-
tiled concrete floor vibrated beneath Julia's feet. Overhead,
an acoustical-tiled ceiling followed the contours of what she
assumed were massive steel beams, and from a corner near
one of these beams fell a little shower of white dust.

People stared at the dust shower, wondering what it
meant.

● ● ●

George Hochenauer and Wilma were in a comfortably furnished basement room below the old Flatiron Building. It was a large room, furnished very much like a traditional English gentlemen's club, with groupings of comfortable easy chairs around small tables and reading lamps. The furniture was old and soiled, having been salvaged over a course of decades from the offices of departed tenants, many of whom had skipped without paying their final rent. Another inelegant feature was the tangle of pipes and electrical conduits that covered the ceiling. Still, it was a good room, cozy and welcoming.

It was intended for the use of building staff members and their invited guests. In normal times it was used for brown-bag lunches, pinochle games, and afternoon naps. Most of the tenants did not even know it existed. Hochenauer was an exception. He was a long-term tenant and was on especially friendly terms with the maintenance crew. They liked him because he helped solve repair problems and also because they felt he was one of them. His speaking accent was honest Bronx. He was not like the young climbers who moved in, stayed two years, disdained the neighborhood, and dreamed of the day they could move uptown. And so Hochenauer possessed a key to the basement clubhouse.

About a dozen people had congregated there to wait out the wind. Hochenauer and Wilma had brought survival packs with them, but these were not the survival packs recommended by *Seven Days*. True, the packs did contain a few stale sandwiches and some candles and flashlights. But the main contents were abundant supplies of vodka, orange juice, and Mother Fletcher's.

Hochenauer was aware they would need water as well as alcoholic beverages to survive, but he did not think that would be a problem. Except during rare periods of drought, water is abundant in Manhattan. It is delivered to the huge city by underground conduits, most of which would escape any disaster that happened on the surface. If electric power should fail, Hochenauer reasoned, pumps would no longer operate to raise water to high building floors, but you would still be able to get water by tapping pipes underground.

And if that failed, he knew, you could always resort to ground water. Manhattan has plenty of that too. In midtown Manhattan, the average water table is four to six floors below street level. Very low sub-basements must be pumped continually to keep them dry. Hochenauer knew that the old Grand Central Building, for example, had seven levels below the street. The bottom two would be submerged most of the time without pumping. In the light of that, it seemed to Hochenauer that the people of New York, given no more than ordinary human cleverness and will, would always find something to drink.

"Ah, this is the life, innit, Hoke?" Wilma was saying contentedly.

"So far, so good," Hochenauer agreed, relaxing in an overstuffed armchair. "Yeah. I gotta say there could be a lot worse places to spend the night."

"You think this old heap is gonna take the wind?" Wilma asked, switching in an instant from contentment to anxiety.

"That's what I think," Hochenauer replied. It was the truth. He felt secure down here in the clubroom. The only sign of the wind's fury was a low rumbling sound, transmitted to the basement by the old building's steel skeleton.

Wilma changed to yet another mood. "I sure hope old Kramer's okay," she said. She sounded as though she might be about to start crying. "You think he's okay, Hoke?"

"Sure," Hochenauer said in what he hoped was a tone of jovial optimism.

The optimism did not take. Wilma said, "I mean, us sitting down here all cozy and everything, and him out there someplace."

"Yeah, well—"

"Poor old Kramer. I feel sorry for him, Hoke."

"Will you quit worrying about Kramer, for God's sake?" Hochenauer said, exasperated.

Wilma started to cry. "He ain't got nobody, Hoke."

"But he don't *want* nobody!"

Wilma cheered up immediately. "Yeah, that's true, innit?"

It was indeed true. Earlier in the afternoon they had tried to get Kramer to come to the clubroom with them. Booker's was closing. The patrons were all leaving. Only Kramer remained at his usual place at the end of the long bar, staring morosely into space, making no move to go.

"We're closing, Kramer," the bartender said kindly. "Time to go home." Other patrons waited to see what would happen.

"What are you closing for?" Kramer wanted to know. "Ain't night yet, is it?"

"The wind, man, the wind!" the bartender explained. "Look out at the street there." He gestured toward the grimy front window. "See how it's blowing already?"

Kramer shrugged. Nothing that happened outside Booker's made any difference to him.

"You gotta go while it's still safe," the bartender went on explaining, trying to be patient. "I'm responsible, y'unnerstand? I gotta send you home while you can still get there."

Kramer shrugged again. The bartender's problem was no concern of his.

The bartender went on arguing with less and less patience. Finally he phoned his brother, who lived next door. They were both big men. Politely and with great care and gentleness, they lifted Kramer off his stool, hands under his thighs so he could maintain his sitting position. He still held his half-full drink. They carried him out the door and deposited him carefully at the curb.

Hochenauer and Wilma started to walk away, carrying

their heavy survival packs. The gale was not yet bad on this side street. They had progressed about half a block when Wilma looked back, then stopped.

"We oughta take him with us, Hoke," she said.

Hochenauer was not enthusiastic about that idea. "He won't come," he said.

"But we oughta try, at least. Look at him, sitting there all by himself! We can't just leave him there, Hoke!"

"Why not? All by himself is what he wants to be."

"But we oughta try anyway."

Hochenauer looked back at the lone figure sitting at the curb, finishing his drink in his usual slow, methodical way. It seemed to Hochenauer that the man looked perfectly content—or to put it more accurately, no less content than he ever looked. Hochenauer said, "Nah. He's okay. Let's leave him alone."

"But Hoke, he's a human *bean*!" Tears were running down Wilma's fat red cheeks.

Hochenauer had to admit that Kramer was a human bean. He recalled that Kramer had said good evening to him once, and on a couple of other occasions had nodded in response to a greeting. "Okay, let's see what he says," Hochenauer agreed reluctantly.

But it was as expected. Kramer had no interest in going with them, or indeed in going anywhere. They stood in the rising wind and argued with him, but the only response they got was an indifferent shrug. Finally, frustrated, they left.

"Feel like a walk, old lady?" Hochenauer asked. "Could be a long night. Be good to stretch our legs."

"Well, okay, but this survival pack is awful heavy."

"Just a short walk. Your pack gets too heavy, we'll stop and rest."

By going slightly out of their way, they came out on Fifth Avenue a few blocks north of the Flatiron Building. This was Hochenauer's favorite view of the funny old structure. At twenty stories it was the tallest building in its immediate neighborhood. It reared into an open space of sky, capturing the charmed gaze of any pedestrian walking down the avenue.

Once in a while, in both engineering and art, something wonderful arises from a set of circumstances that seem at first to be nothing but a damned nuisance. Such was the case with the Flatiron Building, Hochenauer thought. Nobody would have designed this building for fun nor dreamed it up in an attempt to be arty or original. It came into being because of the annoying way in which Broadway meandered diagonally across the otherwise tidy square grid of Manhattan. Where it crossed Fifth Avenue and Twenty-Third Street, it created a narrow triangle of land that was generally thought to be useless as a building plot.

The speculator who bought the plot around the turn of the century, paying a ridiculously low price, was not quite sure what could be done with it. He called on an architect and a structural engineer. Their first reaction was to laugh. Then they got intrigued. And in time they produced the building that some thought was art, some thought was an example of commercial expediency, and some thought was a joke.

Hochenauer thought it was all three. It was art for profit, with a sense of humor. The building's narrow prow pointed straight up Fifth Avenue. Walking toward it from the north, you saw only the bow windows of the prow at first. The initial impression was of height and narrowness. The building looked like a thin, round tower. But as you drew nearer, the outline of the roof gradually shaped itself against the sky. Hochenauer had known this building for many years, but he still experienced the moment of pleased surprise as the shape asserted itself: "Oh! It's a triangle!"

Hochenauer and Wilma walked down Fifth Avenue with

the rising gale at their backs. The spiderweb intersection at Twenty-Third was a nightmare of multiple-gridlocked traffic. For a change, it was pedestrian country. The two walked to the Flatiron's triangular island under the sullen stares of motorists who were not going anywhere. At the prow of the island, Hochenauer paused and turned for one last look at the city before he ducked indoors.

It was a proud and soaring city, he thought. Ten blocks to the north was the towering Empire State Building, 102 stories high, with five acres of windows. Hochenauer imagined he could see its top beginning to sway in the wind. He knew that was an illusion. Tall buildings do sway in high winds—sway by as much as two feet in some cases—but the movement is seldom visible to the unaided eye. Nor can it be felt by people inside the building. It becomes a problem only when you are on a high floor, look through a window and see another tall building close by, swaying in a different rhythm. That can be very disconcerting.

The swaying is not dangerous. At least, Hochenauer thought, it hasn't been up to now. Structural engineers take it into account when designing tall buildings. They also allow for torsion, the tendency of buildings to twist in high winds. Every building is carefully designed to take the maximum in wind forces that can be expected in its particular region.

But today, Hochenauer thought, they'll have to take more than the maximum. What will happen?

He did not know. It scared him to think about the possibilities. He thought some of the most vulnerable-looking structures might prove to be the toughest, simply because engineers had worried about them the most. There was the Port Authority's World Trade Center, for instance. Hochenauer did not like that twin-towered colossus down at Manhattan's southern tip. In his opinion it lacked imagination and good humor. Its windows were narrow and recessed, giving office denizens the impression of looking out of a cave. But that was because of the massive, closely spaced pillars that ran from the towers' tops all the way down to the ground. Though Hochenauer disliked the twin 110-story slabs, he had to admit they were solidly rooted.

A building that had the opposite effect on him was the Citicorp Center, on Lexington Avenue uptown. To Hochenauer, this was an example of stunningly imaginative design. The entire building rested on four gigantic pillars or stilts. These stilts were not at the four corners, but in the middles of the four sides. The result was that the four corners hung out over the walkways, unsupported. Looking at this building made Hochenauer dizzy. But he knew that the very unusualness of the design had led to more than an ordinary amount of worry about wind. At the building's top was a science-fictionish device called a tuned-mass damper. It was essentially a colossal slab of concrete on rollers in a bath of oil, so designed that it would counteract swaying and torsion in high winds.

"Well, I hope this crazy city works," Hochenauer muttered, gazing up Fifth Avenue.

"What's that, Hoke?" Wilma shouted over the wind.

"Nothing," he shouted back. "Let's get down to the clubroom."

That had been three hours ago. Now they sat in the Flatiron Building's basement with a dozen others, listening to the rising rumble of wind as transmitted by the steel around them. Above the rumble, faintly and intermittently at first but then more clearly, Hochenauer heard a high-pitched hum. The building had found its natural resonance and was singing, he thought. Once in a while, too, he thought he heard a distant crash. He wondered if windows were starting to break.

"Are we gonna be okay, Hoke?" Wilma asked.

Hochenauer's first instinct was to tell a cheerful lie. Then he decided not to. He replied, "All I can say is I think so."

18

BY NIGHTFALL THE wind was blowing at well over two hundred miles an hour. It took only another hour to reach three hundred. Most anemometers in the New York metropolitan area had stopped operating by that time. They had been destroyed or ripped away from their mountings, or the structures on which they were mounted had collapsed.

Meteorologists at some airports were able to take continued readings for a time, however, by using airspeed sensors of the kind employed on aircraft. These are not very accurate at normal on-the-ground windspeeds—they won't reliably discriminate between a fresh breeze and a strong breeze, for example—but they are capable of reading the very high speeds reached by jet aircraft.

The wind passed three hundred miles an hour and kept increasing. Nobody was ever quite sure where it stopped.

● ● ●

Edna Jane beckoned Angela into a corner and said, "Ms. Beaulieu, I'm afraid we got problems."

"What *is* it, Edna Jane?"

Angela was annoyed. It was nearly eight o'clock. The party was at its peak of sociability. People were relaxed;

inhibitions were softened; the festive and affectionate mood had driven all the loneliness away. This is always the best but unfortunately the shortest of the stages any party goes through. Angela knew it would soon be supplanted by what she thought of as the overshot stage—that benumbed time in which people are hit by the delayed effects of too many drinks, partial anesthesia sets in, and all meaningful social interaction stops. Wishing to enjoy the brilliant main movement of her party before the overshot stage arrived, Angela did not want to hear about any problems.

But Edna Jane's next words startled her into alert attention. Edna Jane said, "The temporary folks, they gone."

"Gone?"

"Up and quit. Walked out. Every last one of them."

"But—but why, for goodness' sake?"

"Because of the way the building's shaking."

"Shaking?"

"Feel the floor, Ms. Beaulieu."

Angela had not been aware of it until now, and obviously few of her guests had either. But it was true: the floor was vibrating beneath her feet.

"It isn't so bad in here," Edna Jane said. "I mean you don't notice it a lot, maybe because of the thick carpet. But you come in the kitchen, Ms. Beaulieu."

Angela did not want to leave the party, but she was worried enough to follow Edna Jane into the big, shining kitchen. As soon as she stepped onto the red-tiled floor she felt the vibration powerfully. She also noticed that some copper-bottomed pans hanging from a wall rack were gently swaying.

"Listen at this," Edna Jane said, indicating a glass-doored china cabinet. Angela put her ear to the door. She heard the china clinking and rattling softly.

"And look," Edna Jane said. She pointed to the big stainless-steel sink. It was full of rinse water. The surface of the water was alive with shivering patterns of tiny ripples.

"I don't like it one bit, Ms. Beaulieu."

Angela thought Edna Jane was talking about the vanished help. "Can you carry on alone, you and Branch?"

"Well—" Edna Jane looked unhappy.

"Do the best you can," Angela said. They discussed the logistics of the situation for a few minutes, and then Angela went back to join the festive throng. She was confident that Edna Jane and Branch would surmount the problems. She would leave it to them. She did not need to worry.

The wind was screeching and thundering with insane fury. It was so loud now that it was beginning to outshout the party. Angela was annoyed with it; she would have turned down its volume if she could.

"Angela, sweetheart," somebody said behind her. She turned and saw the architect, Peter James Schenker. She had noticed before that he was having a difficult time getting into the mood, and now he looked pale and drawn.

He confirmed the observation. "I'm going to be leaving, dear," he said. "I'm not feeling well. Touch of flu, probably."

His pale high forehead was shiny with sweat, though the room was not hot. Angela asked, "Would you like to lie down a while, Peter?"

"No, I think I'd better just go." He looked extremely nervous. He kept putting his long white hands in his pockets and withdrawing them. This was unusual for him. He was normally a well-controlled man.

"I'm so sorry," Angela said.

"So am I. It's a perfectly lovely party, dear. I really do wish I could stay."

He pecked her on the cheek and hurried away. A thought came to Angela suddenly: *is he worried about the vibration?*

She plunged back into the throng, but she could not recapture her mood of gaiety. The mood would have been wasted on most of the guests in any case, for the overshot stage was plainly arriving. Guests were spilling liquor and cigarette ash everywhere. They were holding conversations in which everybody bellowed non sequiturs and nobody heard a word. They were initiating ponderous sexual fencing matches that they undoubtedly thought were smashingly clever. Angela overheard a young man saying to a young woman, "Shall we talk or fuck?"

Yes, the overshot stage was here. Angela had not drunk much herself; she seldom did and never at her own parties. Now, however, she went to the long bar table for another glass of wine. The caterer's bartenders had deserted. She was glad to see that the guests, needing no special invitation, had begun serving themselves. The Air Force general happened to be at the table, making himself a stiff bourbon on the rocks. He poured wine for her. They wandered back into the living room, talking about his hobby, breeding Great Danes. As they walked, he put his hand on her waist and let it slip down to her buttocks. She did not object. He was a tall, dashingly handsome man in his fifties with a tanned, deep-lined face but a young man's body. He had dark blue eyes of a beautiful clarity. Angela thought it would be nice to know him better. She was thinking of ways to convey this when she was interrupted and beckoned aside again by Edna Jane.

"What *now*?" Angela whispered irritably.

"Branch and me, we leaving, Ms. Beaulieu."

Angela was astonished. "*Leaving?*"

"The building is shaking worse and worse. It don't feel safe. We talked it over, and we—"

"What in God's name has gotten into you, Edna Jane? You can't leave me with this!" Angela waved to indicate the party with its nearly one hundred guests. "Who's going to clean up? You can't go! You can't!"

Edna Jane looked unhappy, but she stood her ground. "I was you, Ms. Beaulieu, I'd tell everybody to go home, and then I'd get downstairs myself, that's what I'd do. This building is shaking itself to pieces, feel like."

"This is crazy, Edna Jane!" Angela was bewildered. Servants were supposed to be loyal, weren't they? They didn't walk out in the middle of a party. It was unheard of! "You can't leave me now!" Angela stamped her foot in helpless rage. "You *can't*, Edna Jane!"

"I'm sorry, Ms. Beaulieu. Please do like I say. Don't stay up here."

Edna Jane put her hand pleadingly on Angela's arm as she said this. Angela shook the hand off angrily. "All right, go! But don't ever come back. Not ever, you hear? And don't come asking me for references either!"

Edna Jane gave her one last, sad look, then turned and left.

Shaking with anger, Angela went into her bedroom to compose herself. She saw that one of her prized nineteenth-century Swiss Alpine watercolors, a long-ago gift from Arthur's mother, had fallen from the wall and was lying on the floor, its glass face cracked. The picture hook had pulled out of the wall. When Angela put her fingertips on the wall she found it vibrating as though some huge engine were laboring inside, or behind, it. But she knew it was only a thin gypsum-board partition wall, and there was nothing on the other side of it but the big, empty elevator hall.

She spent five minutes alone in the bedroom. Then, feeling calmer, she returned to the party. The Air Force general was talking to a feminist author, who seemed angry and was blowing cigarette smoke in his face. He caught Angela's eye. His look said, "Rescue me!" Angela was delighted to be of service. She started toward him.

It was then that the huge north window burst.

It exploded inward with a colossal, high-pitched crack like the sound of rifles. That sound was followed instantly by the roar of a gigantic wind invading the apartment.

Angela was looking into the general's eyes at the instant the window burst. Events happened faster than her reactions. She was still staring at those fine blue eyes when they vanished. She found herself staring, instead, at a crimson spout of blood. A great, spinning chunk of window glass had cut the general's head clear off.

She was still unable to react as fast as the events. She opened her mouth to scream, but by this time the wind had lifted her off her feet. With a tangle of other people and splintering furniture she was hurled violently against the south wall.

She was hurt but conscious, wedged behind a heavy couch. She was screaming but could hear neither her own voice nor other people's above the wind's impossible din.

Furniture was flying and crashing everywhere. Bottles, glasses, and chinaware smashed against the walls, rolled, and skidded along the floor. The west window burst outward. Angela watched in horror as at least a dozen people tumbled out into the shrieking night. One of them was Sarah Millington. Angela could not see faces clearly but had a brief glimpse of Sarah's bright red dress. Sarah seemed to be clinging to an armchair, but it did not help her. She and the chair were both swept out through the window opening.

What made it worse—like some surrealistic nightmare— was that Sarah did not fall down toward the street. A freakish wind eddy hurled her upward instead. Angela watched, screaming hysterically, unheard. She last saw her friend upside-down, mouth wide open, flying up toward the roof.

All the lamps in the living room had been smashed, but some recessed ceiling lights avoided damage and stayed lit. Things and people whirled and tumbled about in the eerie dim light amid incredible noise. The heavy black top of the grand piano flew open, broke off at the hinge, went cartwheeling across the room and punched into the south wall a few feet from Angela's head. If it had hit her, it would surely have killed her. It punched clear through the wall and vanished. The wall was also a flimsy partition made of thin gypsum board over wood studs, with a plastic honeycomb material for soundproofing. The wind tore savagely at the opening made by the piano top. Half the wall disintegrated in seconds. Angela felt herself tumbling. Her head hit something hard. She blacked out. When she came to, she found herself in the elevator hall.

She was in a corner, lying in a pile of debris: pieces of furniture, bits of wall, shards of glass. Other people were lying around her, some moving, others still; most were bleeding. Many had their mouths open, but their cries and screams could not be heard. The wind screeched around the great oblong hall with hellish fury, gusting first in one direction, than another. It seemed less powerful here than in the apartment, but it was too strong to allow walking. Angela watched a man struggle to an all-fours kneeling position, then fall on his side as some white, flying thing hit him on the temple. He lay still, staring at her, his mouth open in an inaudible shout of rage or pain.

The big white-walled hall was lit by recessed lights, a few of which still burned. The air was full of whirling dust and debris, but Angela could dimly see the elevator doors some thirty feet from the corner where she lay. Could she crawl to those doors? Perhaps, but would the elevators still be operating?

For possibly the first time in her life, Angela was forced to pay attention to the way things worked. Nobody else was going to take care of this problem for her, not this time. She tried to assemble what little she knew about elevators. What would happen to high-rise elevators in a disastrous situation like this? Perhaps some floors of the building were damaged even worse than this one. In that case, could the damage extend into the central shaft and prevent the elevators from moving? Or could their electric power be cut off? Or might they simply be grounded by some automatic safety device?

Slightly beyond the elevators was the door to the stairs. Angela thought: if I can make it over there, I'll be all right. Maybe the elevators will be working. If they aren't, well, okay, I'll go through that door to the stairs. If I can walk down sixty-eight flights of stairs, fine; and if I can't, that's okay too. The stairwell will shelter me from the wind. One way or another, I'll be all right. *I'll be all right*!

She was surprised by her own calm. The hysteria that had seized her before was now burnt out. She felt icy and detached. She was not even greatly troubled to discover that her left hand was covered with blood and completely numb. She could move the wrist feebly. She guessed that the wrist was probably intact but the hand might be broken in more than one place. It did not seem to matter.

She began to crawl on her stomach like an infantryman under fire. The wind screamed around her ears. She crawled over shifting mounds of debris and past inert human forms. One plump-bodied woman lay staring at the ceiling. One leg was folded under her back in a position that would have been impossible except for the most supple acrobat. Angela guessed the woman's spine was broken or dislocated. "Poor dear," Angela muttered, aware that not even the loudest shout could be heard above the wind. She gently moved the woman's leg in an attempt to make her more comfortable. The woman's head rolled to one side. The eyes did not blink, move, or change expression. Angela realized that the woman was dead.

"Nadine Parker," Angela said into the wind, suddenly remembering the woman's name. A college president, a bright wit, an altogether amiable soul. Angela reached out with her good hand to touch Nadine's face, but a thundering wind gust abruptly moved the body, and a gush of thick, dark blood erupted from the mouth.

Sobbing, Angela fought her way to the elevators. She struggled to a kneeling position, from which she could just barely reach the signal button on the wall. When she pushed the button, however, no lighted directional arrow appeared.

She became aware that a man was kneeling beside her. His face was so battered and caked with blood that she did not recognize him. He clutched her shoulder and shook his head. She guessed he was telling her that he had already tried the elevators and found them unresponsive.

She pointed toward the stairwell door. He nodded. They crawled to the door and struggled to open it. It was a firestop door, metal-clad and heavy. As soon as they pulled it slightly ajar, the wind did the rest. The wind flung it open with such savage force that its hinges ripped out of the frame, and it fell to the floor.

Hoping other people would see the open doorway and follow, Angela crawled through. The stairs were made of gray-painted steel and concrete, with a gray railing and gray walls all around. She struggled to a sitting position and started down the stairs on her bottom. The wind's force diminished markedly as she went down. Finally, holding the railing with her good right hand, she was able to lift herself to her feet.

It was windy in the stairwell, but not so windy as to make walking impossible. It was also noisy, but the noise was of a different quality from that up above. It was a hollow, echoing, metallic noise. A booming noise, as though several empty iron drums were rolling down the stairs. Mingled with that was an intermittent squealing sound that made Angela clench her teeth. It was like fingernails on a blackboard, only vastly louder.

With sudden terror, she realized what that sound was. It was the scream of a tortured building. It was the ghastly squeal and jangle of a huge steel framework twisting.

The terrible sound was magnified here in the building's hollow core. Angela imagined she could hear great girders bending, joints stretching, rivets popping. She was suddenly aware, once again, of the vibration beneath her feet. The stairs were not merely vibrating, however; they were shuddering. The shuddering rose and fell rhythmically like the oscillating whine of a plucked, tense wire.

I've got to get out of here. Got to, *got to*! . . But hold it, slow down. Panic won't help.

Angela commanded herself fiercely: *don't panic*! You've held yourself together so far. Don't throw it all away. You can get out of this if you keep your wits about you.

Sixty-eight flights of stairs. Could it be done? Of course, why not? Walking up all those stairs would be impossible for anyone but a seasoned runner or mountain climber, but walking down them should not be inordinately taxing to anybody in reasonably good physical condition. Angela removed her high-heeled sandals. She thought: I'll take them in easy stages. Ten flights, then stop and rest if I need to.

She looked behind her. In the dim light from a bare ceiling bulb she saw that the bloody-faced man and several other people had followed her down the stairs to the point where she had stopped. They were all looking at her, crouching and sitting in various attitudes of numb resignation. Their clothes hung from them in ribbons. One woman was virtually naked except for a pearl necklace. Her scalp was bleeding. She seemed unaware that a trickle of blood ran continually down the side of her face and dripped onto the stairs.

Angela wondered: why are they all sitting there staring at me? Then she realized that they were waiting for guidance.

In their fear and pain and confusion, they had decided that she would be their leader. Where she went, they would follow.

She had not asked for the job and did not want it. The idea of it frightened her. She had never been the kind of person who sought leadership, not since college days, anyhow.

But leadership, once thrust upon you, is very hard to shake off. Angela looked back at her sorry platoon of followers, tried to put on a confident expression and was surprised to find her face responding with what felt like a quite convincing smile. She pointed down the stairs. Then, moving slowly and deliberately, she began to descend.

The others followed. She did not know why; nor did they. Perhaps they were attracted by her air of calm deliberation. Perhaps they detected some hint of steel in her—something whose existence nobody, least of all she herself, would have suspected until this desperate hour. It had lain inside her all her life. It had never been needed before.

They collected other people on the stairway as they went down. On two floors, as on Angela's floor, the wind had ripped the firestop doors off their hinges after apparently bursting windows and tearing down interior walls. The wind screamed through the doorway openings on these floors and made navigation of the stairs difficult. On several floors the lights were out. Somehow Angela kept her battered platoon moving downward.

She lost count of the floors. She thought she was somewhere near the forty-fifth when she became aware that the building had started to tilt.

She became aware of it by accident. They had stopped to rest on a floor landing. The woman with the bleeding scalp, weak from blood loss or shock, swayed and began to fall. Somebody caught her. Her pearl necklace broke during the struggle to hold her up, and the pearls rained on the concrete floor. At first they bounced in all directions. But then, swiftly, a frightening order imposed itself on their random motion. They all began to roll in the same direction. They flowed toward one wall, bounced against it and stopped, lined up almost as neatly as they had once been lined on their string.

Angela stared at them as the implication grew clear. The floor was tilted. It was not enough of a tilt to be detected by human senses, which are notoriously inefficient at such judgments in a closed space. But it was enough to bring a great bubble of fear into Angela's throat.

She knew a good deal of sloppy workmanship had gone into the vaunted New World Center. Floors were not as level, nor walls as vertical, as they should have been. Indeed, Edna Jane had complained often that things were always rolling off the kitchen countertops. But the tilt in this stairway landing was more than just a workman's mistake. It was too pronounced. Something else was wrong.

The building was starting to fall.

Every muscle in Angela's body tensed, ready to hurl her down the stairway at ankle-breaking speed. She wanted to run and run, and scream and scream.

Instead, she clutched the iron rail so hard that it hurt. I won't panic, she thought. I will not, *will not*.

She smiled at her ragged little group, pointed downward and said, "Let's be on our way." They could not hear her above the thundering and metallic squealing that echoed up and down the stairwell, but they seemed to get the message from her face and posture. With dogged fortitude, some helping others, they resumed their long, long descent.

The squealing grew louder. The tilting seemed to grow more pronounced, but Angela could not tell whether that was real or imaginary. She wondered: when it really falls, when it finally topples over, will we feel it happening?

• • •

Peter James Schenker had been one of the last riders to go down in the elevators before they were grounded. He found the lobby level crowded with people. They drifted through the arcades and shop areas, some of them looking frightened, some happily expectant, some lost, many drunk. Schenker pushed through the crowds in rising panic. He had to get out of this building before it was too late. He had to!

Going to Angela's party had been a mistake. He had allowed himself to be talked into it by Jelly Jack Barrow, among others. "How's it gonna look, Schenker?" Barrow had said a few days back. "Suppose this Beaulieu dame gives the story to the gossip columns. You're the architect of the building. You're gonna be in New York for some TV thing. But you're scared to go to a party in your own building? Jeez, Schenker. I thought you had better publicity sense than that!"

Schenker had argued that his reason for wishing to turn down Angela's invitation was not fear but inconvenience. He wouldn't have wanted to go to the party even if it had been held underground, he insisted. This was true to the extent that he understood his own motives. But he allowed the argument about bad publicity to sway him. And shortly after arriving at the party, he began to realize that he *was* afraid.

Two hundred miles an hour. Three hundred. Four hundred. Those were terrible winds. Airplanes were designed to take them. Buildings were not.

Leaning against the grand piano up there in Angela's sixty-eighth-floor aerie, Schenker had felt the first faint vibrations through the bones of his hand. A little later he had begun to feel the floor vibrating under his feet. As far as he could tell, nobody else at the time was aware of anything unusual happening. But Schenker knew. His building was being subjected to forces beyond anything it was designed to handle.

His initial vague worries changed quickly to a sharp and specific fear. This great building, the crowning achievement of his life and work: it could not take winds over two hundred miles an hour. Not sustained winds. Sooner or later, *it would fall*.

Every building is a compromise of one kind or another. *Every* building, from a little two-bedroom cottage to a colossus like the New World Center. Schenker had not deliberately or carelessly designed a weak structure. No architect or engineer does. But there were other considerations to balance against the wish to make the structure strong. Expense was one consideration. Openness of design was another: the wish to have large areas of unobstructed floor space rather than forests of pillars. Compromise, compromise: that was the nature of the builder's art. Schenker had always felt the compromises he had worked out for the Center were good ones. Still, he was aware of areas of weakness. He would have eliminated them if he could, but it had proved impossible.

Of course no two architects or structural engineers would approach the same problems in the same ways. There was always fuel for controversy, even for bitter argument and *ad hominem* charges and countercharges. If the building fell, Schenker knew there would be those who would accuse him of incompetence. The general public, not fully understanding what the accusations were about, would lap up the tasty sauce of scandal. Schenker knew he could be ruined.

But I did my best! he insisted to himself, almost in tears. I'm not a bad architect! The building would have been all right in ordinary weather. Nobody could have planned for something like this!

He pushed through the lobby crowds, trying not to cry. "You can't plan for something like this!" he kept muttering aloud. People looked at him oddly. He knew how he must look: a tall, angular man with flowing white hair and a look of madness. He did not care what they thought. He had to get out while he still could.

But when he got to the Center's front entrance, he stopped. The wind out on Park Avenue was shrieking so loudly that he heard the gigantic sound not only with his ears but with all the bones in his body. The thick, gray-smoked, reinforced glass that rose from floor to ceiling was crisscrossed with cracks like transparent snakeskin and in some places was visibly bulging inward. The revolving doors were spinning intermittently—stop-go, stop-go. Outside in the screaming night, dust and street trash rushed past horizontally, illuminated by outdoor lamps. As Schenker stood and watched, a larger object bounced against the broken gray glass and flew away. It was a white metal patio table, probably from somebody's rooftop garden. Schenker had only a fraction of a second to look at it, but in that quick glimpse he could see that the thick metal top was folded and crumpled like paper.

To go out in that wind would be certain suicide. Schenker fled back into the building. He wandered around, scared and muttering. He found himself in the hotel lobby, staring up at the high ceiling. He imagined the monstrous weight of the building above, all those millions of tons of steel, concrete, copper pipe, electrical cable. Dizzy, he leaned against a marble-sheathed pillar, then jumped away from it as though it were red hot.

The massive pillar was shaking.

It was one of the building's main supporting pillars. Steel and concrete, with a decorative outer skin of black marble, it carried the building's weight solidly down into the ground, where it was anchored against the immovable Manhattan granite. It was not supposed to shake in wind. In earthquakes, yes. Like all New York buildings, the New

World Center was designed to withstand what are called Zone One earthquakes: moderate in intensity and infrequent. You expect to feel earthquake tremor on the lower floors of a building such as this. You do not expect to feel wind.

Schenker stood and stared at the pillar, horrified. Then he saw something that frightened him still more. This part of the lobby was floored with great slabs of the same shiny black marble that sheathed the pillars. There was a line of grout where floor and pillar met. As Schenker stared at the pillar's base, he saw that the grout had pulled away from the marble. There was an eighth of an inch of space between the grout and the pillar.

It was impossible! He knew the grade of grout that had been used throughout this building—even knew the brand, for he was a stockholder in a company that manufactured grout and had been careful to specify that company's product. It was a good, serviceable grout, and he knew from years of experience that it did not shrink. In an application such as this, bonded to marble or stone on a base of concrete, it should not pull away at the joints even after years of fluctuating temperature and humidity.

Only one thing could make it pull loose: an unstable base. Either the floor was moving, or the pillar was.

Schenker then saw something else, or thought he did. Horror piled on horror! There was a hairline crack running across one of the marble floor slabs. Schenker fell to his knees for a closer look. Yes, it was true! And now, from this closer observation point, he began to see other cracks. He crawled around the pillar, aware that he was weeping openly now but making no attempt to hide it. Oh, God! Cracks everywhere! The building was breaking up!

Schenker leaped to his feet. "It wasn't my fault!" he said pleadingly to the circle of bystanders who had stopped to gape at him. "You can't plan for something like this!"

Sobbing, he ran back toward the main entrance. He had to get out before the building fell. Nothing else had any importance now: nothing but the overriding need to get out from under the terrifyingly huge weight that towered into the sky over his head.

He ran to one of the revolving doors. It was spinning at high speed as he approached it, but then it stopped abruptly. He hesitated, then stepped into the recess. A new, fierce eddy of wind started it spinning again. The door segment behind him slammed into his back. He was shoved forward and ejected onto the sidewalk outdoors. The wind seized him immediately. Screaming in pain and fright, he rolled down the sidewalk at terrible speed. He flew off the curb and smashed head-first into a gridlocked car. The blow broke his neck and killed him instantly, which was merciful. The body continued to fly, bounce, and scrape down Park Avenue for several blocks. It crashed into a building and rolled up the wall like a giant spider climbing. It fell through a blown-out window and came to rest in what had been a dentist's office. By that time an arm was missing and virtually every other bone in the body was broken in several places.

● ● ●

Ed McRoyden was ready for the electric power failure when it came. He had a big five-cell lantern and a supply of spare batteries. Far below the ground, he was in total darkness for a few seconds when the power went out. Since all of Manhattan's electricity is delivered by underground cables, he assumed the problem must stem from a damaged generating, or relay, station somewhere. He found his lantern quickly. Simultaneously he heard the slow, complaining groan of electric starters trying to get three large diesel engines going.

Each engine was equipped with a switch that sensed the

presence or absence of current from the electric company. Any time that current stopped flowing, the switch automatically closed a gap in the battery-to-starter circuit. With luck, the engine would start. Finally, when it revved up to cruising speed, a clutch-like mechanism would engage the generator, and current would start flowing to replace the missing supply from the power company.

It was all supposed to be automatic. On paper, it was charmingly simple. But it did not always work.

Two of the three engines started in the usual boisterous diesel manner. The third one—the same one that had balked before—did not.

One of the two working generators supplied power for lighting in this basement area. As the lights came on, McRoyden went to the balky engine and scowled at it. He changed the switch setting to manual control and turned off the starter. It clanked morosely to a stop.

"What are you, a prima donna?" he shouted at the big cold engine, over the roar of the other two. "You want to be coddled? Okay, I'll coddle you, by God! How do you like *that*?" He kicked the engine's nearest floor support savagely with the reinforced toe of his boot.

Then he turned on the starter again. This time, the engine came to life with an obedient bellow. McRoyden never understood why. With diesels, you often don't.

● ● ●

Angela and her ragged little platoon of survivors had been facing a difficult problem when the power failed. It happened at the worst possible time, Angela thought.

The scalp-wounded woman had just collapsed. It was while they were wondering what to do that all the stairwell lights went out.

It was blacker than the blackest night. The building screamed and shuddered. One metallic screech was so loud and so close that Angela thought the very stair on which she was standing had wrenched loose from its supports. She thought: this is it. The end. But the stairway did not fall away beneath her. It lurched, then seemed to steady. The rhythmic shuddering resumed.

Somebody was clutching Angela's left arm, the one with the broken hand. She thought the person was screaming but could not be sure. She did not know what to do. We ought to pray, she thought wildly. She shouted, "Everybody kneel! We'll pray!" But she doubted that anybody could hear her above the building's colossal shriek. Defeated and full of depair, she started to cry.

Inexplicably, the dim stairwell lights came on again.

Angela found herself staring at a gray-painted wall. An inch-wide crack extended from floor to ceiling. She was sure that crack had not been there when the lights went out.

Even as she stared at it, a second crack raced jaggedly across the wall to join the first. A foot-wide triangle of gypsum board fell from the juncture of the two cracks, hung by a flap of its cardboard facing for a moment, then tore loose and dropped to the floor.

Trying to hold down her rising panic, fighting to appear calm, Angela bent over the woman who had fallen onto the stairs. A Congressman's wife; Angela did not know her well. What *was* her name? "Come on, dear," Angela coaxed, tugging gently at the woman's arm with her good hand. "Not much farther now."

The woman opened her eyes, looked up at Angela for a second, then turned her face away. "No," she said. Angela had to bend close to hear her above the building's screech. "No. It's no use. I won't make it. Go on without me."

"What nonsense!" Angela shouted at her. "Get up on your feet this minute!"

The woman looked up at her in evident surprise. Then she began struggling to sit up. Some of the others helped her. They finally got her standing, clutching the railing with both hands.

With Angela once again in the lead, they continued their slow descent. Angela felt very tired. Her left arm was beginning to ache severely. She had lost count of the floors to such an extent that any guess could have been wrong by more than ten either way. She was also losing track of time. She just kept plodding downward, one stair at a time, mechanically and without awareness, like a sleepwalker.

She was jolted back to full awareness by the ghastly voice of the building. The scream suddenly began to rise crazily in both volume and pitch. It hurt Angela's ears. She had been holding hard to the stair rail with her good right hand, but now she let go and raised both hands to her ears to muffle that unbearable shriek. She lost her balance and fell heavily against the opposite wall.

She tried to right herself and found that she could not. It took her a few seconds to understand what was happening. Until she did understand, it was like being in one of those nightmares in which the legs won't respond to a command to walk or run. She felt as though she were attached to the wall by invisible elastic bands. Every time she tried to push herself away and stand upright, she was pulled back.

Then she knew. The strange force pulling her against the wall was the ordinary, unmysterious force of gravity. The building's lean had abruptly become more pronounced. She had fallen toward the downward side.

To get back across the stairs to the rail, she would have to walk uphill. Once her sense of balance was oriented, it was not difficult. She looked behind her and saw that her group was still with her. Then she continued the long walk down the tilted stairs.

Suddenly an entire large section of wall disintegrated and vanished. Angela found herself staring into an echoing blackness in which the building's screams and groans were

eerily distorted and magnified. In the dim light she could
see part of an exposed steel girder and also, just behind it,
something that moved in the wind that thundered up from
the darkness below. What was it? Yes, of course: a woven
steel cable. Angela realized she was looking into the elevator
shaft.

The sounds coming from that cavernous black hollow
had the timbre of an other-worldly choir, like colossal
human voices. They howled, wailed, screamed, and moaned
in despairing dissonance.

The stair beneath Angela's feet abruptly shifted. Its tilt
grew sharper. She clung to the stair rail. The tilt continued
to increase. Her feet began to slide out from under her.

She knew this was the building's death. It was falling.

The dim stairwell light went out. She was in total
darkness, surrounded by huge din and confusion. She lost
her grip on the rail and could think of nothing to do but curl
up like a fetus. Things crashed around her. She felt herself
falling, then rolling. Blasts of wind surged past her in all
directions. She came to rest on something that instantly
gave way, then fetched up against something else. Teeth
clinched, eyes shut tight, knees drawn up, hands and
forearms clutched around her head, she endured by not
thinking. Thinking was not possible—which was probably
lucky, for it might have driven her insane.

The noise rose to a volume such as she had never heard
before in her life, and then it subsided. Nothing remained
but the roar and howl of the wind. The building's screech
had stopped.

Angela felt herself and her surroundings. Her left hand
was completely without sensation, but as far as she could
tell everything else was in working order. She seemed to be
lying in a V-shaped trough formed by two flat surfaces.
Wind rushed around her, but nothing else moved.

The darkness was total. She sat up cautiously and looked

around. She could see nothing in any direction.

She asked in a loud voice, "Is anybody here?" There was no response. She shouted the question. Nobody answered. She heard nothing but the rushing of the wind immediately around her and a distant roaring sound.

The wind around her was not violent. It was more like a strong breeze. She had the impression of being enclosed in some kind of sheltering space. She felt over her head. Something hard, cold and rough-surfaced was up there. She slid forward on her bottom. Her feet came to an edge and hung out in empty space. Beyond the edge she could feel nothing in any direction with her feet. She slid back to her original position.

"Is anybody else here?" she shouted again. There was still no response.

She was alive and undamaged except for her hand. That was something to be thankful for. But she did not know how thankful.

• • •

Simon Pollock was scared. So were the two dozen others on the bus. They stared out the windows at a scene of continuous, violent destruction. Every few minutes the violence seemed to rise to a climax, after which, instead of slacking off, it would get worse.

It was night. The young Japanese man had started the bus's engine and turned on the heater and headlights. As though in a shared desire not to endure terror in the dark, other drivers had done the same. At first all the headlights pointed north, the direction they had been traveling on the one-way avenue. But then the wind began to push cars around. Lighter cars shifted first, then heavier ones, and finally large vehicles like the bus. Now the lights pointed in all directions. Further illumination came from some of the shabby little stores on both sides of the avenue. Apparently this section of the city still had electric power. The wind had smashed windows and blown out lights, but some interiors were still intact.

The bus was shuddering. A continual rain of flying objects big and small bounded and rolled on its windows. There was so much noise that individual impacts could not be heard. Nor was it possible to speak any longer. Even shouting into somebody's ear was useless.

Pollock watched helplessly as a little blue Honda in front of the bus turned broadside to the wind and tipped over. There were two occupants in the car. He could see their frightened faces in the windows. The little car fell on its side, then rolled onto its roof. Upside-down, it slid until it hit another car, which was also sliding. Both fetched up against the front of the bus. The bus was being turned toward the left, so that its right side was presented to the wind. It was leaning on vehicles to its left. Pollock could feel the right side lifting as the wind tried to tip it, but for the moment it was staying on its wheels.

The surface of the street was no longer visible. It was covered by a swift-flowing river of broken glass, trash, and bigger objects, including smashed office furniture. Pollock assumed much of it came from the office building nearby. A big, gray metal desk was wedged between the bus and a truck. Something that looked like the wrecked hulk of an electric typewriter had punched through the windshield of another truck and stuck there. Pollock thought he could see a human form in the driver's seat. The form had not moved for a long time.

Pollock walked restlessly to the back of the bus to see what was happening in that direction. In the headlights of jumbled cars he saw the row of sooty old buildings that had once been to the bus's right. One of them, a small hotel, was a few stories taller than its neighbors. It had seven or eight floors. Its front was narrow, but it seemed to stretch a good distance back from the street. Pollock could guess at its interior design. It was undoubtedly like thousands of other small hotels. On each floor a long narrow corridor would run from front to back, and on each side of the corridor would be doors that opened into cheerless little rooms.

Pollock did not know immediately why his wandering gaze was drawn to that one old building. There was something odd about it, but what?

Then he knew. The building was rocking.

A wind load of frightful power was pushing against its broad north wall. Pollock could not see that wall, but he could see the building's narrow front clearly, at least the lower part of it. The wall was of brick. As Pollock watched, horrified, large cracks opened and closed at the wall's northern corner like grinning mouths. Each time they opened, they grew wider and longer. Finally they did not close any more. They simply widened. Bricks fell out and were torn away by the wind.

The old building had received an injury from which it could not recover. It would fall to the south if the wind kept pushing it, and it would fall to the north if the wind should suddenly and miraculously stop. One way or the other, its life was over.

Pollock hoped nobody was still on its upper floors. Undoubtedly all the north windows were gone by now, and most of those on the lee side were probably destroyed, too. Anybody caught up there would find no shelter in the rooms but might huddle in the corridor. The floor of that corridor would now be rocking, tipping like the deck of a ship.

Pollock looked at what he could see of the upper stories. There was a single column of small windows in the very center of the hotel's narrow front. Almost certainly these windows marked the front end of each floor's central corridor. They were meant to provide ventilation and light, but in all likelihood they had been stuck shut for years and were opaque with grime. Now, however, all their glass had been ripped out. It must be wildly windy in those corridors, Pollock thought. For a second he thought he saw a face appear briefly at one of the window openings, but it was too dark up there to see anything clearly. He hoped what he had seen was in his imagination.

The gaps in the brickwork were steadily widening. Pollock knew he was seeing a classic demonstration of why tall, old brick structures are particularly vulnerable to high winds. As long as a brick wall has nothing more than the straight-down force of gravity to contend with, it is as strong as any other kind of wall. Indeed, its very weight is part of its strength. Each brick is held in place by the massive weight of other bricks above it. But when a high wind pushes against the wall and tries to uproot that side of the building, the direction of forces is reversed. The wall now "goes into tension," as structural engineers put it. Instead of pushing down on itself, the wall now tries to pull itself apart.

In a situation like that, ordinary brickwork mortar does not serve effectively as a glue to hold bricks together. In fact, some mortars are so ineffective as glues that segments of old brick walls can be pulled apart with the bare hands. Pollock watched the old hotel unglue itself in just that way. As each crack opened up, bricks at the top of the crack were relieved of the ponderous weight that had held them in place for decades and would have gone on holding them for decades longer if left undisturbed. But now, with the weight removed, bricks simply fell away and were carried off by the wind.

A crack bigger than all the others had appeared at about the level of the second floor. The entire top of the aged building was leaning to the south, hinged on its south wall. As it leaned more and more, the second-floor gap enlarged.

In the near-darkness up there Pollock could see parts of the exposed interior. He saw stumps of broken-off wall studs and a white object that he thought might be a bathtub. One doorframe was uncannily intact, with the door still clinging to its hinges. As Pollock watched, the door was torn off and blown away.

To his horror, he then saw that somebody was clinging to the doorframe. He could not tell whether it was a man or a woman. He or she had apparently sought refuge in the corridor and was now finding that refuge ripped apart. Pollock thought with sympathetic anguish: what a nightmare to live through! The wind would probably have torn off all the victim's clothes, so the naked body would be exposed to flying glass and other debris. But the anguish did not last long. The doorframe came apart. It and the clinging refugee were snatched away by the screaming wind. At the same instant the top of the old building was collapsing on a smaller building to its south. The crash could not be heard above the screaming wind. Dust and debris exploded up and out in all directions, and then were instantly carried off. Pollock had a last glimpse of the hapless refugee vanishing into this cloud, flying, tumbling end-over-end.

Shaken, Pollock turned and started toward the front of the bus. All the passengers had instinctively moved to the lee side, the left. He could see Cissy Medina's dark head not far behind the driver's seat, where the young Japanese man still sat. Pollock groped his way up the aisle, moving with difficulty because the bus was heaving up and down as the wind tried to tip it over.

Something long and thin suddenly punched through a window to his right, shot past him a few inches from his face, and embedded itself in the left side of the bus like a spear.

The tail end quivered, then stilled. Pollock stared at it. It was a crumpled street sign. It was difficult to read in the dim light, but he thought it said eighty-something street. It had traveled more than thirty blocks.

Wind invaded the bus through the broken window. The front windshield and rear window both ripped away. Pollock felt himself tumbling with other people amid an incredible noise. Somehow he managed to grab the overhead luggage rack and hold on. More windows burst. The young Japanese man was scooped out of the driver's seat and hurled out into the shrieking night, followed by other passengers. One of them was Cissy. Pollock saw her for the last time as she stopped herself momentarily by grabbing something near the front of the bus, perhaps the steering wheel. He thought she was looking at him, and he thought he received her message. *It could have been worse, Simon,* he thought she was telling him. *Suppose we had never met?*

"Cissy!" he howled. "Cissy!"

But she was gone.

The bus tipped over onto its left side. It was resting partly on a truck and some crushed office furniture. It pivoted on top of the truck like a giant seesaw. The front end dipped down. The wind caught the rear end and lifted the bus until it was standing on its head. The bus stood poised like that for a moment, then fell on its roof amid a jumble of other vehicles.

Wind blasted through the bus. It tore Simon Pollock loose from his handhold and shot him out through the opening where the bifold doors had been. It lifted him high, high over the street, over the low buildings, then still higher. He saw lights below. He started to tumble head-over-heels, but then stabilized himself by instinctively spreading his arms and legs.

I'm flying, he thought wildly. Flying! He was conscious of one pure, bright moment of exhilaration. At last, in the very last minute of his life, he was doing what he had always dreamed of but had never expected to experience. He was soaring in the sky like a hawk.

He opened his mouth and uttered a single great shout of triumph. And then the wind hurled him back to the earth. The impact was so violent that he had no chance to feel it. He died immediately, still shouting his triumph.

● ● ●

All the lights went out in the *Seven Days* archive area, including the lounge room. There were rumbling noises all around. Somebody lighted a Coleman gasoline lantern on a low coffee table. The harsh white light threw people's shadows on the walls and accentuated the fear in their eyes. They looked around uneasily.

A teenage girl started to cry. She had told Julia her name was Karen. She had only just graduated from high school and was one week into her first full-time job in the *Seven Days* circulation department. The department had been dismissed at noon, but she and some friends, too excited to go home, had stayed in town for lunch and then had found themselves trapped by the unannounced shutdown of the city subway system. Her friends—three other girls, none as old as twenty— huddled nearby.

"Do you think it's safe down here, Ms. Mead?" Karen asked. She and her friends were sitting on the floor. She looked up at Julia imploringly.

Julia started to reply that she was not qualified to make such a judgment, but then she decided on a more soothing answer. This girl doesn't want engineering facts, Julia thought; she wants me to play Grandmother. She wants me to pat her on the head and say, "There, there." Julia restrained herself from doing that, for she was not a grandmotherly personality and knew she could not have pulled it off successfully. Instead she said, "It feels safe to me, dear."

"But this whole place keeps shaking." Karen looked at the shadowed walls fearfully. "Do you *really* think it's safe?"

"Don't worry," Julia said. "It's a well-built building."

This statement was not altogether candid. The *Seven Days* building, completed and certified for occupancy in 1960, not long before she joined the company, had never been entirely satisfactory. It seemed to Julia that she was always on the phone to the maintenance department about something going wrong. The heating and air-conditioning had never worked right despite years of tinkering. Cracks were forever appearing along wall and ceiling plaster joints. The maintenance chief had tried to soothe her irritation by asserting that all buildings have problems. It was naive to expect perfection, he said. Julia did not clearly understand why one couldn't expect perfection, considering how much one had to pay for construction and maintenance, but she finally was able to resign herself to the world as it was and to stop fretting.

"Suppose we get trapped down here," Karen said in a high, small voice. "I couldn't *stand* that. Trapped down here in the dark!" She hugged herself and shivered.

The girl is going to work herself into hysterics, Julia thought. She leaned forward on the sofa, reached down and touched Karen on the shoulder. "We'll be okay," she said.

At that moment there was a loud crack from a corner of the big room. Julia jumped, felt Karen jump under her hand, felt Arthur jump next to her on the sofa. Everybody in the room turned to look at the source of the sound. The corner was in a far end of the room, darkly shadowed. People pulled out flashlights and shone them down there.

For a moment they saw nothing out of the ordinary. At that end of the room a partition wall, painted a sunny yellow, ran under one of the massive beams that were spaced across the ceiling. In the corner where the loud sound had seemed to originate, a doorway was set into the yellow wall. The door was open. It led, Julia knew, into a narrow room that housed microfiche viewers.

Then someone said, "Oh, my God!"

They all seemed to see it simultaneously. They rose to their feet in unison, staring.

One of the doorposts was bent, snapped in the middle. The crack they had heard had been the sound of its breaking.

Even as they watched, the bend became more pronounced. The other doorpost was bowed toward the broken one, giving the doorframe an unnatural hourglass shape. The bowed post snapped. The frame continued to distort, as though being slowly but inexorably squashed downward from above.

Julia realized with sudden terror that that was exactly what was happening. The massive beam overhead was either bending or sagging, resting its colossal weight on the doorframe and the rest of the yellow wall that ran beneath it. That wall was not meant to support weight. Its structural members were standard two-by-four-inch wood studs, whose only duty was to provide a firm framework on which to nail a gypsum-board surface.

The door's top hinge tore away. The door sagged and hung quivering at a crazy angle. The yellow wall was now making a continuous, sharp crackling noise as the beam's unimaginable weight gradually settled down on it, snapping two-by-fours like toothpicks. The sheetrock surface was tearing loose and hanging in strips and flaps. Elbows of broken studs pushed themselves through the sheetrock, made openings, and gradually enlarged them. It all seemed to be happening in ghastly slow motion. The great beam was not settling fast, but it could not be stopped. Incredible weight must be bearing down on it from above.

"What's happening, Arthur?" Julia asked, grabbing his

arm. "Is the building coming apart?" She realized that her voice, normally low and slow, was coming out in a much higher register than usual.

Arthur touched one of her hands with his but otherwise stood perfectly still. "It looks as if the building is shifting," he said. "Or leaning, perhaps. The weight—it must be shifting to the wrong places." He spoke loudly to be heard over the cracking and groaning of the slowly disintegrating yellow wall, but there was no detectable fright in his voice.

It's important to keep it that way, Julia thought. She was aware that Karen and her three friends were huddled in a tight clump, looking first at the crumpling wall and then at Julia and Arthur. The young women's eyes were wide with panic. They were begging to be led to safety. One of them was whimpering like a puppy. Karen kept saying over and over again, "My God, oh my God, my *God!*" Her voice was sometimes a whisper, sometimes a squeal.

Well, Julia thought, in a situation like this, no grandmother worth the name would let herself give in to hysteria. When she spoke, she copied Arthur's voice. She spoke loudly enough to be heard, but her tone was low and calm. She said, "We'd better find some other shelter, don't you think?"

He nodded. "Yes, but the question is—"

He was interrupted by several events that happened simultaneously. The sound of the crumpling yellow wall grew louder, and so did the rumbling from other parts of the building. At the same time the great beam started to become visible. It had been covered with a wood framework to which acoustical tile had been stapled, but now the framework was distorting as the beam sagged, and tiles were falling off. The beam was revealed as a huge "I" of rust-red steel. At the same moment that it came into view, something white fell between Julia and Arthur and bounced off both their shoulders. It was not heavy, only startling. It was followed by a shower of dust.

Julia looked up. It took all her self-control to swallow the cry of fear that rose into her throat.

The thing that had fallen was an acoustical tile. Directly over their heads was another colossal beam. It was either sagging or twisting. Julia thought she could see its motion, but she knew that might be merely a trick played by a panicked mind. More tiles fell as she stared upward, revealing both the steel beam and the flimsy wood framework to which the tiles had been attached. The framework was being subjected to unaccustomed tension as the beam changed shape or position. A nail popped loose, and a stick of wood flew across the room end-over-end.

"This way, I think," Arthur was saying in a matter-of-fact tone. He gestured with his flashlight toward the end of the room opposite the disintegrating yellow wall. The light showed another yellow-painted wall with a doorway set into it, also under a huge beam. But there was no indication so far that this beam had begun to shift or sag. The wall and doorway were intact.

Julia shouted to the group: "This way out! Follow us!"

People gathered survival packs and switched on flashlights. The owner of the Coleman lantern picked it up, causing the wall shadows to dance eerily.

"Come on, girls," Julia said to the little clump of teenagers. But now they were frozen. They were clinging to one another. They could not let go.

Julia gently disengaged one of Karen's hands from the cloth of another girl's jacket. "We'll hold hands, " Julia said. "Make a chain."

The terrified girls did not seem to understand at first. But after a few frustrating seconds, Julia got the hand-to-hand chain organized. Other frightened people joined the chain. With both hands thus occupied, none of them could hold flashlights. Luckily, some people who were more stoical fell in behind them. With Arthur and Julia leading the way, the group filed through the doorway in the intact yellow wall.

Julia had just passed the doorway when something in the wall snapped. This beam, too, was starting to move. Karen squealed with fear and tried to pull her hand from Julia's, obviously wanting to run. Julia held on firmly.

"Just follow me, girls," she called back over her shoulder. "Keep your cool." She was pleased to find her voice low, calm, and strong. "Hold tight."

One of the girls broke out of the chain and started to run, but she was restrained by another girl and eventually linked hands again. "That's the way, girls," Julia shouted encouragingly. "It won't help to go tearing around in all directions. Just hold on. We'll get there."

Get where? she did not know. But the frightened girls followed her in mute obedience. Just like ducklings following a mother duck, she thought, briefly amused.

They walked through cramped, narrow-aisled archive rooms, then emerged in a small elevator lobby. The single elevator that served this subterranean floor was waiting for passengers with its twin doors open, but it was without electric power. It might never rise again.

Arthur paused. The group stopped behind him. They still heard the loud rumbling all around them, pierced occasionally by a metallic clanging. But the ceiling over their heads looked undamaged so far. It was a plain, smooth white ceiling— gypsumboard, Julia sumised. She examined it nervously and saw a few cracks, but she thought they could have been there for years.

Arthur came back to stand next to her. "I'm not sure if I'm leading us right, but it was all I could think of," he said, speaking into her ear to overcome the noises of the building. "I tried to visualize what would happen if a building like this should be pushed over by a wind. It seemed to me we'd be safest on the windward side."

"That would be the north."

"I think so. If we're dealing with tornadoes whirling around every which way, then no amount of figuring can help us. But if it's a straight wind from the north, then—" he shrugged.

"As least it gives us something to try. We can't just stand here chewing our fingernails, can we?"

"Or wetting our diapers," he said, gesturing with his head at Julia's little string of ducklings.

"Don't be unkind, Arthur," she chided. "The poor things are badly scared."

"You're right, that was unkind," he agreed. "If you want the truth, Julia, I'm scared, too. As scared as I've ever been in my life."

He did not sound scared, however. He sounded perfectly calm—just a man solving a problem. Julia hoped she sounded the same.

He said, "Unless I'm completely disoriented, that lounge we were in was somewhere near the south side of the building. Wasn't it?"

Julia thought for a moment. "I think so," she said uncertainly.

"All right. Now what I've been trying to do is visualize a tall building being pushed toward the south." He sounded very much like a professor delivering a lecture, Julia thought. His voice was even, measured, even dry. "The weight would shift onto the south wall, wouldn't it? Whatever was under the building on that side—the foundation, the supports—would be crushed under more weight than they were built to take."

Julia saw it in her mind's eye. "Not only weight," she said. "There might be a sideways push, too. Beams would get pushed off whatever they were supposed to rest on."

"Exactly. I think what we saw in the lounge was something like that starting to happen. But it would only happen on the downwind side of the building, it seems to me. Wouldn't it?"

"Yes!" Julia agreed, still visualizing it. "The other side wouldn't crush down. It would lift up."

"So it seems to me that's where we belong. Somewhere north of here."

The floor under their feet suddenly shuddered violently. There was a loud crash from the open elevator doors, and dust poured out into the small lobby. When the dust cloud thinned, they saw that a concrete block the size of a suitcase had punched through the elevator roof and embedded itself in the floor.

Shining her flashlight upward, Julia saw that the cracks in the lobby ceiling were enlarged. Even as she looked, one edge of the ceiling board pulled away from its adjoining wall. A strip of paper joint tape flopped down, raining white plaster dust.

The building's breakup seemed to be following the group. "We ought to keep moving north," Julia suggested. Arthur nodded and led the way through a doorway at the northern end of the lobby.

The entire building seemed to be shaking now. As they walked in single file down corridors and through drab-walled utility rooms, dust and small pieces of debris fell on them in a continual rain. They came at last into a big room in which the walls and ceiling were covered with copper and plastic pipes of various diameters. Julia assumed they were water pipes. Gauges and color-keyed valve handles sprouted from the pipes like flowers in a strange garden. In the central floor space of the room were half a dozen big blue machines, bolted to the concrete. Julia thought these were probably the pumps that daily lifted thousands of tons of water to the building's high floors. Without electric power, they were now dead metal hulks.

There was no doorway from this room that allowed any further progress toward the north. The man with the Coleman lantern and several other people made a quick search of surrounding rooms and corridors. They came back to report that, as far as they could tell, this was indeed the northernmost end of the basement. The two dozen refugees settled down to find what comfort they could on hard wooden benches and a hard floor.

And then the building fell.

The steady rumbling they had been hearing increased abruptly to a roar like close thunder, mixed with higher-pitched clanging and screeching sounds. The solid concrete floor shuddered. At the south end of the room the end farthest from the huddled group, a water pipe burst, and then another. Julia and others shone flashlights down there. What she saw was a scene from a nightmare. There was a thicket of pipes attached to the ceiling, hanging from metal straps and rods. The pipes were writhing like worms.

More pipes burst. Some dribbled water; some sprayed water briefly, then stopped; others spurted continuously. Some of the water was hot. The room quickly filled with steam. None of the spray reached the group, but water on the floor began to flow around their feet.

The pipes writhed more and more violently. Supporting rods and straps tore loose from the ceiling. Pipes sagged and fell. Now the entire ceiling at the south end of the room was visibly moving. In this room the ceiling consisted of rough wood planks laid across naked steel I-beams. The planks were shifting. Some were sliding apart, while others seemed to be jamming together and arching up.

A huge I-beam at the south end of the room was lifting. Up, up it rose, an inch at a time. It pulled pipes and planks up with it. An arm-thick electrical cable had lain across its top. The cable broke. A four- or five-foot length flopped down into the room and hung swaying from the rising

beam. But it stayed there only for a second. Unimaginable
forces farther away were pulling on it. It was drawn up over
the top of the beam and vanished.

Karen was screaming. Julia held the girl's hand tightly.
Another girl started to scramble to her feet, but Arthur
caught her and pulled her down onto the bench where he
was sitting. He spoke into her ear. Julia could not hear what
he said, but she felt the calming force that radiated from the
man. She watched as he gently raised the back of the girl's
jacket and pulled it over her head. The girl leaned forward,
put her face between her knees and covered her head with
arms and hands.

Julia remembered receiving similar instructions aboard
an airliner once, in preparation for a possible rough landing.
She indicated by gestures that others ought to cover up in
the same way. Not all had jackets or coats, and not all were
limber enough to touch head to knees, but most managed to
work themselves into some kind of protective position. Julia
was starkly aware that none of this would be of the slightest
help if chunks of concrete or other heavy objects should fall
on them, but the head-covered position seemed better than
open exposure. Besides, it felt comforting.

She had one last look around before curling into the
position herself. The room was now so full of steam and
dust that nothing was clearly visible any longer. There
seemed to be a yawning black gap where the rising steel
beam had been. Ceiling planks and other objects big and
small, none clearly identifiable, were raining down around
the big blue water pumps. Julia had the horrifying impression that one object was a human head. Her flashlight beam
glanced off what looked like a single staring eye. In a
fraction of an instant that brilliant dead eye imprinted itself
indelibly on her memory, and then it was gone, buried
beneath other objects and obscured by dust and steam.

Julia closed her eyes and curled up.

The bench on which she sat was shuddering, and so was the concrete floor beneath her feet. The shuddering rose rapidly to a crescendo, then abruptly stopped. So did the metallic clanging and screeching sounds. The only sound left was a steady roaring.

The pump room was suddenly invaded by wind. It was not a particularly powerful wind. It was gusty, blowing first in one direction, then another.

People uncurled themselves and sat up. They shone flashlights here and there, trying to figure out what their situation was.

They looked at each other's faces. They were smothered with dust, and some had minor cuts and bruises, but they were all still alive. That was the first fact that made itself understood in their numbed minds.

Looking up, they saw that the ceiling in their end of the room was still intact. Planks rested on steel beams, which rested on concrete pillars. Everything seemed firm and orderly.

But the ceiling at the other end of the room was gone. Flashlights revealed nothing but a great, gaping blackness. The steady roaring seemed to come from that blackness.

"Do you know what that is up there?" Arthur said into Julia's ear.

She knew, but for a time she did not understand how she knew. She shouted back, "Yes. It's the night. The open air. That sound is the wind."

She was puzzled by her own answer. But then the elements of the situation grew clear to her one by one as the fog of fright and confusion drifted away. It was apparent that the *Seven Days* building had fallen away from them, toward the south. They were sitting in a northern end or corner of the basement, several floors below street level. As the building toppled, parts of the basement level and foundation structure were uprooted. But a break in the structure occurred somewhere above them, perhaps at ground level. The aboveground part of the falling building wrenched itself away from what lay below, including their corner.

So here they were, huddled in a little half-roofed enclosure perhaps thirty feet down, frightened but safe.

"I think the worst is over for now," Arthur said over the noise. "As long as the wind doesn't blow us any new surprises." He was mopping his hard, lined face with a handkerchief. "Believe me, Julia, I've never been so happy to say something is over."

"You seemed as cool as a cucumber throughout," she commented.

"Pure play-acting," he said. He put his handkerchief in his pocket. Then he held his hands out in front of Julia's flashlight. They were shaking.

• • •

It was Danny who first saw the pigeon. Stunned, with one wing broken and half its feathers missing, it had revived and struggled out of the great wind-driven mound of trash that was pushing through the plywood doors. It could not fly and was not even trying to. It simply came walking aimlessly across the floor, and Danny said, "Look!"

That was when they became aware of their predicament.

Pushed by the frightful force of a wind that had reached at least three hundred miles an hour, the trash mound had forced the doors open despite the heavy cartons placed against them. The mound was now inexorably advancing into the long, narrow basement room.

The mound's leading edge had nearly reached the foot of the stairs leading up to the restaurant. Walter, the young man with the thick glasses, went up the stairs and tried a second time to open the steel-clad door at the top. Two other men also tried. The door would not budge. It was evident that the restaurant's management, though not much concerned about thefts from the storage basement, had gone to greater pains to keep burglars out of the restaurant proper.

The last man to try the door was almost trapped by the advancing mound of debris. It crept across the foot of the stairs just as he was coming down.

The three dozen people in the storage room stood and looked at the mound that was rapidly eating up their space. It stretched from floor to ceiling and from wall to wall. It moved forward with a rolling motion. Material and objects continually came into view at the top, cascaded down the front face and eventually were buried at the bottom. It was made of paper, dust, shards and slivers of glass, pigeons, bits of furniture, and other objects that seemed to get larger as time went on. Kim saw an automobile tire, a suitcase, an executive-style swivel chair.

And then she saw something else that her mind at first refused to identify. It was a human hand, cut off at the wrist. A woman's hand, with pink-polished fingernails and a large ruby ring. Kim stared at it in horror until it vanished beneath an avalanche of splintered glass.

The mound rolled on. Kim looked behind her. The only way out of the storage room now was through the sidewalk delivery doors. Some people were already standing near the stairs that led up to those doors in the ceiling. But nobody was going up the stairs. The two black iron doors were shuddering violently in the ferocious wind that blew across them up above. It was plain that to go through those doors and out onto the sidewalk would mean certain death.

The doors were making a loud, metallic thundering sound. Dimly, above that noise, Kim heard somebody shouting something about a retaining wall. It was the white-haired old lady. "Use all the crates and cartons!" she was yelling. "Make it high and thick. Get your backs into it, girls!"

"Right on, Granny!" agreed Suze, the young woman with orange hair. Everybody began to carry and slide heavy cartons into position in front of the advancing trash mound. They formed a wall that gradually grew higher. As the mound continued to advance, some tried to scoop at it with their hands so as to slow its forward motion. But there was so much broken glass in it that they had to give that up.

Suddenly the entire basement shook as though hit by an earthquake. The ceiling lights went out. Over the metallic sound of the iron doors Kim heard a rumbling that seemed to surround her completely. It reminded her of the sound made by a subway train pulling into a station. The floor vibrated beneath her feet. The noise continued for several minutes, while people fumbled in the dark for flashlights. Then, as flashlights flicked on one by one, the rumbling gradually subsided.

Kim was relieved to see Nick holding Danny not far away. Everyone was unharmed. The storage room was just as it had been before, except for the absence of electric power.

And except for the mound of debris. It had continued its inexorable crawl. It was spilling over the top and around the ends of the incomplete retaining wall.

"Let's go!" Granny shouted. "We've got to stop that monster before it eats us alive!"

Frantically, her troops hauled cartons and crates to the wall. But the task was hopeless now. The top of the incomplete wall was already partly covered with spilling trash, so that there was no flat surface on which to pile the next higher course of cartons. In any case, the pressure of wind behind the mound was so great that the finished section of the wall was being pushed out of shape. It was obvious that the wall would not have held for long even if completed. They lacked enough time and enough cartons and crates to make it as thick as it needed to be. They stood back, defeated.

The wall slowly vanished beneath the advancing mound.
"Oh boy," somebody said. "What do we do now?"

"Maybe praying would help," Granny suggested. "Anybody know a good prayer for a time like this?"

Nobody answered. The thirty-odd people stood huddled together at the back end of the storage room, staring at the oncoming mound. Some stood at the lower end of the stairway leading up to the sidewalk doors, but nobody had yet been tempted to go up and open the doors. In the end, Kim surmised, some would. Some would panic. She felt fear rising in her and all around her. She guessed there would be some who would have a special problem with claustrophobia. Trapped in a dark space that was getting ever smaller, some would decide in the end that death outdoors in a killer wind was preferable to death by suffocation or crushing down here. She fought to keep her composure and hugged Danny against her side.

The foot of the mound was now about ten feet from the stairs. People huddled closer together, gazing at the monster in the uneven illumination of flashlights. The iron doors rattled and drummed overhead.

A woman began to recite the Hail Mary prayer in a high, sing-song voice. Some other Catholics joined in, but most in the crowd did not know the prayer. When it was finished, a man said a prayer in Yiddish. Granny then tried to lead the group in saying the more widely known Lord's Prayer. But the response to that, too, was sporadic and unenthusiastic. It did not surprise Kim. She knew from her AA experience that praying is not really as great a comfort as advertised, except to those of the deepest piety.

The mound advanced another two feet. People pressed backward against each other. Danny began to cry.

Instinctively, without thinking about it, Kim began to sing. What came from her throat was the grand old Protestant hymn, "Abide With Me." She might not have chosen that hymn if she had thought about it, for the words are gloomy in places. But her choice was immediately endorsed by the group. The lovely old song was familiar to people of all faiths, lacked any sectarian propaganda, and gave itself readily to harmonizing by ear. One by one, people joined in whether they knew the words or not.

As soon as she heard Danny and Alice Wenska and other women taking up the melody in the soprano register, Kim dropped down to the alto part. Nick and some other men picked up the bass. As usual in amateur choirs, there was a shortage of tenors, but the gap was filled handily by the two clarinets. One played a high, clear straight tenor, while the other danced around the part, straying into the alto and soprano ranges when the time seemed right.

Many people did not know the words. Kim overcame that difficulty by simply repeating the first verse until all were familiar with it. The harmony grew richer, the voices stronger and more confident.

The steady advance of the trash mound pushed people closer and closer together. They put their arms around each other. The acoustics of the gradually shrinking cellar were churchlike. The music bounced off the thick concrete walls and returned subtly enlarged. Kim felt tears running down her cheeks.

There was another episode of thundering around them. As before, the floor shook. This episode lasted a few minutes, as the first one had. The group kept singing.

The mound was now about four feet from the stairs. Soon there would be no more floor space to retreat into. People nearest to the mound were already getting dust and glass slivers on their shoes.

The thundering and floor vibrations stopped. Still the group sang on. There was something different about the music now, but Kim did not know what it was. She puzzled over the change. What was it? A greater clarity, she thought. But in what way?

Then she knew. "Hey!" she shouted, pointing upward.

The singing stopped. The only sound left was a distant rumbling and a clinking of glass from the still-advancing mound. The black iron sidewalk doors overhead were still.

Walter had noticed it at the same time as Kim. He was already on his way up the stairs. He felt one of the doors with the flat of a hand, then put his ear against it. The group watched him in tense anticipation.

"Well," he announced at last, "I sure can't explain this, but there's no more wind up here."

"How can a wind stop that suddenly?" somebody asked.

Walter shrugged. "I told you I couldn't explain it. But you can come up here and listen for yourself. If there's any wind blowing on the other side of these doors, it's no more than a breeze."

Nick said, "There's still a hell of a wind blowing somewhere. This mound is still pushing forward."

"Well, what'll we do?" Walter asked him.

"We open the doors. I don't understand it either, but out there, maybe we've got a chance. Down here we've got none."

Walter unfastened the stout bolt under the doors and very slowly pushed one door open. He poked his head through the gap and looked around. Three dozen people below waited in anxious silence for his report.

He pulled his head back down. "I'm not sure exactly what I'm seeing up there," he told the group. He pulled a flashlight from his belt. "But there sure isn't any wind to worry about."

He poked his head up through the door gap again, then thrust the flashlight through it. After a while he pushed the door wide open, allowing it to settle against its retaining rod. Slowly and cautiously, he mounted another step, then one more, so that those below could see only his legs. He spent a long time up there examining his surroundings. Finally he came back down the stairs, looking puzzled.

"This is going to sound crazy," he said. "There's a sidewalk up there, all right. I know it's a sidewalk. I can see the curb, and a street with cars on it. But the funny thing is—there seems to be some kind of roof overhead."

"A *roof*? What kind of roof?"

"I don't know. My flashlight is pretty dim. It's a roof that's way up high over the street. It slopes. It's shiny."

There was a short, puzzled silence. Then the entire group started up the stairs. Walter opened the second of the two doors to facilitate the exodus. By the time the last of the group stepped out onto the sidewalk, the trash mound below was covering the bottom two stairs and climbing fast.

Three dozen people stood huddled together on the sidewalk, silently shining flashlights upward and around.

Finally somebody said, "My God!"

The roof that Walter had seen was a building. It had toppled across the street and was leaning against another building on the other side. Flashlight beams picked out shiny wall sections and the windows of what had once been offices. A few of the windows were inexplicably intact, but most were missing their glass. Some had jumbles of office furniture and equipment wedged against their frames, hanging out over the street. Directly overhead, Kim saw a protruding corner of a large buff-colored metal cabinet, perhaps part of a computer. Even as she looked at it, it shifted its position in the window, and a shower of dust dropped on the group below. The signal was clear: it would not be safe to stay here.

The collapse of this building and perhaps others explained the thundering and vibrations they had felt down below. Evidently the collapse had happened in such a way as to create a wind-sheltered hollow space, roofed over by the toppled building, blocked at both ends by impenetrable rubble.

The street was a shambles. The wind had made its terrifying power felt here before it was blocked off by the collapse. Cars and trucks were jumbled against each other in wild disarray, some upside-down or on their sides. A few still appeared to have their motors running, for there was a smell of exhaust smoke in the air, and some cars had their headlights on. All around the cars and all over the sidewalk were piles of broken furniture and drifts of glass and debris.

A constant, low rumbling sound came from somewhere far away. It might have been the wind. In this hollow, however, only a light breeze blew.

Human forms and faces were visible in some of the car windows. Most were still. But one man had climbed from a tipped-over truck and was now making his way unsteadily toward the group, looking dazed but unhurt. In an upside-down Isuzu nearby, a woman and child were signaling frantically that they were trapped and needed help. Some from the group went over to see what they could do.

A car on the other side of the street abruptly burst into flames. Kim also saw smoke starting to drift out of one of the blown-out windows overhead.

"We ought to get out of here in a hurry," she said to Nick.

"You're worrying about this thing collapsing?" He pointed to the toppled building over their heads.

"Yes, and also the fires. My guess is this whole place will be an inferno before long." She gestured to indicate the hollow space around them.

He nodded, catching her meaning immediately. "Yes," he said, "you're right. Not enough wind. Where did we read that?"

"Somewhere in the research."

She remembered it clearly: an arresting fact in an otherwise dull scholarly paper. Wind up to a certain velocity will fan many kinds of fires and make them more fierce. City and forest firefighters all fear and hate wind for that reason. But really high winds—winds above the strength of a Category Two hurricane—tend to have the opposite effect. These winds will blow out a fire the way you blow out a candle. Indeed, certain intractable fires that cannot be controlled by any other means—oil- and gas-well fires, for example—can be extinguished by blowing them out with dynamite.

These same high winds will also prevent fires from getting started. Kim's guess was that there were few fires in New York at this moment, no matter what terrible destruction the wind had wrought. However, it seemed likely that the widespread ruin would create many situations in which fires might start when the wind died down. These fires would start first in sheltered places like the hollow in which the group now stood.

Kim looked around the hollow for an exit. She saw none. The building across the street was almost hidden behind piles of rubble, great chunks of concrete and twisted steel girders that were too big to clear away by hand. The only visible part of the building was a blank wall of gray stone blocks. There were no doors in that wall, nor any windows.

On Kim's side of the street, a side entrance to the Italian restaurant was clear of rubble. It was not far from the sidewalk delivery doors. She went to it and tried it. It was a heavy steelclad door like the one they had tried from below, and was just as securely locked against intruders.

Kim consoled herself with the thought that the door probably did not lead to any safe haven anyway. The group needed to get underground before there were further collapses or fires. The restaurant's storage cellar was of course blocked with debris. Even if they did get into the restaurant, they would probably find there was nowhere to go.

Kim turned from the door. At that moment the burning car's gas tank erupted in flames. An orange ball of fire rose to the windowed ceiling formed by the toppled building. Some furniture wedged in a window began to burn.

Nobody seemed to be hurt by the eruption. Several men and women helping the trapped pair from the Isuzu looked shaken, however. They were undoubtedly wondering if the flames would spread to other cars nearer to them.

There was a sudden, loud rumbling noise. The ground shook for a few seconds, then stilled. Dust and debris fell from the fallen building's windows. Apparently the building had shifted. Kim heard a metallic crash near her and jumped in panic. The buff-colored computer cabinet had been dislodged and had fallen to the sidewalk. She was just thinking how lucky it was that the computer had missed everybody when something hit her on the head. She was in a shower of books. She covered her head and pressed herself against the restaurant door. The books were followed by an umbrella, a desk calendar, and finally, a snowstorm of fluttering papers and file folders.

She looked up at the building. Its weight must be enormous. How long would it stay propped up there?

She wondered if the New World Center had withstood the wind. Mother, dear Mother, she thought. And the *Seven Days* building? Had that tremendous crash anything to do with it? Her father had been up there. She knew him to be a tough and resourceful man, but what could he do in a disaster like this?

The toppled building shifted again. A telephone handset fell from a window and danced crazily on its spiral cord. Kim saw Danny clinging to Nick's leg, looking frightened.

More books rained down around Kim. She next saw Nick standing in the street, looking down at something near the curb. Perplexed, she saw him kneel for a closer look. She started toward him, and then she understood. He was looking down into a storm drain.

"If we can get this cover off," he said, "this could be our exit. It looks comfortable enough down there."

"Isn't it smelly?"

"Not particularly. It isn't a sewer, it's only a storm drain. There's street garbage in it, sure." He shone his flashlight down through the grating. "Orange peels, stuff like that. Probably some rats." he grinned up at her. "Don't worry, I'll protect you against the rats."

"My hero," Kim said sourly. She was not enthusiastic about rats.

Others had gathered around. Several men bent to the task of lifting off the grating. It was ponderously heavy, but it moved. The group then climbed one by one down iron rungs to a narrow concrete walkway below. The woman and child rescued from the Isuzu were hurt and needed to be helped, but all others made it easily enough.

Strangely, it was more windy down here than on the surface. A strong breeze blew from the blackness of the tunnel. Nick had already started walking toward the breeze. He waited until the entire group was assembled on the walkway, then led a single-file march.

They walked crouched, holding flashlights. The tunnel was about five feet high. A spaghetti of utility pipes and cables ran along its top. To the left of the walkway, a stream of trash-laden brown water flowed in the same direction as the breeze. At intervals, smaller pipes intersected the main tunnel at right angles. Kim surmised these were drain outlets from the basements and sumps of individual buildings.

The only rat she saw during the march was sitting in the

opening of one of those smaller pipes. The rat regarded the passing group with bright-eyed interest, then retreated into the darkness of the pipe. Kim shone her flashlight into the opening. The rat was sitting with its back to her, nonchalantly scrubbing its whiskers.

She was relieved to note that the rat was plump and glossy-furred. It was obviously eating well and so would have no pressing need to come near the group. Kim recalled reading that rats, unless goaded by starvation or some other great discomfort, prefer to avoid human company. That made her feel better, though not much better. She was not perfectly sure the information was correct. But it must at least be true, she thought, that life in a city storm drain would be heaven for a rat. Warm in winter, cool in summer, with a perpetual supply of food from the streets above: what more could the average rat want?

So Kim reasoned. It was a comfort of sorts. But she still kept nervously shining her flashlight into dark places as they walked.

The breeze strengthened. A steady roaring sound echoed along the tunnel, and that also grew stronger as they proceeded. In time they came to the source of both breeze and noise.

It was another street grating. This one was apparently open to the sky and exposed to the full force of the shrieking wind. Kim and others stood at the bottom of the access well and shone flashlights upward. Wind screamed across the holes in the iron grating high above them. Some of its force was deflected downward. It came down the access well and blew along the tunnel in gale-force gusts.

There was no need for any discussion. One by one, the underground travelers found places to sit on the walkway and rummaged in their survival packs for food and drink. There was nothing to do but wait.

19

WHEN THE SUN came up over New York the next morning, the wind had died down to Admiral Beaufort's range of normalcy. There were occasional gusts of about fifty miles an hour. For most of the day, however, the sustained wind was no stronger than what the admiral would have called a fresh breeze.

● ● ●

George and Wilma Hochenauer and some other refugees emerged from the basement of the Flatiron Building. They were puzzled to find the lobby dark, though their watches said it was morning. Flashlights revealed that the thick glass swinging doors at one end of the lobby had been ripped away, and a great drift of rubble and trash had pushed through the opening and blocked it. The doors at the other end were still there, protected by an upside-down car that had blown against them. Broken furniture and other bits of debris were piled on and around the car. A few chinks of daylight showed through this pile.

After an hour's work, they cleared a space to climb through. They stood on a clear patch of sidewalk and looked around, awed.

In later years, what Hochenauer remembered most clearly about that moment was the vast silence. New York

City had never been that silent in all his lifetime, nor in many generations before him. Even at its quietest, even in the slow dark hours between midnight and dawn, this huge city had never slept. There was always some kind of activity to generate sound. There were always cars and trucks. There were always people. New York had not been completely silent for as much as five seconds in two hundred years.

But today it made no sound at all. Hochenauer heard nothing but the mournful sighing of the wind.

The old Flatiron Building still stood. Virtually all its windows were missing, and part of the roof line seemed to have been torn off, but the basic structure still reared solidly against the partly cloudy sky.

Smaller buildings in the immediate neighborhood had suffered diverse fates. Some looked only superficially damaged. Others were nothing but mounds of broken brick. Some leaned on others. Some had fallen into the street.

Farther away, some taller buildings were no longer there. The skyline of the city as Hochenauer knew it had undergone a violent and radical change.

The streets all around him were completely jammed with smashed vehicles, building rubble, and the contents of people's offices and homes. Nothing moved anywhere, except smoke. Hochenauer could see clouds of it rising over many parts of the city. There seemed to be a major fire downtown in the Wall Street district, and in the other direction he saw a black pall that he judged to be somewhere near Central Park's southern edge.

Seeking a different view, he started to climb over a pile of debris. He accidentally dislodged a green metal file cabinet. It slid down the pile, making a clanging noise that sounded startlingly loud in the overwhelming silence. Hochenauer looked for a firmer place to set his foot. He found himself looking into the staring eyes of a dead man who had been hidden by the file cabinet.

Hochenauer covered the man with something that he thought might have been a bedspread.

The sun came out briefly from behind a cloud and shone peacefully. Wilma began to cry.

"It's all gone, Hoke!" she said. "It's all broke up!"

He went to her and put his skinny arm as far as it could reach around her waist, then patted her great bottom fondly. He did not say anything. He understood that her sorrow was for others, not herself. He and she had, in fact, lost hardly anything personal in the wind. They possessed virtually nothing of material value. Their only real treasure was each other.

The sun dodged behind a cloud, then came out again. Hochenauer finally saw some movement a short distance up Fifth Avenue. Some people's heads were visible behind a vast pile of steel and concrete that had once been a building. It seemed to Hochenauer that the people were moving very slowly, as though dazed by the enormity of the destruction around them.

And now some others were emerging one by one from the basement of the Flatiron Building. They gathered around Hochenauer and Wilma, staring in silence at the ruined city. The breeze sighed and moaned through the immense stillness.

Wilma was still crying.

Then a noise came from somewhere. It was not far away, perhaps half a block, behind some buildings. Hochenauer could not identify it at first. Then he had it.

"You know what that is, old lady?" he said.

"No. What?" Tears were running down Wilma's shiny red cheeks.

"It's a bulldozer. Somebody is already starting to clean

up the mess."

"They're gonna rebuild it, you think?"

"Sure. Good as new. Better, maybe. Safer."

Wilma cheered up immediately.

• • •

Arthur Beaulieu and Julia Mead stood with others near a massive pile of rubble that had once been the base of the *Seven Days* building. They had climbed from their below-ground shelter and believed themselves to be at or near street level, but it was impossible to know for sure. No streets or sidewalks were visible.

The sun shone peacefully. The breeze sighed and crooned.

"What now, Arthur?" Julia asked.

He had spent much of the night thinking about that. He said, "Well, the first step is to look for a small press I can operate under these conditions. And a mechanic to repair it. And a generator to power it."

She looked at him. "You're going to start up *Seven Days* again?"

"Of course. Or at least a crude substitute to begin with. People are going to be starved for news, Julia. And besides—"

He paused. He disliked sentimentality and did not know how to say what was in his mind. Julia prodded him: "Besides what?"

He gestured at the devastation all around them. "New York City has collapsed," he said, "but that doesn't mean we've collapsed does it?"

She took his hand. "No, it doesn't. If this new *Seven Days* of yours is taking job applications, would you consider me?"

"I wouldn't consider running it without you. And I'm

hoping some of the others will drift back to us in time. Charlie and Adelaide. My daughter Kim and that young fellow Pacifico. Do you think they will?"

He did not voice his fear that Kim might not have survived the wind. That possibility was too painful to contemplate for the moment.

"I think it's more than likely people will drift back," Julia said, answering his question. "We ought to set up shop somewhere in this neighborhood if we can. If people want to find us, this would be the logical place for them to start looking."

"Yes. And also—" he gestured again at the rubble that had once been the magazine's building—"somewhere under there are the archives, Julia. Even if I have to camp here for the rest of my life, I'm not going to let them get lost. Sooner or later, somehow or other, I'm going to see they're retrieved."

"Wherever you camp, Arthur, I'll camp with you. And Arthur—"

"Yes?"

She looked at the rubbish-strewn ground, then up at him. "I think we might as well get married now, don't you?"

Surprised and delighted, he hugged her to him. He had been urging marriage for years. She had steadfastly refused, for she harbored what he had always thought was a too-delicate sensitivity to the opinions of other family members. She did not want to give any appearance of trying to move in on his fortune.

Now the fortune had ceased to exist, at least in its former shape. Not only had *Seven Days* been physically destroyed, but so had financial institutions and records everywhere. Banks, stock exchanges, customer account books and computer memories: how much of the world of money lay buried, perhaps never to be resurrected? Did money itself even exist in any meaningful form anymore? Arthur had no idea how all these questions would sort themselves out, but it was perfectly plain that old concepts of wealth had undergone a violent transformation.

It then occurred to him that city and state governments, perhaps even national governments, might also take a long time to reestablish themselves. He asked, "Where do we go for a marriage license?"

She looked surprised at the question, then laughed. "I hadn't thought of that."

"I think we'll have to be content with common law for the time being."

"All right. In that case, I now pronounce us man and wife."

"Is it permissible to kiss the bride now?"

"It's mandatory, Arthur."

● ● ●

Angela heard voices startlingly close to her in the dark. She had not heard them approaching. The acoustics in this wrecked building must be strange, she thought.

"I'm here!" she called out exultantly, full of new hope. "Can you hear me?"

"Yes, we hear you!" a man's voice shouted. "Keep talking! Sing, or something! Whistle!"

Angela shouted, "I'm here! I'm Angela Beaulieu, and I'm alive, and I'm here! Oh, thank God you've found me!"

She saw flashlights then. A woman's voice said, "There she is!"

As the lights illuminated her surroundings, Angela saw that she was lying in the arms of a huge L-shaped steel member, amid a tangle of other steel shapes, woven steel cables, and jagged lumps of concrete. She was only a table's height above a flat-topped girder that sloped down to what looked like solid footing, where her rescuers were. Now that she could see what was below her, she began to slide down off her resting place.

"Do you need help?" a woman called up to her.

"No, I'm not hurt except for my hand." Angela got her feet onto the sloping girder and walked down it. Half a dozen people waited for her below. She had the impression of being in a large empty space shaped like an irregular tunnel, full of debris. Off in the more distant darkness she could see other people's lights and hear shouts.

Her rescuers helped her down off the girder. She found footing on something that rocked a bit. "Is it safe to walk here?" she asked.

"As far as we can tell," said a man with a British accent. "We're in an elevator shaft. It's lying flat on the ground. No farther to fall, you know."

"We're near the bottom of the building," a woman elaborated. Her accent was pure Brooklyn. "Least, it used to be the bottom before it fell over. Were you tryna get down the stairs?"

"Yes. So were a lot of others. Have you—"

"Yeah, we found some still alive. Lemme see that hand."

Angela held her hand out. The woman shone a light on it. It was grossly swollen and discolored. "That don't look too good," the woman commented.

"No, but I'd call myself lucky anyway," Angela said.

"Right you are," said the man with the British accent. "Come on, we've got a sort of first-aid station rigged up close by."

Angela was impressed by the resilience and competence of her fellow New Yorkers. "You've saved my life and I've never even thanked you," she said apologetically, picking her way across debris between the man and the woman.

"You saved your own life, more likely," the man said. "Getting down near the bottom of the building—that's what did it, you know. A few floors higher, you wouldn't have come through it."

Angela puzzled over that for a moment. Until now she had not tried to visualize precisely what had happened to her. She asked, "Was there more damage higher up?"

"Lord, yes! We haven't explored the whole building, but the higher we go, the worse it looks. I envision it like a broomstick falling over. The top would move faster than the lower part, d'you see? So if you were near the bottom, you know, you could actually be let down pretty—well, gently, if that's the right word."

"You gotta excuse him, he's English," the woman explained to Angela. "He don't talk straight, but his heart's in the right place."

"I'm sure it is," said Angela, feeling fond of the pair.

"The fact is," the man went on, wholly unperturbed by the interruption, "a few floors above you the whole inside of the building was squashed flat. We've only found a few people higher than you were. Live people, I mean."

"Some were in a sad shape too," the woman said. "Like we got one guy, claims he's the mayor of New York!"

"Millington?"

"That's what he says. He *could* be, I guess. His face is so banged up, he could be Donald Duck, for all I know. But if he's the mayor, what was he doing around here last night? Why wasn't he down at City Hall where he belonged?"

Angela kept silent. She did not want to talk about her party. She supposed that Millington and other guests might have walked down the stairs a flight or two behind her own group of survivors. In all that huge noise and confusion, she had not been aware of anything except her immediate surroundings.

She saw light ahead of her. After making some turns and

ducking beneath a steel I-beam that was bent like paper, they emerged suddenly into bright daylight. Angela stopped walking for a moment while her eyes adjusted.

They were in an irregular-shaped flat area among mountains of rubble. It was like being at the bottom of an enormous bowl. Angela could not see anything over the bowl's edges, which towered against the cloud-dappled blue sky. The floor of the bowl was made of black asphalt. Angela guessed she was standing on what had once been a street, perhaps Park Avenue itself. Since she could not see any of New York's familiar landmarks, she found it impossible to orient herself.

People were milling about in the flat area, absorbed in various tasks. The air of purpose and bustle made Angela feel good. She thought: this is my New York! This city is not just going to lie down and whine over its fate!

Her rescuers led her around a massive peninsula of rubble and along a makeshift pathway of planks to another open area. This was the first-aid station, where, eventually, a woman doctor named Snade bound Angela's hand with a bandage made from a shirt.

"You should get the use of the hand back in time," Dr. Snade said. "The bones may not knit perfectly. I'm sorry. I'd do more for you if I could."

"I can see what you're up against," Angela said. "Is there something I can do to help you?"

Dr. Snade was a tall, bony woman with long, lank hair. She looked very tired. Like everybody else she was dirt-smudged and dressed in tatters. She said, "Yes, you certainly *can* help. We're desperate for just about everything, even simple things like bedding. Something for those poor people to lie on, something to cover them with." The doctor gestured at rows of injured patients lying on the bare ground.

Angela said, "I'll organize a search," and turned to go.

"Even a bottle of aspirin!" Dr. Snade called after her.

Angela was considering ways of recruiting a task group when she saw a familiar face. "Edna Jane!" she shouted.

Edna Jane Cullum turned and saw her. The two women ran to each other and embraced tightly. "Oh, boy, Ms. Beaulieu, am I glad to see *you*!" Edna Jane said happily.

Angela gave her a squeeze, then stood back and grasped both of Edna Jane's hands. "Listen, Edna Jane," she said, "it's a whole new world we're in now. I've been thinking about this. Yesterday I was rich, but now—now all I am is a survivor. I can't have you as an employee any more, Edna Jane. Do you see that?"

"I see that, Ms. Beaulieu."

"But I'd like to have you as a friend."

"You got that, Ms. Beaulieu. You surely have got that."

"I was hoping I had." Angela raised one of Edna Jane's hands to her lips and kissed the work-roughened knuckles. "But if we're friends, we're equals. From now on you call me Angela."

Edna Jane thought about that for a second. Then she said, slowly, "Well, I don't know about that, Ms. B. I been with you twenty years, near as I can remember. It ain't all that easy, changing a twenty-year habit."

She was right, of course. Angela's suggestion had been too glib. It had a tinny echo in Angela's own ear. She thought it sounded like a suggestion from one of those TV shrinks: perfectly wonderful advice which, in real life, few would care to follow.

Angela did not know how to resolve the dilemma. She and Edna Jane stood looking at each other, sadly puzzled.

Then Angela was struck by an inspiration. "Well, all right," she said, "if you want to call me Ms. B., you go right ahead. And I'll call you Ms. C."

Edna Jane laughed, delighted. "You got yourself a deal, Ms. B.!"

"A deal Ms. C.! Now enough of this nonsense, my friend, we've got work to do." Angela explained Dr. Snade's needs. Edna Jane said she recalled seeing blankets or towels in a basement room. They went to look.

Picking their way through wreckage, they traded accounts of survival in the wind. Edna Jane and her husband, Branch, had sought refuge in the New World Center's basement along with hundreds of others. When the huge building fell, part of the basement structure collapsed under it. The other half of the basement remained intact, saving the lives of those who were lucky enough to have chosen that side of it. Ed McRoyden and Amanda Grewen had not been so lucky.

"I *never* been so scared!" Edna Jane said. "When the building fell down, all the lights went out. Because the emergency generators, see, they all in the side of the basement that collapsed. Otherwise we'd still have power now, I reckon. But there's me and Branch looking for our flashlights in the dark, and the whole world falling down on our heads, sound like. Hoo-*ee*!"

"Darkness makes everything twice as bad, doesn't it?" Angela agreed. "I'm lucky the generators lasted as long as they did. When it went dark for a minute on those stairs, I was ready to give up. I just wanted to sit down and cry. But then the lights came on again, and I made it down to the bottom. If it hadn't been for those lights, I'd be dead."

Edna Jane smiled at her and seemed about to make a comment, but at that moment they saw Spencer Millington, the mayor. He was sitting on a block of concrete just outside a busy entryway that led, Agnela assumed, into the intact part of the basement. His face was cut and bruised, but he was still recognizable to anybody who knew him personally. He was staring fixedly at the ground.

"Spence," Angela said, stopping in front of him. He did not seem to hear her. She said, "Spence Millington!" This time he looked up at her and Edna Jane, made a small dispirited gesture with one hand, then looked down at the ground again.

"Spence, there's a lot to be done," Angela said. She had not meant to scold him, but she could not keep the scolding tone from her voice.

"Leave me alone, I'm hurt," he mumbled.

He did not look as though he had more than superficial injuries. Certainly no bones were broken. Angela said, "Sitting there will only make you feel worse. People need leadership, Spence."

"I'm hurt. I hurt all over. Go away."

Angela looked at Edna Jane, who gave a shrug of resignation. The mayor had failed his city. He had not been of the slightest help before the disaster or during it, and it was quite obvious that he was not about to salvage himself now. His spirit was broken.

Angela sighed. "All right, come on, Ms. C.," she said, turning to go. "Let's get on with it."

"I'm right behind you, Ms. B."

• • •

They came up from the storm drain and stood amid piles and drifts of debris, looking around at what had been New York City. For a time, all talking stopped.

The sun shone. The breeze sighed softly.

A piece of pink cloth, dislodged from some high perch, came flapping down lazily and drifted behind a wrecked bus that was lying on its side. A yellow taxi was parked on top of the bus. There were people in the cab, but they did not move. Nearby was something that looked like part of an aircraft tail assembly, blown from some airport miles away.

Pacifico was standing behind Danny with both his hands on her thin little shoulders. Kim was standing next to him, holding his arm. Everybody was holding onto somebody.

Trish and Suzanne were huddled in a tight clump with the tiny woman they called Granny, who seemed at the moment to be providing most of their support. Alice Wenska and Walter were clinging to each other. It was a moment of fear and uncertainty, yet it was also strangely serene.

Pacifico looked at Kim. "Do you want to see if we can find the *Seven Days* building?" He hesitated at his next thought. "And look for your father?"

"Yes. You and Danny—you'll come with me?"

"Naturally."

"And I want to look for my mother, too, at the New World Center."

Pacifico looked around. The familiar landmarks of his native city were changed and obliterated. He did not know where he was.

He turned to some others standing nearby and asked if anybody knew their whereabouts. People climbed to the tops of rubble mounds and surveyed the surrounding scene. Some buildings still stood. By piecing clues and hunches together, the group arrived at a consensus. This provided a fix on where the *Seven Days* building and the New World Center ought to be. The *Seven Days* building seemed to be the closer of the two.

Pacifico said to the group, "Kim and Danny and I are going back to the *Seven Days* building, if we can find it. Anybody feel like taking a walk?"

He was pleased, though he did not clearly understand why at first, when the entire group of thirty-odd people elected to go along. People gave diverse reasons: they wanted to find food and water, they needed medical supplies, they wanted to explore the extent of the devastation. These reasons were all perfectly sensible. But there was another reason that nobody articulated, and it was the most important reason of all. The group did not want to disband.

Some people talked cheerfully, others just looked about in shock and amazement at the incredible extent of damage the doom wind had wrought.

Pacifico felt buoyed and comforted. You can always count on New Yorkers, he thought. In their untidy and maddening way, they always find a route to survival. Survival is bred into them. It is what they do best. They always seem to be plunging into or struggling out of one crisis or another. But they are people of a special breed. They walk through the valley of the shadow and come out the other side saying, "Crisis? Whaddya mean, crisis?"

Pacifico was not worried. He knew his city would come back to life.

FREE!!
BOOKS BY MAIL
CATALOGUE

BOOKS BY MAIL will share with you our current bestselling books as well as hard to find specialty titles in areas that will match your interests. You will be updated on what's new in books at no cost to you. Just fill in the coupon below and discover the convenience of having books delivered to your home.

PLEASE ADD $1.00 TO COVER THE COST OF POSTAGE & HANDLING.

- -

BOOKS BY MAIL

320 Steelcase Road E.,
Markham, Ontario L3R 2M1

210 5th Ave., 7th Floor
New York, N.Y., 10010

Please send Books By Mail catalogue to:

Name _____
(please print)

Address _____

City _____

Prov./State _____ P.C./Zip _____

(BBM1)